Take the first step beyond
the threshold with courage
in your heart and curiosity
in your mind.

29.09.21

PARIAH'S LAMENT

AN OF METAL AND MAGIC CORE STORY

Richie Billing

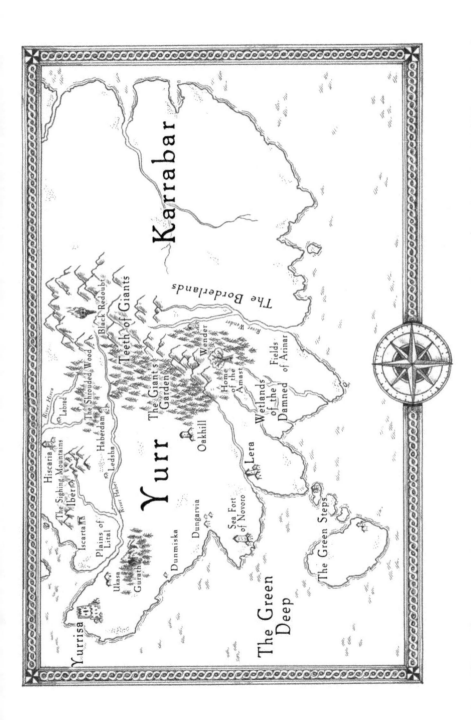

For Mum, Aunty Peggy and Nana, who taught me never to give up.

A thousand thank yous to JM for giving me a shot, to Mark and Chris for their patience and time, and to Anna for her sage advice.

Note to the Reader

YOU HOLD IN YOUR HANDS something very special. This book is an *Of Metal and Magic* CORE series. All CORE stories take place in the same epic fantasy universe, the magical world of Soria. The OMAM Core project includes dozens of authors, whose tales of adventure and intrigue overlap, reference, and influence each other. All official CORE narratives are part of a single unified canon.

Each series is an independent project, designed to be a stand-alone work that can be enjoyed all by itself. But the real magic comes from reading multiple series and discovering the many points of intersection and convergence that our many authors have created. The depth of our world is further enhanced by short stories and worldbuilding pieces you can read for free on our WEBSITE.

At *Of Metal and Magic*, or OMAM for short, we strive to create and publish the best in traditional and epic fantasy. This all began with the collaboration of Richie Billing, JM Williams, and handful of other authors, as we developed the world of Soria beyond a handful of notes scribbled in a colleague's notebook, into the living, breathing history you are about to experience.

All OMAM projects have the potential to expand into larger collaborative worlds—indeed, this is one of our primary goals as a publisher. But nothing beats a CORE series and the complexity we've added to the world of Soria.

Thank you for picking up this title. We hope you enjoy your time reading about our world as much as we enjoyed creating it. For sure, there are many more stories to tell. But for now, enjoy *Pariah's Lament.*

Episode One: Shifting Shadows

To hold faith in one's self, in one's convictions and choices, is, when you come to think of it, a curiously difficult thing. The corrupting tendrils of doubt forever stalk the door, and often in our lives the strength of that door will be tested. Our beliefs will be ridiculed, and indeed we may altogether be cast aside by kith and kin and those we hold dear. But to maintain that faith, when it's shared by no one else, is a sign of true strength and character. For our faith will forever be tested, and sometimes it will break, but never can it be destroyed. Believe in love, in truth, in friendship and honesty. Believe in yourself, and believe that someday things will change for the better.

From ***The Forgotten Daggers*** by S. T. Harris

One

THE HURRIED PATTER of Edvar's steps echoed along the cobbled street. Shutters covered the windows of the hunched stone houses he passed, the candles inside long extinguished. From an inn at the corner of a narrow side street drifted a buzz of chatter and the jingle of flutes and harps. Like moths seeking a flame, a handful of people stumbled toward the commotion. Edvar left them in his wake.

Wheezes of a kind he'd never heard before rattled in his burning chest. Despite the cool ocean breeze that brought with it the smell of salt and seaweed, sweat ran down the side of his face and into his patchy beard. He was thankful his jerkin and breeches were both dark. He would have to ease off the pipe, go on a few more walks, or gods forbid, start drilling with weapons again.

A shed-like carriage turned onto the street ahead, pulled by a team of chestnut rounseys. Edvar willed further haste into his legs and caught up to it, hopping onto the rear platform. He sucked in air, steadying his breathing, while the wheels rolled over the loose stones. It was times like these he lamented having spent much of his life with his nose dipped between the covers of books. Now he regretted it.

Over the slate roofs loomed the parapets of the first of the keep's three walls. The torches of the gatehouse lit up the teeth of the iron portcullis, transforming it into the gaping mouth of some beast from the depths of the Green Deep. Edvar jumped down as the carriage veered right, steadying himself with his hands as he hit the ground.

"Cheeky bastard," the teamster called out after him.

Edvar ran for the gate. At seeing somebody charge toward them, the two guards hefted the spears from their shoulders and crossed them to bar his path.

"Woah, woah, woah," called the smaller of the two, a stubby-nosed man with a thick brown beard. "What's your business?"

"There's no time for this. I passed you little over an hour ago. Just let me through!" Edvar made to move by them. They shoved him back.

"We don't remember and you ain't coming in, so beat it or we'll get stabby."

"The keeper's in danger!"

The guards guffawed. "From who? The kid councilor has a small army guarding him."

"I *am* Councilor Edvar!"

They laughed once more. "Yeah and I'm Makos the Mighty."

The hurried jangles of the warning bells reverberated from the keep, shattering the quiet like a stone through a library window. Edvar looked up at the Iron Tower before turning to the idiot guards, who gaped at him, wide-eyed. Together, they scrambled through the gate.

Why is that bastard always right? Edvar thought, cursing his informant, Mag. Soldiers emerged from doors, pulling on armor, buckling belts and baldrics. Officers yelled orders and led men and women up the motte. *How did they reach him?* Poison seemed most likely. *Always poison.* Edvar had practically interrogated those working in the kitchen and stores to ensure they could be trusted. Guards were stationed day and night at the well and outside the wine cellar, and teams checked the food that came into the keep. Had someone betrayed him? Had he missed something? He must have. *I'm as useful as a fingerless archer.*

As Edvar reached the third and final wall, shouting erupted from the battlements. Before he could look up, he took a blow to the head that knocked him to the ground. Hard.

Flashing lights dazzled his vision and more than once darkness closed and ebbed. Ringing consumed his hearing, the taste of copper flooded his mouth. Eyes unfocused, he saw a figure clad in black getting to their feet. Their face covered, save for their eyes, which looked at him as a starved dog would a chunk of meat. He saw a glimmer of steel in the figure's hand. Edvar pushed himself up onto shaky legs. His attacker swung. Edvar clumsily ducked. Stinging pain erupted in his forearm, but it didn't stop him from charging, shoulder first. They both fell to the ground in a tangle of limbs. Edvar grabbed at the blade. A fist struck his face. More landed with twice the force and something cracked. He rolled away, blood gushing from his nose. When he forced open his eyes he found his attacker standing over him.

In that fractured state of mind, Edvar thought of one thing alone: he'd failed. His keeper, his father, his people, his country, and above all, himself. What future lay ahead for them? Torment, turmoil, death? He could have prevented it. Should have done more. His father had been a fool to place so much trust in him. *Perhaps then we're both fools. We have that in common, at least.* Edvar closed his eyes and awaited his fate.

Pain didn't come. His vision took a moment to focus, and when it did, he saw his attacker on the ground, the bolt of a crossbow sticking from the rogue's thigh. Guards swarmed over them, jabbing with the butts of their spears. Edvar sank back and, before his head hit the ground, the clamor around him faded.

Two

Consciousness returned with a sudden, painful throb. Edvar opened his eyes to find himself in a drab, windowless dormitory upon a bed that offered as much comfort as a pile of spiked maces. Candles flickered in sconces between more beds that stretched along the wall to his right. All empty.

He was still clothed, boots and all. With his elbows, he pushed himself up and recoiled from a sharp pain in his left forearm. The room around him turned upside down. Saliva flooded his mouth and, after a swift and panicked battle, the urge to vomit overcame him. He leaned to the side of the bed and let loose a garish mess. Footsteps pattered against the stone floor.

"Couldn't you have done that in the bucket?" a woman asked. Edvar rolled onto his back. She was dressed in the grey robe and white headdress of the House of Benevolence. Her lips were pursed, brows and amber eyes angled with annoyance. She could not have seen more than twenty-two summers; no older than himself.

"I didn't realise there was one," Edvar croaked.

"On the other side of the bed."

"Ah. I'm sorry." Edvar held up a trembling hand in apology.

She huffed and made to walk away.

"Wait. Where am I?"

She turned, hands on her hips.

"Yurrisa."

"I know that. Where in Yurrisa?"

"The keep's barracks."

"The Keeper—what happened?"

"No idea. Nobody tells me anything." With that, she disappeared through a door, muttering to herself.

Edvar forced himself to sit on the edge of his bed. He breathed deep, trying to steady the room. He felt better for emptying his stomach, but his mouth was dry as sawdust and filled with the taste of sour milk. Wincing, he rolled up his bloody sleeve and found his left arm bandaged from elbow to wrist. He had no clue as to the severity of the cut, but it was certainly the worst pain he'd ever felt.

With the aid of the stone wall, he stood and followed the woman through the door. Each step intensified the throb at his temples and more than once he had to stop. Outside, it was still dark, the wandering moon falling toward the horizon. He staggered to a barrel of water used by soldiers when training and plunged his head into it. The coolness refreshed him, and then he drank deep before sloshing water around his mouth to wash away the taste of blood and bile. The ripples settled and, by the light of a nearby torch, he caught his reflection. And panicked. His long nose was bent to the right, almost certainly broken, and the skin around his Yurrish amber eyes had turned the shade of plums. He ran a hand through his dripping shoulder-length hair and found it matted with blood. With a grimace, he parted and pushed it back behind his furry, bear-shaped ears. Edvar wasn't handsome by traditional Yurrish standards, lacking the strong, angled jaw, full beard and broad shoulders characteristic of many men. And now he had a wonky nose. *Perhaps it'll be an improvement.*

A small army of soldiers buzzed about the circular bailey. With unsteady steps, Edvar passed the pillared entrance of the Great Hall and the Vault of Iron with its etched doors, and approached the imposing Iron Tower. Half a dozen guards stood sentry. They admitted him without pause. Edvar couldn't find the strength to ask them whether or not the keeper lived.

Inside, he hesitated at the bottom of the spiral staircase. Soldiers and chirurgeons assistants came hurrying down, empty buckets and blood-stained bundles in their hands. He stepped aside for them, anxiety strangling his words, and began his ascent.

Edvar wouldn't know what to do if Ashara died. He wasn't sure he could handle it, not so soon after the death of his father. Those lonely days still followed him around, sat in their home before a cold hearth, no candles, utter silence. And the realisation circling around his mind that nobody was coming to make it better.

But the implications of Ashara's death extended far beyond Edvar's feelings. The widowed keeper had no heir. His only son had died at birth and his nieces and nephews had been taken by the Paler, a terrible fever that swept through the nation before Edvar's time, claiming thousands of souls, young and old. The lack of an heir mattered greatly, for there was much more to the role of keeper than governing the realm. Above all, they had to maintain the ancient oath to keep sealed and secure the Vault of Iron. Locked away in that dusty place was the Dagger of Ulara. And locked away with good cause. The magical weapon possessed the power to level towns and slays thousands.

Unless an heir was appointed, there would be a struggle like no other upon Ashara's death. Edvar had no doubt those on the Keeper's Council would make a move. And there was another who stalked the throne like a winter-starved wolf: Tesh, Keeper of neighboring Karrabar and the Vault of Bronze.

To the relief of his weary legs, Edvar reached Ashara's bedchamber. A guard stood in each of the four corners of the landing. In between them hung tapestries depicting heroes and proud moments in Yurrish history that came to life in the light of the braziers. His father was in some of them. Two more guards stood on both sides of the arched doorway. One knocked on the door, and a few moments later, the wispy, white-haired head of a woman appeared. Byden, the most senior of all chirurgeons in the city, nodded for Edvar to enter.

Crimson streaks were spattered across the stone floor, the tapestries upon the walls, the furs and sheets lying beside the bed. Upon the bed itself lay Keeper Ashara, eyes closed, skin pallid. A deep gash ran across his chest, surrounded by half a dozen shallower cuts. Bandages covered both shoulders, arms and hands.

"He lives," Byden said in her soothing voice.

"What in Soria happened?"

"The guards found him fending off the assassin with that candelabrum." Byden nodded in the direction of a bronze candleholder at the foot of the bed. Blood was speckled on the shaft and all along it were cuts and chips where Ashara had blocked the blows. "He's always been a fine swordsman, though never as good as your father." A wry smile carved itself into her stony face.

Edvar frowned. How could she be so calm when the keeper lay dying?

"The assailant escaped out the balcony and used a rope to get down onto the battlements," Byden said.

"That explains how they came to land on my head."

"Ah, I heard of your heroics. Just like one of your father's stunts," Byden said, grinning. Edvar liked the old chirurgeon. She was someone who truly cared for the welfare of others, yet she was oddly indifferent toward death.

"There was nothing heroic about it. Quite the opposite, in fact," Edvar said, peering about the balcony for clues. It was too dark for any meaningful search. "How did they get onto the balcony?"

"Climbed down from the roof."

"But there were four guards stationed up there."

"All lie cold," Byden said solemnly.

Every other window in the tower was a mere slit, designed with defense in mind. Yet Ashara's chamber had a balcony, a feature Edvar recalled his father counseling the keeper to remove for this very reason. Ashara had laughed off his concerns.

A groan from the bed had Edvar rushing across the room. Ashara's eyes flickered.

"Ed," he said, voice raspy.

"Sire. How are you feeling?" Edvar asked.

"I've had better nights. Water." Ashara was unable to grip with his bandaged hands, so Edvar held a cup to his lips. Sip by sip, he emptied it. "My mouth's drier than a dragon's arse."

"They've not dented your sense of humour, I see."

Ashara smiled, amber eyes still alight.

"What happened?" Edvar asked.

"As I changed for bed, the balcony doors swung open and in charged the assassin. I hear you've already acquainted yourself. You look worse than me." His lips curled into a pained grin. "There must be some of your father's fighting spirit in you after all."

"If by that you mean getting knocked out, then yes, in abundance. It was the first time I've ever been punched and I enjoyed it as much as a hot poker to the eye."

Ashara laughed only for his face to contort with pain. "You get used to it. Your father would mock us mercilessly if he saw us beat up like this." The smile faded from his face. "I miss him. More than ever."

A silence descended. Byden fluffed up the pillows behind Ashara's head then bowed and departed. Edvar stewed over Ashara's last comment. If he'd done his job properly, Ashara wouldn't be missing him. But how could Edvar blame him?

"It's my fault this happened. I should have anticipated it, put more soldiers on the roof, insisted on putting a couple on the balcony. Even just reinforced the door." He paused, searching for words that eluded him and then resolved to sigh. "Can you find it in your heart to forgive me?"

"Do not be such a fool, Ed. You couldn't have done more. I was unconvinced by your fears of an attack. I refused the guards on the balcony. If anything it is my fault. And whatever wrong you think you've committed has surely been rectified by your stopping of the assassin." He smiled, and Edvar felt a little better. "I may miss your father, Ed, but that is not to say I do not have faith in you. He would be proud to see you now. But we have been lucky. Somehow I still breathe, and that gives us an opportunity. You must help me find out who is behind this."

Edvar swallowed hard. "I will. And when I do I'll make sure they pay."

"Dealing punishment is not as easy as you think. Let that trouble weigh on my conscience." Ashara lay back, eyes bunching with pain. "Who do you suspect?" he said through gritted teeth.

"Tesh."

Just hearing the name filled Edvar with unease. Since Tesh had ascended to the Karraban throne, violence had plagued the Borderlands. Skirmishes, raids, murders. Upon the waves, Yurrish fishing boats had been attacked, merchant vessels seized by pirates. To Edvar, it seemed a means of Tesh proving himself a strong and brazen leader.

Instead of war, Ashara had brokered for peace, but it had come at a cost: land. And not just any strip of greenery, but the Fields of Arinar, the location of the final battle of the War of the Damned and the resting place of thousands of Yurrish men and women. In the eyes of many, those were sacred lands, and the news of their annexation had been met with bitter hostility, not just from the Yurrish people, but from Edvar's fellow councilors too.

But avoiding bloodshed was the right course of action; of that Edvar was sure. Peace had reigned between the two nations for centuries. Nobody wanted a return to the Age of the Damned and the death and destruction wreaked by the powers contained in the Vaults. Many harsh lessons had been learned, but men liked to fight. Indeed, it was all they seemed to do.

"Do you think we did the right thing, Ed?"

"Yes. It was a chance worth taking. Lives should never be sacrificed for mere pride."

Ashara fell silent a while, eyes closed. He looked twenty years older.

"The rest of the council think it's Tesh too," the keeper said at last. "The moment I awoke they were in here telling me their theories. I fear I cannot trust them anymore. Whether I can trust anyone save for you, Ed. Or am I just being paranoid? It's hard to know when swimming in an ocean of doubt."

Ashara closed his eyes again.

"Shall I have them watched?" Edvar asked. Spying on his fellow councilors was a risky move. If caught it would signal a clear declaration of mistrust and that would lead to open political warfare, at times more deadly than that on the battlefield, or so his father used to say. It wouldn't be easy spying on them too. They had eyes and ears of their own around the city.

"Do you think we should?" Ashara asked.

"I fear we have even fewer friends in the city than we thought, but I have faith in my people."

"Bring me daily updates." Ashara closed his eyes and sighed, sinking back into his pillows. "I feel as if I've been fighting in the front rank for a week," he muttered.

"I'll leave you to rest, sire."

Ashara gave no reply, and by the time Edvar reached the door, he was soundly asleep. He hurried down the stairs, headache replaced by a fire of determination in his chest. He had to make amends, and that began with the assassin.

Three

No matter how hard Isy scrubbed, the remnants of last night's pottage wouldn't budge. She had debated leaving it; the iron cauldron was black after all. But her mother and father would brand her lazy, and they detested nothing more than laziness. She scrubbed harder.

The floor still needed sweeping, the hearth too. Outside, the vegetables had to be tended and, from the growing chorus of clucks, her father hadn't fed the chickens. Another job for her list. Isy cleared her mind, went on working, and finished about an hour before midday, her preferred time to venture outside without harassment.

The mud of the road sucked at her tattered leather boots, a quagmire after incessant rains. Autumn circled like a hawk. The wind grabbed at her woollen green cloak and homespun dress. The hand-me-downs from her cousins never fitted, always too wide at the waist and short of length. She pulled her cloak tight about her, bundling it around her hands to keep away the biting chill. Isy looked like a typical Yurrish girl—bright amber eyes, high cheekbones, pronounced brow over a thin nose that flicked up at the end. Her hair was more russet than the common brown, her ears more round and not as protrusive or furry as some people's in town. But one key feature distinguished Isy from everyone else, something she tried to hide with the grey shawl wrapped around her neck and face. Her black birthmark covered the skin around her right eye and cheek like a great blotch of ink upon a sheet of parchment. It was the reason for her misery, the source of her derision. The superstitious and devout in Haberdam called her the "Cursed One", touched by an evil that brought foul luck to anyone that came into contact with her. Isy wondered whether her father had come to believe the stories too, so little time did he spend in her company.

Where love for her father should have been, she felt nothing. It'd been that way ever since he'd attacked her with his axe. A decade on, she could still smell the ale on his breath, see the hate in his eyes as he came at her with that rusted blade. Isy was closer to her mother, though more out of a sense of duty than love. The few times she'd defended Isy, her father had turned his ire on her, and Isy hated to see her mother bruised and bleeding because of her. So they were distant yet faintly attached.

Tension filled her chest whenever she left the house. Today was no different. Her home was located on the eastern side of Haberdam, near the top of the valley in which the town sat, and close to the Shrouded Wood where she spent most of her free time. The meandering River Haber flowed through the woods and down into the town, splitting it in two. The wood mill, granary and smithy clung to the eastern bank, shipping logs, food and wares downstream to the capital, Yurrisa. One of the town's two inns and a score of taverns populated the bank opposite, and bunched around both banks were hundreds of squat, rectangular houses of stone, wood and thatch. Smoke, rising from their chimneys, fragranced the crisp morning air with burning peat and logs as it drifted up beyond the watchmen's round tower that loomed at the edge of town like a protective parent. The town square was where she was bound, to the Chronicler's Repository, the only place within twenty leagues that had books for public use. And today a new shipment was due. With it, Isy hoped, was *The Trials of Myra the Maid*, a book she had longed to read ever since a travelling tinker named Irma had told her about it at the Autumn Fayre eight summers ago.

Isy left the main road and took a quieter route behind the potters and masons. She hurried past the back of the saddler's shop, pinching her nose at the stench of drying hides, and turned onto a more frequented lane that led to the town square. At hearing voices and laughter, she bit her lip. Isy didn't know the reason behind her mark, if indeed one existed. Nobody else in Haberdam had one, nor had she seen any of the merchants, rivermen or travellers who visited the town with one either. It caused no ailments, brought only scorn. For nineteen summers she had cried and endured, hoping that everyone would see past her mark to the person beneath. That hope had waned and in its stead a carapace had formed to ward against the ceaseless torment. She'd learned, in the harshest of ways, that as much as she wanted to, she couldn't control the behavior of others, only her own reactions and responses—a truly difficult thing to master. She'd had plenty practice.

In the center of the square, a group of young boys and girls chased a small leather ball around with sticks, a game known as *lingas*, and one that often ended with the sticks turned on each other. On the right side of the square was the Haber Inn, the grandest building in town after Baron Rijkard's manor. Outside of the three-story inn, painted a deep green with red sills and architraves, a couple of bushy-bearded men unloaded from a cart barrels and casks broad as their shoulders. Another man, hair much greyer than the laboring pair, sat upon a bench on the inn's front decking, puffing on the pipe clamped between his teeth. Giggles drew Isy's gaze to the other side of the square where three women, all Isy's age, were enjoying the attention of a pair of young rivermen.

Like a mouse leaving cover, Isy scurried across the square and reached the Chronicler's Repository. A feeling of sanctuary washed over her as she clicked the door closed behind. She breathed in the smell of must and paper and stepped deeper inside. She came to a panel hanging on the wall, Keeper Ashara's words etched into it.

"Take pleasure in the writings of others. Open your mind to their words, for they can empower you with the tools to transform the world."

Isy's father had chiselled and hung it. "What a load of bollocks," he had said to her mother at the time. "No words have ever sorted a problem of mine. I'd rather let my fists do the talking."

Isy heard a rumble of voices. "Hello?" she said, edging further into the dusty archive. In the middle of an aisle, she found an open cellar door.

"You foolish boy!" came a shout from within. The bass voice and city accent undoubtedly belonged to the chronicler. "This is one of your few duties. I cannot even begin to think of all the countless hours wasted because of your wretched incompetence." The thump of leather covers and ruffle of papers punctuated his tirade.

"This entire section wouldn't even serve as kindling," the chronicler went on. "I don't understand how you can be so shortsighted. Do you not respect our profession? Do you loathe our precious ink and paper?" More bangs and crashes sounded, and then the angriest shriek yet. "These are all ruined too!"

Isy retreated from the aisle and sought refuge amongst the rows of cluttered bookshelves. Tall and untidy stacks of tomes and parchments filled the aisles. Most of them, Isy knew, were records: outcomes of the town's hearings, debts owed, harvest yields. Riveting reads. Scattered amongst them like gold in a river bed were the books she devoured: history, geography, and, above all, tales of adventure. Stories that helped her escape.

At the end of an aisle there was a window looking out over the square. Isy could see the three women from earlier. Margo, Freya, and Lesa. They had all mocked and bullied her throughout her life. Seeing them walking together, laughing and joking, triggered a sharp pang of emptiness in her chest. It wasn't that she wanted to be out there with them, rather she longed for that sense of belonging they shared, to feel that connection of comfort, trust and love with another person. She focused on her reflection in the window, saw the black stain upon her face. *Maybe I really am the Cursed One. Bound to a life of misery and loneliness.* She reached out to the glass, only to pull back her hand at the thud of footsteps behind her.

Isy ducked behind a stack of books. The wild grey hair of the chronicler came into view, and almost instantly, his beady eyes spotted her. His brows furrowed and, muttering under his breath, he hurried up the stairs to his office, slamming the door behind him, which sent the window beside her rattling. Isy had grown used to such reactions.

"Sorry about him." Vil staggered into view, an unwieldy pile of books in his grasp. Like Isy, the young chronicler's assistant was subdued, though when together they found they had much to discuss: the books they'd read, the people around town they hated, the places Vil had visited with the chronicler. Unlike everyone else in Haberdam, he treated her normally—his eyes met hers and didn't wander to her mark, he asked questions about what she liked and the things that annoyed her, listened without interrupting, laughed at things she said, though never mockingly. He was the closest person she had to a friend.

Isy could see over the books in Vil's grasp his mop of curly brown hair. Vil was short by Yurrish standards. His neck was stooped and shoulders far from straight, the result of years of reading and scrawling and little else. He had a fondness for cake, which showed in his sagging gut. And he had large amber eyes that always glistened as if he was close to tears, something he blamed on the plants and flowers.

Vil bent his knees to place the books on an already packed desk, and the top one fell. Isy took a quick step and caught it just before it hit the ground.

"Nice catch," Vil said in his nasal voice. He set down the books, and the pile toppled. He sighed. Isy wanted to laugh until she noticed a shallow cut above Vil's left eyebrow.

"How'd you get that?"

"Oh? A book hit me." He hurriedly picked up the books, dabbing at the cut with his sleeve.

"You mean he hit you with a book?" Isy asked, gathering the tomes at her feet.

"Not deliberately."

"I hope one of these bookshelves falls and crushes the fat bastard."

Vil's face contorted as if he'd trodden on glass. "Shhh! He might hear you." He signaled for her to follow him into the storeroom. "He has the hearing of a cat," Vil whispered once she was inside, closing the door behind them with the care of a thief.

"What was all that shouting about?" Isy asked, leafing through the pages of a dusty book that contained records of cabbage yields.

"Some of the books in the cellar have gotten moldy. Pages blotchy and rotting, some falling apart."

"How's that your fault?"

"I was meant to keep an eye on them."

"And did you?"

He shook his head.

"Well, you'll have a nice scar to remind you not to forget again. I've got plenty such reminders."

Vil looked at his feet.

Isy could resist no longer. "Did it come?"

His eyes met hers and, fighting a smile, he set off, weaving his way through stacks and piles until he disappeared from view. The excitement in her chest swelled like the banks of the Haber after a storm. He returned with a book, covered in a black cloth, and handed it to her. With care she unwrapped it, biting her bottom lip. She read the golden letters on the front cover. *The Trials of Myra the Maid.*

"At last!" She couldn't resist the urge to cradle the book to her chest and then she flung an arm around Vil and squeezed him too. "I cannot tell you how sick I am of reading about perfect men winning the hearts of perfect women by slaying dragons and monsters and legions of evil men. Just once I wish there would be an ending without kisses and rainbows. And here it is!"

Vil grinned. "It's our only copy so look after it. He made me sleep in the cellar for a week the last time I lost a book. You should see the size of the spiders down there."

"With my life," Isy said, wrapping it up and placing it in her satchel beside her waterskin and lunch. "Thank you, Vil." She wanted to hug him again, but she wasn't sure whether she'd overstepped the boundary. Most people were afraid to touch her. Some even changed their route if they saw her coming. She resolved to squeeze his arm a little. His cheeks reddened, and Isy felt a rush of heat in hers, too. Conscious of what she was doing, she pulled her hand away, grabbed her bag and left. As she stepped outside, her mind filled with the prospect of temporary escape, of peace and comfort, alone.

Isy found herself whistling along with the blackbirds as she followed the dirt road to the Shrouded Wood. Trees lined the way at irregular intervals, the spaces in-between filled with grass, nettles and ferns. Already leaves were beginning to wither. In the height of autumn, the forest around Haberdam was breathtaking with its hues of gold, brown and orange, before winter made it look a place abandoned by life.

At a cluster of wildflowers, she departed the road and followed a narrow trail, almost overgrown with the recent rainfall. A short and steep walk led to a sloped clearing of long grass, and there, at the peak, Isy took a moment to savor the sight that sprawled before her. The many thatched roofs of Haberdam filled the bowl of the valley. The River Haber cut through the town and flowed on through rolling emerald hills sprinkled with sheep, goats and cows. It all seemed so peaceful, yet it was a place in which she found no peace. She longed to live her life alone in the forest, far from here. It was a dream, one that in dark times kept her sane.

In the middle of the clearing, she found her spot—a patch of flattened grass—and set down her bag, hurriedly unwrapping the book. She stroked the brown leather cover, tracing the letters of the title with her fingers, and, after opening it, took a whiff of the page. Isy had just a handful of possessions, most of which were books. Growing up, some of the girls had straw dolls and, when they grew older, were given bows by their fathers. All children in Haberdam were trained to shoot, and despite everyone's repulsion, that law applied to Isy, too. With her keen sight, she'd proven a fair shot, but she had no interest in it. Besides, her father refused to give her a bow.

Isy fell into the words before her, each one a step deeper into a new world, a step further away from reality. She pulled out her bread roll and ate it without taking her eyes from the page, breaking only to blow crumbs from the paper. She grew ignorant to the bees buzzing about the flowers around her, and the tiny flies tickling her hands and arms. Until the snap of a branch pierced the veil.

Her heart ceased to beat, book forgotten. Biting her lip, she rose to her knees and scanned the trees in the direction from which she thought the noise had come. At hearing nothing else she slowly returned to her spot, picked up her book, and heard another snap. Closer.

This time she stood, book left on the ground. Her knees trembled. A rustle off to her right told her something was moving. A feeling of defiance ran through her. She refused to be afraid of whoever or whatever lingered beyond her vision. This was her happy place. How dare they threaten to ruin it?

She could not say where she found the courage, but she moved toward the sound. She reached where she thought the rustling had come from and peered into the murky trees. Another snap of a branch echoed from deeper within. Isy picked up the sturdiest stick she could find and crept closer, heart pulsing in her ears.

Behind a stout tree she halted, looked around the other side. Not a leaf stirred. For a while she waited, eyes never still.

Isy exhaled her tension with a sigh. *Probably a deer.* She cursed herself for being such a paranoid fool. Shoulders easing, she turned back toward the clearing and saw a sight that stilled her heart.

Four

Edvar was sick of stairs. His head felt like it had been used to sound the warning bells, and with each step up the prison tower, the throb behind his eyes intensified. The more he tried to make sense of things, the less sense they made. While he suspected Tesh of Karrabar, he had no real idea who was behind the attack. His fellow councilors had made clear their lack of support for the keeper's attempts at appeasement, though Edvar could see through their protestations. War brought opportunities. Increased demand for weapons, armor, and food meant higher prices and greater profits for those who owned the supplies, and they all had their fingers in such pies. *Could they be working against the Keeper? Stirring up the people against him to drive their own agenda?*

The longing he felt for his father was becoming harder to ignore. His old man would have known what to do, how best to protect Ashara. *He wouldn't have let this happen in the first place.*

Edvar had dismally failed, and yet somehow he clung on. He needed to redeem himself, and now he had an opportunity to do so.

Upon a bare and dimly lit landing near the midpoint of the prison tower, he met his least favorite colleague, Mara. She sat rigidly on a bench outside a guarded door, gaze aimless, her mind no doubt lost in some bitter or scheming thought. Her silver hair was fixed in a tight bun, indigo dress, with matching jacket, neat and uncreased, despite the late hour.

"Mara," Edvar said in greeting. They shared little affection, but Edvar strived to keep terms civil; fewer headaches that way. Mara's narrow eyes scoured his face before she gave the slightest of nods. Edvar could hear the rumble of a man's voice beyond the iron-studded door to the assassin's cell. Two steel-clad women, Mara's personal guards, stood on either side.

"Who's in there?" he asked.

"Rakar."

Her answer heaped a barrel of oil onto Edvar's fires of suspicion. The meticulous treasurer was a quiet, unassuming man, his hairstyle never deviating, face always shaven, the colour of his clothes forever muted. Edvar couldn't remember him being late for an engagement, and he always displayed appreciation for the contributions of others. Rarely did he mix himself up in dirty work like interrogating prisoners.

"How long has he been in there?"

Mara's eyes narrowed. "An hour or so."

Edvar stepped toward the room. Out of the corner of his eye, he saw Mara scowl. Her guards made no move to stop him. Opening the door, he locked eyes with Rakar, who sat facing a woman with skin a pale, bluish hue. Bandages covered her thigh where the crossbow bolt had struck. Beneath her chair, a small pool of blood glistened in the weak light offered by the room's only candle.

"Can I help you?" Rakar asked.

"I'd like to speak with her."

"I'm not finished."

"An hour seems plenty long. What are you discussing? The intricacies of the copper trade?"

The woman sniggered, and Rakar shot Edvar a hellish look. Edvar decided to tip the balance in his favour. "The keeper's orders," he said with a shrug. Technically they were.

"Ten minutes," Rakar said, getting to his feet, the legs of his wooden chair scraping against the stone floor. He slammed the door behind him, a move out of character for a man so calm and composed.

"Slamming doors is such a childish thing to do, don't you think?" Edvar said, taking Rakar's seat.

Off somewhere in the shadows of the windowless room came an occasional drip, no doubt the source of the dank stench. The candle in the sconce upon the grimy stone wall offered a weak resistance against the void and illuminated the peculiar face of the assassin. It was not a trick of the eye—her complexion was indeed a subtle blue, with blotches of dark green all over her skin. Ice-white hair, tied back in a tail, cropped a pockmarked face. Above her leaf-green eyes, a jagged scar, badly healed, ran across her forehead. She certainly wasn't Yurrish and possessed none of the pinched, mole-like features of the Karrabans. *Where in Soria is she from?*

"What's your name?" Edvar asked. He stared into her eyes, seeking clues. Her lips remained pursed. "An unimportant question I suppose. So let's cut the crap shall we, because judging from that wound time's not on your side..." A reaction, at last—the wryest of smiles.

"Does it hurt?" she asked, pointing her bound hands at his blackening eyes and cut nose.

Edvar swallowed a grain of annoyance. "Where are you from?" he said.

"Why does that matter?" Her accent was thick, unlike any he had heard before, her t's sounding like d's.

"I suppose it doesn't. The only thing that does is the name of the person who sent you."

"And what makes you think I'm not acting alone?"

"You're neither from Yurr nor Karrabar so have no clear motive. The timing. The fact it was pretty much a suicide mission. Do you need more reasons?"

She laughed, causing her face to contort with pain. "What if someone did send me? Why should I tell you anything?"

"Because if you don't, the pain you feel now will be like a mere prick to your fingertip."

She grinned. "I've heard of you. The one so young and wise. Perhaps what they say is wrong. I see youth and little else. You're just like the rest."

Edvar felt a prickle of heat in his cheeks. He scratched his patchy beard. "What do you mean?"

"The old are set in their ways. They fear change, and when they are faced with it, they return to what they know. So often it is violence." She pushed herself up in her chair. "It must be hard being younger than them, having them envy your youth."

Edvar saw an opportunity. A sore point. A crack in the wall of resistance. He feigned embitterment. "Having them order you about, expecting obedience and respect. Such things must be earned. They aren't entitlements," he said.

The woman stared at him, sizing him up, and he met her gaze. He wondered how she'd gotten that scar. Had she been enslaved? Abused? Manipulated or betrayed? In an unexpected turn, he found himself pitying her, the woman who had hours before tried to kill him and Ashara.

"I know how you feel, and I want to help you," he said.

"But only if I help you."

Edvar nodded. He shuffled his chair closer, voice lowering. "You have nothing to lose and everything to gain in giving me the name of the person who put you up to this."

"You're wrong, baby face. I'm already dead."

"That's not true."

"What do you know? You cannot save me. I give you the name, they'll cut off my head, stick it on a spike and brand me a heathen. You let me live, and my head will end up far worse off than on a spike. I trust no man." She hawked and spat on the floor.

"I give you my word." Even as he said it, his words felt hollow.

She scoffed. "Your word? Pretty little promises mean nothing. Tell me, did you give your word to protect your noble keeper? Did that stop me from cutting him up?"

"It stopped you from getting away with it."

A bout of pained coughing cut short her burst of laughter. "I should have killed you. You're a pathetic excuse of a man. I can see the fear in your eyes. You're just a kid playing in the world of grownups. I bet your mother and father are ashamed of you."

He knew she was goading him. To his dismay, he felt himself slipping down the walls of the trap.

"Didn't like that one did you? Is Daddy disappointed?"

Edvar lunged across the table. He grabbed her jerkin, pulled her scarred face to his. He could see rings of gold around her pupils, smell the sweat of her body and foulness of her breath. Her mirth grew.

"I did not think it would be so easy to get you off your feet. You really are just like the others."

"I'm nothing like them," Edvar shouted in a voice he didn't recognise.

Her smile faded, and with it went his anger. He released his hold and looked at her, confused at how much she'd managed to rile him. His father had taught him ways to keep his composure, and he'd used none of them here. He'd squandered his chance at getting what he needed. Failure once again embraced him.

He turned to the door, headache returning and with it a sudden wave of fatigue.

"A coin casts a large shadow," the assassin murmured, as Edvar twisted the handle. He looked back over his shoulder, puzzled by her words.

"What?"

The expression upon her face indicated she'd say no more. Edvar shook his head and left her to the cold hands of Mara.

He trudged back to his chamber, craving clarity, but the streets were shrouded in fog. Maybe tomorrow would bring a light to burn through the haze, though he had little hope that it would.

Five

A towering silhouette snuffed out the light of the sun.

Dread pulsed through Isy's body, paralyzing her limbs. It took a step closer, revealing it to be a hairy man with iron-grey skin, dressed in a brown robe that stretched to his ankles. Other than his giant size, he appeared Yurrish, up to his neck. Beyond that, things became warped. His eyes grabbed her attention first. Bulbous and frog-like, they were broad as the rims of tankards, spaced a palms width apart, and lunar-blue in colour. A shudder raced down her spine when he blinked. In between those moon-like eyes was a stubby, wide-nostrilled nose and below it a mouth that lacked lips, though it was hard to see with the mass of wiry brown hair smothering his cheeks and chin. The hair atop his head was similarly coloured and tied in a long plaited tail that hung over his shoulder and stretched down to his waist. Poking out from underneath were large, rat-like ears.

Isy's mind couldn't comprehend what she saw, nor could it muster any thought on what to do. Turn and run. *Run where? He will catch me.* Shout for help. *But who would hear, who would come?*

A sweat-inducing heat rushed through her body. He... it... didn't move. Just stood and stared, face revealing nothing. Isy could stand it no more. She shuffled backwards.

With a swiftness that belied his great frame, the frog-man darted toward her, and before she could properly turn, hands firm and engulfing gripped her shoulders. A sudden weakness overcame her, and she felt unable to resist as he threw her over his shoulder. She wanted to cry out but found no breath to do so. She rose and fell with his lumbering strides and slowly realization dawned. A throat-burning scream erupted from her lungs. She punched and scratched, and when his giant hands stilled hers, she flailed her legs. Her toes struck a solid back. He tossed her to the ground, his demeanor seeming more annoyed than infuriated as he pulled out a rope and began to bind her ankles and wrists. Isy did not relent in her cries and soon her efforts were rewarded. The brush before her rustled.

A figure emerged. The savior she had so often read about, the gallant hero come to rescue the princess. Only she wasn't a princess and the man who stepped into view no hero, but another of the frog-men. He was dressed in identical garb, skin just as grey, with his hair in a plaited tail, like his companion. His eyes were smaller and closer together and his beard was fashioned into three neat plaits. He spoke words that sounded Yurrish, though nothing recognizable, and mixed in were clicks of the tongue that baffled Isy further. Clearly, they were discussing her, pointing and looking in her direction. Who were they? People from an old cautionary tale told by grandmothers to their grandchildren? Isy had never known her grandmothers, though she'd read the stories. In the reaches of her mind she recalled some about wild men, but nothing that matched those who stood before her.

The second man knelt and looked her in the eye. Isy turned away, instinctively hiding her tainted face. Coarse and hairy fingers touched her chin with a gentleness she was unaccustomed to. She didn't resist as he moved her head to face him. He traced her birthmark, not in fear or repulsion, but with intrigue. His touch was almost calming, his massive, ice-blue eyes holding a look of benevolence. He muttered something to his companion, who nodded and moved to stand behind her.

The atmosphere seemed to shift, a blissful moment torn asunder like a butterfly in a hurricane. A hand pulled open her jaw, the force unrelenting. Panic gripped her. She tried to scream but could only grunt. Out of the corner of her eye, she saw the other man pull something from inside his robe and the next thing she knew, a cool liquid trickled over her tongue and down her throat.

A grimace-provoking bitterness filled her mouth. Searing heat burned her gullet and wound its way through her body to sit in her stomach like a lump of coal plucked from the heart of the fire. All she could do was gasp, and with that, she keeled over and fell into nothingness.

Six

Isy awoke with a start. It was dark, so either she'd slept a few hours or an entire day. Her head felt like it could have been either. The foul taste of offal filled her mouth, but no longer did her insides burn. A heavy fur cloak had been wrapped around her shoulders. Wrists still bound, though ankles now free, she pushed herself up on elbows and looked about. She lay close to the mouth of a shallow cave. Impenetrable darkness embraced her, though to her right she found a sky pockmarked with stars and the white tear of the wandering moon, which shone into the cave to provide some light. Two pairs of luminous eyes hovered in the gloom opposite her. There was no campfire. *Perhaps they think someone will come looking for me.* Her father, she imagined, would be straight to the Haber Inn, toasting his first drink, maybe even buying a round for everyone else. Her mother would fret and may even explore the outer reaches of town, but her father would discourage any real search. No doubt he would argue their miserable daughter had run away, abandoned *them*. It was what he did; shifted fault onto others.

That would be the end of it. A brief search, conclusions drawn, and onto whatever trifles the next day brought. Nobody would miss the Cursed One. They would more likely celebrate the lifting of the supposed curse they believed she carried. Maybe they'd even start an annual feast day filled with singing, dancing, music and games. Somehow, from somewhere, a positive thought emerged. *At least now I am free of them.* It seemed her life as she knew it was gone. What lay before her was likely worse, and, like anything unknown, troubling to the point of nausea. But now, at least, she was free of the torment that had crippled her for nineteen summers.

The two frog-men muttered to one another. Her initial captor tossed something in her direction: a pouch made from thick woven leaf. She caught it with her forearms.

"Eat," said the one with the plaited beard. Isy looked at him, surprised at hearing such a strange looking man say such a recognizable word.

"You speak Yurrish?" she asked, food forgotten despite her grumbling stomach.

"Little." His words were more like enunciated grunts.

"What's your name?" she asked, feeling hopeful but unsure why.

His eyes narrowed. "Na-me," he repeated thoughtfully.

With her bound hands, Isy pointed at herself. "Isy", she said, sounding it out.

The one who had taken her frowned, but the other nodded. He pointed at himself, copying Isy. "Kora," he said, clicking his tongue before the 'k'. He pointed at his kinsman: "Tulasc," he said. He muttered in his own language to Tulasc. Isy heard her name mentioned and Tulasc turned to her and nodded. Questions flooded her mind. It'd taken this much effort to get their names, would they be able to answer anything else?

They watched as she ate, which, despite the darkness, made her conscious of her mark.

"Why did you take me?" She grabbed and tugged at her shirt and pointed at herself. Tulasc squinted. Kora shook his head. "Where are you taking me?" she tried again, mimicking moving legs with two of her fingers.

Tulasc's brows furrowed further, but Kora seemed to understand.

"Aena," he said. All his answer did was add to her confusion. They allowed her to finish her berries and nuts and then stood.

"No hit," Kora said.

Tulasc approached her and, with as much effort as lifting a stick, hefted her over his head and placed her bound wrists around his neck to carry her on his back. Something felt odd. Where she anticipated feeling the bones of his spine, she instead found what felt like a shell—the thing she must have kicked earlier.

They descended from the cave and into the lightless forest, their gaits smooth despite the steep and uneven terrain. Her eyes soon grew heavy, yet she resisted sleep. They could kill her at any moment, and this Aena place they carried her to may also spell her end, but curiously she did not feel afraid. She knew what pain and torment were and she was moving away from them. If anything, she found a sense of curiosity building.

Seven

Isy opened her eyes to find the forest lit in the haze of dawn. The pace of the frog-men hadn't altered, but the landscape around them had. Drastically. Wakefulness came swiftly, and she craned her neck to take in as much as she could.

The trees were the biggest things she'd ever seen, so stout they would take twenty paces to walk around, and thrice the height of the watchmen's round tower in Haberdam. Some were smothered in shamrock-colored vines and moss, and all bore mighty branches from which sprouted lush leaves that clustered at their peaks where they battled for sunlight. Around the great, snaking roots were ferns bigger than children and through them Kora and Tulasc moved, the latter carrying Isy upon his back.

From the descriptions she'd read, Isy guessed this was the Giant's Garden, the vast forest that surrounded the base of the Teeth of Giants. But how could they have travelled so far so soon? It was fifteen leagues or more from Haberdam, over difficult terrain.

Tulasc stopped. Kora turned to him and Tulasc whispered something in their own tongue. Kora's expression changed. Isy thought she recognized concern in his bulbous eyes. His ears twitched. Isy could hear nothing but the soughing wind, the rustle of leaves. Kora's head snapped around to look at Tulasc. Upon the next breeze, Isy heard something too. A scratchy shriek.

Skraa. Skraa. Skraa.

She wanted to ask what it was but knew they couldn't tell her. There was no opportunity regardless. They set off at a sprint. Trees and foliage flashed by; she couldn't believe the speed with which they ran. Kora pointed ahead at a fallen tree, the moss-covered trunk hollowed by woodworm. At a crouch, they moved through it, halting a third of the way in. Kora knelt, peering through a crack in the bark. Tulasc set Isy down next to him.

Skraa. Skraa.

Louder. Isy couldn't begin to imagine what it might be. To force these frog-men into hiding meant it must be something ferocious, bigger, uglier. Isy was afraid to breathe. Her heart pounded in her ears. At hearing a sudden thud above her head, she nearly let out a yelp. The creature scratched as it moved, like crows on a wooden roof. Another thud. Followed by another. Isy looked at Kora, who clasped his hand over his mouth. She understood. *Be quiet.* He needn't have worried.

Skraa.

Arms trembling with adrenaline and fear, she pushed herself up to peer through a crack in the wood. Birds. Twice the size of a hawk, their feathers were a deep, shimmering blue. They had black eyes, ringed with orange, with beaks just as dark, and straight and pointed like a dagger. Never had she seen such a bird, though she'd heard of them. A creature spoken of almost mythically in Haberdam. Blue ravens.

"Death comes with the blue raven."

Or so the old saying went. Some said they were the reason behind the tradition of teaching the children of the town to shoot a bow. If true, it must have been an old reason. Nobody she knew had ever seen one.

Three more birds swooped into view and began to dig at the mud with taloned feet. More cries sounded behind, above, all around. Those Isy could see looked up in the direction from which the other caws came. They scurried across the ground with blinking swiftness, beat their broad wings, and took to the air, answering with screeches of their own.

Isy nearly lost consciousness holding her breath. Her mouth was dry and her entire body trembled feverishly. The piercing cries faded from earshot. Kora and Tulasc exchanged a nod and then Tulasc picked her up. Without making a sound, they left the cover of the hollow tree. Silence lingered over the forest, a quiet that came with the presence of predators. The frog-men gazed in every direction, ears twitching, eyes never still. Isy looked around too. Out of the corner of her eye, she saw the leaf of a fern bobbing ever so slightly. She watched it, unsure whether or not it was the wind. A black eye blinked amongst the leaves, and the next thing she knew, blue feathers consumed her vision. Isy cried out and buried her head into Tulasc's back. The frog-man moved. She heard a grunt, then a thud. When she opened her eyes, feathers were floating to the ground. Kora stood a few feet away, a slingshot in hand, while at Tulasc's feet, the bloodied bird twitched as its life escaped.

Once again, they set off at a run, following no trail at all that Isy could see. They kept the same pace for what felt like an hour, and when they stopped neither of them appeared tired. Was this a dream? Had she fallen asleep in the meadow and still lay there now, safe and close to home? The rope chafing the skin of her wrists and the odious smell of nuts and sweat emanating from Tulasc reminded her of the reality. He set her down and they shared a skin of water. The two frog-men conversed and Isy's gaze wandered. Behind a small tree, she saw something pale and sharp poking out from the other side. When she neared she realised it was a jagged piece of bone with morsels of red and brown hanging from it. She peered around the tree and found a skeleton of a doe. Skin, muscle, ligament, organs—everything—had been stripped.

"Paska," Kora said, walking up behind her. He made a pair of wings with his hands. Paska was their name for the blue raven, she guessed. The birds had done to this deer what they would have done to them. She swallowed hard.

They continued on at a steadier pace, seemingly content the threat was gone. The sun fell away, shadows grew, and the forest remained peacefully still. Isy began to lull into a sense of ease, her lids growing heavy; until she caught a scent that dispelled her fatigue, one she knew from back home. It grew in potency; she could taste it now, and she gagged. It was the smell of decaying carcasses at the back of the saddler's workshop. The smell of death.

Perhaps it reminded her of her own vulnerability, but at that moment, panic struck her heart like the bolt of a crossbow and filled it with fear of her own end. The urge to get away overcame her, and she hefted her arms up over Tulasc's head and pushed herself away. As soon as her feet touched the ground, she bolted into a thicket of ferns, ignoring the shouts of Kora and Tulasc. She tore through the brush and chanced a glance over her shoulder to see if they followed.

Something slammed into her chest. Her head hit the ground, the wind fled her lungs. Gasping and stunned, she opened her eyes and focused them on a spearhead hovering over her neck. Holding the spear was one of Kora's kin. A woman, more slender and gaunt than the two men and much less hairy. She answered the calls of her kin with a whistle and soon the duo appeared, mumbling in their language.

With the final, harsh realization that no hero was coming to rescue her, Isy broke into tears.

Episode Two: Heavy Burdens

Everything changed the day I received Uren's letter. I knew from his brevity that he had found something of peculiar interest. It was indeed a tomb not far from Drummnaught belonging to, he believed, an old king. In it, amongst a horde of other artifacts, he had found a chest containing tomes, scrolls, maps, a scabbarded sword with an elegantly bejeweled crossguard, and an item I found particularly curious—the tooth of a shark, fastened in a necklace. Uren had shown little interest in it. Instead, his excitement had been absorbed by a book that he had managed to partially translate. It spoke, he said, of great weapons forged with a magic so powerful they had to be locked away in vaults. I knew immediately what Uren wanted me to do. Find them.

From ***The Forgotten Daggers*** by S. T. Harris

One

EDVAR STEPPED OUT of the shadows and into brilliant tricolor light. The morning sun flooded through the stained-glass windows of the Chamber of Assembly and onto the round, well-polished oak table where the Keeper's Council conducted its affairs. He was the last to arrive.

After the tumultuous night he'd had, getting out of bed had proven a struggle. Sleep had beckoned to him like the prettiest courtesan in the tavern and all his throbbing head had wanted to do was rest in her comfortable bosom. But what sleep he'd gotten had been fitful and he'd awoken with an ill feeling in his stomach. The cause of that, he knew, was not the bang to his head, nor the cut to his arm, but the prospect of this very meeting.

Edvar briefly met Mara's gaze. She'd changed clothing in the few hours since their last encounter, wearing a long, seaweed-colored skirt, tight to her legs, with a matching velvet cloak. Her role on the Council was to oversee security and policing. She would do anything to deflect the scrutiny onto others, namely him.

Next to her sat Levanwe, something of a permanent fixture in the keep having served Ashara's mother, Alysa, too. Unlike Mara, she was more prone to a smile and appeared almost innocent with her cropped white hair and small, crooked stature. Edvar knew it masked a wicked and merciless side. Levanwe was regarded as something of an oracle when it came to trade and commerce, over which she presided.

General Malfan sat beside her. Stout as a barrel and about as tall as one too, the balding old man marched wherever he went, the bushy grey moustache that dominated his face bouncing with his strides. Unsurprisingly, he presided over the military.

Opposite Malfan sat Niskima, glaring at Edvar with her hook of a nose almost pointing at the ceiling. She was a woman who took great pleasure in looking down at others, something she had ample opportunity to do with control over the realm's agriculture.

Rakar sat next to her, his eyes fixed on Edvar as the young councilor made his way to the table.

"My apologies for the tardiness. It's been a... rough night," Edvar said, taking his seat beside the treasurer.

"It's been a rough night for all of us, yet we made it in good time," Mara said, words cold as the bottom of the Green Deep.

"Quite. Sleep is unimportant in such times, Edvar," Levanewe said.

Let me sit down at least, Edvar thought as he poured himself a cup of watered wine. It was going to be a long morning.

Rakar began. "The attack on the Keeper is, I'm sure you'll agree, a deeply disturbing incident, and serious questions must be asked as to how it happened."

A few glances Edvar's way. He hid his clenched jaw with a feigned sip of wine. Ashara's security was his responsibility, as well as intelligence generally. The last thing he needed was to be preached to, though it was to be expected. The assassin was right. The old liked to lord over the young, this lot in particular. They seized any opportunity to pounce upon his inexperiences and naiveties. Not once had they extended the olive branch.

Rakar went on.

"From what I understand, the assassin managed to get onto the roof of the Royal Tower, murdered those standing guard, and climbed down to the Keeper's balcony."

"How in Soria did he get onto the roof?" asked Malfan, voice much deeper than expected for such a small fellow.

"She," corrected Rakar. "It's a question we're still trying to answer," Rakar said, half-glancing at Edvar.

"Did she reveal anything in your interrogations?" Edvar asked, looking at Rakar, then at Mara.

"Little," Mara said. "After I used the meat grinder on her hands, she fell unconscious."

Mara's use of the meat grinder was renowned. Nearly everybody spoke after they'd had a finger or two ruined. And she forced them to watch, pinning open their eyelids if necessary. That was the worst part, Edvar imagined.

"Can we please hold off on the torture?" Edvar said. "We need her alive—she's the only one who can help us identify who's behind this."

"And what do you propose instead? Because whatever method you tried last night achieved nothing," Mara spat.

Anger rumbled in Edvar's chest. He did all he could to keep it there. He didn't want to say something he'd regret, not when he was supposed to be keeping tabs on them for Ashara. He broke his gaze with Mara and took another sip of wine.

"Thank you for your efforts, Mara," Rakar said. "Please let us know how today's interrogations fare."

The others murmured their thanks too. Malfan looked like a dog with a lamb shank, moustache bobbing as he nodded. Edvar kept silent.

"Edvar, what have you learned of the attack? How did the assassin breach the keep's walls?" Levanwe asked.

"I hate to say it, but you assured us you had things covered. What in Soria happened?" Malfan added.

"I'm still trying to ascertain what exactly occurred. Unfortunately, my questioning of the assassin didn't lead to anything, but I would speak to her again today, if there is anything left of her."

Mara stiffened, and for a heartbeat, her eyes flicked to Rakar.

"What of all these informants you boast of? Have they not uncovered anything?" Niskima asked, words hacking at him like a butcher's cleaver.

"I have every one of them seeking clues. This morning the questioning of all the keep's staff will begin. I fear somebody helped the assassin get inside the keep."

"Did you not make these checks before?" Malfan asked.

"Of course. I informed you of my progress at our last meeting. Did you not read my report?"

Silence answered. Edvar knew the thoughts swirling around each of their minds. *He is unfit for this job. Useless. A mere child.* Edvar swallowed another hot coal of anger.

"Who could be behind this?" Rakar put the question to everyone. Not a hint of his demeanor suggested he had anything to do with it, his face etched with grief.

"Tesh of Karrabar is the obvious suspect," Niskima said. Levanwe sounded her agreement.

"He has sought nothing but war since he took power," Malfan said.

"Why treat for peace then?" Rakar asked.

"A smokescreen, to knock us off-guard, make us an easier foe. If he removes Ashara then he's free to invade," Malfan said.

"He's certainly the likeliest option. What of other suspects?" Edvar said. Once more, silence fell. Eyes met eyes.

"We could speculate all day. The information we possess is scant at best," Rakar said. "Until all of the facts are clear, we must not act. We must continue to probe our contacts for information and see what comes to light."

All nodded and made noises of consent.

"Edvar, what security measures are now in place?" Rakar asked. "We must ensure no further harm befalls our Keeper. Lock him in his room and wrap him in plates of steel if you must." At the mention of 'harm', his voice wavered with emotion.

"I have twice as many soldiers guarding his tower. Twenty of the finest archers upon the ramparts, a quad of crossbowmen stationed on the balcony, and the watch upon the battlements has been doubled. It would take a small army to get to him."

"Good. That is all we can do. Defend while we uncover the truth. I'd be grateful if you could send me a report on your added defenses," Rakar said in a dismissive tone akin to a father addressing his son.

Something inside Edvar's weary head snapped. "Do you not trust me, Rakar?"

"I did not say that."

"You implied it. Indeed, you all seem to think it was me that was behind this, judging from your attitudes."

"The Keeper's safety isn't our responsibility. It's yours," Mara said.

"Questions have to be asked," Levanwe said, that sinister edge flashing in her eyes.

"Well, I have questions of my own, starting with you, Rakar. Why were you the first into the interrogation room? I don't think I've ever seen you within half a mile of that tower."

"Our Keeper nearly died, and still might, no thanks to you," Mara spat.

The verbal jab proved one too many. Edvar hurled his cup across the room, spraying Levanwe. Tuts and gasps erupted around the table. Cheeks burning with rage, Edvar stormed from the room. The force with which he slammed the door behind him stirred a rattle from the armor of the surprised guards outside.

Two

Hours passed and Edvar still seethed. His mind and body yearned for sleep, but he was tense as a drawn bowstring. He had no appetite, no thirst, no desire at all other than to unleash his rage upon his fellow councilors, Mara above all. Over and over, he came up with clever, witty and cutting ripostes that he wished he'd said at the time, and berated himself for not having done so. And he obsessed over the next steps. How would they react? Would they try and remove him? And what would the Keeper say? He'd promised to stay close to his co-councilors and in one idiotic swoop, he'd pushed them a league away.

Edvar sighed. From his desk drawer, he pulled out his pipe and tabac box, engraved with a scene from the Battle of Martyr's Head. His father had led the victorious side that day. Glorious Harada the Great. Edvar's mother had the box made after the battle as a gift to her husband. She'd died giving birth to Edvar. Whenever he had asked his father about her, he had received silence in response. And now, he'd never know what she was like, a fact that weighed heavily on his heart.

Edvar took a long drag of his pipe after stuffing the bowl and lighting the brown leaf with a taper. He eased into his padded chair as he exhaled thick, white smoke. He closed his eyes, put thoughts of his parents out of his mind, and with pipe between his teeth, steadily puffed in and out. Slowly, his mind began to de-clutter.

He slipped into a brief, peaceful sleep, and when he awoke, the pipe still hung from his lips, leaf now ash. His headache had eased, and his stomach gave him a nudge for food. When he opened his eyes, the first thing he saw, through the narrow window opposite, was a sky clear of cloud, the color gentle, bright.

Edvar rose from his chair to a chorus of clicks and looked out of the window. He could see half of the keep, its baileys, and most of the sprawling city beyond. Many of those who resided in the keep's towers preferred the coastal view. Like his father and Ashara, Edvar preferred to look over the city he was charged with serving. *What a poor job I'm doing.*

He sighed at the thought of the meeting earlier that day. He'd acted so naively—exactly how they'd wanted him to behave. It'd been planned, no doubt, and he'd taken the bait. Not only was his credibility damaged, but Ashara's too, for it was him who had appointed Edvar to the Council after Harada's death. Edvar couldn't afford to be so foolish again, if he had any of Ashara's goodwill left at all.

A knock on his door snapped him out of his thoughts. "Yes?"

The door opened a crack and through the gap appeared the haggard, squinty-eyed face of Darnell.

"Got something for you," Darnell said in his raspy voice.

"Please, come in," Edvar said.

Darnell was a Watchman. He spent his days and nights policing the streets of Yurrisa. Edvar had recruited him at a time of unrest in the Watch, after Mara had orchestrated a massive change in structure that saw many Watchmen relieved of their jobs. Darnell's loyalties had frayed as a result; he craved justice for his banished friends, something Edvar had promised to give him.

From his quiver, Darnell pulled an arrow that looked like any other and handed it to Edvar, who nodded his thanks and slipped him a couple of silver coins. Darnell bowed and departed. As soon as the door clicked shut, Edvar unscrewed the arrowhead and pulled out from the hollow shaft a rolled-up piece of parchment. He scanned the short message, and for the first time in what felt like a long time, his lips, ever so slightly, curled into a smile.

Three

The prison tower was the oldest and least aesthetically pleasing of all the keep's towers, so it found its natural role. Its bare stone walls were blackened with age and rough as thorns. The stairwells were suffocating and ill-lit—indeed, the tower didn't have a single window.

Edvar climbed the stairs, wondering in what state he was to find the assassin. A day in Mara's care may well have ruined her altogether. He thought he'd gotten the wrong floor when he saw just one guard standing outside the assassin's cell—or rather slouched against the wall, his conical half-helm tipped forward over his eyes. Last night there'd been six, all awake.

"Who's in there?" Edvar asked, moving toward the door.

The guard bolted upright, the back of his helm clanging against the wall. "Nobody, sir," he said loudly in his flustered state.

"What do you mean 'nobody'?" Edvar opened the door. Indeed, the room appeared as if it had never been occupied. Edvar looked at the guard.

"She died, sir."

"When?"

"A few hours ago."

It was the last thing Edvar wanted to hear. The wound to her leg was bad but not fatal, and last night she'd showed no signs of fever. Mara must have pushed her too far. *Or was it deliberate?*

"Who was in here today?"

The guard stuttered. "Lady Mara, sir. Her guards too."

"That all?"

The soldier nodded. Edvar studied his flushed cheeks, watched eyes that were unable to settle.

"What's your name, soldier?"

"Myshal."

"Have you heard of The Black Redoubt, Myshal?"

Myshal nodded, less vigorously this time. "What soldier hasn't?"

"I've often wondered what it would be like to be stationed there. The perpetual ice and snow. Winds to bite away flesh. I heard in the worst winters, your fingers and toes fall off, but not before something else. Do you know what it is?"

Myshal shook his head, looking like an animal wary of a trap.

"Your balls, and then your cock. Probably the worst of it all, though, is the boredom. Nothing to do but chop wood and stick more logs on the fire, waiting, hoping, praying for that signal to come so you can light the pyre and discharge your duty."

Any soldier would sooner charge alone at the walls of an enemy keep than go to the Black Redoubt. The beacon tower had been built during the War of the Damned, after the Karrabans had found a way over the Teeth of Giants and wreaked havoc on the north. There had been no cause to use the beacon since, but it was forever manned, often by the most incompetent and useless of soldiers, or those in need of punishment.

"Myshal, I'll ask you once more. Lie to me and I think I'll arrange a little trip for you. Who visited the assassin today?"

Myshal swallowed hard and looked at the ground. "Councilor Mara, her guards, a serving girl."

"And..."

"Councilor Rakar."

Edvar bit his bottom lip. Thoughts exploded in his mind. *Back again? But why?* Had *he* in fact hired the assassin and dealt with her before she could say anything? *That's madness*, Edvar almost said aloud. Surely it was just circumstantial? He was, after all, the least ambitious of all the councilors and the most honest; the treasury had never experienced a discrepancy under his tenure. And such a coup could not be achieved alone. Edvar could see Mara being involved, but the others... no. Or had Rakar acquired support from elsewhere? Karrabar perhaps...

Cluttered thoughts clashed and ricocheted off the walls of his mind. The throb at his temples was returning. He needed answers, and the starting point, he hoped, was Myshal.

"Have a seat, soldier. I have a couple of questions for you. Best close this door. Keep out that chill."

Four

"Isyyy! Isyyy!"

The rush of the River Haber, crashing and churning against rocks and boulders, drowned out his shouts. Vil had set out that morning with his fires of determination well stoked, but now futility plagued his efforts and the hours already spent calling to no avail were taking their toll on his hope and belief.

Two nights had passed since Isy had disappeared. Her father, Tamlin, hadn't mustered even a half-hearted search. On the night of the first day, he was in the Haber Inn and didn't leave till dawn. Vil had seen Isy's mother looking around the town, though she hadn't strayed far beyond the boundary. Nobody else had offered to help. Indeed, nobody seemed bothered at all.

The mud of the river bank was slick and lined with jagged rocks. Already he'd fallen and grazed his hands. In the chill of late afternoon, they throbbed, just like the rest of his body. He had spent longer on his feet today than he was used to, dwarfing the average distance of his daily ambles around the town and bookshelves of the store.

But Vil couldn't sit idly. Since he'd heard of Isy's disappearance he'd been unable to settle, pacing the stacks, staring out of the windows in the hope of seeing her. He'd bitten his nails down to the bed, and the chronicler had scolded him too many times to count for making more mistakes than usual.

He didn't know why he felt so agitated. He hadn't
known Isy all that long, and beyond their chats when she
came to the store, he didn't speak to her. But there was
something magnetic about her. Was it the sound of her
laugh, or the way her eyes lit up when she smiled? Or her
sharp wit and the fact she listened to his words when others
ignored them?

He did not understand the hatred toward Isy. Yes, she
had a significant mark on her face, but that was the extent of
it. She didn't smell unlike most people in this gods-forsaken
town, nor was she diseased or cursed with ill luck as
everybody claimed. If anything, Vil's days were often better
after a visit from Isy. As selfish a thought as it was,
particularly given how miserable he knew her life to be, he
didn't want her to go. She was the closest thing he'd ever
had to a friend, and in that sense, he feared abandonment
again in his life. But to his knowledge, she had never left
Haberdam before, though she'd often spoke of her desire to
leave. With each passing hour, his fears grew that
something more sinister might have happened.

At a bend in the river, the bank he walked upon rose
steeply. From it jutted a jagged and monstrous rock. Behind
it was a cave, he had learned thanks to Isy. It was one of her
hiding places.

Vil breathed in his doughy gut and skirted around the
edge of the outcropping, using the rocks poking up from the
water's surface to balance upon. A smile came fleetingly to
his lips, the memory flashing in his mind of him falling in
the first time she had brought him here. How she had barked
with laughter. This time, he made it around with dry feet
and stood before a narrow crack shaped like the claw of a
mountain bear. He peered into the void, so dark it was as if
the idea of light had been forgotten. Darkness did not instill
him with fear as it once had. Not since the days he had spent
trapped in the archives of the Grand Library, locked away
and forgotten about, slowly dying and utterly powerless to
change the course of his fate. Even now, a decade on, tension
filled his chest at the thought of those long, lightless,

hungry days. He exhaled it away and stepped up to the cave mouth.

"Isy!"

He waited for the echo to fade, then shouted again.

"Who you lookin' for?"

Vil spun round, heart skipping, to find a young, bearded man, with a mop of tousled brown hair, looking down at him from the bank above. In his hand he held a small fishing spear, the flint point emitting a dull twinkle in the afternoon sun.

"Nobody," Vil sputtered.

"You must be lookin' for someone if you're shoutin' down there."

"My dog. I've lost my dog."

"What kinda dog?"

"A... Yurrish Red."

"Ain't seen no snapper runnin' 'bout down 'ere. What you say its name was?"

"Ba-rd."

"Baaard?" He frowned. "You takin' the piss?" He turned away from Vil. "Oi, Pikey. 'Ere a min."

The breath caught in Vil's throat. *Not another one.* His pathetic lies wouldn't withstand double scrutiny. Another young man, about the same age as the first, came into view. He too carried a spear and, with his thicker beard, shaven head, patched clothes and scar dividing his left eyebrow, looked rougher than his companion. Vil had never seen them around the town, but he hadn't lived in Haberdam long and wasn't one for socializing.

"What's this you've found, Mosh?"

"This weird chubby kid. Shoutin' down this cave he was."

"What you shoutin' down that cave for, tubs?"

"I've lost my dog," Vil said, battling to keep his voice from breaking.

"Yurrish Red called Baaard, he says," said Mosh.

"Funny name for a dog."

"That's what I thought. Tell me this then, tubs, why was you shoutin' 'Isy'?"

Vil dug his thumb into his palm. He willed his mind to produce a response, but it wouldn't comply.

Pikey piped up. "Ain't that the name of Tamlin's kid? The cursed bitch who vanished?"

"Yeah, it is," said Mosh. "You ain't lookin' for that monster are ya? We don't want her coming back. Since she's been gone, Bert the Beak caught a catfish long as his boat and Mikah's snared more rabbits than he has all year. You lookin' on cursin' us all again?"

Pikey skidded down the sloped bank and landed in the shallow water before Vil. Mosh followed, albeit less gracefully, and banged his knee on a rock. He tried to hide his pain as he willed himself to stand tall beside his friend.

"Is that who you're looking for?" Pikey asked in a menacing voice.

All but Vil's quivering lips froze. He had no clue what to do, only felt a powerful urge to flee. But to where? They were blocking the way ahead and he couldn't swim. Into the cave? He didn't trust himself to keep his feet in the gloom; he'd stumble and fall. *What choice do I have?* He turned and scrambled inside.

"You know what my pa always said, Mosh? Guilty men always run."

Vil fought for his footing on the uneven ground, toes connecting with rocks, dipping into holes. To his amazement, he didn't fall. Neither did his pursuers. The thrum of their steps filled his ears. Any moment he expected hands to reach out and grab his cloak. The thought injected further haste into his weary legs, the risk of any moment crashing into rock disregarded.

Over the beat of his heart, he realized the sounds of pursuit had quietened. He didn't want to stop, but he wasn't sure whether they still followed. In the end, he halted. A stone scuffed against the floor. Voices murmured. They weren't far behind.

An idea entered his mind. Vil stretched out his arms, seeking the wall of the cave. After some aimless groping his hand connected with cold, moist rock. He hunkered down against it, bunching like a frightened hedgehog.

"Where in Soria has he gone?" Pikey asked.

"Lunatic. I ain't seen nobody run in here before. Lars said he saw a wild man come out of here once," Mosh said.

"You believe any old shite that storyteller says. You need to start thinkin' for yourself."

Vil could hear their labored breaths, smell their unwashed bodies.

"It's so dark you could lose your cock," Mosh said.

"Wouldn't be hard with that acorn you've got."

"Shut it. Come on, let's go back. My knee's killing me."

"Shut up about your knee. He can't be much further. Come on, be a man."

"I am a man..."

To Vil's relief and astonishment, the voices trickled out of earshot. Butterflies fluttered in his chest—he'd duped them! Never had he fooled anyone before. But his elation faded quickly—he still had to find his way out.

Holding his breath for fear of making a sound, he set off back in the direction he had come, padding along like a cautious cat. Hearing nothing behind him, he upped his pace and soon the grey light of day built against the walls. Never in his life had he been so relieved to see trees.

Vil joined the trail to Haberdam. He longed for the comfort of his bedroom, the crackle of the fire, body slowly thawing, steam rising from a mug of tea, a new book to sink his teeth into. *How can I enjoy any of that when my friend is out there alone?* Had she fallen and hurt herself? Was she attacked by a bear or wolf? He'd heard them howling before. Maybe it was something worse, like the wild men Pikey had mentioned, if indeed they were real. Or perhaps it was something more monstrous altogether—another person. No, he could not rest until she was found. And with nobody else looking, it was down to him.

The sky darkened, the afternoon giving way to dusk. Vil hoped to have covered more ground by now. Raised in Yurrisa, he was used to stone beneath his feet, not mud thick enough to claim a boot. A voice in his head bellowed for him to go home. Things were simpler back in the store. Stacking shelves might be mundane, but it was stress-free and warm. The urge nearly overwhelmed him as he walked by the first wooden houses of Haberdam. His feet cried out in pain and the blister on his left foot had almost certainly burst. The chase had exhausted him physically and emotionally. But he had just one place left to look, and his least favorite of all: the Shrouded Wood.

As he began to rise up the eastern hillside toward the looming trees, wispy tendrils already veiled the ground, snaking through fences and around houses. Vil pulled up his hood. He passed Isy's home: a single-storied rectangle with a stone foundation, wooden walls and thatched roof. Isy's mother, Yari, looked out from the only window. Her gaze fell upon him. Beside the house, he saw Tamlin, Isy's father, chopping wood. All of his concentration was on his task. Vil knew people dealt with grief in different ways: crying, laughing, pretending nothing had happened. He couldn't help but wonder whether Tamlin felt no grief at all.

Soon, houses became a rare and alien sight as trees, bushes and flowers came to dominate the land beside the road. He realized he ought to be looking for signs of Isy and turned his eyes to the ground, already covered in the first fallen leaves of the season. Most things at a distance were blurred for Vil, and up close wasn't much better. Growing up, the other orphans under the care of the chroniclers could see distant things that he could not, or details he could not discern. He was used to it now and didn't let it trouble him, but sometimes he wondered what it would be like to see like everyone else, particularly now, when he needed it.

Vil squinted, and things cleared enough for him to make out some details: the obvious circle of a hoof print; a deep groove of a wagon wheel. Those things were heavy. Isy was smaller than he was, and certainly skinnier. Once more he felt the futility of his efforts and the idea of giving up and going home returned, yet his legs continued on.

The fog thickened. This road led all the way to the Teeth of Giants, the near impassable mountain range that ran along much of the border between Yurr and Karrabar. Vil wondered why there was a road leading there at all. To his knowledge, nobody ever went there. Off to his left, he saw a trail cutting through the long grass and into the trees. He glanced back, judging where it could go. It seemed about right in terms of overlooking the town. He took out his collapsible lantern from his bag—a cunning device he'd swiped from the Grand Library in Yurrisa. Isy had spent a half-hour folding it up and down the first time she'd seen it. Vil lit a candle, placed it inside, and ventured into the murk.

His chest felt as if a pile of books had been heaped upon it. He angled his light in a sliver, illuminating trees stout and thin and the twisted arms of nettles, thorns, and briars, which emerged from the misty gloom to grab at his clothes. He couldn't understand how people felt at home in the woods. It was all so hostile.

He kept to the trail, though at times it seemed to vanish and he began to worry he'd lost it, until it reappeared again. His cheeks brushed the web of a spider and, in a panic, he hopped about and patted himself down. His light extinguished. The voice calling for home was louder than ever, but it fell silent when off to his right he heard the rustle of leaves.

In his mind's eye, Vil saw a great wolf with teeth bared, padding toward him. The sharpest thing Vil carried was a quill. *Had anybody managed to kill anyone or anything with a quill? Makos the Mighty would have no trouble. So too Riad the Bold, or One-Eyed Osalot. What would they do now? Not freeze and cower like a toddler parted from his mother.*

The heroes he admired in the adventure stories he and Isy loved so much were always so fearless, regardless of the obstacles before them. That is how he wished to be. And so, just like them, he pushed back his shoulders, puffed out his chest, re-lit his candle, opened wide the shutter of the lantern, and walked on into the unknown, even if it meant his end.

He found no source of the noise. Soon the trees fell away and he stepped into a sloped clearing, a welcome respite from the choking embrace of the forest. He followed a trail of trampled long grass and came to a flattened patch. His light fell onto a bag. Then a book. He rushed forwards.

Isy's bag lay open on the ground, waterskin beside it, mostly full. On the floor, covered in slugs, was the copy of *Myra the Maid*. He hated slugs. He couldn't see what purpose they served other than to cause mess and disgust when trodden on. He flicked them off, checked the pages and, to his dismay, found that the slimy bastards had begun eating the corners. The chronicler would lock him in the cellar for months for this.

Of Isy, there was no sign.

Dusk had taken hold, and even with thoughts of matching the bravery of his fictional heroes, he lacked the courage to call out Isy's name. *What happened to you?*

Here she had sat not long ago. She had eaten her lunch, sipped her water, read just a few pages of the book, or so her page marker suggested, and then left. Vil began to worry, a concern of a much graver kind. She had not intended to leave. She was taken. *Could she have been ...* He could not bring himself to think about it.

Vil scanned the rest of the flattened grass and was relieved to find no trace of blood. But there, in the corner, hidden amid the gloom, was the faintest of trails. It led toward the trees on the opposite side of the clearing. The answer to whatever happened lay at the end of that trail, of that he was sure. He had some food and water left and plenty of candles too. His heart urged him to go on, yet the voice in his mind yelled at him to go back.

Vil focused on the ground and, once more, set off after his friend.

Five

"I heard it was the Shade of a Dragon."

"You believe any old hokum, Gob. Some toothless poppy smoker was shouting that in the market this morning. It was obviously them Karraban bastards."

"What makes you so sure, Robi? Did you ask the assassin yourself?" said a gruff third voice.

Robi gave no reply.

"Maybe he was in on it," said the voice belonging to Gob.

Laughter rippled from the table behind Edvar. The three men were tanners, the least difficult of all working men to identify: stained clothes and hands and stinking of a peculiar cocktail of rotten flesh and mint. They rubbed themselves with the latter to mask the stench of the former. Nobody could bear their presence long enough to tell them it didn't work.

"If it wasn't the Karrabans who else would it be?" Robi spat back.

"I thought we'd established it was you."

"Seriously, Dano. You know what this means?" Gob said in a solemn tone. "War."

"They've just made peace, why would they go to war?" Dano asked.

"Who knows? Keepers are just as crazy as everyone else," said Robi.

PARIAH'S LAMENT | 71

"If you were Keeper Tesh, I suppose it's the best time to attack. One of the first things I learned in the army was to try and take your enemy unawares. Better odds of staying alive, and that Tesh is a military man," Gob said.

"Stabbing men in the back is the coward's way. If you're gonna fight, fight like a proper man," Robi said.

"Says the man who's never fought in his life," Dano said.

"I had my reasons for not signing up. You know that," Robi said, humorless.

"I'm twisting your balls. No need to get so serious all the time. We're all dying, Rob. Each sip of mead a step closer to the grave. If death is fated to come fighting for the people I love, so be it. And that includes you, you shriveled old prick."

Edvar sipped his whiskey, stifling a smile. He reveled in the vibrant conversations he heard in the taverns and inns of Yurrisa. Alcohol loosened the tongue, removed the shackles of the mind, and above all, gave courage to those who lacked it. They were excellent places to glean information. But it was not the purpose of his current visit. He had a meeting, and she was late.

"Did you hear the story about the duel?" Gob said.

"The Keeper fighting off the assassin and sending him over his balcony?" Dano asked.

Robi nodded. "I heard they're still picking bits of him up."

Edvar tried to keep his eyes from the front door. Constantly glancing in its direction would seem edgy, suspicious. He had to appear at ease, like one of the punters, weary after a day's work. To aid the lie he wore a disguise of second-hand clothes bought from the market in Skimar, one of Yurrisa's poorer districts. The scuffed woolen breeches and stained blue shirt itched so much he now knew what it felt like to be a stray dog. His battered leather boots bunched his toes together, nails digging painfully. They were deliberately ill-fitting—few people in this part of the city wore shoes that fit. Some had funny gaits from the resulting blisters and corns. But the people of this part of town were sharp, attentive. Nice boots stood out a mile.

The door opened. Edvar's shoulders eased with the relief of recognition. Lavia stepped inside with a confident grace, at ease in her new surroundings when others would hesitate. Unlike most women in Yurrisa, her dyed raven-black hair was cut short to her neck, revealing her dainty, bear-like ears. Her round eyes, like the amber of autumn leaves, regarded Edvar for just a moment, then moved to the next face, seeking opportunities, identifying risks. She weaved between tables, chairs and leering men, her slender figure helping her through the slightest gaps. Edvar wouldn't lie; whenever he saw her, he felt a pang of excitement. He locked eyes with the serving girl and signaled for two whiskeys. Lavia slid onto the bench facing him.

"Good to see you," he said with a smile.

Lavia shrugged, indifference in her eyes. The courtesan was in her mid-thirties but looked ten years younger, her cheekbones high, nose straight and slight. Her pale skin was free of the lines of age and when she smiled her face radiated warmth enough to heat a long-cold hearth. Edvar was still learning his letters when his father recruited her. He could see why. She was sharper than most lords and barons, and certainly more engaging. She had many regulars around the city, a number of whom were rich, influential men and women. The kind of people who could conspire to oust the Keeper.

"Sad news about your Keeper," she said. "He was one of the better ones."

"He isn't dead."

"Not yet. You know what happens—worse men grow jealous of better men, and in their pathetic bitterness turn to the knife. They'll finish the job. Or at least try."

The serving girl arrived with the whiskey. Edvar dropped a few coppers extra onto her wooden tray. A smile flashed across her mousy face and she returned to the bar, ginger hair swinging as she went.

"And who are they?"

Lavia smiled, sipped her drink.

"What's your news?" Edvar leaned in, hushed voice lost in the clamor of the tavern.

"There's a target on your back."

"My back?!"

"Why are you so shocked? You're the last pillar propping up the Keeper."

It did, of course, make sense. Edvar simply hadn't considered the reality of it happening. His initial flurry of outrage dissipated, and in its place came concern.

"Do you know who's ordered it?" he asked.

"No."

Edvar slumped back against the bench, shaking his head. "What exactly have you heard? Because this isn't the first time I've supposedly had a target on my back."

"A friend of mine works down in Ukasa. She heard the crew that runs the town debating whether or not to take the contract."

"A contract now?" Edvar's shoulders sagged as he exhaled a worried sigh. This seemed serious, and right now he wasn't sure he had the fight to deal with it. Packing his things and riding as far from Yurrisa as possible felt preferable.

"I don't mean to trouble you further, but you do know you're being watched?"

Edvar made to turn and received a prompt kick in the shin. "Are you thick as firewood?"

"Of late, yes."

"There's a couple over by the hearth. The woman can't stop looking at you. And before you get excited, it's not lust in her eyes." Lavia drained her glass and looked at him expectantly.

"Is that it? What about the attack on the Keeper?"

"Oh. That." She rolled her eyes.

Heated voices erupted behind them. The unchecked laughter and chatter in the room simmered.

"Yeah, I am saying that!" The voice belonged to Robi. "A man who can't judge his enemies isn't a man I want leading Yurr!" He was squaring up to a man a head taller, with fair hair and a wild beard that covered much of his face.

"You speak treasonous words, friend," the taller man said in a rumbling voice, folding his thick, defined arms, no doubt earned laboring on Yurrisa's many farms.

"I speak what everyone else is thinking," Robi spat.

The taller man looked around the room. Nobody offered a syllable.

"Ashara is weak, and everyone knows it," Robi said. "We should have gone to war with Karrabar and now look. We're going to get invaded and where is he to protect us? On his deathbed is where! We need to fight back!"

"We're sick of war," a young man shouted from the corner. "You old bastards don't have to fight. We do."

Voices filled with brewing aggression rang out from all corners of the tavern.

"We were young once too."

"We've buried sons and daughters."

"You can't let bullies walk all over you."

"Exactly," Robi said, waving his arms about. "But I bet this lanky prick's never been bullied so he can't wrap his fat head around it."

The taller man stepped up to Robi.

"Come on then! I've had bigger dumps than you," Robi shouted.

In a blink of an eye, the taller man swung at Robi. The sound of fist against cheek echoed through the room. Robi crashed into a table, hit the floor, and chaos erupted. Tankards and glasses were first into battle, indiscriminately hurled, followed by stools, swinging arms and flailing bodies.

Edvar and Lavia sought cover under their table.

"This is the effect of your Keeper," she said seemingly unfazed by the riot unfolding around them. "He divides opinion."

That wasn't Edvar's primary concern at that moment. "Hurry, what news of the attack? You must have something for me," he shouted over the ruckus.

"Nothing. Everybody's got their own story of what happened. One thing that sticks though is that you got your arse kicked. Can't hide those bruises, eh?" She laughed to herself.

"Who are they saying is behind it?"

"That mad bastard Tesh, of course."

"'A coin casts a large shadow'. I don't suppose you've heard anyone say that?"

Her eyes narrowed, searching the drawers of her mind. She shook her head. "What does it mean?"

"Good question."

A trio of clay cups smashed before their table, showering them with shards and ale. Men grappled drunkenly with each other. Punches aimed and missed. Stools shattered against backs, bottles against heads. How anyone knew who was on whose side was beyond Edvar, but what did it matter to these drunken fools? In the midst of it all lay Robi, creator of chaos, sprawled upon the floor, unconscious. Edvar saw a gap in the fighting. "We should get out of here."

Edvar and Lavia weaved through the bodies occupying the floor, out cold, groaning, bleeding. They stepped outside into a throng of confusion and panic. People shouted for the Watchmen. Edvar angled away from them all. Lavia grabbed his arm.

"Aren't you forgetting something?" She looked unimpressed, as if she'd caught him cheating her.

"Ah, sorry. My head's up my arse." He reached into his tattered jacket, pulled out a small coin purse and slipped it into Lavia's hand. Her fingers closed around it, and she made to walk away. Edvar held onto her, pulled her back to him.

"If you hear anything at all, I want to know immediately."

She looked into his eyes. "Got it." And with that, she slipped back into the crowd. Edvar had no doubt she could handle herself. Indeed, she was probably the most dangerous person in the tavern that night.

With the sounds of the brawl fading, he reflected on another fraught effort to glean information. Each door of inquiry had been slammed so hard in his face it had floored him. All he had was that stupid riddle. *A coin casts a large shadow.*

Earlier that day, while wallowing in his room after the meeting, he'd assembled every type of Yurrish coin, had shuttered his windows and lined them up, holding a candle to each to see which one cast the largest shadow. A silver japara won the contest, but its shadow was hardly large. Edvar had studied every detail of the japara: the crude portrait of Ashara with its comically pointed chin, the few words etched on the other side—loyalty, valor, victory. He picked those words apart, rearranged letters. Three hours he would never reclaim. He had to try it, though, to at least rule out the option and focus his efforts.

The two guards who had stopped him the night of the attack were on watch at the gate. This time, they saluted, and one even gave a bow. Edvar reciprocated and when he looked back, found them squabbling.

Every window in the Royal Tower was alight. No shadows for assassins to hide in. But after witnessing that brawl tonight was the Keeper safe anywhere? He loathed admitting it, but it'd shaken him. Mistrust and disillusionment had spread like a plague across the city, and he wasn't quite sure how. Prior to Karrabar's provocations, Ashara had been untouchable. He created jobs, kept taxes reasonable, borders safe, harvests consistent, justice fair and decisive, and above all, he kept the Vault of Iron secure. A perfect leader. A man who did not serve himself but his people alone. Edvar had been certain their policy of appeasement with Karrabar would have garnered support.

Once again, Edvar found himself fruitlessly walking to Ashara's chamber, scrambling to formulate an excuse for his failings.

Six

Flickering shadows danced across the tapestries upon the wall, giving life to the scenes they depicted. Peat bricks and logs crackled in a hearth framed by great slabs of stone, with a broad iron grate before it to keep any flares at bay.

Ashara looked worse than the night before. He was in the grips of an intense fever, shivering incessantly despite sweat covering his pallid skin. His cheeks were gaunt and drained of vitality. As he stood beside his bed, Edvar contemplated how in just a matter of days this strong, confident and capable man had been reduced to a weak, fragile wreck.

With a start, Ashara's weary eyes opened. Edvar didn't know what to say, where to begin, whether he should burden this sick man with more ill news.

"Gods, Ed." Ashara's teeth chattered. Edvar pulled the wolf-fur blanket right up to Ashara's chin. He couldn't think of the best way to explain things, so he just let it out.

"I've messed up, sire. Again. I lost control at the meeting this morning and left before the end. The rest of the day I wasted pitying myself when I should have been investigating, and now the assassin is dead." Edvar's voice broke. A tear came to his eye. He blinked it away.

"I feel like everything I do worsens things, and on top of that one of my informants tells me I'm being hunted." Edvar couldn't bring himself to look at Ashara until that moment. The Keeper's eyes were bunched with pain. "I'm sorry, sire.

I fear I am useless to you, that you would be better off without me."

"No," Ashara muttered. Over and over he repeated himself, shaking his head, eyes closed. "Not now. Not now. He's coming for me, Ed. I've seen him. I see his eyes. Yes. Yes. He will kill me."

Ashara's eyes were bunched so tight it was as if he was trapped in his mind.

"Who means to kill you, sire?"

"I can see him standing over me. My sword is in his hand, and it drips with blood. My blood."

"Who?"

"Tesh."

"He is better than me, Ed. Men do not forget. They keep pain in their hearts. Always, forever." Ashara's teeth ground in sudden anguish. Slowly it eased and he fell quiet, as if his struggle was over.

Tesh? Do not forget what? As far as Edvar knew, Ashara and Tesh hadn't met before the peace conference in Wender, and neither Keeper had revealed anything to suggest they had a history. Indeed, all they had done was glare at each other in silence. What had happened between them? Going off Ashara's ramblings he could only speculate. But could such feverish mutterings be trusted at all?

Edvar reached for a cloth on the far bedside table to wet Ashara's brow. He found a strip of parchment beside the cloth, ends curled and marked with a waxen seal.

Wender is ash and cinders. Karrabar marches west. Prepare for war.

It was signed by Baroness Ura. The quaint town of Wender lay in her barony and was just a few leagues from the newly negotiated border between Yurr and Karrabar. Given its location, it had served as host for the peace conference between the two nations.

Edvar trusted Ura. Seeing her words set his cheeks afire with shame. It confirmed that he'd been wrong about Tesh. The Karraban Keeper had played them. All along his intention was war and death. And look what their misjudgment had cost—the lives and homes of the hundreds of people who called Wender home.

"Help me, Ed," Ashara muttered, eyes still closed. His hand reached out, searching for Edvar, who grabbed it. He was surprised by the strength of the keeper's grip. "He comes, Ed. You must save me. You must save us all."

Seven

The rain renewed the wetness of Isy's cheeks. Dozens of towering, stick-like humanoids stopped and stared as she was carried through what appeared to be a makeshift camp. Raindrops pattered against dome-shaped shelters that were made of wattle and daub and covered with moss. They were huddled together in the spaces between pine trees, oaks and the odd beech. White smoke rose from small fires before them, and more strands drifted through holes in their tops.

More of Kora and Tulasc's kin emerged from doors, their clothes ragged and dirty, eyes even bigger and more bulbous amid grey, gaunt faces. The sight of it all set Isy's heart racing. She buried her face into Tulasc's nut-scented hair. With wrists and ankles bound, it was the only move she could make to flee.

Kora approached a shelter and pulled aside the rag covering the doorway for Tulasc, who stooped as he entered. He set Isy down, turned and left without a word or glance. The strands of light shining through the material that covered the door eclipsed as someone stood in front of it, blocking her path. Isy turned and regarded her prison cell.

A beam of light shone in through a hole in the center of the roof, illuminating a circle of stones filled with ash. Bunched together around the firepit were six heaps of moss, flattened and shaped like mattresses. Wrists and ankles still bound, Isy crawled over to the nearest one and rolled upon it. It was more comfortable, at least, than Tulasc's back. A strong smell of sweat and feces came to her nose, but it didn't linger, and the more pleasant scent of pine needles replaced it. Now she just wished she could rid herself of the rope around her numbing wrists and ankles. Perhaps then she could attempt to escape again.

Isy yearned to know what they wanted with her. She'd read stories about the Ancients sacrificing people to change their fortune with the gods. Would such a fate be any worse than her life now? Indeed, what was her purpose in Haberdam? To serve as a punch bag for her father? The cure for the boredom of the children? The chickens she tended to everyday lived more fulfilling and purposeful lives. What did it matter now, anyway? Her fate, it seemed, belonged to these frog people, and if it was death they intended, that prospect did not fill her heart with as much darkness and despair as it first had.

Two people entered. One was a young woman with brown hair fixed in a plait that hung over her right shoulder. Her iron-grey complexion matched that of the dark-bearded man behind her, who carried a pail of water. He set it down before Isy, then began to build a fire. From a wicker basket the woman took a small bunch of mushrooms, a wooden bowl filled with nuts, and another filled with some kind of carrot-colored paste. She placed each one before Isy. Neither of them could tear their gaze from her.

"Where am I?" Isy asked. She could feel tears welling.

Their slender, inhuman lips remained pursed. Flames began to beat away the dimness of the room. They stood and turned to leave.

"Wait," she said, scrambling after them on hands and knees. "Where am I?!"

They glanced back at her before they departed. Tears overwhelmed Isy's pitiful dam. She returned to the mossy bed, curled up in a ball and silently sobbed.

Eight

When she opened her eyes, she was in her room in Haberdam. The curtain possessed the same holes. Straw tickled her back. Chickens clucked outside. Definitely home. Isy got out of bed and opened the door to the common room. It was dark, as if she'd awoken in the dead of night.

"Ma," she called. No reply. Stepping further into the room she heard a whistle and halted. Her first thought, or rather her hope, was that it was the wind, yet in her heart she knew it was a person. She left the house. It was darker outside than it was indoors, the sky a starless void, yet the darkness soundlessly writhed like a knot of snakes. She passed houses lit in a moon-like glow, despite no light source. Where she expected to see some houses, she instead found gloomy pits.

A scream howled along the road, sharp and brief and filled with terrible fear. She felt compelled to go to it. She ran, and as she moved, she heard it again. Louder. When she heard it a third time, familiarity struck, and she slowed to a stop before the Chronicler's Store. It was smothered by the same shifting shadows from the sky. Another scream echoed from the open threshold. Isy stepped inside.

Laughter trickled along the corridor, wicked, hissing, filled with glee. A sound that had haunted her life. She hastened her step, moving through the stacks, trying to escape the snickering. She reached the aisle with the cellar door. Open. She hurried down the steps, laughter in her ears.

A closed door stood in the cellar wall ahead. She tried the handle. Unlocked, to her relief. She burst inside and recoiled from a blinding whiteness.

Black spots flashed in her vision. When it adjusted, she made out the silhouette of a man standing before her. The light emitted from him. The sight filled her with hope and joy so pure it moved her to tears. She ran toward him but as she neared he began to shrink, the light dimming. She was close enough to touch. She reached out, tripped, fell...

Isy bolted upright. Sweat glued her fringe to her forehead, clothes to her body. She didn't dream often, but when she did, they came with a feverish intensity. Plus, she could never make sense of them. The same went for her most recent experience.

She crawled to the bucket of water, splashed her face. The grazes and scratches from the chafing rope stung like a score of bee stings. A fire still burned, and she wondered how long she'd slept. Beside the bucket was the food they'd left, and for the first time in her life, the sight of nuts had her salivating. She tucked into them, and then she turned to the mushrooms. After devouring them all, she moved onto the orange paste. This she approached with more caution, first sampling a bit. It tasted how it looked: like carrots. After washing it down with water, the rag door rippled. Kora entered, a small axe in his hand.

Isy shuffled away from him. In two strides he was over her, his massive hands engulfing hers. He grabbed her ankles, brought the blade of the axe toward them, and cut her bindings.

"Co-me," he said, holding the rag open.

Two other frog people met her outside, each carrying the biggest spears she had ever seen. Thick as a sapling and stretching beyond the height of their already giant wielders, both ends were tipped with broad, wicked points that looked like murderous spades. The faces of those who carried them were covered with hoods, though she could still sense their great eyes upon her; she doubted they missed anything. Kora signaled and they led on down the trail.

Isy had to half-run to match their strides. She caught up to Kora. "What's going to happen to me?"

The slight contortion of Kora's face told her he wasn't sure what she asked. "We say," he said, pointing ahead, though all Isy could see were more trees and wattle domes. She could hear children and babies crying, a man shouting. More people were about now, it seemed, and all eyes fell upon her. Isy saw thin faces dominated by black ringed eyes that possessed a look Isy could relate to—utter helplessness. She angled her face to the floor, swept her fringe over her mark.

The trees thinned and the forest brightened. Through the boles to her left, she saw the vibrant green of a grassy clearing and clouds of black and grey smoke rising from a half dozen fires. She caught a smell that made her gag— burning swine and hair, mingled with the scent of a latrine pit on a baking summer's day. When the trees receded altogether, she uncovered the source.

Piles of corpses. The bodies of Kora's kin.

Limbs hung lifelessly over one another. Eyes stared without direction. Mouths hung ajar. They lacked any dignity or grace, merely heaped, ready to be burned. A cloud of flies buzzed around them and a handful of youths, mouths and noses covered with rags, had the unenviable task of trying to keep them away with leafy branches. Pinching her nose did nothing to stop the smell. It clung to her taste buds; she had to fight to stop the bile rising from her stomach. She'd seen dead bodies before, but washed and perfumed, and never so many.

What looked like a small wooden altar stood beside the pyres. A frog-man stood upon it, speaking to a trio of people who were hunched over in grief. More stood before a low-burning pyre, holding hands. Seeing all this told Isy much about Kora and his kin. That they cared and loved and hurt just like everybody else. Had the scale of the dead simply overwhelmed them? A ravaging illness could do that. A decade or so ago in Haberdam, a fever took a fifth of the population in a week. Her father had lamented that Isy hadn't been one of them. Isy was similarly disappointed it hadn't killed him.

A hand touched her back. She looked up to find Kora gazing down at her, his eyes wet with tears.

They left the clearing and came to a dome with a banner hanging from a nearby tree. It was sky-blue in color, with a white criss-cross border. The bottom end was frayed and it appeared to have been slashed several times, but the focal image was unobscured. A man and a woman stood in the center of a circle. They were stick-like and white as bone, limbs overlapping and stretching out to the edges of the circle, as if holding it in place. Isy could not begin to fathom what it meant.

Kora held open the material covering the doorway. This could be it. Her life over. She tried to absorb her potential final sights, but the images of the piles of bodies overwhelmed everything else. She looked up through the canopy at the bleak slate sky, and the first drops of rain fell into her eyes. She detested rain. It kept her indoors, trapped with the people who made her life a misery. *How fitting.*

Isy exhaled and stepped inside.

She found a room much grander in comparison to the one she had earlier slept in. Small torches burned upon wooden posts around the edges. Fur rugs covered the floor and colorful tapestries, patterned with abstract designs, hung from the ceiling. In the center of the room was a roaring fire, around which sat three white-haired women garbed in flowing, vibrantly-colored robes: one purple, another green, the last blue. Even with stooped necks and backs they seemed tall. Their creased skin was a silvery hue and despite the firelight, their eyes, the color of ice, glowed with experience, wisdom and a vigor that belied their age. The most ancient-looking of the three, dressed in purple and sitting in the middle, spoke.

"Welcome, Isy."

Her accent was thick as treacle. Isy realized her mouth was ajar and closed it.

"My name Aena. This," she said, indicating the hook-nosed woman to her left, dressed in blue, "is Gosha. And this, Wema," she said pointing to the woman in green on her right. "We are Guides of our people: the Amast. Come. Sit." Aena held out her hand to a cushion of moss on the opposite side of the fire. Seeing no other choice, Isy took it. When she sat, Kora drew his axe and grabbed her wrists. She winced momentarily but felt stupid for doing so when he cut her bindings.

"We sorry for tying you, Isy. We fear you run and we understand why you want run. We look different to you..." Her face contorted in a peculiar fashion, mouth stretching wide. A smile, Isy guessed?

"You look white as clouds. We get you something?" Aena asked her.

"I-I'm fine."

"You have questions, we answer all. But first, we explain why you here." More than once when Aena spoke, she paused to think of her next word, and her pronunciations almost stumped Isy completely.

Isy managed a nod, battling with the accent.

"For many turns of the sun, the Amast hidden. We believe peace, love, together. Hate broke us in past. Never again we let it happen." Her great hands with their long, bone-thin fingers reached up to cover her heart. "No being other than Amast ever set foot on soil of our home. Until a man appear. He look like you. He see us and flee. Days later, he return with more men. Many. They carry swords, axes, fire. They cut my people, my friends, my family. Women, children. Everyone. Then they burn our home to the ground.

"Some of us escape. We flee west. Because of our wounded, we had to stop. Sickness spread around our camp. Now, many hungry. We too weak to go on, yet cannot stay with winter coming. It why I send my Kora to find help. He find you.

"More Amast die each day. To survive cold that come soon, we need help. I too weak to travel. But I the only one who understand Yurrish, and poorly as you hear. What I know I learn long ago and my mind is…" she waved her hand, searching for the word. "Bad," she settled on. "We hope you, Isy, can help. We need guide to teach us your tongue and show us way to your leader so that we ask for refuge."

"Who? Baron Rijkard?"

Aena hesitated, brows furrowing. "I do not understand."

"The person in charge of my town is called Baron Rijkard, though most people call him Baron Prickard."

Confusion deepened on the faces of the three Guides.

"I thought Keeper Ashara leader? A man great and honorable. A man who love his people."

"Ohh. The Keeper. I suppose he is."

"Would he help?"

"More likely than Rijkard. The baron's greedy and tight-fisted with his coin. But the bigger problem is the people who live there. They're cruel and wicked. They would sooner see you dead than help."

Aena frowned. "Can you take us to Keeper?"

"To Yurrisa? It's the other side of the country! And I've never been there before."

Isy regretted the sternness of her tone, but annoyance stabbed at her resolve. These Amast had abducted her, carried her who knew how far without explanation, led her to believe they were going to kill her, and dropped her into a world she had no knowledge of, into a crisis far bigger than her. Not to mention, the idea of going to a city as big as Yurrisa terrified her.

"Please, Isy. You must. We need help, or we die."

What can I say to that? Do I even have a choice? I couldn't leave if I wanted. "But why me?"

"Kora found you reading. He believe you know well your language."

"That doesn't make me qualified to teach. I've never taught anyone anything! You're not *that* bad at Yurrish. Why can't you teach them?" Isy asked.

Aena sighed. "I try. We have no Yurrish words to read. Sound alone too hard and we run out of time. But more, we need guide leading us to those that help." Tears fell from Aena's eyes, indeed from all of their eyes. They were each utterly helpless in this the most desperate of situations. Sitting idly while around them their people, their very existence, withered and died.

Pity welled in Isy's heart while confusion gripped her mind. What they asked of her bordered on madness. Teach? Guide? Things she had never contemplated before. Her whole life she had been ignored or abused, and now somebody wanted her help? She bit her lip and looked at the faces of the elderly Amast women before her, at their giant eyes wet with tears. She and she thought of those decomposing bodies out in the clearing. Of the look of fear and helplessness in the giant eyes of the children.

"I will help," Isy said. *Though I'm not sure that I can.*

Episode Three: Bumps and Bruises

Uren sent me west, to the remote and sheer cliffs of Midara. The sea and I have never agreed, so across land I went. Steam trains only carried me so far, and then it was by horseback through country thick as its people. The weeks it took gave me time to ponder. Had Uren finally lost his mind? All that time alone in tombs and catacombs could loosen a man's grip on reality. Magic daggers... What was magic but the sleight-of-hand tricks that children delighted in? My doubts in Uren grew with each mile, and when at last I smelled the salt of the sea and saw the looming and desolate cliffs of Midara, I was quite convinced that he had sent me on a quest of his fantastical imaginations.

From **The Forgotten Daggers** by S. T. Harris

One

AENA WALKED AT a snail's pace, aided by a great, gnarled staff. Isy looked at Kora and the other Amast around them and saw no hint of impatience. She shook her head. Only the night before had Aena impressed upon Isy the urgency of their plight. At least now she understood why the old Amast guide couldn't go to Yurrisa; Keeper Ashara would be ten years in the grave before she arrived.

They reached a broad wattle shelter nestled beneath a stout oak, its boughs hanging low like a hen shielding her young with her wings. Kora held open the heavy material covering the doorway, and one by one, they stepped into gloom. Aena's assistant hurried to light a fire, and with sticks and moss snapping and crackling, the brightening glow revealed small wicker baskets around the edges of the room. Aena muttered something to her assistant, who went to one of the baskets and removed the lid. From inside she pulled a sheaf of parchment and handed it to Aena.

"Amast write everything down. And we paint. Records of our pasts. Hundreds of years. Now it all ash. We took what we could, but this nothing compared to what was."

Aena sank into a cushion of moss beside the fire. Sitting cross-legged, she held out a trembling hand to her assistant, who passed her a slender pipe with a purple leaf stuffed into the bowl. Kora held to the bowl a lit taper and Aena inhaled for what seemed like minutes. An aroma of wild flowers filled the room. Aena exhaled smoke thick and white that coiled and constricted as it rose. Her grimace of exertion eased, shoulders sagged. She looked at Isy, that peculiar smile upon her face.

"Sit, Isy," she said, holding her hand out to a mossy mound beside her. Isy obeyed.

Fire lit and Aena settled, her assistant and Kora bowed and left the hut, to the thanks of Aena.

"We weep for lost writings and pictures," Aena said, smoke escaping her mouth as she spoke. "We try to replace, but work is much." She leafed through the pages in her hand, then passed them to Isy.

"I knew we need help, so began to write Yurrish words I know to teach Amast. Not many."

Isy took the parchments and, holding them to the light of the fire, scanned them. In a shaky hand, Isy saw Yurrish words. Basic ones, mixed with the odd long one, the latter badly misspelled. There were sentences, too, as random as they were wrong. How anyone could learn from this, Isy wasn't sure.

"You speak it very well," Isy said in as polite a tone as possible.

"Thank you. Had good teacher. He a hunter from Iber named Par." Once more she smiled in her bizarre, contorted way. "We met in forest long time ago. He gave me book and I learn more from that. It funny how I not forget, yet I forget what happen yesterday." She chuckled, and when her laughter died, took another pull on her still lit pipe.

"We have reeds and feathers and inks to write with, and parchment. Lots," she said, puffing smoke. "You add to what I began?"

Isy bit her lip. "Like I said, I've never taught anybody anything before, and like you, what I know I have learned from books. I've never had a proper teacher. But I'll try."

"Language more than words. It how we act, how we sound. Amast not know Yurrish people, how you act. Like trying to learn songs of birds, we only can guess. But I help too. I tell you what Amast say and teach you Amasti. Between us, we do well."

Some of the tension shifted in Isy's shoulders at hearing that. She wasn't *completely* alone.

"Most important, we need guide. Amast not left woods for two thousand turns of sun. Not until Kora and others went find help. We not know how find your Keeper."

That makes two of us, Isy thought.

Aena puffed on her pipe, eyes on Isy, unreadable despite their great size.

"What if we go all that way and the Keeper refuses to help?" Isy asked.

Aena's eyes flicked to the fire, smoke rising from lips slightly parted. They glistened with tears; Isy took that as her answer.

"Do you know anything of the men who killed your people?" Isy asked.

Aena shook her head. "Had shields like full moon with yellow star in middle."

"Karrabar..." Isy muttered.

"You know?"

"The emblem belongs to Karrabar, the realm bordering Yurr. They have a new Keeper, Tesh. And he decided to make a new sigil. The guiding star, he calls himself." *Like an arse hole.*

"I not understand why he attack us."

"No doubt because you're different. I'm abused and degraded where I'm from, even by my own parents, all for how I look."

"Your face?"

Tears obscured Isy's vision, though her voice held firm.. "I was born with it. They say I'm cursed."

"By what?"

Isy looked at her, wanting to explain, but feeling only futility at the prospect. "I don't want to talk about it."

"Another day, perhaps." Aena smiled, and Isy couldn't help but smile too, despite her sniffles and tears.

Aena went on. "Our past has pain too."

"What happened?" Isy sniffed and wiped her eyes.

Aena took another lengthy pull on her pipe, eyes bunching closed as if pained by the memories. She exhaled a cloud of white smoke, opened her eyes, and began. "Before stone castles, Amast a tribe in land you call Wetlands of Damned. To us, Urasa. In Amasti, means haven, happy. Was beautiful place, filled with plants and creatures, now gone from world.

"Time pass, Amast thrive. Borders expand. Explorers travel far. One, a woman named Edela, went far north. Deep in mountains she find something that change Amast forever.

"An ancient dagger of terrible power. Thing of magic. Stealer of souls. Amast made weapons to channel magic of dagger. Horrible weapons that kill many, many people. Some Amast reject it as evil. Others saw chance."

Isy knew well the tale of the two daggers of power: Ulara, the Yurrish dagger, and Silusa, the Karraban dagger. They were known as the stealers of souls; indeed, both names meant 'soul' in their respective languages. They were used to wage the worst war in the histories of Yurr and Karrabar. Some of the stories from the War of the Damned had haunted Isy's dreams for months after reading about them, things so heinous they were beyond the comprehension of even the most murderous individual. She was just glad both weapons were locked away far underground, and thankfully forgotten about in the minds of most people. But never in those stories had she heard of the Amast, nor a third dagger of power belonging to them.

"It began war amongst Amast. Some try destroy dagger. Others try take for themselves, for greed and power. They won. The Betrayers they known as, but call themselves Builders.

"Led by Betrayers, Amast conquer land. Enslaved others. The biggest flaw of Betrayers was ignorance. They blind to fact they changing, ignored that power came at cost. Lots of Amast changed how they look. Over many turns of sun, Amast warped. Grow bigger, stronger, can see in dark, can hear things far away. Became what you see now. Because of magic of dagger."

Isy thought that was a somewhat polite description. She could put it no other way: the Amast looked like giant, gangly anthropomorphic frogs.

"The Transformation was end of Amast. They thought it disease first, and that began Cleansing. Amast slaughtered like lambs. But Transformed fight back. Bigger and stronger, they beat Amast Empire. Amast that survived, our ancestors, left ruined Urasa and started fresh here in north, where we live in peace ever since, doing best to forget pain of past."

Aena's pipe extinguished. She emptied the ash into the hearth. "Well, child, I exhausted. Even chatter tiring with age." She pushed herself up with the aid of her sticks. Isy moved to help, but she waved her away.

"Rest, child. You had long day. You need be fresh. Tomorrow you deliver first lesson." Her lips curled into a smile.

Two

Sleep eluded Isy, though her body pleaded for it. The knot constricting in her stomach forced her into a ball. At first, she wondered whether it was the carrot paste, but she came to accept it was the stress of the situation. Learning of the existence of the Amast had shattered the world as she knew it. To reel against the truth was to give in to fear, just like those in Haberdam did with her marked face. Being like them was the last thing she wanted. And the Amast were desperate for help. *Desperate.* The piles of bodies were evidence enough of that. *There will be more of them if I refuse.*

But how could she teach a group of people who didn't understand her and whom she didn't understand either? Being confined or hidden was what she was used to, not standing before an audience. *What if they ask me a question? What if I don't know the answer? What if I can't teach them anything? What if they die because of my failure?* A maelstrom of thoughts battered her mind. At least she had Aena to help. The kindly old Amast woman seemed to possess inexhaustible patience. *I hope it's inexhaustible.*

The thorn in Isy's foot was the *how* of it all. With no experience of teaching and, beyond what her mother had shown her, no experience of being taught, she had no reference points. She decided to start with the basics: "hello", "goodbye", "my name is..." That would do for tomorrow. Having something of a plan eased the tension in her stomach enough for her to entertain the idea of sleep.

It felt as if she had closed her eyes for just a few minutes when a hand shook her awake. Kora crouched over her. Isy started and sat up.

"We go," he said with, she guessed, a smile. His mouth pulled more of a grimace, but his blue eyes lit up.

"I'm not ready," she croaked.

Flustered and with annoyance stabbing at her temples, she tossed aside her blanket. Too little sleep always left her in a short mood. Something else was at work, though. She got like this whenever she had to do something she didn't want to do. She scrambled together her parchments upon which she'd scribbled some words. Kora offered to carry them for her. Nobody had ever done that for her before. It improved her mood a little.

The crisp morning air bit Isy's cheeks as she stepped outside. It wasn't until she caught the fetid scent on the breeze that she remembered the mounds of bodies waiting to be burned. They didn't head in that direction, though, to her relief. Kora took her east, to another part of the camp. They stopped at a small clearing, sheltered by branches, where a number of cook fires burned. Hanging over them were pots little and large, the steaming contents stirred by Amast men and women. Isy recognized the woman who'd beaten her down. She was smiling, and for a moment Isy thought the grin was for her, until Kora walked into view and her eyes, blue as a winter sky, followed him. She handed him a wooden bowl, and with reluctance, one to Isy too. By then her smile had faded.

Steam rose from the watery green contents. It smelled like rosemary and mint, tasted like it too. She didn't like mint. Her father loved it. After a few sips she grew used to the bitterness and found distraction in the sights around her. Children sat upon mothers' laps or stood close by, clinging onto legs or hands. A few of the younger ones sobbed. Even more had cheeks wet from tears. Despondency and confusion consumed their moon-like eyes. Isy could only imagine what they had experienced. Witnessing family members being killed, seeing loved ones—their protectors—distressed and afraid, hearing and smelling fear and death. *How could a child come back from that?*

When they'd finished their soup, Kora led on, and to Isy's dismay, the woman who had hit her came with them. Isy trailed behind the Amast pair. They stopped before an unremarkable shelter close to the bank of a stream where people were washing their bodies and clothes. Inside, Isy found a confined yet homely room. Red woven carpets covered the floor, and a small fire provided a warm light that repelled the shadows. Two Amast sat cross-legged around the fire. A thin-faced woman, and Tulasc. The woman wore a nut-brown robe, lined with fur. Her hair was a similar hue, plaited in what appeared to be the common Amast hairstyle. Her complexion was lighter than Tulasc's, like the fur of a grey squirrel. Eyes, like two great cornflowers, were locked upon Isy. The woman who had walked with them sat down with her kin by the fire.

Kora placed a giant hand upon Isy's shoulder. "Isy," he announced.

In chorus, they repeated her name, the sound like a swarm of bees. Kora led her to the woman who had hit her. "Pekira," he said. Isy forced a smile. Pekira didn't make such an effort.

Next to her was the thin-faced woman, Yera, who was a shade more welcoming than Pekira. Beside her was Tulasc, who grunted at her in what Isy judged a friendly way. Kora repeated their names a few times so Isy could get used to the lilts and clicks of the tongue. He set down her parchments on a crude table beside the fire and took a seat beside Yera.

Silence barged into the room and grabbed Isy's throat, strangling her words. She chewed her lip. Was she to start now? But Aena said she would be here to help. Sweat began to form under her fringe and a sudden feeling of self-consciousness washed over her. She half-turned away from the group, swept her hair to cover more of her mark. She bit deeper into her lip, trying to think back to the plans she had made the night before, but it was as if an eclipse of ravenous moths had gotten to them.

"H-hello," she said, and awkwardly waved. She nodded at them, a signal to repeat.

They looked at her quizzically. "H-hello," they said with uncertainty, glancing at one another, before mimicking her wave.

Horns sounded outside to cut short her anguish. Short, frantic blasts. All of those in the room shot to their feet and hurried to the door. Isy followed.

The horns continued to ring out, coming from deeper in the forest. In between blasts, Isy heard something else. A sound she recognized, growing steadily louder.

Skraa. Skraa. Skraa.

Hundreds, if not thousands.

Over the tips of the trees, the flock of paska grew like spilt ink. Prey in sight, their calls became harsher, louder. Isy's first reaction was to flee indoors, but nobody else moved. Their eyes were elsewhere.

"Aena!" Kora bellowed. The ancient Guide was making her way toward them, her assistant urging her along.

Skraa. Skraa. Skraa.

The first of the paska swooped down upon a fleeing Amast man, digging talons deep into his back. He swung his arms, trying to bash the ferocious bird that murderously pecked and clawed.

Kora ran toward Aena. Isy wanted to go after him, though she wasn't sure why. The others pushed her inside and quickly began to gather whatever they could to block the doorway—tree trunk chests, the table, firewood. Kora all of a sudden leapt through the doorway, grappling with a paska. Shrieks and feathers filled the air. The bird's dagger-like beak pecked and snapped. It seemed deranged, as if it lacked control over its actions. A blade flashed and the flapping wings stilled.

Tulasc lowered his spear and helped a bleeding Kora to his feet, though the Amast man didn't seem troubled at all by the wounds on his hands and arms. Pekira and Yera had barricaded most of the doorway now and held their shoulders against the blockade. Thuds barraged against it.

Beaks appeared in gaps too narrow for them to squeeze their feathered bodies through, and they shrieked their frustrations.

The thudding subsided. Outside they could hear the cries and calls of the paska, the screams of the Amast, and now the scratch of claws against the wattle of the dome. They were tearing their way in. Tulasc ran to a long sack of woven material and almost tore it open. From inside he pulled a handful of spears. The Amast hurried to take one. He pushed the last into Isy's hands and she nearly toppled with the weight of it. He pointed at the ceiling and walls and thrust upwards with his own spear. His message was clear. *Stab and kill whatever comes through.*

They spread out in a circle, backs to each other. The spear was near twice Isy's height and too thick to wrap her fingers around. Branches snapped above their heads. Scratchy caws sounded from all directions, as if the paska were talking to one another, coordinating their assault.

Sunlight exploded above Isy. Sticks and twigs showered down upon her. The head of a paska punctured the roof and screamed. She froze. Kora, beside her, wasted no time. In a flash of movement, his spear cut through the neck of the bird. It stirred a chorus of piercing wails from the others.

More cracks in the shelter erupted all around, and the battle began in earnest. Before the Amast had killed one paska, another had either made a fresh gap or emerged through an existing one.

The wall before Isy suddenly parted. Sunlight blinded her vision. She could not shield her eyes for fear of dropping the spear. Squinting, she aimed as best she could for the light and charged. She felt it connect with something, heard a cry.

Behind her, Yera shouted something and Pekira answered her. Isy had no time to turn and look. Another hole emerged above her head. With all the strength she possessed, she hefted the spear up and, with her momentum, thrust it at the hole. The paska recoiled with a shriek. When she turned back to the first hole, another was halfway through, beak snapping. Isy swung down, straining her arms to keep control, and severed the bird's blue-feathered wing in half.

Isy glanced around her. The sight of blood running down Kora's back caught her breath, but it seemed to have no bearing on the ferocity of his movements. Indeed, all of the Amast moved with improbable swiftness, wielding their spears as if they were mere sticks. They showed no signs of fatigue, each strike precise and fatal.

The tide of paska waned. Blood dripped from the ceiling. Beams of light shone through from all angles and in those rays floated feathers and motes of dust. Isy could no longer hear the piercing caws of the paska outside, nor the screams of the Amast.

Kora peered out of a hole for a good few minutes, then moved to the door and dissembled the barricade. One by one the others followed, spears raised, Isy last of all, clutching hers with trembling hands.

Most of the Amast, it seemed, had made it indoors, but the weak frames and rag doors were beyond ineffective. The surrounding domes had been torn to shreds in parts, holes gaping where paska had poured in, the inhabitants overwhelmed by sheer numbers. Dead paska were piled at the bases of many domes and some lay in pathways where they'd killed each other, fighting over the bodies of the Amast.

Kora led them down the trail in close formation, moving around strips of torn, blood-stained clothing, blue feathers, and morsels of pink and grey flesh. Nobody's head remained still. They stopped at the shelter closest to the spot where they'd last seen Aena. Like many of the others, great gashes had been torn in the walls and roof. Kora glanced back at the group before he entered.

They may as well have stepped into an abattoir. Bile rose from Isy's stomach and she battled retches. Everywhere she turned she saw blood. Dripping from the wattle walls and wooden chests, speckling and staining the furs and rugs upon the floor. Pools lay around the bodies of two Amast who were nothing more than skeletons, their clothes shredded, flesh, muscle and organs stripped. Not far away was, Isy guessed from what was left of her clothing, Aena's assistant, body pecked to the bone. She lay upon a chest that was splintered in parts, with a paska-sized hole in the center of its lid. Kora and Tulasc moved what remained of her body aside and opened the chest.

Aena lay inside, body intact, save for a stain of red around her left shoulder and breast. In her hands, she held the neck of a paska, almost lovingly. Kora held his fingers over her nostrils, then straightened and nodded. She was alive.

Three

Edvar hefted his shield just in time. Wood clapped. A numbing shockwave raced up his arm before the rim of the shield snapped back to strike his forehead. He reeled away, seeking respite. Sweat dripped into his eyes. The leather armor over his gambeson served as a radiator, and his chainmail shirt grew heavier with each swing of his blunted sword.

Camos slashed once more. Edvar caught it with his sword. No sooner had they clashed did Camos strike again, and again, forcing Edvar behind his shield and driving him further back. With a combination swifter than his cannonball gut suggested he was capable of, Camos batted away Edvar's shield, then his sword, and with his own shield, caught Edvar square in the face. Edvar hit the floor. Flashing lights obscured his vision. The copper taste of blood flooded his mouth. Something blocked out the sun. Edvar lacked the will to open his eyes.

"Give your opponent half a chance like that and you'll have worse than a bloody nose," Camos said in his gruff voice. He held out a hand and lifted Edvar to his feet as if he were light as a kitten. Edvar felt about as dangerous as one.

Camos's greyshot hair was greasy and unwashed and tied back in a scruffy ponytail. His thick beard, similarly colored, smothered much of his face and almost hid his brown, mournful eyes. His father used to call him "Slice" for the number of scars he had.

"You did better than yesterday," Camos said, returning his sword and shield to their racks. "But you're a way off keeping that fat head of yours on your shoulders."

Edvar slumped onto a bench beside a water barrel. "It's not *that* fat."

"You're an archer's dream, pal." Camos handed him a wooden cup. Edvar dipped it into the barrel and drank deep, poured more over his head and face, and washed away the blood trickling from his throbbing nose. *Again, the nose. It'll be crooked forever.*

They were in the second of the keep's three baileys, in the mustering yard before the barracks. A few other soldiers sparred with shields, swords, and spears. Earlier he'd seen a giant of a man swinging a spiked ball the size of a tree stump. He hoped Camos didn't pair him up for a sparring session; it was the kind of sadistic thing he'd do. Upon the walls, a few crossbowmen watched on with mirthful expressions, until a sergeant berated them and sent them on their way.

"You've got your father's frame but none of the muscle," Camos said. "You move like him. That hunched gait. I thought I was watching him again."

Edvar was sick of everyone comparing him to his father. *What about me? I'm my own man.* "If only I could fight like he did, hey," he said. He couldn't get angry with Camos. It was the old warrior's way of showing affection. He'd served in the Yurrish army with Edvar's father and was one of his most loyal and dependable men. But the curse of the veteran is loss. Camos had few remaining friends. When he wasn't in the training yard, he was in the tavern, trying, no doubt, to forget.

"You'll get there. Nothing in life comes easy," Camos said.

Edvar downed another cup of water. His body was awash with aches and throbs. He longed for a warm bath, a hot meal and undisturbed sleep. *I have no time for any of that.* It'd been nearly a week since the assassination attempt and he'd gleaned next to nothing. The interrogations of the keep staff proved useless, his informants silent as door mice, and surveillance efforts had yielded naught. Each of his fellow councilors had kept to their routines—no unusual meetings, no conversations with unknown individuals. After two days of tracking, he'd found Mag, his informant who'd warned him of the assassination attempt in the first place. He found him in an alleyway in Skimar, throat cut, mouth stuffed with what looked and smelled like horse crap. Not a hint as to who could have killed him.

It wasn't uncommon for informants to turn up dead. It was the nature of the game. No risk, no reward. But this felt deliberately inconvenient, and it hadn't helped Edvar's growing paranoia. He felt as if he was being chased through a labyrinth of dead ends, all the while the walls and ceiling were closing in to snuff him out.

But he strived to climb out of that pit of despair. Resuming weapons training had reduced his feelings of helplessness and reminded him what it felt like to be confident and powerful, beatings from Camos aside. And for once there was good news from the Borderlands. There was no sign of an imminent Karraban invasion. The attack on Wender appeared to be a raid, and a devastating one at that—over two hundred dead; houses, shops, and barns torched; scores of rapes; countless pillaging; slaughtering of livestock. Wender and its people would carry the scars forever.

There was word of a train of people headed to Yurrisa, another to Oakhill—home of Baroness Ura—and even some venturing as far north as Haberdam and Labrad—the furthest distance from war possible. Who could blame them? The Yurrish response, according to Malfan, after having convened a meeting with his generals, was to sure up the border and hold tight. *And he criticized our policy of appeasement?* It was one less thing to worry about, at least, and any opportunity to reduce his growing list of troubles Edvar would seize.

The pressure was building like an angry carbuncle. Each day brought something new to weigh down his soul. And tomorrow morning was the first council meeting since he'd stormed out. The scrutiny would be suffocating. The prospect provoked a sense of dread, but he had to face it. Ashara needed him. Now more than ever.

"Oi, you paying attention?" Camos snapped.

Edvar had caught a few of Camos's words: something about stance and moving his feet. His lack of response set Camos off.

"If you wanna learn how to defend yourself, you need to listen." His tone grew angrier with each word. Spittle went in Edvar's mouth. "This isn't some piss take. This is life and death. Your father knew that, the Keeper knows that, but none of you poncy councilors know. Do you know how it feels to line up against thousands of men all determined to kill you? How it feels when the first cries of charge ring out? What it's like to stand in an arrow storm, watching your brothers and sisters in arms die?

"When you were a kid, I told your father to give you military experience. He said no. He said you had no interest, only in books. Well, I say there are some things that you can't learn from books. Some things you must do and feel to truly understand."

Edvar endured his admonishment. He'd grown unused to being scalded like this. His father had regularly done so, and in his defense, it was often deserved. Edvar was lucky, he supposed, that he only had one parent to berate him for his wrongdoings, though sometimes he wished he'd had two. Edvar knew Camos was right; he was just trying to impart advice the only way he knew how.

Edvar's gaze wandered across the bailey. Disappearing through the gatehouse toward the city, he glimpsed the purple and grey cloaks of Mara and Rakar. An urge to follow consumed Edvar's heart, though his mind branded him a fool for considering the idea. If they spotted him, that would be it for his seat on the Council. Repeated and grievous failures, lashing out in their previous meeting, and then spying on his colleagues. The Council would not stand for it and what could Ashara do to stop them in his current state?

But Edvar was fraught with desperation. He needed something, anything.

Edvar stood, Camos berating him still. "I have to go." He removed his chainmail shirt and hurried after them, adrenaline deadening his aches and pains.

"I'm not finished!" Camos shouted.

Edvar waved without turning. Camos would beat him twice as hard for that tomorrow. The old warrior never let anything slide.

He entered the last bailey, a clear, grassy area some four hundred paces long, and saw the pair approaching the gate ahead. Edvar slowed to a walk. There wasn't any cover here, save the storage sheds lining the gravel road, used by the archery corps. Hanging on the side of the closest cabin were a few russet cloaks. He nabbed one, a staff too, casting a glance in the direction of the archers practicing nearby. Someone would be punished for losing their gear, but for Edvar it was a small price to pay.

Edvar swept the cloak over his shoulders, pulled down the hood, and stooped over the staff. The frail old man was a favorite disguise of his—the aged carried less of a threat in many people's eyes, though it was sometimes a challenge to keep up with those he pursued while maintaining character.

Despite the high street bustling with people heading in myriad directions, Edvar never lost sight of Rakar and Mara. They turned down an adjoining street leading to the Merchant's District, a place popular with the city's elite and an area Edvar tended to avoid—those who congregated there were firmly wedged up their own arses. Nevertheless, he was partial to the mead of the Winged Star. The rabble thinned and Edvar hung back, eyes never off the pair ahead. His heart threatened to leap from his throat. Any moment one of them could turn and see him and that would be it. The voice of reason within him cried out to turn around, yet he pressed on.

Over the din of footsteps and chatter came the rush of the fountain, and soon he saw the sparkle of its spray in the sunlight. The brilliant obsidian sculpture loomed above all else, a magnet of attention. Carved waves crashed into the shore and rose up like a tower, upon which sat a young boy and girl, holding together over their heads a pail, water gushing from it into the broad, circular bowl below. It was known as "The Waves of Life" and was crafted centuries ago by Cretor of Cadine. It paid homage to the Green Deep and River Haber—the givers of Yurrish life, bringing food and water—and to the men and women who founded Yurrisa.

Around the edge of the square, crammed shoulder to shoulder, were a dozen eateries and taverns. On the west side stood the Theatre of Yurr, one of Yurrisa's grandest buildings, an impression cemented by its flight of marble steps leading up to its entrance, where four pillars, marble too, supported a great archway. The finest inn in Yurrisa, The Keeper's Right Hand, faced it. Beside that was the epicenter of the Yurrish economy—the Merchant House. It was a towering building, painted white save for its sills and architraves, which were black, and hanging above its doorway was a figurehead of a mermaid that once sat at the head of The Green Explorer, one of Yurrisa's most famous military ships. Beside it were a tailors shop, pigeon lofts, a shipwright, and an armorer. The rich, however fat, needed armor to at least look the part. Indeed, it was all that most of them were good at.

People gathered around the fountain, sitting, chatting, playing games upon tables, or listening to busking harpists, singers and fiddle players. Nearly all were dressed in robes of silk and velvet, brightly colored and worn in a similar fashion. These people followed trends as if their lives depended on it.

Edvar fell in amongst the crowd. Up ahead he could see Rakar and Mara slow before the fountain. Mara glanced over her shoulder, right at Edvar, her eyes staring into his soul. An urge to stop gripped him. Had she spotted him? Was his disguise *that* pathetic? But she turned back and they continued on, deeper into the crowd. Rattled, Edvar hesitated.

From the direction of the docks marched a band of sailors, headed for the Merchant House. The captain strode before his crew, grey mutton chop sideburns sweeping across his cheeks like waves. Four of his men carried a large chest on their shoulders, and another half-dozen more surrounded them, hands on sword hilts. They crossed the path of Mara and Rakar. When the sailors moved clear, Edvar's fellow councilors were nowhere to be seen.

Edvar scanned the square, trying his best not to seem obvious. It was as if they'd fallen through the ground. He wanted to straighten his back, enhance his view, but that would give away his disguise. He continued on, angling to the side of the square, feigning the need for a rest. Why had he thought this a good idea? It was madness! All risk and no reward. What evidence could he really hope to obtain? And he'd offended Camos in the process. *What's happening to me?* It was as if his ability to think had fled him.

Edvar stood and made for the keep. He cast his gaze across the square once more, still dumbfounded by their sudden disappearance. He happened to lock eyes with a man. Copper-skinned with dark hair tied back, he had a closely cropped beard, divided by a scar, which stretched diagonally from cheek to chin. His beady eyes never strayed from Edvar. Eyes that possessed one desire alone: kill.

Without thought, Edvar ducked down the nearest side street. When he glanced back, the man was in pursuit, purpose in his strides. Edvar strained his legs, disguise abandoned. Had they known he would follow? Was it all just a trap? It seemed so obvious now that he was standing in the middle of it. *How could I be so naive?*

He abruptly ducked down an alleyway and sprinted toward the other end, the hours of training that morning beginning to take their toll. Before he turned off it, he glanced back to find the man racing after him.

Edvar abandoned the cloak. The staff he kept—his only weapon, though he wasn't sure what damage his weary arms could muster. He re-joined the high street, heading toward the smog of the industrial district beside the River Haber. As good a place as any to shake his pursuer.

The streets quietened as he passed rows of squat houses of stone and wood, their only differentiating feature the front doors, which were painted in an array of bright colors. Hurried steps continued to patter behind him.

An iron forge loomed ahead, black smoke billowing from its many chimneys, metal bashing ringing out through windows that couldn't open wide enough for those inside. Yurr was rich in iron and the capital alone had a dozen such forges making everything from weapons and armor to door studs and nails. He hoped he could lose him inside.

Edvar hurried through an open side door and found himself in a pitch dark room. When his eyes adjusted, he saw a great pile of coal, black as a moonless sky, consuming the length of the left wall. The other walls were stained black too. Crashes and bangs sounded from a large rectangular doorway to the right. He ventured through it and received a stun to the senses. Heat struck first, stifling his breath and constricting his chest. Then came a wave of deafening sound that sent his ears ringing.

Furnaces lined the far wall, fires like pits of hell roaring in small holes at their bases. Not far away were a dozen rows of anvils of varying sizes, and standing at them were men and women bashing and shaping white-hot iron. Nobody seemed to notice Edvar. He looked around, searching for a place to hide. An iron framework hung over the furnaces and led to the windows and roof high above. With no better options, he ran to the closest ladder and began to ascend.

A few of the rungs wobbled, but the urge to flee prevailed. As he neared the top he glanced down and what he saw propelled him up the last stretch. No sooner had Edvar found his feet on the narrow iron walkway was the man half-way up. Edvar struck out with his staff. His pursuer read his intentions, moved a few rungs down, and grabbed onto the end and pulled. Edvar relented his grip before he went with it, and grasped the rail for balance. His attacker climbed up onto the walkway and drew a stubby yet sharp dagger from his belt. Edvar backed away.

Below, flames rushed and roared as workers stoked the furnaces and beat iron. He tried to recall Camos's training but his thoughts held like soup. The man came forwards. *What would Pa do? Not cower like a toddler and await his fate.*

A roar erupted from Edvar's lungs, lost amongst the racket of the forge, and he charged with his shoulder. He pictured the blade plunging into his back, but it didn't come. They both fell, Edvar on top of him. Edvar's first instinct was to disarm. He scrambled for his attacker's blade hand and felt a terrible sting in his palm. Not bad enough to stop him from grabbing onto his wrist and, as Camos had taught him, he dug his thumb into the base of the hand and twisted. Edvar felt the vibrations of a scream but couldn't hear it. The dagger fell to the ground far below.

Edvar pushed back and swung at the dark-haired man, each blow falling in time with the bashes of the hammers below. With their face more crimson than pink, he ceased.

"Who sent you?" Edvar screamed down his ear, over and over, shaking him by his collar. The man was too dazed to respond, but Edvar didn't care. He hauled him further over the edge and bellowed the same question.

A dart flew past his face. Edvar spun round and found another man, dressed all in black, hurriedly reloading a single-handed crossbow. The man in Edvar's grasp seized his chance. He lurched forwards, struck Edvar hard at the temple, which caused him to lose his grip on his collar. The dark-haired man grabbed at Edvar's jerkin but could find no purchase. He fell from the walkway to the ground below.

Edvar scrambled to his feet to find the crossbow pointed at him. This was it. Now he had truly failed, and all the fault was at his feet. The other councilors had been right all along: he was just a naive fool, a simpleton easily played. Edvar closed his eyes, awaited the bolt to end his life. Seconds passed like eons to the sounds of hammering. He opened his eyes, found his attacker scrambling with his crossbow. The string had drawn but the bolt had jammed.

Hesitation did not enter Edvar's mind. He sprung forwards and, supporting himself on the railings of the walkway, pushed his attacker with both feet over the rail. He landed on his back not far from his lifeless companion, vacant eyes staring up at Edvar.

Edvar's limbs crumbled beneath him. To the unloving sounds of the forge, he began to sob.

Four

The heat of the fire burned through Isy's skirt. She loved to get as close as she could, reading by the flickering glow, watching shadows dance across the page to bring life to the words.

Weariness seeped to her marrow. Like the previous days, she had spent the best part of thirteen hours in the dingy dome shelter, teaching the Amast in her hesitant, uncertain fashion, as well as scribing out lists of words for them to read. All the while, everyone else in the camp helped rebuild after the attack of the paska. It didn't feel right sitting around talking and reading when others needed help, others she felt more confident of helping than those she was teaching.

That said, the Amast had made good progress, in part down to their unwavering determination to learn, though at times their concentration waned. Tulasc struggled the most, his pronunciations hilarious if nothing else. The four of them spent every waking moment practicing and helping one another. After six lengthy lessons, they could converse in basic terms in a broken fashion. The Keeper might smile, at least.

The more time she spent with the Amast, the more her understanding grew as to why they were so invested in this plan. They were homeless and dying and this, they believed, was their last hope—reaching out to people who knew nothing of their existence. Isy could see no other option for them, and if indeed she was committed to helping them, it meant that she was going to Yurrisa.

Apprehension churned in her gut. Nobody, not even her parents, had accepted her for the way she looked. How would two hundred thousand people react? How would they take to the Amast? Would they do what the Karrabans did and kill them? Would she get caught in the crossfire? Yet again fear of death circled her mind. A week ago, the prospect hadn't troubled her. Now it filled her with dread. What had changed?

A ruffle by the doorway drew her out of her thoughts. Kora stooped before her, a bundle of scrolls in his hand. Isy beckoned him to the fire. He sat beside her, placing his papers down next to him. Snaps and crackles filled the silence. Kora looked like he was searching the flames for words and a couple of times he glanced at her, only to turn back as if he'd forgotten what to say. The appearance of the Amast was still unusual to Isy. It was their eyes above all, so amphibian, each blink like a lunar eclipse.

"Aena teach me more so learn fast. You teach me?" Kora stuttered and paused between words which made him a little testing to listen to, but he was doing well, especially given his poor teacher.

"Of course. Starting with what you've just said." Legs crossed, she shuffled away from the fire to face Kora.

"Aena is your grandmother." She sounded out *grandmother* slowly so he could mimic.

"What grandmother?"

"Mother of your mother. Aena."

Kora nodded, placed his hand over his heart. "Mother of my mother," he said.

Isy had visited Aena three times since the attack and on each occasion her skin had further paled, her wrinkles deepening to ridges. The bird she had strangled had buried its beak deep into her shoulder, leaving a nasty open wound that had since become infected. Now she lay in the grips of a fever, yet to awake. Isy hoped she would soon.

"My mother, Misendi. Killed by men. My father die trying to save. I help Aena. I could not help."

"I'm sorry," Isy said, tears in the corners of her eyes to match Kora's.

"What for? You no kill them?"

"It's something we say. Sorry for your loss."

They fell silent again until Kora turned to his papers, handed them to Isy, and their lesson began. Hours passed like minutes. Isy taught her language, Kora his. Her tongue clicking drew mirthful reactions from Kora and she broke down in laughter of her own. She couldn't recall ever laughing so deep and freely before. And she had experienced it here, far from home, far from anything she knew or understood, with someone who, even with eyes five times the size of her own, did not see her birthmark. He saw her for who she was, not how she appeared.

Kora returned the following night. Isy hoped he would. He brought food: a roasted red root that looked like a stubby parsnip but had the texture of potato, and a small bunch of mushrooms covered in honey. Like the night previous they taught more of their languages, ate, laughed.

Beyond Kora, she found the Amast truly wonderful people. Each day men, women, and children came to her door with clothes, food and fresh water—things they all lacked themselves, and all in the midst of grieving for the loss of their loved ones, if not to disease than by the beaks and talons of the paska. Thankfully there hadn't been any more sightings of the blue birds, and ever since the attack, people's eyes watched the sky instead of Isy. A welcome relief.

Some things troubled her, though. Sleep had become a thing to fear, her dreams twisted and terrifying. One recurred in which she found herself lost in the Amast camp, the cries of paska at her back, screeching down her ears. Always she ended up in the clearing with the dead bodies. She had dreamt another of being carried to one of those piles upon a makeshift bed by two Amast men. The body they placed her upon was Kora's, his eyes wide and vacant.

After another sleepless night, Isy made her way to the shelter that had become their classroom. She recognized some of the Amast she passed and exchanged smiles and waves, and one child even ran forward to give her a hug. Laughing, she realized something—she had no fear of walking about in the open. No urge to skulk about or hide in bushes. Her birthmark was almost forgotten. In fact, nobody here seemed to notice it at all.

She passed the clearing with the pyres. The bodies were gone, devoured by the paska. The smell had drawn them from far and wide and it was here they had congregated. The remains had been placed on one big fire, and now only a few charred splinters and shards of bone remained. Losing the bodies of the dead pained the Amast tremendously. They had been robbed of the chance to say their final farewells to those they loved. The smell was gone, at least.

The paska had killed a hundred and ninety-three altogether, including the two other Guides, Gosha and Wema. Kora had said that before the Karrabans came, there had been over five thousand Amast. Now, little more than five hundred remained, many sick and weak.

Isy's students were waiting for her when she arrived. She was greeted by "good mornings" and "hellos". It seemed such a long time ago that she had taught them those words, yet it had only been a week. They'd packed much into the days so far. Her eyes met Kora's and she looked away, feeling heat rise in her cheeks. She set down her papers, composing herself.

"Kora!" A young Amast woman with copper hair burst into the room. Isy recognized her as one of those caring for Aena. Kora didn't hesitate. In a few strides he was out of the dome and down the trail. Like the day of the paska attack, the others made for the door too, and Isy followed. She tagged behind while they muttered in Amasti. She caught the odd word but they spoke too quickly to understand. Was Aena awake? Or... Aena was the driving force behind all of this. Losing her would be like losing not just the oars, but the rudder too. Dread stabbed at Isy's gut.

A crowd had gathered outside the dome where Aena was being cared for. They fell silent and parted when Kora reached them. Isy and the others followed behind. Through the press of bodies, Isy saw Kora kneeling beside Aena's bed. She was awake, but she looked her worst yet, clutching her grandson's hand with emaciated fingers.

Isy caught a few of her whispered Amasti words. "No more time. Our end. Get help." Aena grimaced, her eyes bunching closed. Kora spoke to her in swift Amasti. She did not answer. The lines around her eyes eased until calmness returned to her face. A veil of stillness fell over her body, and Isy knew that life had slipped away.

They did not resume their lesson that day. When darkness descended, they began Aena's cremation. The Amast filled the clearing and the forest around it. Even the wounded and sick left their beds. Isy didn't know Aena well at all, but the sight of so many mourners was a testament to the person she no doubt was. Isy had decided against getting closer, opting instead to watch from a rise overlooking the clearing. Those earlier feelings of belonging had faded. What she had grown used to had changed again. She did not know the songs, the rituals, the conventions. Now, more than ever, she felt like an outsider. A return to what she knew.

They began to sing. The women first, in harmonic tones, soft and low. Then they stopped and the men took over, just as harmonious but deeper. Back and forth they went, singing to each other. The sound of grief and longing, of a sorrow too deep to express in words alone. Then it ceased, the snap of flames in the breeze the only noise. Eyes turned north to the body of Aena. She lay upon a wooden platform, carried by four Amast men, Tulasc and Kora two of them. Her body, save for her face, was cocooned in grey linen. When they reached the beginning of the crowd, they stopped, lifted her body high and passed it to those closest. The song resumed, this time men and women singing together as Aena made her way to the square. Isy couldn't stop the tears falling from her eyes. She had never heard a more beautifully harmonious yet sad sound.

When Aena's body arrived at the clearing, their voices grew in volume. She was lifted onto a great pyre of moss, sticks, twigs, and logs and surrounded by wildflowers of blues, purples and whites. Isy thought it much more dignified than being buried in the ground to feed the worms.

An Amast woman dressed all in white, who Isy knew to be named Escara, ascended the dais. Escara shouted a few words and with the torch in her hand, lit the pyre. The flames grew quickly, licking, ensnaring, before engulfing Aena altogether. Save for the occasional whimper, all were silent. It stayed like that as the flames lulled. Until a horn rang out. The same sound that had heralded the coming of the paska, cutting through the quiet like a knife through flesh.

Even from her position, Isy could hear the intake of breath. She saw fear ripple through the crowd. Two blasts meant danger. Heads turned to the night sky. Mutterings grew. Everyone, it seemed, expected the second blast.

Eyes shifted toward the camp entrance. Two torches approached, moving fast, and headed for the clearing. Now Isy wanted to get closer. She set off down the road. The density of the crowd had eased. Some, fearing trouble, hurried back to their shelters. She weaved her way through them, recognizing the odd Amasti word. "Paska", "Outsiders". When she reached the edge of the clearing, her progress was halted. The elongated bodies of the Amast boxed her in like a thicket of trees. All she could see were legs, back and arse. She hopped and jumped. Futile. A hand touched her arm. An Amast man, bigger than most of those around them, looked down at her with that warped Amasti smile upon his face.

"Sit on my shoulders?" he asked in his own language, pointing.

Isy smiled, nodded, and he bowed down for her to clamber upon him. Over twelve feet up, she had a better view than anyone. Beyond the dying pyre, the crowd parted. The torches of the returning Amast melded with the others. Kora met them. Even from her enhanced angle, Isy couldn't see a thing.

Someone shouted her name. It sounded like Kora. Others repeated the call. Heads turned and a line of bodies parted, stopping at her. The Amast man lowered her down and like a child expecting a telling off, Isy trudged toward Kora.

For the first time, she saw those who had arrived. Two Amast men stood before a bundle of dark and dirty rags lying on the ground. The taller of the two had a broad and vertical scar upon his stone-grey cheek. The other had a brown bandana wrapped around his forehead and a huge spear slung over his shoulder. Both sets of pale, bulbous eyes held weary looks. The bundle upon the floor moved and Isy realized it was a person. Kora nodded and the scarred man hauled them up.

Isy squinted. He was Yurrish. Dirt smothered his face. Dried blood caked his nose. His curly hair was a tangled mess of leaves and twigs. His cloak was torn, his boots covered in mud, soles peeling. There was no mistaking who it was.

"Vil!"

Tears flooded her eyes. Someone came. Someone cared enough to look for her. The little chronicler's assistant who complained about the countryside, shivered at the slightest draft, and paled at seeing even the shade of blood. Of all people.

She raced forwards, threw her arms around him, squeezed him so tight he gasped. "Isy," he said.

"Vil."

Five

"Where are we, Isy?" Vil huddled close to the fire. Still, he shivered. With some reluctance he'd washed the dirt from his face but was yet to touch the nuts and berries the Amast had left for him. Isy had caught him glancing at them longingly more than once.

"Somewhere in the Giant's Garden."

"Giant's Garden?! That far? What are these ... things, Isy?" he spoke in a whisper.

"They're not things. They're called the Amast."

"A-what?"

"Amast. I can't believe you came, Vil."

"How could I not come? And I'm glad of it now. Kidnapped by these monsters. We have to leave. Come on, let's go, while it's still dark."

Isy laughed.

"What's funny?"

"You are. Do you know the way back? What would you do if a flock of paska swooped down at you?"

"Paska? Isy, I don't know what they've done to you, but we have to get out of here."

His comment struck a nerve. "They've done nothing to me. I'm helping them."

"How?"

She told him in brief about the plight of the Amast, the attack by the Karrabans, the sickness ravaging them and their plan to seek help from the Keeper. Vil shook his head and the stab of annoyance at Isy's temples grew.

"Don't you see? Once you've helped them, they'll kill you," he said.

"Why in Soria do you think they'll do that?"

"Because you do not know them."

"And nor do you." Isy stood and made for the door. Before she left, she turned to him.

"For the first time in my life, I've lived with people who haven't looked at me and seen only my mark. With these alien people, I'm more at home than I've ever been amongst my own."

She left before he could respond. Why was he so deaf to her words?

The hero she had longed for had arrived at last. Never in the stories did the hero and princess argue. Never did the princess refuse to leave her captors. *I am no princess.*

She went to find Kora.

Episode Four: Into the Cold

"Upon that cliff once stood a great city known as Yurrisa," Uren had said. Here, in the center of where it ought to have been, all I could see was wind-swept grass. Other than my grazing mare and the gulls that occasionally swooped by in the hope of finding food, not a soul could be found.

For days I explored that rugged stretch of coast and found nothing but unremarkable rocks. I dug pit after pit, each one deeper than the last. Hope numbed the pain of my blistered hands. Each day, always the same. No finds, and a greater sense that Uren's quest was futile. My misery compounded in the height of a storm. Rain poured into the hole I had labored hours to dig. From the pit of my lungs I roared my frustration. Who is more at fault: the liar, or the fool that believes him?

From *The Forgotten Daggers* by S. T. Harris

One

WITHOUT BREAKING STRIDE, the Amast bobbed beneath branches, weaved and twisted through boles, never under threat of losing balance. It was like a dance, and Isy was mesmerized. Kora led the way with Pekira close behind. Yera and Tulasc brought up the rear, and in between trudged Isy and Vil, their branch-snapping stomps betraying the silence the Amast worked so gracefully hard to maintain. In the glow of the moon, broken by naked trees, Isy glanced back at the hunched form of Vil.

"I will not help these thieves," Vil had said when Isy first asked him to show them the way to Yurrisa.

"Please, Vil. You're the only person I know who's been there. We can't go to Haberdam. You know what Baron Rijkard would do. Keeper Ashara's the only one who can help."

"Why don't they kidnap somebody else?"

"We don't have any more time for this. We need *your* help."

"We? When did you become one of *them*?" Isy had never known him capable of such poisonous anger. It reminded her of her father.

"When all of my own cast me aside."

"Not all."

"Please, Vil. For me?"

Vil had, with great reluctance, agreed, an agreement that came close to collapsing when he heard that they must go by foot. They had no mounts and the nearest river, which the Amast called the Qathi, led to the south coast, through the Wetlands of the Damned. Vil had judged it about a hundred leagues away over hills and across rivers, which would be a two to three-week walk, if they could keep a good pace and the weather stayed fair. The Amast intended to do it in less time. With their swiftness and endless endurance, Isy didn't doubt it.

Kora abruptly halted and Isy walked into the back of Pekira, who turned and hissed at her.

"What is it?" Isy whispered, ignoring Pekira.

Kora gave no reply. Fear of the paska had driven them to travel by night. The impenetrable gloom, the unrecognizable sounds, never completely sure they were headed in the right direction, all set Isy on edge.

"Are we stopping?" Vil asked. "My feet are fit to fall off." Isy's feet cried out in pain too. Her boots were chafing her toes.

"No time for breaks," Yera snapped. The reaction surprised Isy. The Amast generally possessed unfaltering patience, or so it seemed to Isy, but they'd not taken well to Vil. Since they'd left the camp, he'd persistently complained; it was annoying even Isy. Often she caught him staring with furrowed brows at the Amast, with a look in his eyes Isy knew well, and not one she associated with Vil. It disappointed her, but she understood why he felt as he did. His world had been torn asunder. Vil was a man who lived by routine, contented when in control. With that stripped away, it left an uncomfortable, fearful mess, which made coming to terms with the existence of the Amast more difficult for him. No greater fear existed than that of the unknown, and at the moment, the Amast were very much unknowns.

"Wind tricks ears," Kora said.

The group uttered a collective sigh. They continued on, and only when the first rays of dawn broke through the trees did they stop. Beside a stream, they found a shallow cave and there made camp. The Amast unshouldered their woven travel bags and double-ended spears, and sat down on the cold earth with their backs against the lichen-covered stone. None of them showed any signs of tiredness. An exhausted Vil staggered toward the stream.

"Here," Kora said, offering his water skin. Vil looked at him and after a moment's hesitation, took it and drank. Isy hoped it was a sign of a change.

Two

Isy felt as if her eyes had just closed when Kora shook her awake. Rain pattered against the rocks outside the cave and rippled the stream beyond. She could not gauge the time, so grey was the day. The Amast were on their feet, ready to go. Vil lay huddled in a dark corner of the cave. Isy approached him.

"Vil, we have to go."

"I'm too tired to move."

"You know they'll just carry you if you don't get up."

He made a noise like an angry dog and, as if propelled by his annoyance, stood. He never spoke another word until, at dusk, they stopped again at the edge of a vast meadow of long grass.

"Why have we stopped?" Isy asked Kora.

"Why didn't we stop hours ago?" Vil chimed in. Pekira scowled at him. Vil countered with one of his own.

"We watch grass for movement," Kora said.

"What do you mean, 'movement'?" Isy asked.

"Cats hunt here."

"What, like mountain lions?"

"Ikata. Hear everything, but you not hear them until they leaping for your throat," Tulasc said.

Fear seemed to soften Vil's angry shell. He shook his head at Isy with a look that said, *what in Soria have you gotten me into?* The meadow spread wide before them, how far exactly Isy couldn't say with the encroaching shadows of night. The pouring rain left blades of grass trembling, suggesting that something was moving through it. Like Vil, she had no desire to go through there, but she trusted Kora and the others.

"Here," Kora said, handing Isy and Vil a slender spear each. "We use for throwing but they do for you."

The color further drained from Vil's face as he took the polished wooden spear. Isy found it much wieldier and a good deal lighter than the one she'd used to fight the paska. If attacked, she could defend herself. Or try, at least. It felt strange to be in a position to do so after a whole life spent fleeing. The churning anxiety in her stomach eased a little.

Pekira led the way into the long grass, scything what she could with a sickle-shaped dirk and stomping flat what remained. The grass at their flanks loomed way over Isy's head, but not as tall as the Amast, who scanned over the top, heads never still. It went that way for what felt like hours. The clouds eventually shifted and unleashed the light of a full moon, a reassuring beacon amid the void.

Ahead, Isy could see the shadowy form of trees—the resumption of the forest, she hoped. With a smile, she glanced back at Vil. He was dragging his feet, eyes to the ground. Behind him, further along the trail they'd forged, Isy saw a glimmer of eyeshine in the moonlight, right at the edge of the long grass. She stopped dead, her heart too. Yera, bringing up the rear, saw her looking and followed her gaze. She too halted, ears twitching. She brought up her spear. The grass to the left swayed. On the right too.

"Ikata!" Yera shouted. "Both sides."

"We not far. Hurry!" Pekira said. Scything abandoned, the Amast quickly outran Isy and Vil's human legs. As they passed, Tulasc and Yera lifted Vil and Isy and carried them. The long and sodden grass buffeted Isy's face. She could hear animalistic grunts of exertion in the grass around her. The image of fangs and claws leaping toward them consumed her mind.

"Faster!" Kora shouted.

The dark, spindly shapes of trees rose above them, and then the Amast were free of the long grass, maintaining stride as they weaved through boles that seemed to appear from nowhere. Yera's grip on Isy tightened.

Before the rocky remains of a former stream, they halted. Isy and Vil regained their feet and in a circle they all stood, clutching their spears. Isy scanned the gloom for sight or sound of pursuit. After a few still minutes, the tension in her shoulders eased.

"We must've out-ran them," she muttered to Vil.

As the final word left her mouth, the shadows before her shifted. Yellow eyes erupted from the void, descending on Vil. Without thought, Isy brought up her spear, held strong her arms. The stone point sunk into the neck of the ikata. Warm blood spattered her arms and trickled down the shaft, over her fingers. Mouth agape, she looked down at what she had slain—a beast the size of a large dog with shaggy brown fur, striped grey. It had imposing black-padded paws, tipped with thick claws, and a long, slender tail. Its head was as big as a pig's, with a stubby snout housing rows of intimidating teeth. She'd read about Yurrish mountain lions. Seeing them in the flesh was something altogether different. Judging from the wide eyes dominating Vil's pale face, he wasn't sure what to make of the situation either.

"There are others," Pekira said. "They circle."

"Keep moving," Kora said.

Only when the sun rose did they stop. Fatigue, it seemed, was beginning to overwhelm even the Amast. Everyone sat with backs to tree trunks or rocks, drinking deep from water skins, wiping sweat from brows or kneading achy muscles. Vil collapsed on his back, chest rising and falling. The Amast exchanged looks amongst themselves, eyes flicking to Isy.

"Only fiercest Amast hunter kill ikata," Tulasc said, looking at Isy. "You not hesitate. You have hunter's instinct." Isy's cheeks burned. Her mouth opened but instead of words, she settled for a smile and a nod of thanks. Vil sat up and looked at her.

"I would've died if it wasn't for you. Thank you, Isy."

After dropping back to check for signs of pursuit, Yera reappeared with no word of ikata, though she couldn't be sure they weren't still following. Pekira climbed a looming tree and shouted down what she could see.

"Small lake in bottom of valley. Beyond, trees and hills."

"Beyond hills is town called Ledsha." Kora said, turning to Vil. "Isy says you know way from there."

Vil looked at Kora, then Isy, and nodded. "I've made the journey only once. The road west from Ledsha leads to the highway. That'll take us all the way to Yurrisa."

Pekira jumped down from the tree.

"How far to lake?" Kora asked her.

"A mile."

"We shall rest there."

Vil sighed.

Three

Isy couldn't recall the last time she'd submerged both head and body underwater. The cold stole her breath and brought with it invigorating wakefulness. She was glad to be clean of the sweat and dirt of the road and the blood of the ikata. Clouds drifted by overhead, the lower ones ominously dark, those behind a purer white. *Just like my face.* It would rain again soon.

She jumped about on the bank to get dry, rang out her hair and put on the clothes the Amast had made for her: a coarse brown robe that stretched to her ankles, with a dividing cut in the middle, ending just above her knees to allow for more movement. Underneath she wore her linen shirt, breeches and boots from home, and over her shoulders she fastened a fur cloak, complete with a deep and snug hood, again made by the Amast. It was warm as sitting next to a roaring hearth.

Back at their camp, Tulasc and Yera were answering Vil's questions about the ikata. Kora and Pekira were beside the lake with their throwing spears, hunting fish. Isy savored the scene. Harmonious. Calm. What a true family ought to be like—something she often imagined but never experienced. Isy sat beside Vil.

"Thank you again for saving me," he said.

"I'm still not quite sure what happened," Isy said.

"You were a hero. That's what happened."

Isy smiled. She couldn't recall anybody calling her a hero before.

"Something I've learned these past few weeks is that fear can control your life, paralyse you," Isy said. "To beat it, you must fight back. Take the first step beyond the threshold with courage in your heart and curiosity in your mind. We've both done things we'd never thought we'd do. Who'll ever believe our stories?"

Vil laughed. "Well, they'll at least make a good book."

"When this is over, we'll write it together."

In the hours that followed, they sat around the fire, eating fish and practicing Yurrish. Vil began to contribute too. Isy was thrilled by the help, and the Amast found his input useful. Indeed, she noticed a shift in the way they looked at him, which buoyed her mood. When at last they came to rest, she slept like the dead.

Isy awoke to rain, falling in a resolute cascade, pounding the earth and drenching the group. The autumnal sun that had visited them that morning seemed a lifetime away. With heads down, they marched on, and soon, through the haze of rain, the lights of a town crept into view: Ledsha.

In the grips of dusk, they reached an overlooking ridge and Yera and Pekira gazed in awe at the hundreds of orange lights twinkling in the valley below. *You wouldn't feel like that if you went down there*, Isy thought.

To Isy's dismay and Vil's audible groans, they steered clear of Ledsha. She longed to be out of the rain she loathed so much, warming herself beside a fire. But the lights disappeared and as Vil had said, they came to the western road—an unremarkable strip of compacted earth about two wagons wide and littered with puddles. Kora judged it safe enough to travel along. The chances were slim of encountering somebody in this part of the realm, and at this time of night and in such poor weather, too. Plus, the Amast would see or hear anyone long before they spotted the group.

The road cut through a forest of ancient pines. The fragrance of their green needles filled Isy's nose. She'd grown used to the pace now. The blisters that had formed in the first days of their journey had hardened and her legs ached less whenever they stopped. Everybody was quiet, engaging in conversation only when something needed discussing. Isy didn't feel much like talking, anyway. Something played on her mind. The further west they moved, a new threat grew. One that made ikata and paska seem like docile pets.

Four

The wind rattled the window, its biting tendrils breaking through cracks in the glass. With his nose, Edvar nudged his woollen scarf further over his face. No fire burned in the empty apartment. Not even a candle to remind him what warmth was. *You'll never know when you'll need somewhere to hide*, his father's voice echoed through the darkness. It was a safe house, one of many his father had kept over the years, and one of the few Edvar still deemed safe. Or so he hoped.

Edvar removed the blankets from his legs and got to his numb feet, walked a few laps around the room to get the blood flowing, and came to stand before the window. It was a couple of hours past dusk, he judged, and the narrow, winding street below was bathed in shadow, save for the occasional strips of light that broke through curtained windows. From *The Leaky Ship* at the end of the street came the continuous din of drunken chatter and laughter. A knock sounded over it. Outside his room?

His heart stilled. He looked with broad eyes at the door for several minutes, then approached it, avoiding creaky floorboards, straining to hear over the rumble of his heart. Too often over the past few days he'd found himself doing this, imagining people with murderous intentions waiting for him out in the corridor. When he found the courage to open the door, sword in hand, nobody was ever there, just like now. He clicked the door closed and slid across the bolt. He was weary to his marrow. An ill-feeling perpetually churned in his stomach, keeping him from sleep, troubling his dreams when he did nod off, and there, waiting for him, as soon as he awoke. He was imprisoned by fear.

Edvar returned to his pallet, wrapped himself up in furs and blankets. He nibbled at some hard cheese. His appetite had waned since the attack. His drinking hadn't. By his side was a green bottle half full of a pungent brew named Potch. Made from grain, it was far stronger than any other Yurrish spirit. Ideal for those sleepless nights.

He hadn't been completely idle since the attack in the forge. He managed to meet daily with his informants, though his fear of pursuit was great. More than once, he'd turned to find ominous-looking individuals following him, and fueled by adrenaline, he'd twist and turn down streets and alleys to lose them. None of his informants had yet to provide a lead. Not even a mere granule. It felt as if he was playing a game of Warlords, moving pieces but unable to see where on the board his opponents' were. Tesh, the Council... *What if they're working together?*

Ambition, not duty, drove the members of the Council; it was how they'd risen to their stations. Indeed, the ambitious rarely felt satisfaction. Once something was achieved they moved onto the next bigger and better thing. A mere taste was never enough. But to turn against the man they'd sworn to serve, who'd gifted them opportunity, power and wealth? Where was their honor? Their morality?

Alone, his fellow councilors lacked the influence to pull off a coup. To succeed they would have to work together. Could their inflated egos allow for such a thing?

The problem gnawing at Edvar was where Tesh fitted in everything. Working with the Council? Acting opportunistically? Both perhaps? Edvar lacked the information to determine. There had to be something more going on. To threaten an end to peace, a peace that benefitted Karrabar so greatly, just didn't make sense. Tesh had proven his boldness in taking the Fields of Arinar. Did he have a conqueror's ambition? No... Edvar sensed something else was driving Tesh, but what?

Edvar checked the window again. Fewer people traversed the road; he judged it time to go. He held his ear to the door before opening it. Content that the corridor was clear, he soundlessly closed it behind him and locked it. Many of the apartments in the building were dilapidated and riddled with rot and decay. Not even the homeless fancied a night inside. A handful of people still lived on the lower floors, and sometimes strays wandered in, but that night, as he hurried down the steps, he saw no one. He stepped outside and pulled the hood of his black woolen cloak as low as it would go. His short sword gave a reassuring tap against his leg. He wouldn't go anywhere without it now. On his other hip hung the stave of a torch. The cool night air nipped at his cheeks. Off to his right, he could see the glow of *The Leaky Ship*. He headed in the opposite direction, following the road as it angled toward the keep.

He reached a small square, packed with people. Their attentions were locked on a man standing in the middle of them all, upon a raised platform. Dressed in a tattered red robe, his grey hair was beyond unkempt, beard too. He waved his arms, voice raised with passion, mist billowing from his mouth.

"Friends, we have been misled! We have been brought up to believe that there is only one way to live our lives, that the freedom we know is all that there is. We have been conditioned to accept it without question. None of us can achieve any sense of betterment beyond what our lives allow for. We are trapped, and yet at the same time, we are the makers of our cage. That is not to say it is any fault of our own. We have been duped!

"Why are we not trusted to govern ourselves, to rule over our own lives and determine our own futures? Why do we need a man in a tower to dictate what we can and cannot do? He bleeds the same blood as we do, only he'd sooner watch *us* bleed!"

The crowd grew animated, nodding their heads, clapping with growing vigor.

"Just look—jobs are disappearing and so too the food on our tables. Soon they'll take our roofs. All the while the rich get fatter in their towers!

"Together we must liberate ourselves from society's shackles. We must rebel and take control of our futures and freedoms. You ask me how? I shall tell you, for there is only one way. Revolution. To revolt against the world we know and struggle for one that is greater and better."

Cheers erupted throughout the crowd. Edvar hoped his muted reaction went unnoticed.

"Revolution, friends, cannot be achieved by merely changing our thinking. We must act, we must seize the day and refuse to let go. That day is now upon us. Keeper Tesh marches to bring our demise while Ashara hides in his keep. The time to act is now. All of us must pick up weapons and fight for what we want, for what we know to be right." The preacher punched his palm. Everyone in the crowd burst into rapturous applause, shouting support and agreement. Edvar swallowed hard and moved on down the street.

Before the treaty with Karrabar, it would have been difficult to comprehend such dissent in Yurr. Ashara had been an idol, so too his mother, Alysa. How had it changed so dramatically in such a short space of time? Surely people could not be so fickle?

This dissident preaching wasn't isolated. His informants had repeatedly mentioned similar meetings and rallies in squares, taverns, even in workshops and factories across the city. All had a consistent theme—dissent toward the keeper. Could someone be deliberately stirring them up? Today's news that two of the largest iron forges in the city were to inexplicably close next week would only lump further coal onto the blaze of frustration. Edvar was growing tired of not knowing the answers, of not being able to understand. Always he'd found a way to solve his problems, but time and time again he was being made to look like an idiot, so much so he was beginning to believe he was one.

The outer wall of the keep loomed above the slate roofs, with lights from torches along the parapets punctuating the darkness. Edvar ducked down an alley. The only life along it was a tabby cat whose eyes widened at the sight of him. He stopped at an iron grid, checked up and down for signs of pursuit, then hefted it aside and, after replacing it, clambered down the rickety ladder.

In absolute darkness, Edvar pulled out his flint and lit the torch. Then he drew his sword. The flickering glow glinted in the steel. An old ruler named Bientas had built these tunnels, a man with more enemies than friends, and when that was the case, a swift exit was a necessity. Bientas, ironically enough, never got to use them. A heart attack took him first, and to his great misfortune, it occurred while on the privy. Armed with a vivid imagination, Edvar had as a child gone on adventures through Bientas's tunnels, discovering lost treasures and defeating evil monsters. He wished life was simple as that again.

The existence of these tunnels was not a secret, though. His father had maps of them, and no doubt others on the council did too. That meant potential traps.

The urge to glance over his shoulder was like an itchy rash. Every time he heard a sound, he lowered his torch, stopped, listened. He hesitated before every turn. Raised his sword, ready to strike. Nobody was ever waiting for him.

At last, he came to the studded wooden door. It possessed a cunning lock. Edvar turned the bone dials to the correct sequence of carved images—flower, bird, fish, flower—and it clicked open. He extinguished his torch with the dry dirt of the ground, propped it up against the wall and slipped inside.

Edvar sheathed his sword and began to ascend the narrow, winding staircase. Eventually, he reached another door, the other side of which blended seamlessly with the wall. Edvar checked before leaving safety and stepped into the storage vaults. Dusty furniture and canvas-covered crates cluttered the room. Only the servants came down here, and seldom so. Luckily, he encountered nobody on the stairs. Four guards stood sentry outside the keeper's bedchamber. All drew their swords and made to attack.

RICHIE BILLING | 140

Edvar waved his hands, removed his hood and pulled down his scarf. Recognition eased the soldier's stances and they nodded in acknowledgement. One of them knocked on the door.

"Come in," the Keeper shouted from the other side.

"Sire," Edvar said, closing the door behind him.

"Good to see you, Ed." For the first time since the attempt on his life, Ashara greeted Edvar on his feet. He looked splendid in a deep blue shirt, open and loose for his healing wounds. Having seen him bedridden for so long, Edvar had forgotten how tall he was, a full head above himself, with a broadness to match. His long, dark hair had been cut back behind his ears—a style he wore in his younger years. They embraced and sat in cushioned chairs before a roaring hearth. Edvar began to thaw. He had a newfound appreciation for warmth and comfort after days in that damp apartment.

Ashara's brows were furrowed.

"What's wrong?" Edvar asked.

"I'm assuming you've not heard the news."

Edvar shook his head.

"Levanwe is dead."

"What?!"

"Her handmaid found her cold in her bed this morning. It seems she passed away in her sleep."

Levanwe dead. Another problem for his mounting pile. He didn't have the capacity to even think about it. Edvar ran his hands through his hair, rubbed his eyes with his palms, grumbled and sighed.

"I owe you an apology, Ed," Ashara said, standing and walking over to put an arm around Edvar's shoulder. "For all the time I was bedridden you dealt with this crisis alone. A truly terrible mess, beyond anything I have known, and it nearly cost your life.

"I am here again now, Ed. The pressure isn't on you alone anymore. By gods, I will bear it all upon my back. They are my burdens to carry. To keep this weight on your shoulders will drive you to madness! Come here." Ashara hauled Edvar to his feet and pulled him into a fatherly bear hug. It was exactly what Edvar needed, and when Ashara at last released him, he felt, in a strange way, lighter. They sat back down and Edvar this time noticed how comfortable the cushioned chair was.

"Drink," Ashara said, handing Edvar a glass goblet of red wine. "It's been too long since we last drank together."

It had. But not that long since Edvar's last drink. Curiously he found no desire to have any of the wine. Out of courtesy, he sipped. "Do you know how Levanwe died? Was she sick?" Edvar asked.

"Not that I was aware of," Ashara said. "She was a fine old age, though. Perhaps it was just her time."

"And you believe that?"

"As much as I believe there are people with octopus tentacles for legs living in Green Deep."

"What are you thinking?" Edvar asked.

"I don't know what to think anymore. If I've learned anything this past month it's that nothing is how it appears. People do unfathomable things for reasons they may not even understand themselves. Especially when temptation is before them. Power, control—they corrupt minds and skew reasoning."

"I think they're all in on it together, the Council," Edvar said. "Alone they're too weak to get rid of you. Together they control most of Yurr."

"They've served me loyally for decades. Swore a blood oath. Why would they be so foolish?"

"Perhaps it's like you say. They want more. What they have might not be enough."

Ashara stared into the flames. "But if they did seek to oust me, do you not think they would have already gotten rid of me by now, especially when I was confined to my bedchamber?"

"It's not through the want of trying. First the assassin, and now they're playing a longer game, I fear. Turning the people against you."

Ashara's face contorted with disbelief.

"No more than thirty minutes ago I passed a man preaching to a crowd of people. He suggested they'd be better off without you, that all you do is tell them what they can and cannot do. The people cheered. And they weren't the only ones. Across the city, there are preachings like this taking place daily and people are buying into them. The crowds continue to grow. Someone is coordinating this, I fear. It's a subtle campaign of propaganda designed to weaken your position."

Ashara slumped back in his chair. Elbows upon the arms, his chin rested on his hands. "Control is slipping from my grasp. Enemies on the horizon. Enemies in the camp. What happened, Ed? When did I become such a blind fool?"

"When did we both?"

"We'll die as fools together, at least." Ashara drained his goblet.

Edvar stared into the flames. *Our enemies may rob us of everything, but they cannot strip us of hope. The only person who can take that away is you.* His father spoke as if he was in the room. Edvar smiled, and a streak of light broke through the dark clouds shrouding his thoughts.

"What would my father do if he were here?" It was a question people often put to him, one that annoyed him every time he heard it, but this time, it was him reciting the words.

Ashara looked at him. Edvar didn't wait for an answer.

"He would not sit here and lament. He would take out his whetstone and sharpen his sword."

A smile flickered across Ashara's face. "You're right." He sat up. "Sometimes the problems consume you so much you forget who you are."

"I have an idea," Edvar said, a rush of confidence coursing through him. Ashara nodded for him to go on.

"Our biggest threat right now is the people. They need appeasing. The only way I can think to do that is if you ride out into the city. People preach that you are weak, that you are too ill to lead. Some even say you're dead. You need to quash the rumors, prove them wrong, that you're strong and able and here to listen to their problems and provide solutions."

"Charge into the belly of the beast?" Ashara said, toying with his beard. Edvar could see the doubt in his eyes. *Or is it fear?*

"I have fought many wars and even more battles, Ed. But the greatest battle of all is that which wages in a warrior's mind. To fight or to flee? Many want to flee, though few ever do. It is those who fear death that die first. I see in your eyes the same fire that filled your fathers' when we first stood together in the shield wall, waiting for the horn to charge. It was a sight that filled my heart with courage. Tomorrow we will win back my people."

Edvar smiled, though in the back of his mind a dark thought persisted: *these next few days might be my last.*

Five

The highway to Yurrisa stretched from left to right for as far as Isy could see. Fragrant pines loomed either side of the strip of compacted earth. A clear-blue sky hung behind them. A day free of rain, at last, or so the sky promised. Dew-tipped grass gently swayed between the trees and road, and standing in a longer thicket at the junction was a post with three arrowed signs. *Yurrisa* was engraved in the one pointing west, *Hiscaria*, the one pointed north, and *Ledsha* east, in the direction from which they had travelled. Hiscaria was a northern town upon the banks of the Hisca River, not dissimilar to Haberdam, or so Isy had read. She had no desire to go there.

"We're not far from a village named Iber. It sits at the foot of the Sighing Mountains," Vil said.

"We must cross Sighing Mountains?" Tulasc asked, stumbling over the name.

"No. They stand to the north. You'll be glad of it when you see them."

"Why they named so?" Pekira asked.

"When I was last in Iber, I heard a tale about a woman who lived at the edge of the village," Vil began. "Her children went out one morning to play. In the afternoon, a storm swept over the mountains. They did not return. She went looking for them and the last place she was said to have searched was the mountains, in the height of the storm. From the peaks, she yelled their names and the people of Iber heard her calls. They say you can still hear her sighs of grief when the wind gusts."

"She find them?" Yera asked.

Vil shook his head.

Isy was sure the Amast believed the story was true. She'd read herself that it was the shape of the mountains that created the sound. A more plausible explanation than the ghost of a grieving mother.

They departed the highway and moved along trails that ran parallel. Not far from the road, Pekira found a wayward pine, its branches sagging to the ground to provide complete shelter. There, the party of six settled for their rest. Isy's lids were closing as soon as she sat down. They must have walked twenty miles a day, at least, for the past week. She managed to snatch only a few hours' sleep when they rested, though it didn't trouble her as much as Vil. Their goal was firmly set in her heart and mind. She could sleep all she wanted once it was achieved.

A few hours shut-eye perked her up, and while they cooked and broke their fast, they practiced Yurrish. It'd become a daily ritual, for a couple of hours while they ate and packed up camp. And as often as they could, they practiced on the move, talking to one another, singing songs, or repeating phrases after Vil and her. Having Vil there made things much easier. She could spend more time with the struggling Tulasc, and had more time to teach Kora one to one as they had back at the Amast camp. He was, after all, the key representative of the Amast and the one with the best grasp of the language.

The Amast's frosty attitude toward Vil had melted away too, and his constant visible discomfort had gone with it. Indeed, he looked altogether different. Slimmer at the waist, straighter of shoulder. His cheeks were thinner, pimples beginning to fade, and his beard had thickened. Whenever they had a chance, Vil got Tulasc to teach him how to wield a spear and Kora how to use a sling. He was poor with both, which provided a few laughs for Isy and the others, but he was trying and for that Isy loved him.

That afternoon, they continued along trails visible only to Amast eyes. The more time Isy spent with the Amast, the more she appreciated their mastery of woodsmanship. Their broad rodent-like ears twitched at the slightest of sounds, noses always sniffing, eyes scanning. They knew every plant and tree, which mushrooms were safe to eat and those that would induce euphoria, where best to look for shelter, and where to find water. Isy was learning as much as she taught. A life alone in the woods may not be a distant dream after all, she considered.

With the final rays of the sun streaking across the land, they reached a break in the tree line and, in the hazy distance, beheld the jagged contours and snow-capped peaks of the Sighing Mountains. Their enormity became lost as they delved into another thicket of pines. The boles soon thinned, and the sound of rushing water came to dominate Isy's hearing. After climbing a small rise, they found the source.

The River Iber was wide as a lake at this particular stretch, its flow swift and turbulent, churning in parts as it crashed into boulders that protruded from the surface.

"If we head back to the highway there's a bridge," Vil said, setting off upstream. The Amast didn't follow. They looked at one another, seemingly conversing with their eyes as they so often did.

"What's wrong?" Vil asked.

Isy answered for them. "There's nowhere to hide on a bridge. If anyone came, we'd be spotted. Trapped."

Kora nodded. Isy knew all too well the paralysing helplessness that came with wanting to hide when stuck in plain sight. "We'll make sure it's clear before we cross," she said.

The Amast agreed, though it was obvious from their rigid postures they felt otherwise.

The bridge was a stone creation that united the banks where the Iber narrowed. Three arches, smothered in vines and lichen, admitted the current. As they neared, the Amast slowed. At the edge of the road, amid the cover of ferns and bushes, they peered across the bridge and along the road beyond. Not far after the crossing, it bent away to the left, hidden by the forest, which increased the tension. For long minutes, they waited and watched.

"Let us go," Kora said. The spring in their step said all of them wanted to run. For prying eyes, that would look even more suspicious. The Amast pulled their hoods as low as they would go and stooped their backs to look smaller. Isy pulled down her hood too, so low she could just see the wet stone beneath her feet. The muffled rush of the Iber mingled with the hurried patter of feet.

"Run," Kora said.

Isy lifted up her hood. Two shapes moved toward them. Riders.

In a few strides, the four Amast were across the bridge, leaving Isy and Vil behind. The riders spurred on their mounts. Isy wished her feet would spring wings. When at last they made it across, she and Vil charged into the brush, finding the others hunkered down a short way in. Kora pointed at the canopy and the Amast began to climb the trees. Pekira helped Vil climb, Kora offered to help Isy, though she didn't need it. She was good at climbing trees. Over the years she'd hidden in a fair few. The river was quieter this high up. Drowning out the rush came the thrum of hooves. Isy bit her lip, held her breath.

The riders slowed to a halt at the point they'd departed the road. One dismounted and examined the ground.

"What you see?" said the man still in the saddle. He held a crossbow over his leg, finger over the trigger.

"Not much in this light."

"People definitely ran into here. And they looked odd. Tall as that branch there, or so it looked from back there."

"That's about eleven foot!"

"You doubting me?"

"With them old eyes, yeah I am. Why don't you go look and prove me wrong? If you're right I'll pay for the ale tonight."

No answer came from the mounted man. He looked up at the branches, right at Isy.

"I'll take that as a no. Come on. We ain't got far till Hiscaria. Keep your mind on that bed. If you're lucky, you might find a woman to warm it with."

Once the sounds of hooves and chatter had faded, the group descended the trees and gathered at the bottom. Nobody offered a word. Isy studied the Amast and recognized fear in their giant eyes. The thin veil of ignorance enveloping them had burst, the harsh realities of the wider world flooding in. The world she knew all too well.

Nobody seemed to settle in the days that followed. The Amast detoured further from the highway. Whenever they neared farms, homesteads or the occasional hunter, they ran or hid. Isy once more felt like her old, depressed self.

Supplies were running low and opportunities to hunt were slim with the pressing need to practice Yurrish and cover ground. Whenever they did get a chance, the Amast returned with slim pickings. But according to Vil, they had just half a week to go, a fact that inflamed Isy's unease. With the events of the journey distracting her, she'd managed to shift the prospect of going to Yurrisa out of her mind. Now, it was becoming harder to ignore, and that grim, paralytic feeling that had accompanied her throughout her life was building once again in her chest. To rid herself of it she could either flee or face it. Fleeing was the easier choice. The difficult part would be abandoning those she had grown to care for.

They'll be fine without me. They're not far now. They can speak Yurrish. They can look after themselves, the voice in her head repeatedly said. But since she'd arrived at the Amast camp things had changed. She had been forced to tackle her fears, discovered that she could best them, and now they no longer troubled her so much. She was tired of being afraid, of running and hiding. Now she wanted to hold her ground, stand up to the world.

But it was becoming clear to Isy that no matter how brave they were, they couldn't simply walk in through the city gates. If the people didn't stone them to death first, the guards would surely arrest them, ending any hope of meeting the keeper. With fate wrested from their control, what would happen? That evening, as they crossed through farmers' fields, she shared her concerns with Vil.

"What do you think will happen when we get to Yurrisa?"

"What do you mean?" Vil asked.

"The Amast have got a point with all this pussyfooting about. You didn't exactly welcome them with open arms when you first saw them. Same goes for me, and you know how people in Haberdam treat me for how I look. How will thousands of city folk react?"

Vil went to speak, then lost his tongue. "I hadn't thought that far ahead. I've been so focused on getting there."

"Will we get stopped if we just walk through the gate?"

"If we walked in with these giants, yes. If we could disguise them somehow, then we might have a chance. They're not that strict in Yurrisa. Keeper Ashara is very trusting of his people, or so he was when last I was there. But it's the people we need to be worried about. They're unpredictably cruel."

Isy bit her lip. Her gaze wandered toward the valley below where a thin wisp of grey smoke rose from a little wooden farmhouse. "I have an idea... but I'm not sure it's the right thing to do."

"Go on..."

Six

In the branches that soughed and creaked above their heads, an owl hooted. Isy's chest grew tighter. She stood close to Kora, whose bulbous eyes were fixed on the farmhouse. Candles twinkled in the square, four-paned window no more than twenty feet away. The smoke of burning turf rose from the chimney to fragrance the chill night air. Tulasc whispered something to Kora in Amasti. Isy looked to Vil at her left side. He returned the gaze, wide-eyed.

"If they have a wagon it'll be in that barn," Isy said pointing at a large wooden shed opposite the house. Isy had never stolen anything before. She knew the pain victims of livestock theft endured—too poor to afford replacements, work slowing down or halting as a result, potentially ruining their livelihoods and plunging them into poverty and despair.

It's worth it, she told herself. Without a way of getting into Yurrisa, their plan would fail and the Amast would die. If only they could explain their plight to the farmer, get him to understand. The odds of that were longer than the River Haber. She would recommend to the group they return the wagon and horses on their way back. If they got that far.

Kora and Tulasc made to stand. Isy grabbed Kora's arm.

"Watch out for dogs. Farmers always have dogs."

Kora didn't reply, and judging from his puzzled look, she was sure he had no clue what she was talking about. *Did we cover dogs in our lessons?*

Kora and Tulasc darted through the shadows toward the barn, moving so low they were almost on all fours. Without making as much as a scuff they reached the wooden building and together, hefted the beam locking the two doors in place. Kora disappeared inside while Tulasc kept watch. A few moments later, they heard the hoot of an owl—the signal. They were in luck.

Isy and Vil left their cover and ran at a crouch to the barn. Isy glanced at the farmhouse door, expecting it to open. She imagined a face appearing in the window, someone banging on the glass. She quickened her pace. Tulasc ushered them inside and closed the doors behind them. They found Kora with a small torch in his hand, standing beside a four-wheeled wagon. A bench for the driver and passengers stood at the front. The rest of it was covered in oiled canvas shaped like a horseshoe.

"Where are the horses?" Isy whispered.

"I can smell them," Vil said.

"Over here," Kora said. He led them to a couple of stalls where two piebald mares were stabled. Isy liked horses. She found them calm and graceful creatures. Often she saw merchants and farmers whipping them in Haberdam and it turned her stomach. *If I was the horse, I'd kick off their heads.*

Vil grabbed a pair of bridles hanging upon the wall and set about fastening them. On their travels around the realm, the chronicler had forced Vil to help the teamsters so he'd picked up a thing or two, though, as always, he seemed unsure of himself, hesitating and fumbling with the straps.

"Kora!" Tulasc whispered. "Light out. Quick." Kora snuffed out the flame of his torch. Darkness and a tense silence enveloped them. Isy's heart threatened to burst her eardrums. Finally, Tulasc spoke.

"Door open. Creature like thin wolf came out. It's sniffing ground."

"A dog," Isy said.

The horses gave gentle whinnies as Vil led them from their stalls and hitched them to the wagon.

"What's it doing now?" Isy asked.

"Still sniffing. Getting closer."

Isy and Vil climbed onto the front bench. Vil grabbed the reins.

"How hard can it be?" he had said earlier during their planning. Isy suspected much harder than he thought.

Kora sat beside Isy. "We're ready," he said to Tulasc. "Open the doors."

With a firm push, the two doors swung with a groan and thudded into the wooden walls. Tulasc stood before the hound, which looked at him wide-eyed. Its ears and tail sprung upwards. Deep, furious barks erupted from its muzzle. It ran straight for him.

Vil flicked the reins and gave a *hiyah*. The mares flicked their tails.

"Vil..." Isy said. The door of the house opened and light poured into the night. It was quickly obscured by a burly, brown-haired man, his face and arms thick with hair. He held a bow, an arrow nocked to the string.

Vil tried the same tact, this time more vigorously. It made no difference. Isy wanted to scream at him. Kora hefted his spear and with the flat side, gave one of the horses a slap on the rear. It worked. The horse bolted and her companion copied. Kora leant to the side and locked arms with Tulasc as they passed, hauling him up. The dog diverted its charge at the sight of onrushing hooves, while the farmer took aim.

"Duck!" Isy shouted.

Her knees hit the wooden footwell, hands over her head. A violent crunch sent a streak of terror down her back. When she looked up she found the shaft of an arrow wobbling where she had sat just a moment before.

"Get us out of here Vil!" she roared.

Vil angled the horses down the road. The farmer shouted. Arrows thudded into the frame of the wagon, whistled by them, punctured the canvas. More dogs barked. Isy looked back to find a pack of deerhounds bounding after them, mouths snapping. They were no match for the longer-legged horses, though, and soon they gave up. The lights of the farm fell from view, and at the end of the winding road, they re-joined the highway. The others emerged from the shadows. There was no doubting the smiles upon their faces, even Pekira, who broke into delighted applause. They clambered into the back and through the night they rode on, the wandering moon inching its way across the sky until it disappeared behind the trees. They didn't encounter another soul.

Isy couldn't sleep. The arrowhead, still embedded in the wagon, served as a sobering reminder of what might have happened. But she was alive, and what a feeling it was. Tingles broke out in waves across her body, spreading down her arms and up to the top of her head. There was a time when she would have welcomed death. Not now. Now she had purpose. A reason to go on. She had felt no greater sense of determination to succeed in all her life. If mountains stood in their path, she would tear them down. She would part rivers, heft fallen trees. Face hundreds of thousands of people without hiding her face.

At dawn, they crested a ridge and there, in the hazy distance, Isy glimpsed the towers of Yurrisa. She bit her lip.

Seven

Through a hole in the canvas made by one of the farmer's arrows, Isy beheld the walls of Yurrisa. Assembled of stone blocks of varying sizes and hues and closely mortared together, they stretched to a dizzying height. The curtain wall embraced just two thirds of the city. The other portion of the population sprawled out beyond, and it was through that bustling collection of farmsteads, houses, shops, workshops, taverns, inns and factories they had rolled that morning.

When they'd reached those first farms at the edge of the city, the Amast and Isy took up their hiding positions in the back of the wagon, underneath a coarse hempen canvas they'd found under the teamster's bench. Even the most incompetent of guards would find them, but at least it kept them out of sight. Vil rode alone at the front. A part of Isy wanted to be up there with him, seeing all of the things she could hear and smell—the strange accents, cooking meats and fish, the gulls cawing overhead, hungry for scraps. But she knew what would happen if they saw her, and the prospect made her nauseous. Now more than ever she had to be brave, and she was determined not give in an inch to fear.

A convoy of wagons, horses and people on foot, some lugging overly packed hand-carts, formed a queue leading into the gate—a vast arch in the wall with the metal teeth of a portcullis poking from the top. Vil had said the gates were open all day, with people free to come and go as they pleased. Now, the guards seemed to be questioning everyone, checking their loads, even hopping into the back of some wagons. Isy's cheeks seared with panic. An urge to flee exploded within her, to slip out of the back of the wagon and run far from here. They inched across a wooden bridge, beneath which was a dry moat filled with sharpened stakes. Upon the battlements, a dozen soldiers garbed in the royal blue of Yurr scanned the crowd below, longbows and crossbows in their hands. Isy began to sweat. Her stomach churned and she took deep breaths to stem the rising bile. What would happen if they were discovered? Arrested? Killed? They might spare Vil, but she doubted the guards would hesitate to cut down a tainted woman and four alien people.

When the walls blocked out the light of the sun, Isy ducked under the canvas sheet and hoped. So still were the Amast it was like lying next to dead. Isy did a fair job of matching them; she could scarcely breathe for her nerves. Voices came to her ears. Then she heard Vil's.

"How do?" he said.

"What's in the back?" a gruff voice responded.

Isy's heart battered her ribcage, seeking escape.

"Stuff I've picked up on the way home from Haberdam. Books, wool, furs. Shite, mostly." Vil's voice didn't quiver; he'd spent the last day practicing what to say and what to do should the outcomes be different. Isy heard the guard chuckle.

"Travelling alone?"

"Nah. Dropped the others off at the edge of town. Farm boys looking for adventure."

"Not much adventure to be had in Haberdam."

"That's what I told 'em."

"Where you headed?"

"The market to try and flog this, then back to my boss's warehouse on Haska Street."

After that Isy heard nothing but the chatter of those waiting behind, the gulls circling above. The guard took an age to answer.

"In you go."

Isy had never heard more wonderful words in all her life. The wagon rolled forward and left the gatehouse behind, and with it some of her tension. She rid herself of the itchy canvas and once again peered through the hole at the city that was just as alien to her as it was to the Amast. A press of people filed by, standing aside to allow the horses and wagon through. Isy could stand it no longer. She wanted to see it all, not just an area the size of her forefinger. She wrapped her blue scarf around her face, covering all but her eyes, and after pulling down her hood, clambered to the front and sat beside Vil.

Inside the curtain wall, the roads were paved with sandstone bricks, their yellow hue faded by time and feet. The buildings were monstrous in size compared to those of Haberdam, their designs peculiar yet beautiful. Some walls were whitewashed, others painted green, blue, orange or yellow. Windowsills and architraves had letters and figures carved into them, too high up and faded to make out. Dozens of shuttered windows were wide open and from them hung circular lines of drying clothes that flapped and spun in the breeze. Clusters of chimneys sprouted from angled roofs of wood and slate, spewing grey smoke into the sky. Isy couldn't smell the fires, though, only feces, piss and body odor.

Upon ledges perched small birds, adding their coos to the continuous din of chatter and soles slapping stone. A few cats lazed about, half an eye on the birds, but indifferent to the throng of people. Along the street came the sound of instruments—flutes, lutes and fiddles, the bass notes of singers too. It was an all-out assault to Isy's senses.

"Welcome to Yurrisa," Vil said, mouth fixed in a toothy grin. "What do you think?"

"Let's just say it's different." Isy grinned. There was certainly an appealing buzz about the place. "I can't believe you kept it together. You even made them laugh."

"What can I say? Maybe I'm a born adventurer after all."

"I'll believe that when you get us before the keeper."

Vil's silence told her everything. They still had no plan to actually get to Keeper Ashara. Vil said he opened his doors to the people to hear their petitions a few times each week. It was their best shot, but where would they hide until then?

"What now?" she asked.

"Head toward the keep and see if we can get in?"

"Where's the ke-... Never mind." Isy cut herself off. As they turned a corner and freed themselves of the imposing buildings, the keep loomed before them on the highest hill in the city. Blue swallowtail flags fluttered upon the three-tiered walls that enveloped the central tower. Isy had read about the keep—the biggest in all of Yurr, boasting formidable and cunning defenses, including a trio of baileys and gates and countless murder holes and defensive contraptions. It had withstood many a siege and never succumbed to capture. Nothing she'd read did it justice. It was the biggest, most awe-inspiring structure she had ever seen.

"How in Soria are we going to get in there?" Isy asked.

Vil didn't answer.

They passed a group of women, a spring to their step, arms linked, laughter following them down the street. Two men with blacksmith's arms marched with fists bunched behind them, determined and humorless expressions upon their faces. Children weaved through the press, barging and shouldering as they went and drawing angry shouts that went unheard. All of these people had something in common—they were headed in the same direction. In fact, *everybody* was.

"Did you hear that?" Vil asked.

Isy shook her head.

"Them women back there were talking about the Keeper. They said he's in the Keeper's Square."

"What? Now?"

Vil nodded. "And it's not far away."

Hope exploded in her chest. The keeper had come to them. *What luck!* A solution seemingly presented to them by fate itself. "Well, get a move on!"

The flow of Isy's excitement came to an abrupt halt when they turned a corner. Thousands upon thousands of people clogged the broad street before them. A few argued and shoved each other. Children cried. Young teens pickpocketed, their livid victims shouting and chasing after them. The pace slowed to a crawl. The horses grew agitated. The mare on the right, which Isy had named Nara, nipped at those who came too close.

"What you doin' drivin' that big bastard through here?" one man shouted in fury.

"Stupid pricks! Move that thing!"

The verbal barrage grew and Isy's cheeks burned. She wanted to shrink away into nothingness.

"We're not going to get through in this wagon," Vil said.

"You think?"

Vil looked a world away from the assuredness he'd oozed before. "We need to find somewhere to park up."

"And then what?"

"Move on foot."

Isy's contorted expression told Vil everything.

"They can stay or they can come with us. With their hoods up no one might notice."

"They're ten feet tall, Vil!"

Vil sighed. "Let them decide what to do. I'm out of ideas."

Isy bit her lip.

"Isy," Kora called from inside the canvas. She took a deep breath, went inside and explained the situation. Silence met her when she finished. Pekira, so often quiet, was first to speak.

"What if we cannot get through all these people? There are thousands." There was no fear in her voice, only doubt.

"I do not know. I feel as uncertain as you do. This may be our best shot, our only shot of meeting the Keeper."

"Isy," Vil called.

She stuck her head out of the canvas. He'd managed to get off the packed road and was riding along a narrow side street.

"Looks like an old storage shed up there. Can you check the door?"

Isy hopped down and inspected the lock. Rusted iron chains were wrapped around the beam. When she gave them a tug, they fell away. *Convenient.* She pushed and reluctantly it swung open. An empty and dusty room awaited inside.

"Perfect," Vil said. Isy closed the door behind the wagon and turned to find the Amast disembarking.

"We will go," Kora said. "I made a promise to my grandmother. I will not fail."

Eight

Edvar couldn't believe how quickly the crowds had amassed. Ashara had made little fanfare on the way down to the Keeper's Square. Edvar hoped the spontaneous nature of the trip would be enough to prevent anyone from staging an attack. Despite that fact, he'd taken no chances. Around the platform he and Ashara stood upon was a small army of spear and crossbowmen, three ranks deep, with more guarding their chosen route back to the keep. Edvar had debated bringing a lesser force as a display of trust, but in the end had thought better of the idea.

Many who had gathered called out to the Keeper with good wishes, waved hands and handkerchiefs. Children sat upon shoulders, smiling and waving too. Ashara reciprocated, grinning broadly. Still, Edvar scanned every face, seeking any hint of hostility or threats. His eyes even scoured the soldiers guarding them. No matter how much he tried to ensure their loyalty, they were Malfan's soldiers, and he did not trust that little oaf one bit.

"Word spread quickly," Ashara said.

"Gossip spreads like dysentery in this city."

Ashara laughed. "It feels like an age ago since I did this. In fact, the last time was when your father was still alive." A more somber expression crossed his face.

Ashara held his hands high and brought silence to the thousands packed into the square and surrounding streets.

Few people could enchant a crowd like Ashara. He was a man worth listening to.

"My good people. I am here to prove to you that I am not dead!" He laughed, and it was met by a great cheer.

Perhaps they still love him after all.

"I wished to stand before you sooner, to reassure you that I am here to defend our lands and loved ones against any evil that may threaten Yurr. That includes those to the east."

Another cheer rippled through the crowd.

"For too long," Ashara began, shouting louder for all to hear, "Tesh of Karrabar has flaunted our peaceful history. A peace that our ancestors died to secure. A peace that has kept us all safe and happy for centuries. I tried to quell him to maintain that peace, to save us all from fighting again. Now it is clear that his evil knows no bounds. That he cares nothing for peace. He will pillage Yurr, destroy our homes, kill our loved ones, unless together we stand against him and say, *no more!*"

The reaction was not as well-received as Edvar expected. *They think he should have known this already. Maybe we should have done. Are we too far gone?*

A commotion stirred in the northern end of the square. Shouts of annoyance and hostility filled the air. The crowd began to part, which caused further turmoil as people barged into and crushed one another. Edvar strained his eyes but couldn't make out what was going on. Ashara hesitated, gaze drawn in the same direction. The attention of the crowd was slipping away. They couldn't afford to squander this opportunity.

Four hooded figures, dressed in brown robes, emerged from the crowd. They towered over everyone around them by a good few feet. And they were headed right for the keeper. More people looked back, craning necks to see what was going on. The group neared and the confused clamor died as people failed to make sense of what they saw. Edvar shared that feeling. His heart beat like a drum. They were inhumanly tall, so tall that it had to be two people, one upon the others' shoulders.

"Crossbows," Edvar ordered.

The line of crossbowmen behind the shield wall raised their weapons, placing them over the shoulders of their comrades. Panic erupted at the front of the crowd, people diving out of the way, children screaming, crying. A space cleared and Edvar caught his first true sight of the approaching group. In front of the four hooded giants was a young Yurrish man with curly brown hair. His breeches and boots were covered in mud, his face stained with dirt and dust. Beside him, he guessed, was a Yurrish woman judging from her slight frame. He could not see her face for the hood pulled down over it.

"Halt," Edvar shouted.

The girl held up her hand and brought the group to a stop. "We carry no weapons," she shouted, accent northern, from Ledsha or Hiscaria perhaps. "We must speak with the Keeper as a matter of urgency," she said.

"Who are you?" Edvar called.

"My name is Isyara. I come from Haberdam. I am a guide to those who seek Keeper Ashara. This is Vil, a citizen of Yurrisa and assistant to the chronicler of Haberdam," the pair of them bowed deeply, followed by the giants.

"What do you think?" Edvar whispered to Ashara.

"I think I've never seen anything like it." Ashara paused, looked on, eyebrows furrowed. "Step forward," the Keeper said. He descended the stairs of the platform and came to stand behind the shield wall. Edvar followed. He noticed none of the giant people wore shoes. Instead, their massive feet, Yurrish in shape and appearance, were smothered in coarse brown hair.

"If I am to hear a word from any of your mouths," Ashara began, "you must show me your faces."

One by one, hoods were removed. Edvar had never heard such a loud intake of breath. The young woman was indeed Yurrish, though half of her face was covered by a raven-black mark. He could not say the same for the others. Their eyes grabbed his attention first, wide as plates, bulbous, broadly spaced and blue as ice. Their noses were long and broad-nostrilled, skin slate grey. The two men had brown, unkempt beards. The two women had their hair tied in plaits. Their arms hung loosely at their side, stretching down to their knees. And their hands, big enough, it seemed, to crush stone, were similar to their feet—covered in dark hair with black talon-like nails.

Edvar couldn't find any words to say to these people, if indeed he could call them that. Judging by Ashara's parted lips, he was struggling too. It was the girl with the mark upon her face who broke the silence.

"Our companions are known as the Amast." She stepped aside and introduced them in turn. Each of them bowed with their left arm held across their chest. The Amast man named Kora stepped forward.

"Good Keeper, we have travelled far to meet you. I am sure you have never laid eyes on the Amast before. Please do not be alarmed by our appearance. We intend no harm to you or any of your people. We come to you in a time of great need. Men wearing the yellow of the kingdom you know as Karrabar massacred my people and destroyed our home. Good Keeper, we seek refuge in your fair kingdom. All we wish is to live in peace and safety. I beg an audience with you so that I can tell you of our plight."

Ashara looked at Edvar. Edvar didn't know what to say. He was moved by these... men and women, wanted to hear more of their situation. For a long moment, Ashara stood and stared, pondering his choices. He ordered the shield wall to part and stepped toward them, to stand before the Amast man named Kora. He towered over the Keeper by some three feet and looked able to kill him with one swing of his massive fist.

Jeers. Boos. Shouts of disgust and outrage, curses and much worse, suddenly exploded from the crowd.

"*Why are you listening to them and not us?*" they cried.

"*We're your people. Help us!*"

"We need your help more. We have no jobs and no money for food!"

Their ire was not isolated to the Keeper but directed toward the group too, who were called unspeakable things. Projectiles flew indiscriminately in the direction of Ashara and the Amast and, in a heartbeat, shields surrounded them. That was the sign for them to retreat to the keep. Edvar ordered their guards to bring the Amast too. Nothing would be left of them if they stayed in the square.

The clamor quickly faded as they hurried up the street, soldiers holding the people at bay. Things had turned with frightening swiftness. Edvar looked over his shoulder at the ambling giants and the wild-looking woman and man following them. *I really am the unluckiest bastard in Yurr.*

Safe inside the walls, the post-mortem began. Edvar instructed the guards to show the Amast to a room in the Iron Tower while Edvar and Ashara went to the Great Hall.

"What in Soria happened out there?" Ashara shouted once inside, tearing off his plated armor. It clanged against the floor. "What did I do to cause so much hostility?"

"It is not you, I fear, sire. It is these... Amast. Things were going better than I hoped until they arrived."

"They are not at fault. If what they say is true they are yet more victims of Tesh's madness. Have you ever heard of these Amast before?"

"No. Never. Not in any of the stories I've heard."

"Do you believe them?"

"I will need to speak to them, but I fear now is not the time." Edvar approached the large bay windows and looked out over the city. He could see masses of people gathered in the streets. Wisps of black smoke rose from fires in the Keeper's Square. In silence, Edvar and Ashara watched as the city they fought so hard for and loved so much, reared up against them. Knocks came from the door.

"Enter," Ashara shouted. The keeper appeared a man renewed, ready for war—the exact opposite to how Edvar felt. The door swung open. "Malfan. Just the person I wanted to see."

Episode Five: Running from Home

Hope is a curious thing. It can blind. It can heal. It can inspire. It can make a man a fool. In our time of greatest need it is often there, a guiding light hovering above us. A reminder that all is not lost until the very end.

I wanted to find Uren's city. I wanted to find his magic dagger. With all my heart, I hoped they existed and that I would arrive at the place he had described to find them waiting for me. As I sat weeping tears of despair upon that cliff, Hope bellowed its laughter. It had made a fool of another man. I longed for nothing more than to pack up and return home, but something kept me there.

From **The Forgotten Daggers** by S. T. Harris

One

ISY COULDN'T MOVE from the window. Lakes of fire burned all across the city. Streaks of flames united them where the people of Yurrisa marched through the streets like angry ants, chanting and shouting and waving their torches. The soldiers who had guarded their retreat from the Keeper's Square had fallen back to the keep and now the people lay siege to the outer gate. Resounding thuds and the groan of wood breached the glass of the window.

"Is this our doing?" Pekira asked, almost whispering.

Isy bit her lip. Her greatest fear had come to fruition—that the people of the city would recoil in disgust at the sight of those so alien. The reaction she knew all too well. The one she ought to have known would come. Instead, she had grown drunk on hope and led the Amast into the mouth of a monstrous dragon. Had she ended any hope of the Amast getting help? She looked over at them, sat on the stone floor, backs to the cold wall. In their huge eyes, she saw resignation, despondency. Yera and Tulasc silently wept, as did Pekira, though she tried to mask it. Kora stared vacantly at the floor. Even Vil, who had loathed the Amast not long ago, had glistening cheeks.

It had started so well. The Keeper had listened to them, had come down to meet them. He could still help. Surely he could calm the crowd, show them reason. He was the legendary Ashara after all. Hero of the people. But they were yet to hear any word from him since being locked away in this tower, visited only by servants who brought bread and cheeses and jugs of water. Isy poured herself a cup, at last tearing her gaze away from the violence. She hated being locked up. Her father had done it to her more times than she could count. She wanted to do something, *had* to do something, to fix this situation. *But what?*

She returned to the window, eyes flitting to the door. Beyond it so much was happening. She needed to know what.

Two

"What in Soria is happening out there, Malfan?" Keeper Ashara's voice resounded through the cavernous hall.

"The keep is besieged, sire. The people seek to break the gates."

"And will they succeed?"

"Well, they outnumber us a hundred to one. If they mean to do it, then yes. Unless we take action to stop them."

"Have you lost your mind, man? I will not kill my own people!"

"They are not *your* people, sire. Not anymore." Malfan unsheathed his sword, the ring of steel echoing. "They have lost faith in you, and we cannot have a keeper the people do not trust."

"And is that to say, my bald little friend, that *you* have lost faith in me?"

Malfan's moustachioed lips remained sealed.

"I thought I could trust you, Malfan. Three decades you've stood by my side, on the battlefield and off. We've saved each other's lives. And is this how you repay me? With betrayal?" Ashara roared.

"It is you who has betrayed this nation," Malfan returned with equal fury. "You stopped trusting us, and your pathetic leadership has plunged us into chaos. An army is invading this land and all you do is give in to them. The man I knew would never have done that. A warrior does not allow his foe to strike a blow unguarded. He fights, and the fight in you has gone. You're a danger to us all."

Ashara laughed as if Malfan had just said the funniest thing he'd ever heard. "Come on then. Let us see how much fight is left in me." Ashara drew his long sword, Runas, the ancient Yurrish word for "blood". It had been in the family for generations, handed down to each keeper. Age had neither dimmed its glean nor blunted its edge. The silver hilt and crossguard, with their crimson trim, shimmered in the light of the braziers, so too the etchings along the flat of the blade, and the ruby pommel seemed to emit a light of its own.

Edvar drew his bland short sword in a much less graceful fashion.

"Do you have enough fight for all of us?" said a woman.

Malfan's lips curled into a smile.

From the shadows at the edge of the hall emerged Mara, Niskima and trailing behind, Rakar. Mara held a dirk that suited her murderous look, and Niskima carried a small flanged mace and buckler. Rakar wielded a short sword. Edvar had never seen him within a hundred yards of a weapon. His lack of experience was evident, the weight of the blade awkward in his grip. Not that Edvar was an expert. They formed a circle around Ashara and Edvar, blocking off the door.

"I gave you all power and responsibility. And here you are, betraying the sanctity of the oath we gave to the Yurrish people," Ashara said. "You would risk everything we have spent centuries building, disrespecting all the pain and strife our ancestors endured in the War of the Damned, all to take control for yourselves?"

"Oh shut up, Ashara," Mara spat. "You were never fit to rule. All you've ever done is ride on the backs of others. And now you take the advice of an incompetent boy rather than from us."

"You stopped trusting us a long time ago," Rakar said. "And that is your failing, not ours. Stop playing the victim. It makes you look even more pathetic. Everything we have done, and will do, is for the sake of this kingdom."

"For the sake of yourselves," Ashara said.

Rakar smiled. "It does not matter anymore. Your reign is at an end. The Good Keeper, the first to be deposed by his own people." Rakar laughed, Mara too. Malfan and Niskima's faces were like stone.

"I'm guessing it was you who killed Levanwe?" Ashara asked.

"She didn't agree with our... methods," Mara said. "The woman had one foot in the grave anyway."

The smile upon her face sent a chill down Edvar's spine. The hilt of his sword squirmed in his palm. His knees trembled. Fear constricted his chest. He tried to alleviate it with a few deep breaths, just like Camos had taught him. *Never let the moment beat you. Breathe.*

The traitors inched closer, Malfan swinging his sword around, loosening his wrist.

"At least you're doing your own dirty work," Ashara said, readying his stance.

Malfan lunged for the Keeper. He swung left and right, a furious flurry which forced Ashara back a few paces. The other three moved in on Edvar. Niskima attacked first, her eyes consumed by a hatred that had brewed for years. She was faster than her grey hair suggested, and it was clear she knew what she was doing, her handle of the mace assured, buckler held high in defense.

Edvar parried a blow and metal rang in his ears. His wrist jarred and began to throb. Rakar and Mara had dropped back a few paces, allowing Niskima to fight alone. Never ones to put themselves in harm's way. Or maybe they wanted Niskima dead. The grey-haired woman attacked again, a swipe aimed at his head. Edvar ducked, rolled his body and felt the mace swing by. It awakened something in him, a realization of the situation. Just like with the assassins, it was life or death, and like then, he had no desire to die. Not today, no matter how long the odds of survival.

He took a quick breath, readied his feet and brought up his sword in defense.

To his left, Ashara and Malfan continued their furious melee. They were tiring, though, the time between blows slower, each strike dealt with less vigor.

Niskima pressed once more, yet to show fatigue, but she was always one for hiding things. Edvar blocked and moved, lunged with a strike of his own. The tip of his blade sliced her side and she cried out. Grabbing the wound, she dropped back a pace or two. Someone else cried out beside Edvar. He didn't want to look.

Ashara clutched at a wound to the top of his sword arm. Blood poured through his fingers, though he still held onto his sword. A smiling Malfan attacked again. As did an infuriated Niskima. The clang of steel rang out once more.

Rakar and Mara had dropped further back, sensing victory. But the injury had knocked it out of Niskima. Her attacks carried less force, sweat lined her brow and her hand kept returning to the gash at her side. Edvar pressed, unleashing a fierce combination, right, left, right, right again, and, with the final blow, raked his blade down the shaft of her mace and severed the hand from her arm. Stunned, Niskima turned toward him and Edvar plunged his sword into her gut. She dropped to the ground, coughing blood. Not far away, somebody else fell too.

Edvar willed himself to look and found Runas embedded in Malfan's neck. A pale-looking Ashara yanked it free and turned to face Rakar and Mara.

"I prefer these odds," the Keeper said, spitting blood.

"You think this is it?" Rakar said, smiling. "Now we do it my way. And I care nothing for honor. Guards!"

The door almost flew off its hinges. Soldiers flooded in, a wave of spears and swords and shields sweeping towards Ashara and Edvar.

"Come on," Edvar shouted, pointing behind the top dais. Ashara didn't move. He couldn't tear his eyes away from Rakar. Only when the traitorous treasurer became lost in the press of charging foes did Ashara relent. Crossbow bolts flew by them, smashing into the wall. Edvar pressed the hidden button, blended in amongst the stone slabs, and the secret door clicked open. They disappeared inside and slammed it shut.

"How did you know of this?" Ashara asked, voice bodiless in the gloom.

"I know all the tunnels and passageways. Grab onto my jacket and don't let go, we've no time to get lost." Edvar set off, relying on memory and intuition to guide him, all the while holding off panic. He'd been along this particular tunnel more times than he could count, and a few times in pitch darkness like this. The footing was even, the ceiling relatively high, though in parts it became a crouch. The one thing he did not like was the closeness of the walls.

Thuds and bangs, shouting too, echoed along the tunnel.

"Sounds like they got in," Ashara said.

"We'll lose them."

At the first opportunity, Edvar turned down an adjoining tunnel, then left at the next junction. He did this over and over until they arrived at a fork. One way would take them to the city walls, the other to the Iron Tower.

The Amast.

They were locked up in the tower. He'd completely forgotten about them. If they were left, they'd be killed. The people had revolted at the sight of them. Rakar would execute them to curry favor, no doubt in the most brutal of ways. He couldn't let that happen, not when he had a chance to lead them to safety. It was an unusual feeling after the past few weeks, the power to actually do some good. But was it worth the risk? He wasn't sure where in the tower they were. They could be stepping into a trap after having just escaped another. He cursed under his breath.

"Why have we stopped?" Ashara whispered.

Three

From beyond the door, Isy could hear shouting, the rattle of armor as people ran by, swords leaving sheaths.

"I wish I knew what was happening out there," Vil said. The color had drained from his face.

"I'm guessing the people don't make a habit of rioting here?" Isy asked.

Vil shook his head. The Amast seemed a little calmer than him, though Isy suspected they were just better at hiding it.

"Your keeper can fix this?" Kora asked Vil. Isy studied the Amast man. If Ashara couldn't, that would be an end to all of their hopes. An end to the Amast. *Have we failed?*

The bolt of the door rattled and the door swung open. The breath caught in Isy's throat. The young man who had been with the Keeper earlier that day stood before them. He was sweating profusely, dark fringe glued to his forehead.

"We must go," he said when his breathing had settled enough.

"What's happening?" Isy asked.

"No time to explain. We have to go now. Your lives depend on it."

"We cannot go," Kora said. "If we leave without help our people will die."

The young man rolled his eyes and stomped his foot. "Listen to me. We must leave. Now. If you don't you *will* die." He pushed the door wider and pointed for them to go.

Isy looked into the young man's amber eyes and saw neither hate nor malice, only desperation and fear. She looked to Kora and nodded.

Isy struggled with the steps as they descended further and further down the tower, each one a different height to the last, though not as much as the Amast struggled with the narrowness of the winding stairwell. It was different from the one they had come up in, far less grandiose and with fewer candles to light their way. Soon there were no candles at all and the stairwell ended before an iron-studded door. The young man knocked three times, twice in quick succession with a pause between the third. A lock clicked open and the door swung in.

Hiding in the gloom was the Keeper of Yurr. Face ghostly white and spattered with blood, he clutched his right shoulder, the white gambeson beneath his fingers stained crimson. "What took you?" he asked the young man through gritted teeth. No answer came. Keeper Ashara turned to the Amast. "I will explain all in time, but for now, I promise to help you if you can help me."

The Amast nodded. "We will help," Kora said. Ashara gave them a weary look of thanks and instructed the young man to lead the way.

They held onto each other to guide themselves through the gloom. The gradient of the tunnel rose and the further up they went, the louder the sounds of the riot became. Dust and rocks showered down on Isy from the ceiling. She could hear women and children shrieking amidst the sounds of galloping hooves on stone. A dog barked frantically in the distance before falling silent. Isy did not linger too much on the poor mutt's fate. She knew that whatever was going on up there, it was humanity at its very worst, worse even than the mobs of children that used to chase her through Haberdam. This mob would tear her friends apart as well as her. Was it some evil spell that made the marauding crowds above act in such a way? No. People didn't need to be enchanted to act like that. They needed no excuse at all.

The sounds above quietened and soon the group came to a halt. The young man muttered just loud enough for all to hear.

"This door opens into the dry moat before the northern gate. There's a narrow path through the stakes and then we must climb a ladder to get to the outer city. Once we're up, stick as close to me as possible, and you'll all have to keep as low to the ground as you can, for obvious reasons," he said to the Amast.

Darkness had fallen and the cold air smelt like Winter Solstice night in Haberdam, thick with the smell of bonfires. They hurried through the stakes and up the crude and concealed ladder and regrouped in the shadow of a saddler's workshop. From there, they moved along darkened back alleys, pausing when they ended to check the open road before moving on. Everyone, it seemed, was within the city walls. Or hiding.

They kept to the shadows until at last they were free of buildings and moved instead through the mud of farmer's fields. At the top of a rise, they paused for breath and looked back whence they came.

Red fire consumed the horizon. Black smoke plumed and formed a roiling cloud. Yurrisa burned.

Isy looked around at her dejected companions. Vil, shivering and bleary-eyed, collapsed on the floor in exhaustion. The Amast were expressionless as ever. The wounded Keeper was propped up by the young man she'd learned was named Edvar. Both men surveyed the chaotic city in disbelief. In their eyes, lit up by the flames of their burning home, Isy saw something familiar: failure.

Four

To never feel true satisfaction is a flaw of man. Always yearning for more, for things beyond our possession. Like all humanity before us, we longed for betterment, for control over our own destiny. Achieving that came at a cost greater than any of us could have comprehended. Power changed us, turned us upon ourselves, fractured us, and left us to die in helplessness.

I remember casting my eyes over the Dagger for the first time, pulsating with the power to change our lives forever. Seeing it then, we should have known a taste would not be enough. It turned us into wolves starved by a winter long and harsh. We abandoned morality, forgot compassion, and in the process, sealed our demise.

Civil war raged for decades, brutal and bloody, like severing your arm with a blunt and rusty knife. Forests became wastelands; cities, towns and villages reduced to piles of rubble. Generations of people wiped from history. No longer did the birds sing, nor did children laugh. Fatigue consumed our souls. We left those apocalyptic lands and sought a new home, far from our tainted past. Somewhere we could forget. Somewhere we could rediscover that which we all seek: happiness.

The final sentence played over in his mind. It was as if those words, written who knew how long ago, were for him. He set down the book and held a taper to his pipe, puffing smoke into the cabin. Of all the many books he'd read, he'd never found one so... intriguing. According to his best scribe, Oska, the original had been written in the hand of the

Ancients. It was a battered old tome brought back by his men
from the Giant's Garden after surveying the land given to
Karrabar in Ashara's pitiful treaty.

He closed his eyes, listening to the creak of the wood as
it bowed to the might of the waves. He'd never been fond of
sailing. Seasickness hadn't plagued him as it had others. It
was the being trapped that he didn't like. He enjoyed his
freedom and there weren't many places to go on a ship.
Perhaps it was why many believed the sailor's life so tough.

Fed up of his berth, he decided to get some air. He
fastened his black leather jacket and donned his fur-lined
cloak, pulled on his boots and grabbed his leather gloves off
the bedside table. He stretched his muscular legs and
loosened his knees, both aching from being sat down for too
long. His bones clicked more than they used to. He was
lucky, though. After decades of battles, the worst of his
injuries were a few scars, the most noticeable being the one
that cut a bald line through his brown, grey-shot beard. His
wavy hair was similarly colored and hung down to his
shoulders. Perhaps his most significant feature was his eyes.
Like polished mahogany, they glistened, and never did they
stay still, always scanning and scrutinizing. They sat either
side of a pinched and crooked nose. How had luck stayed
with him on the battlefield while in every other aspect of his
life it had abandoned him? Was he destined to survive what
was to come, to see out his goals at last? He was not a pious
man—he had seen too many horrors to believe in any divine
purpose—but he wondered.

Mist left his mouth as he stepped onto the deck. The
chill bit at his face, but it was no more than an annoyance;
he had felt true cold before, the kind that dements. It was
dawn, the sun rising back in the direction of home. The
waves were steady and calm. A scattering of cloud drifted
overhead. Along the western horizon, a few stars still shone,
while to the east, red streaks broke forth and lit up the fleet
of carracks, cogs and galleys sailing around his galleon,
their daffodil-yellow sails full in the stiff morning breeze. A
gruff voice broke the tranquility.

"A red morning, m'lord. An omen, perhaps."

Tesh blew smoke from his pipe, gaze not straying from his ships. "You know I don't care for such things, Iljasar."

Tesh's right hand came to stand beside him. "Aye. We bend our own fates, as you say. Did you sleep?"

"A little."

"Nyramo has tinctures that might help. You need your rest as much as anyone."

"I prefer to keep a clear head."

"Lack of sleep will muddle your thoughts worse than a drop of opa."

"I'll bear that in mind." Tesh puffed on his pipe and looked at Iljasar. Tesh wasn't the tallest of Karrabans, who were already a diminutive people, and Iljasar was smaller than him, but what the old warrior lacked in height he made up for in broadness, his shoulders and arms like a woodcutter's after twenty years in the job. His pointed ears, shaped like that of a fox, had an array of earrings and studs, each one bearing a tale that he was all too happy to tell, especially after an ale or three. Age lined his copper skin, around his eyes in particular. And he didn't have a single hair on his body. Those that didn't know him mistook him for a eunuch. Tesh had seen him bed more women than a randy teen in a brothel to know that wasn't the case. "I don't have to shave, at least," Tesh had heard him say too many times to count. It was that kind of attitude that Tesh liked. Finding the positives instead of lamenting. Iljasar hadn't just schooled Tesh how to fight; he'd shown him the ways of the world, about women and love. Everything his father should have taught him, but didn't.

"How far to the Green Steps?" Tesh asked.

"Once the sun rises, we should be able to see them on the horizon."

"What do you expect?"

Iljasar folded his arms, squeezed the butt of his chin with thumb and forefinger as so often he did. "If they're true to their word, we should be able to sail through unopposed. Why? Do you have doubts?"

Tesh wrung the wooden bulwark before him, pipe between his lips. "There are few people I trust in this world. I count no Yurrishman amongst them."

"Let's see what the day brings. We're ready whatever the situation."

Tesh smiled. He remained on deck as the day grew brighter. Iljasar went off berating someone. A cabin boy brought Tesh coffee in a bronze cup. He bowed and left without saying a word. The night shift switched to the day shift and, as they passed him, sailors bowed and saluted, glimpsing then averting their eyes. In his short time as keeper, Tesh hadn't been out much in public. He loathed those that paraded through the streets, feeding their egos off of people's adorations, like Ashara. Tesh was a soldier, a general, spending much of his life campaigning. He missed that life, or parts of it anyway. Things were simpler on the battlefield. Kill or be killed. There were no worries beyond that.

Tesh realized he was clamping down too tightly on his pipe. He eased his jaw. His hatred for Ashara never left him feeling cold. The man had made his life a misery. He had turned his own father against him and stole from his hand the only woman he'd ever loved, and indeed the only woman who had ever loved him. *We were meant to be together and he destroyed it all.*

Tesh's father had shipped him off to the army after that, a broken man, and for all those long years he plotted to take Jessyia back. When she died, that hope faded, and a desire for revenge blossomed, one that had grown to consume his heart and mind. Most nights he dreamt of Ashara, covered in Jessyia's blood, laughing at him in that mocking and disdainful way, a laugh that had followed Tesh around throughout his youth. He hated sleep now. Awake, he could imagine the moment he sunk his sword into Ashara's heart. It would be no less than he deserved.

A bell sounded at the bow of the ship. Lost in thought, Tesh hadn't spotted the six islands that made up the Green Steps, now clear in the distance. They varied in size, the gaps between them wide enough only for small ships, save for that between the final island and the rocky shore—the main shipping channel along the coast. Flames sparked to life on the beacon towers upon each island. Tesh caught the sound of horns. So too, it seemed, did Iljasar, who re-joined Tesh at the bulwark.

"Them lying snakes didn't pass on the message then?" the old warrior said.

"I can't say I'm disappointed. We have our new toys to try out." A smile crept to Tesh's lips, though it didn't linger long.

As they drew nearer, the Yurrish ships appeared from behind the islands: a dozen or so galleys and one four-masted galleon that dwarfed them all. Tesh expected more resistance after the recent attacks along the border. Were their eyes turned completely in that direction? Or perhaps Rakar had done his job after all. *When does a Yurrishman ever do anything honestly?*

It wasn't just the ships they had to contend with, though. Tesh had vivid memories of Ashara and his cretinous mother, Alysa, boasting of the strength of the Yurrish sea defenses—batteries of trebuchets and catapults, enough to sink a great fleet, lay on these islands, or so they said. Now he would see if those boasts held true.

Tesh gave the order to hold position. A deckhand raised a round shield, painted red, and the other ships repeated the order. The Yurrish ships drew a line opposite, blocking the channel. One of the Yurrish galleys, blue mast tipped with a white flag, left the line and sailed toward them.

"Bargaining for peace it seems. We outnumber them ten to one. Who could blame them?" Iljasar said. "Shall I go?"

"Indeed. But I'm coming too."

"What if it's a trap?"

"Then we won't give them a chance to spring it."

Five

Tesh sat at the stern, Iljasar beside him, their eyes never leaving the approaching Yurrish rowboat, a similar size to their own, though more elegantly designed, with a broad hull and the figurehead of a sea serpent at the bow. When they reached a few feet away, the rowers held still their oars. A Yurrishman, who possessed the officious air of a commander, stood.

"Do you mean to declare war with all these ships, gentlemen?"

Tesh studied him. A few days growth covered his cheeks and chin, and bags sagged under his eyes. A drunkard, Tesh suspected. His grey hair was shaven at the sides and longer and slicked back on top. A small yet noticeable scar cut vertically down his left eye. From his wandering gaze, he seemed unsure who was in charge of the Karrabans.

Iljasar stood and responded.

"Perhaps so, good sir. We're off to Yurrisa, to pillage and plunder!" The dozen Karraban rowers laughed and cheered. Tesh found himself smiling too.

The Yurrish commander scowled. "And to whom do I speak?"

"Tesh, Keeper of Karrabar," Tesh said from his seat.

The Yurrish commander stammered and grappled for composure. "If it is war that you intend, then you shall go no further," he said defiantly, hand shifting to the sword at his hip. He drew it a little.

Tesh glanced at Iljasar and nodded. Iljasar kicked the side of the boat twice. The oarsmen threw back the hessian canvas covering their legs and drew crossbows. Before those on the Yurrish boat could react, a storm of bolts darted toward them. Another Karraban lit the oil-soaked rags poking from small pots filled with oil and hurled them at the Yurrish boat. Flames erupted. The survivors of the initial barrage wailed as fire devoured their clothes and flesh. Some dived into the water, only to be picked off by the crossbowmen. All the while Tesh sat and watched.

Horns rang out from the Yurrish boats. More answered on the islands. Iljasar ordered them back to the ship. At hearing a snap and mighty groan of wood, Tesh looked over his shoulder. Clusters of boulders soared into the air, propelled by the great arms of trebuchets positioned upon the island closest. They hung like hawks hunting prey before plummeting toward them.

Iljasar bellowed the order to row harder, faster. The first boulder smashed into the water in front of them, sending foam towering into the air. More fell around them like giant hailstones. A good soaking was the extent of the damage. The rest of the fleet was not so lucky. Men screamed. Wood shattered. Canvas snapped. Half a dozen ships fell to the first volley.

Tesh pushed back his sodden fringe and clambered up the portside rope ladder. Once aboard, the Karraban ships thrust out their oars and surged forward, spreading wide to make it harder for the trebuchets to hone in on an area. More rocky showers hammered down, coming in staggered bursts. Ships sunk. Men died. Tesh's anger surged.

"Faster. Harder," he roared, slamming his fist against the bulwark. The rowers below deck responded, repeating his words rhythmically. The next wave of rocks sailed overhead.

As planned, the Karraban fleet split in two. Tesh led one half toward the Yurrish ships, who'd maintained their blockade. The other half headed for the islands.

With the distance closing, the catapults upon the islands began to loose. Solid balls of iron twice the size as a human head, rained down upon the Karraban ships, tearing through wood, snapping sails and rigging, crushing bone, killing instantly.

Tesh's gaze shifted to the Yurrish ships. He spat at the sight of the white lily of Yurr upon their flags. Iljasar looked at him, a grin upon his face. Tesh gave the nod.

"Rumblers ready!" Iljasar bellowed. The portside oarsmen pulled up their oars and the ship turned to starboard. Upon the deck, men hauled ropes to open scores of wooden hatches on the starboard side of the boat. They backed water and slowed to a stop. Other ships did the same until they formed a line before the Yurrish. They were vulnerable to ramming, but Tesh didn't intend for the Yurrish to get that close.

Tesh lowered his raised arm. A horn sounded. The air sizzled, and there came a fleeting moment of pure silence before the deck beneath him shuddered. Tesh nearly lost his feet. A sound greater than thunder ripped through the air as a score of iron balls shot across the water and crashed into the enemy ships, tearing holes in wood and man alike. Shouts and screams broke through his tinnitus for the briefest of moments before another barrage was fired. Thick white smoke billowed up from below, carrying with it the sweet smell of burning that made him want to sneeze. The volleys continued, the smoke thickening, until the sight of toppling masts and sails became lost.

Tesh coughed, covered his mouth with his cloak. His eyes stung and watered. He ordered a cease-fire and somehow someone heard him. Now it was the turn of the smaller ships. They disappeared into the haze and swarmed upon the battered Yurrish vessels, catapulting firepots and shooting any survivors with bolt and arrow. Soon the ringing in his ears eased enough for him to hear the screams of dying men and women.

When the smoke cleared, he discovered his ships had reduced much of the island's defensive fortifications to rubble. His men had poured out of rowboats and climbed the rocky banks. And upon those rocks, they now fought the defenders. Clashing swords glinted in the sun. Crossbow bolts smashed holes in the Yurrish force, and pikes and spears drove them back toward the center of the islands where the main forts stood. The catapults of the defenders' were seized and turned on the forts, felling walls and roofs and allowing the Karraban force to overwhelm and kill. In the space of no more than an hour, one of the renowned Yurrish sea defenses had been obliterated.

Iljasar turned to his keeper. "What do you think?"

Tesh smiled. Not since the War of the Damned had anyone wielded such destructive and devastating power. With them, he would reduce Ashara and everything he held dear to nothingness.

Six

Each step was harder than the last. More than once Edvar had stumbled and fallen, and as the blue haze of dawn fought the gloom, he realized just how muddy he was. His hands, chilled to numbness, looked like a blacksmith's after a day at the forge. He couldn't see the leather of his boots for the mud upon them. His breeches were now brown, so too his gambeson, and the links of his mail shirt were stuffed with mud. His entire body ached—legs and lower back in particular. They had stopped only to clean and bandage Ashara's shoulder wound, and since then headed north through the forest, moving parallel to the road. Edvar yearned for a hot bath and roaring fire to doze by. *Will I ever enjoy such things again?*

A howling wind sent branches and boughs creaking, shook withered leaves from their perches and stirred those already fallen. Each gust brought the smell of burning. At the top of a ridge, they came to a break in the treeline and looked back in the direction of Yurrisa as the first rays of dawn crested the land. A cloud of grey and black smoke smeared the horizon. The image of Edvar's failure.

No Yurrish keeper had ever been overthrown. Only Ashara. *What will the chroniclers scribble?* The great keeper led, or rather misled, by the incompetent boy adviser. Too young and naïve to uncover a coup plotted under his nose. Chased from the city with his tail between his legs, never to be seen or heard of again. Nothing like his father. A shame to the family. It was everything he deserved.

"What is that?" the Amast woman named Pekira said.

"It is no fire," said the leader of their group, Kora.

Edvar looked to where Pekira pointed. Plumes of smoke—or was it dust?—rose above the trees back in the direction of the road, two or three leagues away, at least. Edvar looked at Ashara. The Keeper, it seemed, already knew what it was and what it meant. Realization struck Edvar like a knife in the gut.

"They're hunting us," Ashara said.

"There are no better woodsmen than the Amast," Isy said. "You can lead us to safety. Can't you?" she asked Kora. She looked how Edvar felt: despondent, shoulders and back slumped with fatigue, eyes dark-ringed and lids heavy. Her voice, though, was full of defiance, of hope.

"There must be hundreds of them to stir up such a cloud," Ashara said. "We must go where horses cannot. There." He pointed over Edvar's shoulder, to the great mountain known as Gurath, an ancient word meaning 'white giant'. The peak of Gurath was permanently covered in snow. It was said that when its snows melted, the world would end. Edvar had visited the foothills of Gurath once before when he was fourteen summers old—a rare expedition with his father. For a week, they had camped, hunted and explored. He had taught Edvar how to light a fire, where best to look for shelter, how to snare rabbits and squirrels, what berries and mushrooms he could eat and which would loosen his bowels. He'd been amazed at how much his father had known, at how able he was. He made it all seem so easy and natural. Edvar had asked him how he had learned such things. *Believe and you will find a way.*

Seven

Isy's legs ached to the bone. Since tumbling over a protruding root, the back of her left leg was tight as a drawn bowstring and throbbed like a pus-filled carbuncle. They hadn't even spent a night in Yurrisa and now they were back walking through dark woods again, heading in the direction they had come from. To travel so far, to go through so much, and then to fail. She could have done more. Should have said more to the Keeper, more to the people to help them understand.

Looking back, confronting the Keeper at that moment was a silly idea, plagued with risks. She'd let excitement and hope cloud her judgment. That poor decision had sparked the downfall of the Keeper and potentially sealed the deaths of the Amast. She was meant to be their guide, their protector, and she had utterly failed them.

Hope was not altogether lost, though. Keeper Ashara had vowed to help the Amast. Only he was no longer keeper, and the wound to his shoulder was taking its toll. His skin was almost luminous in the gloom. If he survived their escape, could he re-take the city with so little support? And even if it was possible, how long would it take? The Amast were dying every day back at the camp.

All of these thoughts battered Isy's mind, chipped away at her resolve, such that they made her want to stop and give up. But fear curiously possessed a power both paralyzing and motivating. No matter the pain she endured in getting away, she did not want to be captured by the riders that continued to pursue them. So she struggled on with gritted teeth, eyes to the ground, avoiding the looming white peaks of Gurath which still seemed so far away.

Dusk quickly descended over the steep valley they navigated through. Brown and rugged patches of bare-branched deciduous trees punctuated the sea of evergreens. For the first time, and indeed one of the most inopportune of times, Isy considered how beautiful the land here was. It reminded her of home... Haberdam. *Not home.* She turned back to the trail to find she'd lagged way behind. Kora was waiting for her.

"They close the gap. We cannot afford to tarry," he said as she caught up.

"Tarry... You can speak Yurrish better than I can now," she smiled, hiding a grimace from the pain in her leg.

"You hurt?" he asked.

She shook her head.

"It's your left leg. You struggle to place weight on it. What happened?"

There was no point lying. Those eyes saw everything. *Except my mark.* "I tripped over a root and strained it, I think. I'm fine, though. Just a twinge."

"Twinge. A new one to me." Kora smiled, held out his hand to pull her up the last stretch of the ridge. She took it, and he pulled her into his giant embrace. "I will carry you if you like? You are light," Kora offered.

"I'm fine," she said. It wasn't as if she'd broken anything, and leg aside she was fine. It wasn't fair to burden Kora too. They all had to struggle along the same path. Not even Vil was complaining. Maybe he'd learned to hide it better. Or was he being brave in front of the Keeper? Maybe he could just handle it more than she could.

The day wore on, and they stopped by a stream, Isy and Ashara fit to collapse. With Yera's help, the young man named Edvar cleaned and bound the Keeper's wound and the Amast woman gave Ashara a root to chew which livened him up.

The wind stiffened in the afternoon to grab at clothes and blow down hoods. Isy shivered as she walked, numb hands wrapped in her fur cloak, fighting to keep her hood close. She lagged at the back, Kora ahead of her, with a gap between him and the Keeper, Vil and Edvar. She couldn't quite believe he was the Keeper of Yurr. It was surreal seeing a man in the flesh that she'd only ever heard stories about. The wound to his arm was very much the opposite of surreal, however. Despite their earlier efforts, Ashara had further paled, and now Edvar and Vil had to support him, which admittedly made Isy feel a bit better about her injury. Pekira, Tulasc and Yera moved in single file in front of them, taking a leisurely stroll in comparison to the Yurrish.

At the top of a gruelingly steep rise, they stopped and the Yurrish collapsed to the ground. The Amast were looking back at the valley below, lit by the final rays of the autumnal sun.

"Do you see them?" Tulasc asked.

"Yes," Yera said. "I see the birds scattering to the east. Is that what you see?"

Tulasc nodded.

Isy's heart sunk. How could they still be following them?

"I will fall back and cover our tracks. We need to know how many follow us, too," Tulasc said.

"Is it worth the risk, Tulasc?" Yera said. "You have no spear. What if they spot you?" The Amast only carried dirks and daggers, their spears left reluctantly in the wagon in Yurrisa.

"The darkness is my weapon."

It seemed none of the Amast wished to argue further with him; indeed, it would likely be pointless. Tulasc, more than any of the others, was stubborn as a weary mule. Within seconds he was out of sight, and once more they continued on to the protesting throbs of Isy's legs.

Darkness had claimed the land now and, unable to see, Isy stumbled and staggered over protruding roots and rocks.

It only served to inflame her injury and more than once she had to bite her lip to stop from crying out.

As she tried to haul herself up a crag, her left leg gave way altogether. She fell back onto stone, the wind knocked from her lungs, the back of her head throbbing in sync with her leg. No matter how much she wanted to, she couldn't find the strength to get up. The muscles in her injured leg convulsed and twitched. Kora's bulbous eyes looked down at her. He hopped down and gently lifted her up.

"Can you hold onto my neck?" he asked her. Isy nodded.

They went on, Isy relieved she no longer had to walk, though her ego felt just as wounded as her body. They were in the shadows of Gurath now, the trees growing sparse, the land rugged and rocky, the gradient increasing. A howl cut through the night, a shriek of pain and fear. It sounded like nothing Isy had ever heard before.

"What was that?" Isy asked, wondering if Kora could feel the beat of her heart against his carapace back.

"It is hard to say."

"It's not Tulasc, is it?"

"I hope not."

With a crescent moon shining down upon them, they decided to take a break behind a stand of rocks, sheltered from the wind. Water skins were handed around, so too nuts and berries and mushrooms. Nothing appetizing, but Isy didn't care as long as it ceased the rumbling pangs in her stomach.

Nobody, it seemed, had the energy to talk, though heads snapped around when they heard bushes rustling nearby. Weapons flashed out of scabbards.

"It is me." Tulasc stepped into the weak glow of the moon.

"Good to see you brother," Yera said, gripping Tulasc's forearm and touching his forehead with her own. The other Amast greeted him similarly.

"What news?" Ashara asked.

"A couple hundred people dressed like the soldiers from the city follow us. I heard their metal suits rattling from a half-mile away. Some of them look different, dressed in clothes more suited to the forest. I nearly ran into one. It is those who follow our tracks and lead the others. I covered our tracks and laid false ones but I cannot guarantee it will work. They have followed us this far. They know these woods as well as we know our own."

"They're Pathfinders, and indeed they are trained in these very woods. You did well, Tulasc," Ashara said. "I thank you for trying." With lips pursed and brows furrowed with concern, the Keeper looked at Edvar.

Eight

Despite the dimness of night, Edvar could see the knowing look in Ashara's eyes. Their options, it seemed, were few. Tired, ill-armed and wounded, they couldn't put up much of a fight. Could the Amast even fight? They seemed such passive and clumsy beings and they carried with them only flint dirks, though they weren't far off the length of a short sword. Outrunning their pursuers was looking less likely. Ashara and the Amast guide, Isy, were close to collapsing. Without rest the flight would be their deaths.

"We must find somewhere to hide for the night and hope Tulasc's efforts work," Ashara said with a grimace.

Kora nodded and once more the group set off to hunt for a hole to hide in. Pekira and Yera went on ahead and soundlessly returned with news of a narrow cave in a crag not far uphill.

By the time they'd scrambled inside the pitch-dark but somewhat warm cave, Ashara couldn't walk unaided and could barely keep open his eyes.

"How are you feeling?" Edvar asked as he sat him down against the wall.

"Like I could sleep a hundred years," Ashara muttered. He shivered like a frightened dog. Edvar removed his own cloak and wrapped it around him.

"I will tend to your wound," Yera said, kneeling down beside Ashara. Vil removed his cloak and handed it to Edvar who bundled it up and placed it behind the Keeper's head.

Tulasc made a small fire using the few sticks and leaves he found lying around the cave, then he, Kora and Pekira left to cover their tracks and find some firewood.

Edvar sat on the opposite side of the fire to Isy. She looked at him with her big, amber eyes, glowing in the firelight. One looked like the sun on a brilliantly clear day, the other a full moon hanging in the night sky that was her birthmark.

"How's your leg?" he asked her. Isy stammered, seemingly startled by the question.

"It's getting harder to put weight on it."

"I can take a look if you like?"

She hesitated, biting her bottom lip. "Okay," she said.

Edvar shuffled closer, and with great care, lifted up her outstretched leg onto his lap. She stifled a yelp and he was quick to apologize. He hoped she couldn't see his burning cheeks in the dim light. With a delicate touch, he ran his fingers along the back of her leg.

"There," she said with a wince as he reached just above her heel.

"I've had an injury like this before. I might be able to ease the tension a little."

"What did you do?" she asked.

"When I was a kid, I tripped over in one of the tunnels we escaped through. I nearly got stuck in there because of it." He gradually added more pressure to his kneading, gauging the right amount from her grimaces.

"Why did you take us with you?" Isy asked.

The question stumped him. His mind had been so consumed by the riots, the attack and getting away that he'd forgotten he hadn't explained anything to Isy, Vil and the Amast.

"I couldn't leave you all there. You would have been killed. Probably in the most horrible of ways in front of the whole city. You did not deserve that. So much has gone wrong, I had to do something right. Now your turn. Why did you travel all the way to Yurrisa? You still have not had the chance to fully explain."

"Well, you know about the Karrabans attacking the Amast. The few Amast who survived fled. They grew weak, sick and could go no further, so set up a camp on the edge of the Giant's Garden. They've been there for months, starving and dying of disease."

"How did you come to find them?"

"They found me, I suppose. Kora and Tulasc kidnapped me."

Edvar laughed, thinking it a joke. Going off her silence, he soon realized it wasn't. "Really?"

"They couldn't speak Yurrish at the time, so I suppose there was no other way to get me to go. When I got there, one of the leaders of the Amast named Aena, what they call a Guide, could speak some Yurrish, and she explained everything. How could I not help?"

"How come this Aena isn't with you?"

"She was killed by birds the Amast call the paska. I know it as the blue raven."

"I've read about them," Edvar said.

"In *Mythos of Yurr?*"

"Yes! It's one of my favorite books," Edvar said with a flutter of excitement.

"Mine too! I think I've read it half a dozen times."

"So why Yurrisa? It's such a long way from the Giant's Garden. Could you find no closer aid?"

"Aena knew of Ashara. She knew how noble he is, how much he loves his people. He is the opposite of Baron Rijkard of Haberdam. That miserable prick would sooner hang the Amast than help. Their home has been destroyed. They have nowhere to go, so Aena thought it best to seek out Ashara, to see if he can give them the shelter, aid and kindness they need. Otherwise, the Amast will perish.

"I'm so sorry, Edvar. We didn't mean to cause all this trouble for you. The Keeper has been overthrown all because of us."

A silence filled the cave. He hadn't blamed Isy, Vil and the Amast for what transpired in Yurrisa and it saddened his heart to hear her blaming herself. "Please, Isy, this is by no means your fault. This is all the work of traitors."

"You are in the west now," Ashara said, half-rising up from beneath the pile of cloaks upon him. "And that means you are my people. I will protect you from Tesh and help you rebuild your lives.

"This entire situation is of my own making. You are all the victims. I am the one who should be sorry and, with all my heart, I am. I will not ask you to help me. That goes for you too, Ed. You have all done too much for me already."

Edvar didn't know what to say, and it was clear from the quiet that followed that everybody else felt the same. Waterskins were once more passed around, so too nuts and berries. The tension eased and Edvar hoped that it had brought them closer together. He shared his waterskin with Isy, who told him the pain had settled in her leg. It was then that the others returned.

"They are camped further down the hill. There are around two hundred altogether and more search the surrounding forest," Tulasc said.

"We have covered our tracks as best we can, but they were not deceived by Tulasc's efforts, and he is the finest tracker of all the Amast, living and dead," Kora said.

"What shall we do?" Yera asked.

The silence in the cave weighed heavy.

"We must keep moving," Ashara said at last. "I am weak, but I have a few more miles left in me."

"My leg isn't hurting as much. I think I can walk," Isy said.

"I agree. We should go," Edvar added. He couldn't settle here in the knowledge that their pursuers were close. They had a chance to put some distance between them and potentially lose them altogether. Only a fool wouldn't take it.

Everyone got to their feet and shouldered the few travel sacks they carried. Vil was first out of the cave. Edvar hung back to offer Isy a hand but saw that Kora had beaten him to it. He turned to follow the others and heard the sound of a horn. Right outside the cave.

"What's going on?" Edvar asked, pushing forward.

"A scout was there," said a pale Vil, pointing at a thicket of trees down the hillside. "He saw me, turned and ran."

"Damn it to hell," Edvar said.

"I'm sorry," Vil said.

"It's hardly your fault, boy," said Ashara. "They would have no doubt found us sooner or later. Come on, we have no time to waste."

They set off at a run across the rocky ground, heading for the cover of the trees, their way lit by the pale glow of the moon.

"They surround us," Kora said, slowing to a stop. Edvar turned around to see shadows darting through the murk. All around them he could hear the rattle of chainmail and armor. Another blast of the horn rang out. The loudest yet.

"Then we must fight," Tulasc said, drawing his dirk. One by one, the Amast drew their weapons.

"You do not have to fight for me," Ashara said. "It is me they want, not you. Edvar will go with you and help your people. If anyone will find a way, it will be him. Hurry, before it's too late." Ashara tried to push Kora away. He did the same to Edvar and it turned into an embrace.

"I will face them as I have faced all of my enemies. How your father and I faced them." Ashara pushed Edvar back and drew his sword, Runas, with his left hand, though he could hardly hold its weight.

"And I will face them with you," Edvar said, drawing his own. He knew in his mind it meant certain death, but fighting for what he believed in, for the man he loved, felt like the right thing to do, the only thing to do.

"I will fight too," Vil said.

"So will I," Isy added. And both drew their flint knives, loaned to them by the Amast.

"I could not ask for finer people to fight beside," Ashara said. He turned toward the approaching enemies and lifted his sword. They stood in a circle, weapons ready. Soldiers filled the clearing, quickly forming a shield wall around them.

"We're trapped," Vil said, voice quivering.

Edvar imagined the crossbows being lined up behind the shields, anticipated the storm of bolts rushing toward them. The pain would be brief, he hoped.

The wall suddenly parted, and a lone figure strode toward them.

"Keeper Ashara," he said, voice deep.

"General Jarat," Ashara answered. "I thought you hated the mountains."

"I wouldn't be here if it wasn't for you. Put down your weapons."

"We have no intention of returning to Yurrisa. Not yet, anyway."

"Nor do I." Jarat moved a little closer. "Malfan got the army to swear an oath of allegiance to him. Not everyone agreed. When we first joined the army, we swore to serve our Keeper and country. Not a fat, useless old general who's forgotten what soldiering is. My loyalty, and that of all these men and women around us, is to you."

Edvar's grip on his sword hadn't eased. He didn't know much about Jarat, only that he was an old-school general who'd served in the Yurrish Army his entire life. Edvar's father had mentioned him a few times. But it didn't matter who he was, or how genuine he appeared to be, nobody could be trusted, least of all the army, the very organization under Malfan's thumb. To Edvar's dismay, Ashara seemed to be buying Jarat's words. The Amast were, as ever, unreadable. Isy seemed desperate to say something.

Edvar edged closer to Ashara, whispered in his ear. "You cannot trust them, sire. Nobody can be trusted after what happened."

"It is a lack of trust that has led me down this path. To dispel all faith in others is to consign us all to death. We would be alone, this group of eight, running paranoid from the world. If I cannot trust a man whose life I have saved more than once, and who has saved mine many more times, who has devoted his entire life to this nation and its rulers, then I fear humanity is broken. If that is the case, I no longer wish to live in a world as cruel as this."

Edvar neither agreed nor disagreed. He just did not want to make the choice when their lives depended on it. He realized then that it was moments such as these that defined a leader. Finding clarity in the most difficult of times; seeing through the mist when all others are blind.

"Trust is hard to earn," said another voice, one Edvar recognized. Into the moonlight strode Camos. The old sword master walked right by Jarat and Ashara and embraced Edvar. "Your father was a true friend of mine, and you don't get many of them in life. I'd never leave his son in need."

Edvar laughed and the tension in his shoulders fell away.

Jarat stepped forward, beside Camos. "We all left the city when word of your escape reached us, hoping to find and protect you. We want you back in your rightful place, keeping safe the Vault, and we will give our lives to see that done." Jarat sunk to one knee. Camos huffed and copied, and one by one the other soldiers around them did the same.

"I give my life to keeper and country." The soldiers repeated in a chorus of allegiance. "To serve faithfully, to guard against injustice and evil, to protect the lands of Yurr and all of its people, and with my dying breath, keep the Vault of Iron sealed." It was the blood oath every man and woman swore when they first joined the Yurrish Army. To hear it said aloud by so many, at a time when Edvar felt so alone, lifted his heart and sent tears trickling down his cheeks.

They rose to their feet and saluted. Ashara stepped forward and embraced Jarat and Camos both. The surrounding soldiers lowered their shields, sheathed weapons and approached the Keeper. Ashara recognized some of those amongst the ranks and welcomed them with names, embraces and slaps on the back. The tension amongst the Amast eased too. Isy and Vil were smiling, relief palpable. Even the Amast cracked a smile in their peculiar fashion.

After nearly two days of being chased, harried by fear with nothing but the will to survive to keep them going, it was over. For now, at least. And for the first time in a while, the news was good. They had allies. Not many, but some, and that brought hope that there were others out there in the realm that still supported the Keeper. Perhaps the battle was not yet lost. No, it was just beginning.

Episode Six: The Swelling Tide

As I watched the sun descend over the horizon after another fruitless day, I hurled my hand trowel off the cliff edge in frustration. Upon my knees, fighting tears, I had the idea of exploring the rock-strewn beaches where I had tossed my tool. My final attempt, I decided. The next day, I prepped my rope and began the climb. It took hours, or so it felt, before I made it to the bottom. I admit that, at the time, my confidence was beaten, and more than once I lost my footing and had to fight to stop from giving up.

On even ground, I scoured the rock-covered beach, examined the cliff face, and found nothing. Kicking at the scree in weary frustration, my toe struck something heavy, and when my curses subsided, I knelt down to find, beneath a thicket of seaweed, a rusted cannonball.

From ***The Forgotten Daggers*** by S. T. Harris

One

BLACK SMOKE SCARRED the southern horizon. Jem couldn't hear the waves buffeting his dainty sailboat, only that terrible, rumbling thunder. A sound he had only heard the clouds make, when the sea god Eulé was angry and sent forth great waves and blinding forks to batter the coast and scorch the land.

Back upon the Green Steps, when the first horns had sounded, Jem had felt no fear. It was the moment he'd been waiting for. The reason why he, a simple fisherman from Dunmiska, had joined the Yurrish Navy: to protect those he loved from Soria's evils. But before he could retrieve his spear and shield from the barracks, an officer had come to him with a summons from Commander Balca. And now Jem was here, sailing away from the Battle of the Green Steps to Fort Novoro, carrying word of the marauding Karraban fleet. Balca had sent only him—it was all they could spare against the Karraban numbers. With thumb and forefinger, Jem rubbed the shark tooth hanging around his neck and asked Eulé to see him to Novoro safely.

With the burn in his muscles subsiding, he lifted the oars and continued to row. When darkness fell, he would raise the sail and pray the Karrabans chose not to pursue. Already a knot twisted in his stomach at the thought of falling asleep at the tiller and waking to find himself surrounded by yellow sails. He wasn't sure he could sleep anyway, not after what he'd just witnessed.

With a good breeze, he would be at Fort Novoro by dawn.
Part of him wanted to continue sailing on up the coast to
home. It had been three years since he last saw his mother,
last caught a glimpse of Abi. He wondered how they fared,
whether the fishing had been good, the potato harvests
plentiful. Soon, as they tended to do, the happier thoughts
made way for the sadder ones. The memory of the night
when raiders from the Northern Isles attacked Dunmiska
had always remained so vivid, even a decade on. With axe
and spear, his father and brother had raced to the aid of the
burning village. Women were raped. Some taken, children
too, never to be seen again. Houses were reduced to ash.
Animals were slaughtered, even the dogs, cats and chickens.

Seventy-two people in Dunmiska were murdered. His
father and brother made up that number. And Jem had done
nothing to stop it. Nothing to help. With his mother he had
watched from their home upon the hill, praying to Eulé,
tears pouring from his eyes as he battled with the urge to
rush down to the burning village in the valley below. He
would have done it if his mother had let go of him, or so he
told himself. Almost as if Eulé had heard their pleas, a
Yurrish galley spotted the raider's ship and came to
Dunmiska's aid. Since that day, the only thing that Jem had
wanted to do was become one of those fearless soldiers who
had run into the village to save lives. It was why, when he
was old enough, he'd snuck away from home and enlisted.

A splash of cold water upon his cheek brought him back
to the present. Jem looked over his shoulder. He could no
longer see the Green Steps, nor any Karraban ships, only
black clouds that, in the setting sun, seemed to be stained
red with the blood of his comrades. He took a drink from his
water skin and resumed his rowing, stopping only when the
last rays of the sun fell beyond the horizon. Every muscle in
his arms and shoulders complained. His hands were dry and
blistered. Sweat lined his skin, and his sodden clothes clung
to him. Jem stood to a chorus of clicks and, after searching
the gloomy horizon behind him, judged it safe to raise the
sail. The wind snapped it to attention, and the boat surged

forwards. He pulled in the oars and almost collapsed beside the tiller.

Fatigue aside, a weight sagged on his shoulders, a realization that he'd so far been able to push out of his mind. His friends upon the Steps, people he would die for, his brothers and sisters in arms, were all gone. Just like his father and brother.

Tears came to his eyes. It wasn't fair. But what did life care for fairness? "Fools try to predict the future, and life enjoys making fools of men," his father used to say. Jem wished he'd inherited some of the man's wisdom.

Jem ate some dried fruit and pork, drank more water, and fought the urge to close his eyes. It felt as if a couple of galleys sagged on his lids. When next he opened them, the world was no longer black but blue with the haze of dawn. He sprung forward. Jagged cliffs and small beaches stood to his right; he was heading in the same direction, at least. He dreaded to turn his eyes to the horizon for fear of finding a fleet of ships.

It was clear.

He eased back into his seat and realized the stiffness in his arms and back. Some rowing, he hoped, would loosen them.

He locked the oars in place, and as he rowed, he scanned the shore, looking for something recognizable. Much of the western coast was unremarkable cliff and rock. He just hoped he hadn't sailed right by the fort.

As the sun rose, the veil of mist hovering over the water lifted, and there, cut into the dark rock of a jutting stretch of cliff, was the jewel of Yurr's naval defenses: the Sea Fort of Novoro.

A quay with two great limpet-covered walls jutted from the cliff like powerful arms, protecting the ships docked within from Eulé's wrath. To Jem's dismay, he counted just fourteen masts. Half full. The rest must be patrolling the northern coast and outer isles, but even with them they were still outnumbered, and what good could ships do against the Karraban thunder?

Along the walls of the quay were circular stations for catapults and trebuchets, but in peacetime, they were kept in sheds beside the fort, safe from salt and water. None were out, ready to defend. They had no clue what sailed toward them, and that made Jem's mission all the more urgent.

The fort itself stretched to three-quarters of the height of the cliff. Two towers, cut out of the rock face, protruded either side of a stout wooden gate. Uniting them was a crenelated wall, again cut out of the cliff, and wide enough for trebuchets and catapults. At the very top of the cliff was a more modest-sized keep, blue flag flapping at the top of each of its four towers. Surrounding the upper keep were more batteries of trebuchets.

It was an intimidating sight to any attacker, a formidable obstacle to overcome. Indeed, it was described by the Yurrish as impenetrable. But the Karrabans had made short work of the defenses on the Green Steps, and those structures had dense and sturdy walls to protect from the wind and the waves. Could they bring down the entire cliff?

The thought of sailing straight home entered his mind again, but like a wave against rock, it clashed with another thought. *Those at Novoro will not stand a chance if I do not warn them.* To protect the people he loved. That was why he was here. If Novoro fell, what hope did Dunmiska and Yurrisa have? To flee would be to fail. Jem raised the blue flag of Yurr and began to row hard. Stitched to the flag were three green strips—the sign he had come from the Green Steps. The quay gates heaved into motion.

Six men awaited him upon the dock. Four of them held spears and shields and wore conical helms, with a blue woolen cloak over leather armor. The two most central men carried swords at their hips, and their cloaks were more of a navy hue and lined with thick furs. They were officers—the darker the shade of blue, the higher the rank in the Yurrish military. A trio of deckhands hurled ropes toward Jem, so they could pull him in. He clambered up the quay ladder and saluted those waiting for him at the top.

"I sense it isn't good news you bring?" said the smaller of the officers, a clean-shaven man with a perfectly round face.

Jem shook his head. "I bear a message for Commander Demiri."

"Better get back in that boat then. Demiri was reassigned last week. Commander Verea is in charge now."

"Then it is him I must see."

The officers exchanged a look before turning toward the monumental fort. There, at the base, the scale was truly breathtaking. Jem could see the dozens of murder holes in the battlements above. The wooden doors of the gate, made from beams the width of ancient trees, opened into a long, tight and dark tunnel. Before they came to that tunnel they passed through three portcullis gates, the walls narrowing at each hold. Jem spotted eyes looking down at him through the murder holes in the walls and ceiling. The tunnel sloped upwards until it opened up into a bright chamber lit by torches and braziers. Locked in place on a set of tracks before the door was an iron roller, nearly the width and height of the tunnel. It was covered in hundreds of iron spikes a foot long or more. Iron chains fastened it to a large winch, used to retrieve the roller after it was released. Jem shuddered at the thought of it hurtling toward him. Impaled and crushed. A gruesome way to go.

"What's your name, soldier?" the round-faced officer asked.

"Jem, sir."

"Nice to meet you, Jem. I'm Wylkes, and this miserable prick is Gundar," he said, sticking a thumb in the direction of the other officer, a bear of a man with a grey shot beard and scarred face. Gundar gave Jem a nod. Jem was sure to return it.

They went up a flight of stairs that wound on for so long Jem was sure the Karrabans had arrived by the time they reached the top. They joined a corridor, its stone walls devoid of decoration save for iron sconces and candle holders, and the occasional dusty shield bearing the white lily of Yurr. Soldiers had better things to do than dust and decorate, it seemed. They stopped at an unremarkable door and Wylkes rapped his knuckles against it. A muffled "come in" sounded from inside.

Wylkes went in first. Gundar waited for Jem to follow before closing the door behind them. Unlike the corridors, this room was much brighter, with an iron chandelier of candles hanging from the ceiling and a fire burning in a hearth to the right. Jem looked at the flames longingly. His eyes drifted to a large map of the Yurrish coast hanging over the mantel, and to the image of a horse-like creature emerging from the water in the south-east corner. Jem had always found stories of sea creatures fascinating. Each night as a child he had sat beside the fire with his father, who told him tales of monstrous squids and leviathans of the Green Deep. Now wasn't the time for reminiscing, though. Before a row of cupboards, cabinets and cluttered bookshelves was a desk of dark wood, and sat behind it was, Jem assumed, Commander Verea.

Jem had encountered many commanders in the Yurrish Navy. All had a certain way about them, a certain appearance: strong and muscular from a hard life at sea, a knowing look in their eyes that spoke of wisdom obtained by staring death in the face. They were capable and accomplished, the kind others respected and listened to. Sat before Jem was the opposite of that. Dark wispy hair clung to Verea's pate, swept across in a poor attempt at covering the pale flesh beneath. Above his furry bear-shaped ears, the hair he still did have was unkempt, mostly grey with patches of brown, and he had a dense moustache with connecting sideburns. His button-like eyes regarded Jem, brows furrowed.

Wylkes and Gundar saluted, prompting Jem to do the same. Verea's scowl eased a little, and his gaze returned to the parchment before him.

"What is it, Wylkes? I'm busy."

Jem heard the creak of Gundar's leather armor as his shoulders stiffened. Wylkes answered.

"This lad brings word from the Steps."

Verea looked up at Jem. "What word is this?"

Jem tried to focus his thoughts. "Yesterday morning we were attacked by a Karraban fleet. Fifty strong. They wiped out our ships and destroyed our forts."

"Impossible," Verea said.

"They have weapons, sir. Powerful weapons that make noises like thunder, only louder and more terrifying. I can still hear them ringing in my ears. I fear I will never know silence again. The towers upon the islands crumbled like clay under their might. Our ships couldn't even get close before they were sunk. They burned what remained to cinders and killed any survivors. Sir, this all happened in no more than an hour."

"Even *The Wayward Prince*? That ship has served for decades," Wylkes said.

"That was first to go, sir," Jem said. "Commander Balca ordered me to bring word, so that you can prepare. They will sail here next, and then to Yurrisa."

All eyes in the room turned to Verea who gazed at his parchment, quill twisting in his fingers. It was the man Jem had yet to hear speak who broke the silence.

"Well? Shall we ready the defenses? Shall we send word to Yurrisa?" Gundar asked, deep voice riddled with frustration. He looked fit to gut Verea.

"What if they do not intend to attack here?" Verea said, looking up at them.

"Are you mad, man? Whether they attack or not, we are sworn to protect this coast. If they get past us they are free to sail to Yurrisa and pillage the towns and villages from here to there. By our honor as sworn soldiers of Yurr, we cannot let them pass unhindered!" Gundar was shouting by the end. The scowl that had welcomed Jem was back on Verea's face, only with added ferociousness.

"I do not take well to that tone, Captain. Speak to me like that again and you'll be begging the Karrabans to kill you." There was venom in his voice, and Jem saw the true man. Someone who wouldn't hesitate to stab another in the back. Cunning as the rat who survives in the sewer when all others die of hunger. Verea didn't need to prove himself on the battlefield to lead. He schemed his way to the top instead.

Gundar and Verea's eyes became locked in a tense silence, until Wylkes broke it up. "What's your order, sir?" he said in as diplomatic a tone as he could.

"Prepare the defenses, and send messengers by land and sea," Verea said through gritted teeth.

The officers nodded and made to leave. Jem too.

"Not you, boy."

Jem's heart froze. He turned to face the commander, who waited for the door to close before speaking. "If you say a word about what you saw at the Green Steps to anyone in this keep, I'll cut off pieces of you one at a time and force you to eat them. Got it?"

Jem looked into Verea's pale amber eyes and recognised something he knew well: fear. Jem nodded.

"Now out of my sight and join the ranks. You'll be fighting on the battlements."

Jem found it hard to move his legs. A terrible feeling gripped his heart and chest and stifled his breath. A rush of heat swept through his body, as if he'd stepped into the kitchen of a keep on feast day. Darkness closed in, like storm clouds snuffing out the sun, and he staggered to the wall of the corridor, slumping against it, savoring the coolness of the stone. Over and over, he rubbed the shark tooth. He wanted to flee, to be far from this place and from the Karraban thunder. He wanted to be back home in his mother's embrace. He would waste no time in telling Abi how he felt. Dammit, he would ask her to marry him there and then, and who cared if she said no. That was nothing to be afraid of. Not in comparison to a fleet of Karrabans.

Slowly, normality returned. To his relief, nobody had seen him, and he didn't want to hang around in case anyone did, Verea in particular. Jem got back to his feet and began to walk.

He found his way to the ground floor and met a maelstrom of panicked activity. Men and women were pulling on bits and pieces of armor, barking orders, issuing responses. The patter of hurried feet was unrelenting. Jem froze. *What should I do? Where should I go?* The last place he wanted to go was the wall. He spied the door leading outside through the press of bodies.

Jem hurried down the quay to his sailboat, trying his best not to seem eager. The quay gates were still open. The desire to flee consumed every thought and feeling, but a voice of opposition spoke out too, telling him to stay, to fight. He reached his boat. Jem glanced back at the great fort. Could it withstand that terrible thunder?

A horn shattered the quiet morning, a deep, long blast that turned higher in tone. He snapped his head in the direction from which it came—the opposite wall of the quay. The horn sounded again. Bells rang out from the keep upon the cliff. Shouting along the walls and around the fort added to the frenzy.

Jem looked to the horizon.

Two

For over a week, Isy had bounced about in the saddle, clutching onto Vil. The chafing was torturous, particularly with Vil's riding. At first, his handle of the mahogany charger was frail and the mare knew it, but Vil's confidence had grown and Isy's grasping of his waist and clothes had eased. He'd since taken to showing her the basics of riding, like the importance of keeping a straight back and moving up and down to the rhythm of the horse. Learning how to ride didn't make her like it any more. But it beat walking and gave her injured leg a chance to mend.

The line of cavalry was six hundred strong, trotting along in three columns, with a small herd of remounts at the back and more pulling a few supply wagons. Jarat had taken most of the horses in Yurrisa in the hope of eliminating the chance of pursuit. It seemed to have worked so far.

In the middle of the line, just ahead of Isy and Vil, rode Ashara, Edvar and Jarat. Yera had continued to tend to the Keeper's wound and after a night of undisturbed sleep, he appeared a man renewed.

Since they'd broken camp that morning, the Keeper and his two advisors had ridden side by side, bodies bent toward one another in conversation. There had been no laughter, no smiles. Isy wanted to know what it was they discussed. Perhaps she would ask Edvar later. She'd found herself beside him around the fire the past few nights and the conversations had flowed as freely as the wine, which never seemed to run dry. Isy was unused to drinking, and the sweet liquid had a knack for loosening her tongue. Edvar had asked her about Haberdam and she had told him everything, from the names she was called to being chased and hunted through the town by the other children, and of the times her father had beaten her.

"I may have been born there, but it's never felt like home," Isy had said two nights before. She and Edvar had been the last by the fire, the others retiring drunk. "They don't want me there. I would leave and never return if only I had somewhere else to go."

"I know this pales in comparison to what you have endured, but when I was growing up, I too was cast aside by others," Edvar said. "I had no friends. I could never find anyone who didn't tease me for being skinny, tall and spotty. They used to call me Spider-Boy and Eddie Long Legs. I spent all my time alone, reading. My father used to say: 'It matters not how you appear, only what you do.' I say it does matter how you appear, sometimes. But he is right— as so often he is, or was—that the people worth spending time with are the people who do not care how you appear, that look into your eyes and see you for who you are. The real person within. Know this, Isy, that how you look may matter to some people, but it does not matter to me."

Isy nodded and blinked tears from her bleary eyes. It all made so much sense. Breaking her conditioned thoughts was so difficult, but she was determined to do it. "This journey and the people I have met have given me so much. I had no life before. Now I know what living is, what purpose and desire feel like. I have found a reason to go on. Hopefully, we still have time to help the Amast."

"You said they are gravely ill?"

Isy nodded. "I have never seen so many dead bodies before. The sight troubles me still. My greatest fear is that we return to their camp too late."

Gentle thuds and the swish of grass brought Isy back to the present. She turned to find Kora jogging toward them. The Amast had refused the offer of mounts. In fairness, even the biggest of destriers would have struggled to carry them. Instead, they walked in their lumbering fashion, close to the back of the line. In the past week, more than a few helmeted heads had glanced in their direction, though none had given them a wide berth, a fact acknowledged and respected by the Amast.

Isy smiled at Kora, and he reciprocated in his grimace-like fashion.

"Is there news of a plan?" Kora asked. Isy gazed further along the line at the three strategos.

"They've been chatting like that all morning."

Kora looked too, ears twitching, seemingly trying to hear them. "Perhaps I will ask," he said and jogged forward toward them.

Through the swathes of white clouds, Isy had been tracking the direction of the sun and was of the belief they were heading north-west. Up ahead she saw a post with arrowed signs nailed to it, and as they passed, Isy saw "Hiscaria" etched into the one that was pointing in the direction they were headed.

"Are we heading to Haberdam?" Isy asked.

Vil hesitated before answering. "I'm not sure. I overheard some soldiers talking about Haberdam before." His eyes were on the back of their horse's neck.

"Vil! Why didn't you tell me?" Isy glared daggers at him and the saddle took on a whole new level of discomfort. A knife laced with poisonous dread stabbed at her gut, but oddly, the tide of anxiety that usually followed did not overwhelm her as so often it did.

Ever since the night she had told Edvar about her life in Haberdam, she'd felt purged of her troubled thoughts. She found a part of her *did* want to return. She wanted to see her mother again, feel the security of her embrace, tell her of her kidnapping, of the terror of the paska and ikata, of her new friends and how she had helped them, and of the great city upon the coast with its giant walls and towers and vicious people. She felt a surge of pride, a feeling that morphed into a determination to stand up to her father, to stand up to her bullies with her head held high in the knowledge that her birthmark didn't matter.

But like a wolf stalking wounded prey, fear lingered. The fear that had ruled her life. The fear of being abused, beaten, killed. She knew she had to let go of it, to lock it away in the past. Otherwise, it would haunt her forever, would influence how she thought and felt about every facet of her life. It clung on like tree sap, and it would take all the courage she had gained to scrape herself clean once and for all. Returning to Haberdam and confronting those fears, she hoped, would help achieve that.

"I'm sorry, Isy. I didn't want to tell you right away. I knew it would be tough, but remember I'm here, so is Kora and the others. You'll be safe with us. And think of the Amast. Why else would we be going to Haberdam if not to get them help? It's the closest town to their camp." Vil half turned his head, a flicker of a smile upon his face. "We've nearly done what we set out to do."

Vil's words thawed her worries. A grin even crept to her lips. Vil was right.

Her friend went on.

"It'll be strange going back. It feels like so long since I left. When I first heard mention of Haberdam, I was glad. I thought about reading beside the hearth, sitting in my cushioned chair, the cat curled up on my lap, purring softly... That thought used to fill me with such joy, such relief. Now it feels hollow.

"I think something changed in me when I went to look for you. Walking through those pitch-dark woods scared me to the marrow, but the idea of giving up never really entered my mind. I had to find you. And I'm here, and I feel proud not to have turned back. It taught me that I can do things the world tells me I cannot, things that even my own mind tells me I'm unable or too weak to do. I learned what it feels like to be alive, to do things that truly matter. Well, more so than emptying the Chronicler's bed pot. I don't know... it just beats reading about people doing great things. We're *here*, doing them ourselves."

Isy smiled, gave his waist a squeeze, and rested her head on his back. He put into words so much of what she was feeling. "If I'm to return home, I'm glad you'll be with me," she said.

The pine trees that had flanked them for so long disappeared on their left side and gave way to a small lake. A flock of white birds covered every inch of a tiny island close to the far bank and made a fine job of filling each fleeting moment with scratchy caws. They didn't quieten at the sight of the small army. Ashara called a halt for a brief rest and men and women dismounted and led their mounts to the water. Still the birds cawed.

Perhaps they sense the unease in the world. Or maybe they warn us of our folly? Isy wondered.

The rest of the Amast approached Isy and Vil, and Tulasc offered Isy a hand down, which she gladly took. She grimaced as her feet touched the ground. Her legs were stiff, arse raw and numb, lower back and shoulders tender. Her ankle was healing too. The swelling had reduced, and it was more mobile than it had been the days before.

"You should walk, little Isy," Yera said. "There is no better thing."

"For you maybe," she said, rubbing her backside to try and rid herself of the dead sensation.

"Here is Kora," Pekira said. Isy turned to find Kora approaching, and with him were the Keeper, Edvar, Jarat and the grumpy old soldier Camos. She put a swift end to rubbing her rump and straightened her clothes and hair. She caught a grin upon Edvar's face. His eyes never missed a thing, though, like the Amast, he didn't seem to notice her mark.

Isy, Vil and the Amast bowed to the Keeper.

"We have a plan and I wanted your thoughts before we finally decide," Ashara said. "We intend to ride to a town not far from here, called Haberdam, and I believe not far from the Amast camp. It is my intention to secure the allegiance of Rijkard, Baron of Haberdam, and an agreement that your people be moved there to recover. We will gather supplies and ride on to the camp of your people. Once war is over I will find land in Yurr for your new home. If you do not agree, we will think of another plan, but all of us, your kinsman Kora included, believe this to be the best course."

Heads turned to Kora, who nodded in agreement.

The Amast looked at each other, and Isy saw tears welling in their bulbous eyes. "Thank you," Pekira said, stepping forward and kneeling before Ashara, head coming up to his chest.

Tulasc and Yera copied, gushing thanks, and then came Isy's own tears. The realization that they had nearly succeeded, that the Amast would be saved, struck in waves of euphoria. For so long it felt as if it would never happen. Travelling all that way only to be chased right back with their one hope of salvation with them.

But they had nearly done it. Success was a feeling she was unused to, and the joy overwhelmed her fear of returning home. Like Edvar had said, it didn't matter what the people of Haberdam thought of her. She had helped save the Amast. What had they ever done besides gossip, mock and abuse?

Ashara had begun talking again. "It has been many years since Rijkard and I last saw one another, and the encounter wasn't pleasant. He is a dissident bastard, defiant at any opportunity, just like his father, and he will not want to agree to my proposal, but by my dying breath I will see that he does."

Isy bit her lip. Excitement ebbed and a bitter taste filled her mouth at hearing that name. Rijkard, a man more stubborn than a tired and lame mule. He had treated Isy as the others in town had—like something foul he'd stepped in.

She remembered her mother petitioning him for protection after Isy had been beaten by the other children so badly her face looked like a rotten plum. He had done nothing. He cared more for his seat of power than he did justice. And that selfish attitude had trickled down to the people. She couldn't even begin to imagine how those in

Haberdam would react to the Amast. How would that affect Rijkard's decision? Isy feared to consider the answers. She was just glad they had a small army with them.

Three

Edvar found himself staring doubt in the face once again as the column trotted into motion. *Have I made the right decision?* Since his last conversation with Isy a couple of nights back his thoughts had been whirring, trying to solve the puzzle in his mind. Ashara and Jarat had wanted to go straight to Baroness Jalden. No other baron in the realm held as much influence and commanded more soldiers. It was the logical first step. Baron Rijkard on the other hand, was the most dissident and had the fewest soldiers. The greatest risk, if anything. But if they went to Rijkard, they could help the Amast, and from what Isy had said, they didn't have much more time to do so.

"Why even bother with Rijkard at all?" Jarat had said.

"Because if we get Rijkard onside, think of the message it sends to the rest," Edvar replied. "The least supportive baron of them all first to declare loyalty. It would extinguish any doubt the other barons and baronesses have and all but guarantee their allegiance. And war aside, Isy tells me the camp of the Amast isn't far from Haberdam. Those that are there are sick and weak and may not hold out much longer, especially with the weather turning. We could help them too and stone two birds at once."

Ashara laughed. "I must say that sounds sensible to me."

"It's a risk, though. What if that prick Rijkard has already sided with the Council?" Jarat asked. "You say he's always wanted independence. What if they've promised to give it to him?"

Edvar frowned. He couldn't deny that it was a possibility.

"Well, if the barons and baronesses have indeed turned on me, better to go first to the one that we can overpower," Ashara said.

"Good point," Jarat said.

"Then it's agreed. Haberdam it is."

The thought now playing on Edvar's mind was whether his plan would offend Isy. He knew how much she wanted to save the Amast, but only two nights before had she told him of how much she hated Haberdam, of how miserable her life there was. And he had manufactured the move to lead her back there.

The Keeper rode up beside him, stirring Edvar from his thoughts. "You seem glum, Ed? Everything well?"

"Yes, sire. Just thinking, is all."

"I can hazard a guess as to what."

Edvar gave him a quizzical look.

"You've been spending a lot of time with that young girl. Isy, is she called? I've never seen you say so much to a woman before." Ashara chuckled. "I know the symptoms of lovesickness, Ed. The endless questions running through your mind. Does she, doesn't she? Should I, shouldn't I?"

Edvar's cheeks burned. "She's interesting. I like talking to her is all." He looked over his shoulder at Isy, further back in the column, her head bobbing along behind Vil. Her gaze was fixed on the ground, eyes holding all of Soria's worries. Edvar sighed.

Four

Vil estimated they'd been away for three turns of the wandering moon. To Isy, it felt like three turns of the sun. The road wound to the left and down a gentle slope to run alongside the River Haber. Its banks were swollen with recent rainfall, churning water a muddy brown from the runoff. At the sight of the first houses of the town, Isy's heart began to race, battering her ribcage in an attempt to flee. Already people had stopped to watch the cavalry file into town. A few children waved at the soldiers—who reciprocated—but most stopped and stared. There wasn't much love for the Yurrish Army here. Haberdam had been sacked by raiders more than a few times over the years and help was always too late in coming. The scars of the past ran deep, and the people here were cursed with good memories.

Like an itch, Isy felt the urge to yank down her hood over her face. She fought it. Vil pulled the horse out of the column and stopped.

"What are you doing?" she asked as he hopped down.

"You're on your own the rest of the way," he said, handing her the reins.

She frowned at him, confused.

"You need to do this, Isy. Remember what I showed you. Keep your back straight and use your legs." And with that, he turned and headed back toward the Amast. It was then that Isy understood. She smiled, looked ahead at the town and the feathers of smoke rising from chimneys, and as Vil had taught her, kicked the mare on.

Isy sat straight and tall in the saddle and looked down at those she passed. The faces she saw contorted with bafflement, confusion and fear. This was a test, by no means her last but certainly the biggest, and Vil knew it. He knew that she had to face it alone, to be brave, to overcome the pain of her life and take the next step forward. He knew her so well. It shamed her that she knew so little in turn.

Wooden houses were replaced by stone as they moved deeper into Haberdam. More and more people gathered in the narrow dirt roads. Eyes were mostly fixed on the Amast and her. Fingers pointed, hands covered mouths. Hundreds of hooves pattered, armor and mail rattled. Dogs, confused and afraid, barked over and over, masking the gasps, the murmurs, and no doubt the curses and mockery—she could still see the leers, though, the movement of mouths.

They arrived at the square, which quickly filled. Through the press of soldiers and horses, Isy saw the door of the town watch barracks swing open. The lanky form of Captain Gerdasa stepped outside. The annoyance upon his face soon dissolved at the sight of so many armed soldiers.

Gerdasa was tall and slender, with a narrow face dominated by a drooping moustache. A conical iron helm adorned his head, attached chainmail draping over his neck and shoulders. He didn't wear the blue tabard of Yurr, rather the purple of Haberdam, complete with its thistle emblem. Isy preferred the Yurrish lily.

Ashara, Edvar and Jarat dismounted. Isy was close enough to hear them.

"Where is Baron Rijkard?" Ashara asked.

Gerdasa stuttered. "He isn't here. May I ask who enquires?"

"Keeper Ashara."

Gerdasa's face bunched and settled into a disbelieving smile. He shook his head.

"If you enjoy your position, Captain, you would do well to fetch him," Edvar said.

"Unnecessary," said a deep voice that carried over the clamor in the square. The volume dropped further and into view strode Baron Rijkard. His black, fur-lined cloak hovered above the mud of the ground. His hair had once been a similar hue but was now speckled with grey. He was clean-shaven, with bright amber eyes set back under deep brows. To Isy, he was the embodiment of sternness.

"It is not often we see the Keeper of Yurr in these parts," Rijkard said. "We are deemed too far from the comforts of the city, or that was the case the last time an invitation was extended." He made no move to welcome Ashara, stopping a few feet before him, beside the gangly Gerdasa. Rijkard's eyes scanned the crowd of soldiers and when he saw the Amast they briefly widened with a mix of fear and panic. Then they fell upon Isy and his heavy brows furrowed.

"We were in the area," Ashara said, maintaining some warmth to his tone.

"I'm sure you were. Let's talk more inside," Rijkard said, holding out his hand for Ashara to lead the way.

"Jarat, see to the camp," Ashara said.

"Aye, sire."

And with that the Keeper and Edvar left. Jarat ordered a small force to stay in the square, with the rest to head to the fields outside the town to make camp. Through the shifting mass of bodies, Vil and the Amast appeared, smiling.

"Your home is pretty," Tulasc said. His gaze wandered about the town, observing the buildings. "I have many questions."

Vil laughed.

"As do I," Yera said.

"I think I'll go give the Chronicler a heart attack," Vil said. "I'll catch up with you all later." He disappeared amongst the crowd.

A pang of panic stirred in Isy's chest at seeing Vil go. What she had to do next made her feel no better.

"Do you want to come to my house?" Isy asked the Amast. The words felt strange. Indeed, it was the first time she had ever invited anybody to her home.

"Lead the way," said Kora.

Isy looked at him, nausea churning in her gut. Kora gave her a smile, and from somewhere one came to her lips too. She nodded more to herself than to anyone else, and began to walk.

Five

Edvar wrinkled his nose. The ill-lit reception chamber of the barracks stunk of cat piss. Before the flames of the hearth, he found the source: a big, monochrome tomcat curled up in a wicker basket. Was the stench worth fewer rats?

Up a winding staircase they went, led by one of the Baron's servants, the silent Baron himself haunting their steps behind. They soon arrived at the top and were led into an unremarkable room with a rectangular four-paned window overlooking the bustling town square. A packed floor-to-ceiling bookcase covered the wall to their right. Embers crackled in a small hearth to their left. Only a series of iron candle-holders broke up the monotony of the bare, russet walls, the paint flaking like dry skin. A wooden desk cluttered with papers and piles of books, as well as a few miniature carvings of peculiar creatures, stood before the window, a padded chair one side and three rickety chairs the other.

"This is my office for when I need to get work done. The guards do a good job of ensuring I'm not disturbed. Can I fetch you a drink? Water? Wine? Perhaps something stronger?" Rijkard asked.

"Water would serve well," Ashara said. Edvar nodded that he too would like some, though he would have rather gone for wine to help ease the pain of days in the saddle. They sat down, Rijkard dismissing his young servant who barely lifted his eyes from the ground. Edvar suspected he'd received a few lashings for looking at the wrong person at the wrong time.

"So, what brings you to Haberdam, though I have an idea?"

"And what is this idea you have?" Ashara asked.

"Why, your abdication of course."

Ashara laughed and shook his head, no doubt masking the same thoughts racing through Edvar's mind: how had those bastards managed to get word here so soon?

"I can assure you I haven't abdicated," Ashara said.

Rijkard sat back, his chair creaking, and looked out of the window. "You can assure me all you like. From what I can see, you're a keeper with nothing to keep. I'm guessing from your entourage that you don't intend to take this lying down?"

Ashara let silence answer for him.

"If I help you, what's to stop the new rulers of Yurr marching here and torching my town and killing my people? A few hundred horses won't be enough to protect them."

"Don't let Jarat hear you say that."

"You have, at least, one of the better generals on your side."

"We have fought together, Rijkard. You are a born leader, and you are true of heart. These traitors who squabble over my throne cannot be trusted. Power has corrupted them and driven them in pursuit of their own ends. They are everything you loathe. I fear they will try to open the Vault."

"And where is the Key of Ulara?"

From under his collar, Ashara took out a heavy chain. It was looped through the ring of an iron key the length of his hand. Ancient words were etched into its stem, and sprouting from its end were three pins, each notched with elaborate key wards. That key alone could open the Vault. Should it be lost, it would remain sealed. Or so was the intention.

"They'll come looking for you if indeed it's their intention to open it. And that prospect pleases me as much as the sight of those creatures you brought with you."

Edvar twitched with anger. He looked to Ashara, who gave a slight shake of his head.

"But you agree that the Vault must not be opened?" Ashara and Rijkard locked eyes.

"Of course. But with the key here and no other way in, you're still to convince me as to why I should risk my people to help you?"

Ashara sighed, and for the briefest of moments, Edvar saw regret in Rijkard's eyes.

"You think me a beaten man, Rijkard? All this land you claim to love so much, it is my family who gave it to yours for helping to ensure the survival of Yurr. That survival is now threatened, and by every fiber of my being, I will not stand idle and allow it to come to fruition."

Rijkard looked unmoved to the point of disinterested.

"You may not find it in your heart to love or respect me, Rijkard, but I know damn well the other barons of Yurr do, and I swear on the soul of my good mother, that if you side against me, I will muster an army and march them here first. But do I even need their help? I have six hundred of the finest and most loyal soldiers in Yurr all over your little town. If I tell them to pillage and burn, they will."

"You wouldn't do that to your own people."

"Wouldn't I? *Your* decision would make them traitors to the realm."

Edvar could hear Rijkard grinding his teeth. The baron swallowed, tore his gaze away from the keeper.

"My loyalty, as it always has been, is to you, *sire*," he said as if someone was twisting a knife in his back.

Edvar shifted in his seat. *How can Ashara trust this man? And it was my idea to come here...* Had he made another foolish mistake? Jarat had argued against it. Was he right? Edvar took a deep breath and told himself to have faith in his convictions. *Easier said than done.*

"I did not doubt it for a heartbeat," Ashara said, upbeat. "Which is why I need something else from you."

Rijkard pulled at the hairs of his beard. "Which is?"

"A few days walk from here, toward the Giant's Garden, there is a camp of a group of people known as the Amast—these 'creatures' as you describe them. The Karrabans destroyed their home and they are in desperate need of aid. I require food, water and able bodies to help bring them back here."

"Here?! You want to bring more of those things here? First, you insult me by bringing back that cursed bitch, and now you want me to harbor more of those... monsters? There'll be outrage. The people won't stand for it." By the end of his outburst, Rijkard was on his feet.

"Then make them stand for it," Edvar said, throwing back his chair in fury. "And the only curse that poor girl has is that she cares too much. She has more courage and dignity than you could ever dream of."

Rijkard scowled, but it did not send Edvar's anger waning. Rijkard broke his gaze and looked to Ashara.

"You need to keep your mutt chained."

"I'm afraid he's chewed through the links." Ashara stood, too. "Have everything ready by morning. We ride at first light."

"We?"

"Indeed. I think you coming to meet our new friends would be a fine idea. And besides, it'll give us an opportunity to catch up."

Judging by the look of incredulity in Rijkard's eyes, he didn't agree.

Six

Isy's steps lacked enthusiasm. The Amast poured a stream of questions in her direction—what were the windows made from? How did they make their thatched roofs? Her answers were growing shorter. It wasn't their fault, she knew. She simply didn't have the headspace. Her focus was on her mother and father. The tension was near suffocating now, and the idea of turning around was growing in her mind. Her legs kept moving.

The people she passed stopped and stared at them. Some even yelped and fled. Once again, she felt the urge to mask her face, but she found greater strength to resist. *What do I have to fear? Nothing.* She straightened her back and shoulders and felt as tall as the Amast.

At the top of the rise in the road, peeking out behind an ancient pine tree, was the wooden form of her single-storey house. A stream of white smoke twisted from the chimney, fragrancing the air with pine. The repetitive sound of chopping wood stilled her heart. She knew who it was. Not much had changed, it seemed.

"Here it is," she almost whispered to the Amast as they crested the rise.

Their white and black goat, Milly, was grazing upon the grass before the house. She looked up at the group and the rate of her chewing slowed.

"That is like tura," Pekira said.

"What's tura?" Isy asked.

"Like that, but taller, with powerful muscles, thicker fur and great horns that curve like my knife. They live around the mountains. I swear by Lefala that I have seen them walking along a cliff face."

"It is so," Tulasc said.

"I'd like to see them one day," Isy said.

The chopping went on—her father round the back of the house, no doubt, oblivious to their arrival. The front door, though, swung on its hinges. Her mother flew out of the house and rushed toward her, shawl slipping from her shoulders and landing in the mud. She looked thin, fatigued, grey hair at her temples, and bags under eyes that streamed tears. Isy couldn't contain her own. They met in an embrace, sobbed into each other's shoulders and held on like they never wanted to let go.

"I thought I'd lost you forever," her mother said.

"You can't get rid of me that easy." They hugged until Isy remembered that the Amast were waiting behind her.

"Ma, I want you to meet my friends." She introduced them in turn and was proud of her mother for not recoiling at the sight of them. Kora gave her a deep bow.

"It is an honor to meet the mother of the woman who has helped save my people." The rest of the Amast copied, even steely Pekira.

Isy's mother gave her an inquisitive look, but Isy's gaze had shifted to something behind her. The chop of wood had ceased, and beside the house, axe in hand, stood her father. He looked as if he'd seen the ghosts of his parents. With squinted eyes, he took a few slow steps toward them, grip on his axe firm.

The weight of a house fell upon Isy's chest. "Hello, Pa," she mustered the courage to say.

He looked at her, then at the Amast, then back at her, unable to settle, unable, it seemed, to comprehend what was before him. His eyes began to twitch, a reaction she'd seen before. More than once. Isy shuffled away. She knew what was coming. Her mother stepped before her. He edged closer. Raised his axe. His deep-set eyes were wide and wild.

He breathed in heavy wheezes, rage threatening to blow him apart. His pace increased. Isy's mother shouted his name, but he did not hear. Lost to anger, his eyes were on Isy and the Amast. He hefted his axe. Isy pushed her mother aside. Kora pushed Isy out the way, and with a long-reaching leg, kicked Isy's father hard in the chest. The axe left his hand and he fell backwards, head hitting the ground, hard.

Isy picked up the axe and stood over the man who had sired her, who had rejected her, who had made her life a misery. He seemed so weak, so frail and afraid, cowering behind his hands, gasping for air like a fish out of water. He began to weep and moan like a dying man. The sound bore into Isy's temples.

Her mother had regained her feet with a hand from Yera and embraced Isy once again. "He's broken. He doesn't speak to me anymore. Just drinks and grunts, works and sleeps. Sometimes he eats. I've heard him muttering to himself. I don't know what to do."

The axe felt light in her hand, its edge pointing down at her father. "I have no love for him, Ma. He has never been a father to me. I always hoped that he could change. The very idea broke him."

Despite her hatred for her father, Isy had no desire to take his life. She dropped the axe on the floor beside him.

Isy looked her mother in the eye. "I didn't run away, Ma. I wouldn't leave without saying goodbye. In kind of a funny way, I was kidnapped, by Kora." She turned and pointed to the Amast man.

Her mother's face contorted with confusion. "Please, you must come inside and tell me all," she said, and they went in, giving her writhing father a wide berth.

The Amast had to crouch to get through the doorway. Tulasc still managed to bang his head. They sat cross-legged on the ground around the hearth. While her mother made mint tea and offered around fresh bread rolls—Isy's favorite—Isy told her tale. For the entire time, her mother gaped, and when at last Isy had finished, she had still found no words.

"Everything is different now, Ma. I feel different. I feel... alive. I suppose what I'm saying is, I can't stay here. If I did, I'd go back to my miserable existence, and to be honest, I'd sooner die than do that."

"You're leaving then?" her mother asked, tears welling in her eyes.

Isy nodded. "Only this time at least I get to say goodbye."

"You speak as if you'll never come back."

"I don't think I will."

Tears ran down her mother's cheeks and she held back a cry, swallowed hard and regained some composure. "I understand." She hugged Isy tightly. "I'm sorry," she whispered through her sniffs.

"You have nothing to apologize for." Isy kissed her cheek.

They sat a while, enjoying each other's presence. Isy told more tales of what she had seen and done, with the help of the Amast who seemed more than at ease, laughing and joking. When at last the deep blue of dusk took hold, they said their farewells. Tulasc bumped his head on his way out. Pekira laughed.

There was no sign of Isy's father outside. Just Milly, chewing as always. Isy embraced her mother a final time and, after a last glance around the house she had once called home, turned and walked away.

Seven

Jem stood motionless while around him chaos unfolded. Orders were barked, answers shrieked. Men and women darted this way and that, their armor and mail clinking and rattling. Despite cracking whips, horses strained to pull catapults and carts laden with stones and iron balls from the wooden sheds lining the quay. Over the clamor, came the steady beat of drums from the Karraban ships.

Jem didn't know what to do, where to go. Everything around him became a blur. His ears rang like they had the first time he'd witnessed the Karraban thunder and his knees almost buckled in fear of experiencing it again. The gates of the quay closed with a grumble, and beyond, the Karraban ships with their yellow sails unfurled, grew in size and number. There was no hope of fleeing now. His fate lay in Novoro.

A deep voice cut through the noise and soldiers stilled and slowed. Gundar had seemingly grown a foot taller. His broad shoulders were clad in polished iron pauldrons, with layered plate covering his chest and legs. In one hand he held an open-faced helm tipped with a black plume of horsehair, and in his other a battleaxe, the blade broad as a guillotine. He looked capable of cutting a Karraban ship in two. Seeing him, hearing him, watching him bellow orders, dispelling panic and inspiring confidence, lifted Jem from his paralysis of fear. His instructions were clear, simple, effective and soldiers listened. Even those trained and well-practised in their drills can lose their way without leadership. Gundar went within the keep and Jem followed.

His shortsword hung at his hip, bow and quiver, stripped of their canvas covers, dangled over his shoulders, and his circular wooden shield, wrapped in boiled leather, was strapped to his off-hand. Verea had ordered him to the wall, but he wasn't sure how to get there and wasn't keen to find out. As soon as they reached the first of the inner chambers, Gundar began shouting orders. But the fifty or so soldiers inside ignored him. Instead, their gaze was fixed on someone in the center of the room. He too was clad in polished iron plate, only with a blue trim. His helmet was a tall, conical creation tipped with a white plume, twice as long as Gundar's, giving him the look of some exotic breed of chicken.

"It is I who command these men, Captain Gundar. Not you." It was, of course, Verea.

Gundar approached the commander, men and women parting for him, until he stood before him like a hulking tower. "And what is it you command them to do?"

Verea's armored fists clenched and he jabbed a finger in Gundar's direction. "I do not answer to you."

"Do you tell them to heat the pitch and stock arrows, to ensure the spike roller is oiled and working?"

"I am tired of your insolence, Gundar. You will do as I say, and I command you to take the wall."

Gundar did something Jem didn't expect. He laughed, but his humor quickly died. "Have you seen what sails toward us?"

Verea's eyes narrowed.

"Well, *Commander*, I invite you to join me on the wall to see for yourself." Gundar held out his hand toward the stairwell, and after a lingering stare, Verea went.

Gundar looked about him, locked eyes with Jem, and nodded for him to follow. Reaching the battlements, Verea slowed to a stop, his mouth catching flies.

"You said fifty ships. Did you lie to me boy?"

Jem moved between the parapets. He too stopped in his tracks. The sea around Novoro had turned yellow for all the sails. The great galleons he had seen from afar bobbed around swells of smaller ships. He could hear the steady and ominous beat of the drums, louder than ever. No thunder. Not yet. "There wasn't this many at the Steps, sir."

Verea's eyes didn't shift from the approaching fleet. "There's no way we can repel them all. There must be at least thirty thousand soldiers on all of those ships. Have they sent an envoy? Perhaps we can negotiate a truce."

"Do you hear your own words, man?" Gundar barked. "A truce? Novoro is all that stands between here and Yurrisa. These Karraban bastards will destroy everything and you want to let them? You're even more of a fool than I thought. You're not fit to lead. Stand down and give us all a chance."

Verea trembled. Jem wasn't sure if it was with rage or fear. He almost slashed Jem's shoulder pulling his sword from its sheath. "I've had it with your insubordination. If you cannot follow my orders, you shall not serve under me."

Gundar's face contorted into a look of terrible anger. In half a heartbeat, the knife at his hip was in his hand, and in the other, it was plunged into Verea's neck, through the gap in his armor. With shock still etched on Verea's face, Gundar lifted him up over his head and hurled him over the wall.

Jem couldn't quite believe what he had witnessed. From the looks on the faces of the other men and women around them, they couldn't either.

"Spread word," Gundar shouted. "I now lead the defense." He put on his plumed helm. "Artillery will be ready to loose at the sound of my horn." Men and women scattered. Jem wasn't sure whether to go with them.

"You, lad. Stay at my side. You've seen these bastards in battle. I want you to tell me everything they're up to. And I want you to tell me more of this thunder."

The sounds of the Karraban war machine grew as Jem recounted everything he had seen at the Green Steps. Gundar's eyes forever watched the enemy fleet but he did not miss a word of Jem's. More than once a soldier came to his side, but he held up his hand to stop them interrupting. It was information he wanted, anything he could use to help him repel these killers from the east. But Jem sensed his dissatisfaction. He could offer no telling detail that would swing the battle in their favor, only set out the storm that would strike Novoro. When Jem had finished, Gundar looked at him. In his eyes he saw for the briefest of moments a flicker of desperation, a glimmer of self-doubt. What remained of Jem's resolve waivered. How could they succeed if their leader, their only hope, did not believe they would? The defenders upon the wall had grown quiet too. Six hundred, at least, stood tall against their fear along the parapets, awaiting the horns of war.

But Gundar was no coward; that much was clear from the fleeting time Jem had known him. His eyes returned to the fleet, and a cold, fierce look of determination descended over his face. He began to walk along the wall, eyes still fixed on the Karrabans. As Gundar had ordered, Jem followed. Soldiers saluted, stood to attention and stepped aside for their new leader. Gundar clasped their hands, slapped their backs and wished them good fortune. And then, to the background noise of the Karraban drums, Gundar stood upon a crenel and addressed his warriors.

"Death sails toward us, but I don't feel like dying today. Do you?"

The Yurrish roared their defiance.

"These Karrabans killed our men at the Steps. They'll kill us too, and then sail on to rape, pillage and murder those we love, those we've vowed to protect. They'll burn our homes, defile our lands, wipe us from history. Are we to stand here and let them? Or are we to kill every last bastard who sets foot on our land and burn those piss-poor ships they call a fleet?!"

Men and women cheered, beat their shields, stomped the floor with the butts of their spears. It rippled along the wall, down the stairs and through the entire keep until, it seemed, the whole cliff shook. Jem roared as loud as his voice would allow, till his throat and lungs burned. It was an exorcism of his fear, a trigger for adrenaline to surge. His body tingled. The grip on his spear tightened. Gundar blew his war horn, a sound that quietened the Karraban drums and shook Jem's bones, sending another wave of power coursing through his body.

The trebuchets hurled their great rocks, and the battle for Novoro began.

Episode Seven: Why We Fight

The joy, or rather, the relief I felt at finding that piece of iron was like learning a loved one had survived a terrible ordeal. My heart had married itself to this cause, and indeed that night, after being driven off the beach by the tide, I gazed over my find like an infatuated teen. I could not sleep, yet dawn did not tarry, and before the sun had risen, I had returned to the cliff to await the retreat of the waves.

Upon the beach once more, I scoured every bit of sand and scree, dug deep, and found naught. I went on further down the beach, risking being cut off by the returning tide. Around a bend, I came to a peculiar formation in the cliff face—a jagged tear in the rock, too high to climb up to, yet frustratingly close. I'd brought a few sticks of dynamite with me. I retreated from their sizzling, and once the ringing in my ears had subsided and the falling rock had stilled, the dust settled to reveal, to my besotted delight, a cave.

From ***The Forgotten Daggers*** by S. T. Harris

One

LIKE A FLOCK of dive-bombing gulls, the great stones of the Yurrish trebuchets and catapults twisted and turned in the air. One jagged chunk struck the bow of a Karraban galley and splinters and shards burst forth to a chorus of cracks and screams. Another great boulder obliterated the masthead of a nearby ship, hurling those upon the deck overboard.

More missed than struck. The yellow tide did not falter.

Driven forward by oars, the Karraban fleet ate up the water, moving in a diagonal line. The trebuchets were taking an age to reload. From his vantage point, Jem could see those on the quay hurrying to winch back the catapults. At the sound of a frantic horn, the arms of the catapults were unleashed and clusters of iron balls and stones rained down on those ships leading the Karraban charge, puncturing hulls, sails and decks.

Still, they came.

The trebuchets, ranges adjusted, loosed again and once more struck a destructive blow. Yet the Karrabans persisted. Yurrish archers upon the quay walls unleashed their first volley. Unfortunate rowers upon the open decks screamed, and the momentum of a number of ships waned, oars falling slack or tangling with others. One talented or lucky archer struck a helmsman, and the galley veered into another, scraping its side and snapping its oars, and, no doubt, the arms of a few oarsmen too.

The Karrabans answered with arrows of their own, archers placed in crow's nests and platforms built amongst the rigging. The air quickly grew thick with darts. Incrementally drowning out the shouts and cries of men and women were the great crashes of stone against wood as the loads of catapults and trebuchets fell. The frenetic scene around the quay wall absorbed Jem's attention. Creeping into the top of his vision, looming behind the chaos, came the first of the great galleons. Its rowers slowed, turned portside, level with the quay gate.

"Sir, the galleon carries the thunder. You must stop it!" Jem shouted.

Gundar looked to where he pointed and nodded. He dispatched messengers to the quay and artillery stations. Jem spotted hatches opening on the portside of the ship. Catapults continued to fire at the galleys, though some quick-thinking engineers had turned their aim to the galleon. Their loads fell short. The trebuchets were still reloading. They were the only ones who had a hope of hitting it, if any of their operators had the presence of mind to know where to aim.

One by one, the great wooden arms of the trebuchets sprung forwards. Huge rocks hung in the air like eagles. Everyone upon the wall had their eyes upon them, hoping they struck, willing them to do so, and despairing as they watched each one splash harmlessly into the water.

It was the turn of the Karrabans, and unlike the Yurrish, they did not waste their opportunity. A long blast of a Karraban horn was sounded. It was picked up by those ships fighting before the galleon. Hurriedly they backed water and maneuvered to create a clear channel. An unobstructed line of fire.

Jem heard a rumble, like that of a rock slide. Half a heartbeat later came the deafening crescendo. White smoke erupted from the side of the galleon, and with it, scores of black balls that careered into the wooden gate of the quay, almost too swiftly to see. Wood split and cracked and flew into the air, the barrage continuous, each bang like a punch to Jem's senses. Smoke choked the quay. Through the haze, Jem saw the catapults ready to loose, but they didn't. The Yurrish recoiled in fear and awe at the terrible sight before them, at hearing sounds only the sky had ever made. Never had they witnessed such terrible power, such swift and effortless destruction.

Gundar blew his horn to order the attack. Before his siren ended, dozens of grappling hooks emerged from the smoke and latched onto the walls either side of the gate. Within heartbeats, Karrbans were upon the walls, hacking down the stunned Yurrish. The trebuchets upon the cliff had heard Gundar's call, though. Their loads came crashing down upon the galleon. The mass of white smoke suffocating the quay suddenly turned orange. Flames roared forth in all directions. A fiery tower rose into the sky. Jem couldn't stand to look at it for its brightness, and he ducked behind a crenel. The thunderous bangs ceased.

Jem mustered the courage to look. Galleys with iron-tipped battering rams at their bow's powered through the splintered remains of the gate. The surviving defenders sprinted from the quay, toward the portcullises of Novoro's keep. Arrows struck them in the back and soon their bodies became lost in a wave of yellow tabards. Gundar ordered the archers to loose at will. Jem stepped up with his own bow, the grip writhing in his sweaty grasp. Karrabans streamed forward along the quay walls. Jem aimed for the space where the walls met solid land, and loosed. He didn't wait to see if it landed, nocking another arrow, drawing and loosing once more.

Volley after volley of darts and stones rained down on the Karrabans, felling them by the dozen. Still they came, momentum unwavering. And then the surge fell away. The steady stream of arrows from the attackers slowed to a trickle.

"Don't say they're beaten already," Jem heard a man beside him say.

Jem tore his eyes from the ground below and looked to the horizon. Fires raged in some of the Karraban ships struck by projectiles. Others had been reduced to planks and rigging, floating on the water. But too many yellow sails still blotted out the blue of the sea, and through the broken quay gates they poured. At their head were two more galleons.

And then it clicked. It had been a ruse, the first wave of attackers mere sacrifices to distract from the advancing ships. Jem looked to Gundar. The colossus of a captain was standing upon the walls like a man devoid of fear, directing the defense like a conductor of chaos.

"Commander!" Jem shouted. Gundar didn't hear. His booming shouts added to the cacophony and drowned out Jem's timid cry. Jem tried again and again until it pierced through the clamor and Gundar looked around. Jem pointed to the quay. The galleons were slowing and turning portside, hatches already open.

Screams erupted above Jem's head. Before he could look up, the body of a Yurrishman thudded into the battlements. He was the first in a torrent of bodies, falling like sacks of grain. Some crashed into unwitting individuals, breaking and killing them too.

The Karrabans had somehow managed to get up there. That was all the time he had to consider it.

Thunder clapped in the quay.

Two

An autumnal breeze nipped at Isy's face, the air fresh with
the scent of recent rain. Tweets and songs emanated from
the leaf-shedding trees, creating a harmonious din that
drifted through the forest. It was disturbed by scores of
hooves churning up the moss-covered ground, the odd
grunt and whinny of a horse as it was stopped from grazing
upon the lush grass, the rumbling voices of men and
women, their intermittent laughter, and the clangs and
jangles of their weapons and armor. Here there was no war,
no strife or worry, just everything living freely, in ignorance.
Who knew how long it would be before any of them
experienced peace like this again, if they ever did at all.

The sheer immensity of the trees in the Giant's Garden
hadn't really struck Isy the first time. In her defense, she
had been in the midst of a kidnapping. Now, she was
completely awestruck. Some of them dwarfed the towers of
Yurrisa, their bases broader than a cruck house. Mighty
arm-like boughs supported hundreds and thousands of
branches filled with lush, awl-shaped leaves, growing
denser as they rose toward the peak. Others couldn't take
their eyes off the trees either, and the column of wagons and
horses slowed, much to the audible frustrations of Baron
Rijkard, riding at the front of the line with Keeper Ashara.
Tulasc and Yera had gone on ahead to scout, leaving Pekira
and Kora to lead the hundred-strong line of cavalry. More
than once the Amast pair had stopped the line and held up

their hands for them to be still and silent. Their ears had twitched, bulbous eyes scouring the trees. Whenever they resumed, mumbling began, calmness replaced with unease.

Isy heard hooves trotting behind her and turned to find Edvar approaching.

"How's that mare treating you? She looked feisty this morning."

"Fine. It's just you she doesn't like." Isy stroked her horse's chestnut neck. Edvar was right, she had looked a lively beast. Seeing the mare stomping and throwing her head had daunted Isy, but from the moment she sat in the saddle, it was as if someone had pulled the docile lever in her mind. Isy had even decided on a name. Luna.

Edvar laughed. "I see you're one of those annoying people who are good at everything. You're as natural a rider as I've seen," Edvar said.

"And how would you know?"

"I know horses."

"I won't ask why." Isy smiled.

Edvar's laughter simmered. He shook his head and changed the subject. "Tell me, why are the Amast always looking up at the sky? At first, I thought they were using the sun to navigate, but we've had this grey cloud hanging above us all afternoon."

"Blue ravens."

Edvar's eyes widened, not with fear, but with curiosity. He looked off into the trees, in the direction the Amast gazed.

"Do you think they would attack us? Surely no bird could be that bold?"

"I've never seen creatures like them. It was as if they had been possessed by some insatiable urge to kill."

"But you survived them?"

"I killed some."

Edvar's eyebrows rose, lips curled into a smile.

"Do you doubt me?" she asked, smiling too. "You can ask Kora if you like. The Amast never lie. I've killed an ikata too. Just as it was about to get Vil."

"Ika-what?"

Isy recounted he tale.

"You're impressive," Edvar said after she'd finished. He grinned. "I don't think I've ever met anyone quite like you. What other beasts have you slain?"

"None. I'm not some murderous monster."

"You're far from that. Here's me thinking country girls didn't do much beside farm."

"You shouldn't believe everything you hear."

"Very true. My problem now is that I trust nothing I hear." Edvar sighed. "I've been surrounded by liars and deceivers for too long. I fear I've forgotten what trust and honesty is."

"Do you trust Kora to lead you safely to the camp?" Isy asked.

Edvar nodded, though none too vigorously.

"Do you trust me?"

He nodded again.

"You can lose trust, but what's lost can always be found. You've been hurt, and you're learning how to trust again. I went through the same thing. Take one step at a time. You're doing well." She smiled.

"You're wise," Edvar said.

"I speak from experience. Whether that makes me wise or not, I don't know. Nobody's ever called me that before, anyway."

She looked at Edvar. He was such an unusual man. Well-spoken and proper, an elegant noble from the city, yet he was light-hearted, conscientious and kind. She didn't find him particularly handsome, and he had a somewhat gangly gait. But she liked his strong nose and his round amber eyes that looked into hers when she spoke. Nobody had ever seemed so interested in her, and she wasn't quite sure how to react. But at the same time, she sensed an uneasiness about him, like he was hiding something, and Isy suspected what it was: his nervousness and insecurities. Isy knew better than anyone the need to harden herself to the stresses and torments of the world, and when that shield was weakened things could quite easily fall apart. Edvar, she guessed, was rebuilding his own shield, and by the sounds of it, a lot had been thrown at him.

Before the day gave way to night, they made camp around the bases of the giant trees. Canvas tents were erected with wooden poles and cook fires burst to life before them, to beat away the encroaching gloom. There was no laughter or chatter. Instead, a tense air hung over the camp. A good portion of the troupe were from Haberdam, and, prior to leaving, had voiced their concerns about the trip into untrodden lands. The edginess of the Amast hadn't helped either, and to top it all the persistent stopping for broken down wagons had ground everyone's patience to brittle sheets.

Isy sat upon a log beside a pine-scented fire and pulled off her boots. The release of tension was phenomenal. She exhaled a sigh of relief, lips curling into a pleasure-filled smile. At her side, Vil was rummaging through his bag.

"What are you looking for?" Isy asked.

"Sausages. I'm sure I had some in here."

"You and your sausages," Isy said as she removed her other boot.

"Aha," Vil said with a grin. He pulled out a small white cloth and unraveled it to reveal four pink sausages, ready to cook. He stabbed them each with a stick, the ends of which he had cleaned and sharpened with his dagger, and propped them up over the fire. He returned to his perch on the small log, their legs touching.

"So, what were you and city boy talking about today?"

Isy cast a suspicious glance at Vil as he awkwardly turned the sausages. "Not a lot. Just talking about the blue ravens."

"Let me guess, he didn't believe you."

"The opposite actually."

Vil fell quiet, turning the sausages. The scuff of feet drew their gaze from the fire and into the light stepped Edvar, a loaf of bread in his hands. He smiled at the pair of them.

"Mind if I join you? I'm fed up of hearing about how big the damn trees are."

"Of course," Isy said, returning the smile. She glanced at Vil, who continued to turn the sausages as if Edvar hadn't arrived. Isy shuffled closer to Vil so Edvar could sit beside her.

They spoke of the slow progress of the day, how the wagons kept getting stuck and of their disbelief at the dozens of spare wheels they'd so far gone through. Tomorrow, they all hoped, would be better. The decision had been made to push on, with the wagons to follow at their own pace—an idea of Baron Rijkard's. Supplies would instead be loaded onto horses as much as possible. Vil complained that would only lame the horses, leading to more delays. Edvar offered no comment, and indeed, it seemed to Isy that he wasn't being as free with his words as he had the previous days. The same went for Vil.

Vil declared the sausages cooked and, with visible reluctance, offered one to Edvar, which he gratefully accepted. In turn, Edvar shared out his loaf, and Isy watched as he cut out a groove in the center of his piece and placed in it his sausage. Isy copied and found it much more wholesome combining the two. And her fingers didn't get as greasy either.

Vil stood up.

"I'm going to find Tulasc. I said I'd help him with the watch." He didn't wait for any response and disappeared into the gloom.

"Is he okay?" Edvar asked, licking the grease off his fingers.

"I think so. He's prone to bad moods." Isy licked her fingers clean too. "Any news?"

Edvar sighed. "Rijkard is still furious at having been brought along, or as he puts it, 'dragged' along. He hasn't opened his mouth save to complain. I've heard him saying borderline treacherous things about the Keeper behind his back, and Ashara has few pleasant words for him in turn. I fear I've given more bad advice in suggesting that he come along. What if forcing them together breaks their already fragile relationship? I tell you, Isy, I really am a fool sometimes. Well, of late, most of the time."

"Rijkard wouldn't turn on him. It isn't hate he glares at Ashara with, more like the way some smaller men look with envy at bigger men. Beneath it all, he's afraid of Ashara. He wouldn't have agreed to any of this if he wasn't. All we can do is hope that his fear holds out."

"You'd do well on the Council I feel," Edvar said.

"What about the other barons and baronesses? Will they keep their loyalty?"

"I hope so. They're all more loyal than Rijkard, so if we can maintain his allegiance, then hopefully that'll send a positive signal to the others. But... I don't know. Doubt seems to follow me around these days. I cannot shake it. I feel little conviction in anything I do."

He looked into the fire.

Isy studied him. "What happened back at Yurrisa, before we came?"

"I'm still trying to make sense of it all." He fell quiet, the crackle of the flames filling the silence. And then he spoke, telling her of the treaty with Karrabar, the assassination attempt on Ashara's life, and how he had lost the confidence of the Council and the people of Yurrisa. He told her of the attempt on his own life and how he had fought and killed his attackers. He spoke with no pride when he described pushing those men to their deaths, and his eyes grew wet with tears, though his voice remained firm.

"I'm so sorry, Edvar. If I'd known, we would've done it all differently. I would've tried to meet you privately, then none of this would have happened. I am such a fool. We were just so afraid of being captured and killed before we got a chance to see the Keeper." She buried her head in her hands and tried to hide from the shame gripping her body. She could not bear to look at Edvar. A hand gently pulled her wrist away from her face. She looked at him, into his eyes, bright in the dark.

"It isn't your fault, so please don't blame yourself. We were too late."

"What do you mean?"

"It didn't matter what we did that day. The Council had made their move. They'd pretty much shut down every factory in the city to incense the people, and the people wanted an excuse to vent their rage. The Council gave it to them. When we returned to the keep, my former co-councilors were already there, waiting. It was going to happen regardless. If anyone is to blame, it is me. It is my job to see these threats coming and stop them from happening. And here we are now."

"That's an awful lot of pressure to have on your shoulders."

Edvar shrugged. "It's the way it is and the only way I've ever known. Sometimes I love it. More often, I hate it."

"By the sounds of it there isn't much you could have done to stop what happened. Some things are just beyond our control. Fate weaves its own paths for us all, and it does not care for fairness. We just have to make the best of it, even when it seems impossible. All we can do is pick ourselves up and take the next step forward. If we fall down again, we get up, until we fall for good."

They fell quiet with their eyes on the flickering flames. Unlike earlier, Isy felt comfortable with the silence. So too, it seemed, did Edvar.

"*Edvar,*" came a call in the gloom.

"Here," he replied.

A round-faced soldier with a bushy beard came into view. "The Keeper is looking for you."

Edvar nodded and looked to Isy. "Thank you. I feel better for talking to you."

"Me too," she said, smiling.

They locked eyes, and then he stood and disappeared into the night, leaving Isy alone.

Three

It was a couple of days later, the hour close to midday, when Yera and Tulasc burst from the brush. It was the first time anyone had seen them in days. Even on their alien faces Edvar recognized a fearful urgency. They waved their arms, beckoning them on, and Kora and Pekira set off at a sprint.

Ashara kicked the side of his horse and went after them, Edvar in tow, guiding his mare through trees thick and thin. Upon the breeze he caught a fetid smell. Tasted it even. Like a feces-filled moat in the heat of summer mingled with the scent of bodies unwashed in years. He coughed, pulled his scarf up over his nose and mouth. Even his horse recoiled, shaking her head and grunting. With the density of trees thinning, there grew a furious buzzing sound, growing in intensity. They rode into a clearing, the soft grass turning to churned mud, as if torn up by the hooves of cattle. Scattered through the clearing were shelters of wattle, canvas and rags, randomly organized. Circular clusters of rocks suggested camp fires, but all were cold. Indeed, it seemed a place devoid of life, and from the smell, Edvar feared it was.

The Amast stopped before the first of the shelters, seemingly afraid to go any further. Edvar and Ashara dismounted, closely followed by Rijkard, the latter holding a handkerchief over his nose. Behind him, rode Isy and Vil, and for a moment Edvar locked eyes with her. Tears ran down her cheeks. Worry was etched upon her face, top teeth biting down on her lower lip. She looked beyond him to the camp and rode forward toward Kora and the others.

Kora called out in his own language. It echoed around the camp. A brief, pain-stricken shriek sounded in response. For a moment, Edvar wondered whether it was an animal. The rag over the door of a wattle shelter shifted and an Amast woman shuffled out. Mere skin wrapped around bone, she ambled toward them, her giant frame hunched and frail. Her huge fingers were like the teeth of rakes, clutching her swollen stomach. Her cheeks were hollow, skin the color of rotten pork, and her huge, round eyes looked like bloodshot moons. Grey and wispy hair clung to her scalp. Her gait lacked balance as she shuffled through the mud. Kora and his kin moved toward her, and she stumbled and fell.

From around the camp, more skeletal figures emerged, hobbling through the mud like beings stripped of their conscious minds, driven only by instinct, the innate desire to survive. Men, women, a handful of children, equally thin and frail, all verging on death. Some pointed to Kora and the other Amast, called out their names. Kora and Tulasc turned to the group of Yurrish and beckoned them on. Ashara gave the order and men and women, pale as the starving Amast, roused themselves from shock and hurriedly unpacked from their panniers food, water, poultices, potions, blankets. The Amast fell to their knees around the Yurrish, grabbed at apples, bread, nuts, berries, and cured meats, and swigged from skins of water. Some of the Amast lacked the teeth or strength to chew.

Isy and Vil went to help the Yurrish volunteers, and the realization struck Edvar that he was standing still, mouth agape. Never had he witnessed such emaciation, such helpless suffering. The tendrils of death were etched all over their bodies, yet despite the torrent of despair, the flames of life somehow burned on. Edvar was amazed anybody had survived in such a filthy place. And what had led them here was the consequence of war and fighting, disputes that seemed so trivial in the face of this: mass deaths, the destruction of homes, the obliteration, nearly, of an entire group of people. Edvar had played his role in it all, and that fact wracked him with guilt.

He dismounted and helped a young man from Haberdam carry a hefty sack of apples. Ashara helped too, two sacks of food upon his uninjured shoulder. Indeed, everybody assisted apart from Baron Rijkard, who continued to scowl beneath his silken cloth. How his heart could remain so cold with such sights before him Edvar could not comprehend.

Some of the first to eat began to vomit. Uncontrollable retching wracked their brittle bodies and left them keeled over in the mud.

Isy shouted.

"You cannot let them stuff their faces! It's shocking their bodies. You must feed them little, otherwise they may die."

Edvar hurried to join Isy, Kora and Yera as they carried out the heinous act of taking food from starving hands. Feeble grumbles and groans, the angriest they could muster, rang out from the Amast. Kora and the others spoke quickly in Amasti, trying to quell them. It took a while for them to understand, and the energy to struggle soon fled them.

Some of Jarat's soldiers did a sweep around the camp. They reported a further twenty survivors too weak and sick to move. Another sixty-six were dead and decomposing in their hovels. They found an area strewn with pyres, none recent, and a mound of putrid bodies, swarmed upon by flies and crows. A hundred or so, they guessed. Only seventy Amast survived, all clinging to life.

Big campfires were lit, and the survivors were given fresh furs and blankets to wrap themselves in. Still the Amast shivered. The cry for food was incessant, each plea grinding away at Edvar's morality. He *was* helping them, if only they could understand. But he couldn't shake the feeling of fault. If he and Ashara hadn't decided to give land to the Karrabans the Amast may have remained unknown to the world, safe and well in their homes. *But I knew nothing of them. And if I did, I would have protected them.* The rationale made him feel no better.

The plan was to give the starving Amast a small amount of food and water every hour, with the frequency and amount increasing with time. Isy had read about famines and starvation in an old history book, she said, and had advised Edvar on what to do. Following her guidance, the vomiting had ceased.

At dusk, the Yurrish set to work burning the dead. Edvar helped carry the bodies. Even with his nose and mouth wrapped up so tightly he could scarcely breath, the smell seeped through, and more than once bile rose to the back of his throat and threatened to go further. The job got easier with the growing darkness, the twisted features of those he carried hidden by shadow. All anyone could smell for the rest of the night was burning flesh.

Edvar awoke the next day upon a pile of soft moss, wrapped in his furs, next to a flickering campfire. He had been so tired the night previous that he had simply followed Isy to a campfire, sat down, and the rest was a blur. An arm was wrapped around his waist, tucked up against his chest, a dainty hand clutching one of his own. He glanced over his shoulder, conscious of disturbing whoever it was, and found a sleeping Isy. In the morning light, she seemed so peaceful. The side of her face that he could see was smooth and lily-white, glowing almost. The black mark consuming much of the other half of her face he didn't mind. Yes, it was unsightly, the skin hard and crusted, yet amongst that darkness was a brilliantly bright eye, and it was her eyes that captivated him most, with their glimmering warmth. He liked too her slight nose with its flicked end, watching her pink clips curl into smiles that inevitably provoked one of his own. Indeed, the very sound of her laughter lifted his mood. Having known what she had endured throughout her life, seeing those rare smiles triggered a sense of satisfaction within him. Never, so far as he could tell, had she forced a smile or laugh, stifled a yawn, fidgeted disinterestedly, like so many of the women he knew in

Yurrisa. Isy had taught him much so far, above all that looks did not matter in the slightest, and he felt in his heart that she had more yet to teach him.

A pain in his groin reminded him that he hadn't emptied his bladder since yesterday afternoon. And he needed to fart. Doing his best not to wake Isy, he removed her hand, pulled on his boots and headed to the edge of camp. After an epic piss and some percussion from the rear, Edvar went to find Ashara. It was a few hours after dawn, the air chill with the rising sun, and most of the Yurrish were only just stirring after a late night spent hefting and burning. The Amast slept beside fires well-stoked through the night, covered in furs and blankets. Their shivering had eased, as had the cries for food. It would take a while for people so big and once so strong to recover. Time was a luxury they no longer enjoyed, and already Edvar's thoughts had turned to the challenges that awaited them still.

Edvar passed the smoldering pyres, and there, in the shadows of the trees, stood Rijkard, alone. Edvar slowed to a stop and watched him. Rijkard's hand rested on the hilt of his sword, his grey-shot hair swaying in the breeze. Was he thinking of the Amast? That he had been wrong to react to them as he had? Did he feel pain for them? Did an urge for justice burn in his chest? Or did he look on with hate and loathing? Edvar approached him.

At hearing him, Rijkard snapped out of his thoughts and turned to regard Edvar.

"Councilor," Rijkard said, looking back at the flames.

"May I join you?"

Rijkard shrugged. Not a no, at least.

"I'd like to thank you once again for coming, Baron. Without yours and your people's help, the Amast would almost certainly have died. An entire group of people almost lost to history, though I fear we may lose them still."

Rijkard turned his head in Edvar's direction. Edvar knew what had provoked it—referring to the Amast as people.

"Seeing all this makes everything else seem so trivial, don't you think?" Edvar said. "I remember once feeling overcome with worry because they'd run out of cheese in the keep. 'What am I to do without cheese?' I asked myself in utter despair. Cheese... these people have had nothing to eat for weeks. Stricken by illness, unable to hunt or forage, unable even to go down to the stream. I can't begin to imagine the helplessness. The loss of hope. Knowing death was inching closer with nothing to halt its march. I can think of no worse torture to mind or body. How any of them are still alive defeats me."

Rijkard said nothing.

Evar continued. "Our squabbling with Karrabar has played its part. I am fortunate that in my lifetime I have never seen war. Now I have glimpsed its ugly face, and I am filled with a fire of determination to see that something like this never happens again."

"You sound like your father."

"You knew him?"

"There were few who didn't. He was the infectious sort. We fought together in Enning's Field against the Oposkans. I had charge of the right of the line, your father had the centre. We took a surprise cavalry charge in our flank and our mid-ranks collapsed. I'm here today because of Harada's fearless charge into the Oposkan horses. I'd never seen infantry charge cavalry and win. Your father never cared much for odds, though, long or short."

"He never spoke much of his battles."

"Few who fight do. We try to forget. I have seen war, lad. And I do not want to march my people to die. Ashara has no power, no army, no hope of taking back his city."

"Not for much longer."

"Words are wind, and anyone from my barony will tell you so. You city folk are full of it. You may think of us as the armpit of Yurr, but we are no man's fool."

"That's not what I think and it certainly isn't what Ashara thinks. Please believe me when I say that. And even if some people did think that of Haberdam, do you think they will for much longer? You are the Keeper's savior, indeed the savior of the whole realm. Nobody will ever forget the brave men and women of Haberdam who stood with defiance, loyalty and honor when their country needed them most. I know you aren't fond of me, Baron, but I admire and respect you for what you are doing."

Rijkard looked at him, eyes narrowing. Edvar gave him the warmest smile he could muster.

Rijkard looked back to the pyres. "Are you hungry, Councilor?"

"I could eat."

"Then let us find us some food and a fire to warm ourselves beside."

Together they walked through the camp toward the food tents. Rijkard kept his silence. Edvar hoped playing up to his ego would work. He'd recognized the flaw in Rijkard's armor during their first meeting. He was a proud man, and such men can grow drunk on praise, crave it, demand it even. He had his insecurities too: a fear of belittlement and insignificance, and a total disdain for disrespect in any form. If he had to, Edvar would pull down Rijkard's breeches and kiss his hairy cheeks to keep him onside.

Four

Isy watched Kora, Pekira and Yera, all physically and emotionally exhausted, slump down before the fire. Vil offered them water and food. None of them took it. Jarat sat upon a log beside Isy, picking at his nails with his dagger. Ashara stood before them all, eyes fixed on the flames, his mind elsewhere. Edvar and Rijkard sat beside Jarat, and as if it had all been rehearsed, the Keeper began to speak.

"Thank you for coming. Time is not on our side and our next steps must be taken swiftly—in just two weeks we must reach Iscarta to hopefully meet with the other barons and baronesses. So here is the plan I propose. First, we must return to Haberdam and muster our forces. Jarat will leave some of his men here to help your people with the Amast, Rijkard." Ashara turned to the Amast. "You will be safe in Haberdam. It is far from the conflict to come. I only hope that, when it is done, I will be in a position to make a home for you."

The Amast looked to one another, expressions blank as ever, and then Kora stood. "Good Keeper, we are truly grateful for what you have done for our people. You saved us from our end. In the ruins of our old life, the Amast vowed never to pick up arms and kill again. We kept that vow for centuries. But we have been gravely wounded, and the threat to our future is great still.

"We have spoken long on this together and all of us wish to serve with you, to help you reclaim what you lost, as you helped us.

"We are not many, but there may be more of us. One of our kin has spoken of another who found this camp. One of our own who had been separated after the attack on our home. There are more Amast, she said, well and healthy, not far away. But this messenger fell ill and died here. We cannot find her body, so we do not know if what they say is true or some dream forged by hope. Tulasc is searching now for signs of the truth. If he finds them, I believe with all my heart that when they learn what you have done for us, they will fight too."

Tears welled in Ashara's eyes. Isy's own tears freely flowed down her cheeks.

"It would be an honor to fight beside you," Ashara said, and he offered his hand to the giant Amast man. The pair shook in the warrior's grip—something Kora had picked up from the Yurrish soldiers.

With the plan agreed, Jarat went over logistical matters before the conference was ended.

Vil approached Isy.

"What are you going to do?" he asked her.

"What do you mean?" She knew what he meant. All the while Jarat had spoken, Kora's words had played on her mind.

"Stay in Haberdam or march to Yurrisa?" he said.

"I decided a long time ago that I'd never go back to Haberdam. I told you this."

"I know. I thought you might have changed your mind. You know, now that we're back home."

"It will never be my home, Vil. Why, are you thinking of staying?"

He took a few moments to answer. "No. But marching to war is a little scary, I must admit."

"Have you not always yearned for an adventure like this? Imagine if Makos the Mighty decided halfway through a quest that he'd had enough." Isy didn't want to admit it aloud, but doubt was infecting her thinking too, eating away at the foundations of her certainty. To stay with the Amast in Haberdam—the place she hated more than any other, the place she was relieved to be rid of and had been happier without ever since—or to go with the Keeper and Edvar and march to *war*? There was a good chance she would die, but death may await her in Haberdam too, especially now that those who lived there had experienced life without her. At least she wasn't alone in her doubts. Vil was clearly thinking of staying too. She could not imagine him fighting in a war. Nor could she imagine herself. But staying was easier for him, though the Chronicler was an abusive bastard. Just not as bad as her father was to her.

Vil looked at her, the tension in his face breaking. "You're right. Besides, I'm quite looking forward to seeing the Henge of Iscarta. I've read loads about it. I think there have been over a dozen battles there."

"How old is it meant to be?"

"Nobody's sure. Some say hundreds of years, others say thousands."

"I wonder who built it," Isy said. They reached their own tents and Isy went straight for her pack of food, pulling out a softening apple. She took a bite and shuddered with the bitterness, but chewed on. It was the first bit of food she'd eaten all day. With mushing up food for the Amast—many had lost their teeth in their deteriorating states—fetching clean water from the stream and helping with bathing and washing, she hadn't had a moment to herself. Her back and shoulders ached from all the lifting. But hers and everyone else's efforts were worth it. And it had all helped to distract her.

Edvar appeared and said his hellos. Vil looked up and grunted. Edvar sat down, and moments later, Vil stormed off without a word.

"What's going on with you two?" Isy asked Edvar.

"Nothing. I've tried speaking to him, but he has no interest whatsoever in conversing with me."

Isy frowned. "He's jealous, I suppose, of the time you and I spend together." She stopped eating her apple, appetite gone. *Why are things always so difficult?*

"You seemed worried at the meeting, and you've helped me with my troubles. I wanted you to know that I'm here if you needed to talk to someone about yours," Edvar said.

She studied him for a moment, wondering how he had read her, and then cursed herself for making it so plain. When she didn't answer, he spoke.

"Are you wondering whether to stay in Haberdam?"

Without taking her eyes off him, she nodded.

"I don't really know what to say to you, Isy. My future is as uncertain as yours. I suppose all we can do is what we feel is best. What feels right."

"And what do you feel is right?"

Edvar took a moment to pick his words. "To stand by Ashara. To fight for him and for all the realm."

"What if that's the wrong thing to do?"

Edvar shrugged and smiled. "Then I shall be wrong. I know Ashara and I know him to be true and honest. There is nobody better to guide us through this madness and see us to safety. With all my heart I believe that."

"So you would die for him?"

"I nearly have. Twice, now."

Edvar began to open up like one of the books she loved to read so much. He told her the things he had deliberately omitted the last time about the run up to their escape from Yurrisa. Tears came to his eyes when he explained how he had run away and hid, thoughts and feelings that she could tell he had bottled up and tried to ignore; she too was used to doing so. He spoke of his father and his legacy and the pressure that weighed on his shoulders; of how Ashara had been an uncle to him growing up and a father to him since he had lost his own; and of the guilt he felt for having misguided Ashara. By the time he had finished, Isy felt a connection deeper than before. And crucially, she knew what she wanted to do.

"Can I come with you?"

Five

Jem was lost in a sea of white. A single-toned squeal pierced through the veil. It grew painfully loud, and the whiteness dimmed, tendrils of shadow seeping in. Distant rumbles came to his ears, like thunder on the horizon. *Like thunder.*

The ringing gave way to those crashes and bangs, each one coming with the beat of his heart. His eyes flickered open. Slate-grey clouds hung above. Dust hovered in the air, rocks and debris showered down upon him. He raised his throbbing head and looked around. Men and women, hands over their ears, cowered down behind the crenellations of the wall, fear etched upon their faces, consuming their eyes, paralyzing their bodies. A few defiant individuals continued to loose arrows. For many, it was the last they shot. The Karraban thunder smashed the parapets to bits, obliterated siege engines, battered the cliff behind them and knocked from it great chunks of rock that tumbled down to crush those below. The ringing in Jem's ears eased enough for him to hear the screams. They became the backdrop to the rumbling of the Karraban thunder. Only one thought entered Jem's mind: flee.

On his hands and knees, he scurried toward the closest stairway. He felt no shame in running. Anyone who stayed up here would surely die, and he would be better off alive. Or would he?

Other soldiers, it seemed, thought the same. Gundar at last sounded the horn to fall back and those still breathing surged toward the nearest stairways. With the press of bodies thickening, they ground to a halt as they waited for people to descend the narrow staircase. Soldiers fell by the second to the Karraban thunder, taken out by falling rocks, some big as wagons, crushing groups trapped in the bustle below. The stone beneath Jem's feet rumbled more and more. The dust was choking. Grit sat in his teeth, got into his eyes. Hands pushed him forward, crushing him against those in front. The stench of urine and loose bowels was thick —the smell of fear, of death. Jem was certain this was his own too. Trapped, helpless upon a collapsing wall. This wasn't the way he wanted to go. He pushed forward with everything he had, inched closer, and fell to the ground.

Jem began to slip downwards to the right, toward the sea. He looked back and saw his comrades disappearing into churning clouds of dust as the wall crumbled. Jem scrambled for purchase and found nothing. Further and further he slipped, panic growing, until a hand grabbed his wrist. Jem shot upwards where more hands grabbed him and hurled him through the stairway door. They hurried down the steps, shoulders clashing with each other and the walls. Panicked breathing sounded all around him. Screams echoed after them and with it the rumble of thunder and falling rock. The legendary fort of Novoro was crumbling into the sea.

Jem's knees were weak, his confidence battered. He followed the grim patter of feet, the rattle of chain, plate and scale. The same thought, it seemed, ran through everyone's mind. They were going to die.

At the bottom of the steps, they entered a broad torch-lit chamber. Jem's eyes were immediately drawn to the great roller lying before the sturdy wooden doors. On the other side of those doors, making their way up the sloped passageway, were the Karrabans. The roller, with its countless rows of spikes of differing heights, each one sharp as a freshly forged spearhead, had been hefted up a curved platform in order to set it off with greater momentum.

"On my signal, let it loose and open the doors," Gundar said.

The shouts of the Karrabans echoed up the tunnel.

"Now!"

A soldier triggered the mechanism and the spiked roller began to move. Another group of soldiers removed the heavy wooden beam from the doors and opened them wide. The roller gathered speed, the metal chain to which it was attached rattling. It disappeared into the gloom of the tunnel, pace quickening, quickening, until a wave of screams and gurgled cries erupted as spikes punctured, pierced, shattered. The rattling of the chain ceased, the roller's momentum lost, and the winchers set to work lugging it back. It returned a bloody mess. Once in position again, the roller was loosed. This time the screams and cries were fainter, and Gundar ordered the roller back. The four winchers pushed the arms of the wheel and abruptly fell to the floor, the wheel spinning loosely and striking one of them on the head. The chain came rattling up the tunnel and struck a knockout blow to the helm of an unwitting woman.

"Bastards have cut the links," Gundar growled. Close the gate." The order couldn't have come soon enough. Moments after the beam was placed across the doors, the pounding of axes and shields rang out against it. The doors surged inwards. The beam groaned. A battering ram.

"Shoulders against wood," Gundar bellowed. Being one of those closest the gate, Jem was pushed forwards and joined others placing their weight against the door. He dug in his feet, though they skidded against the stone, and braced for the next blow. It nearly knocked him to the ground. A couple of others did hit the floor. Quickly they regained their position.

The battering did not relent. Jem counted each blow—it distracted from the pain—and on the twelfth, the beam splintered. Spears sprung forth through the crack between doors, deflecting off armor, finding fatal gaps. Men and women screamed and recoiled in pain. The ram struck again, the beam further broke. More spearheads jabbed and lunged through the widening gap with furious intent. When next the battering ram struck, a clay pot, flames burning within, flew through the gap and shattered in the middle of the Yurrish. Blinding orange flames exploded. A great ball of fire spread across the chamber, licking skin, blackening armor, singing hair. Heat roared against Jem's cheeks, and he turned his face away, toward the gate, just as the ram struck again. The surging door struck his forehead and knocked him flat on the ground. For a moment, all turned black, until the warm trickle of blood down his face prompted him to open his eyes. He regretted it. His comrades were afire, waving their arms, tearing at the straps of their armor. The smell of singed hair filled his nose, and slowly screams filtered through over the ringing in his ears. More bodies were burning all around him, others dying from wounds inflicted by blades. Almost in slow motion the gate burst open, and with it came a swell of Karraban bodies. Hands grabbed his tabard and hauled Jem to his feet.

Jem found himself amongst a tide of retreating Yurrish, moving up another narrow staircase. More than once he stumbled over the uneven steps and was hefted back to his feet by the woman behind him. The hurried patter of feet echoed upwards, the sound of Karraban voices too, and then the enemy was there, thrusting and lunging at the two women behind Jem. They batted away the blows with their circular shields. But a wicked spearhead landed under one of their guards, and she stumbled. Before Jem could leap to her aid, a Karraban spear sunk into her throat.

Jem drew his sword. He had no shield, so around the guard of the other woman he hacked and slashed, jabbed and lunged. He heard a scream. His first kill, maybe. He didn't have time to consider it further. Felling one Karraban wouldn't be enough to repel them. His arm trembled with exertion, sword heavier in his grip with each swing.

With Jem and his comrade holding the Karrabans back, they retreated upwards, step by step. A hand grabbed Jem's shoulder and he chanced a glance to find a flat-faced Yurrishman with a great battleaxe standing behind him. He pulled Jem back and stepped forward to relieve him from his desperate defense.

Jem hurried up the last few steps and through the doorway. He stepped into a long chamber with a low ceiling and narrow walls, lit by torches held in sconces upon the walls. Gundar was there issuing orders, and when he saw Jem, gave him a pat on the back that nearly knocked Jem off balance. Pride stirred in his chest. The heroic woman at last made it through and the thick iron door was slammed shut and bolted. The flat-faced man was nowhere to be seen.

The Karrabans hammered against the door almost instantly. Jem felt fit to collapse. Blood ran down his sword arm from cuts he hadn't realized he'd sustained in the melee. He chose not to look at them, and instead breathed deep and steadied himself. Gundar was at the other end of the wide chamber, organizing ranks for the next stand. Jem staggered toward them, and as he passed through the shadows between torches, he crossed a strip of metal grating.

A couple of hundred soldiers were locked into a shield wall, twenty wide and ten deep. At their head stood Gundar. Jem, somehow, was in the third rank. Whenever they had trained, he had formed up in the seventh or eighth. Only the strongest fighters made up the early ranks, and he had never been regarded as that. Someone shoved a fresh spear and shield into his hands. He barely had the strength to hold them up.

The repeated beatings of the Karraban rams bored into Jem's mind. He winced as the iron door hit the floor. The sound echoed through the chamber, until all that could be heard was the flames of torches and beating hearts rattling chainmail. Blood and sweat clammed his face and dripped from his nose and brow.

The roar of the Karrabans almost split the rock beneath Jem's feet. They erupted from the door and charged at the Yurrish line like rabid dogs. Hundreds of them, eyes and voices wild and filled with a lust for blood. They passed over the gratings and Gundar gave the order. The lever was pulled and a bed of iron spikes sprung forth from the ground. Battle cries turned to screams and wails. Jem was grateful for the shadows masking the carnage.

The Karrabans hesitated, and Gundar seized the chance to order their few archers to loose. A sleet of darts whistled through the air, felling a score of men. The Karrabans hurried into a shield wall which quickly gathered more spines than a hedgehog's back. Their formation rippled, their center opened, and from the gap came the iron door, clanging against the grating.

Gundar ordered the spikes raised in an effort, Jem guessed, to shift the door. They snapped up, some puncturing through, others denting and bending the thick iron. Gundar ordered them lowered once more.

"It's jammed, sir," came a frantic cry.

Soldiers rushed to help the poor bastard trying to shift the lever, but the Karrabans had already seized their chance. Over the door they charged, shields hefted against the Yurrish arrow storm, bearing down on their foes.

The clap of wooden shields filled Jem's ears. He was forced back a few steps, and Gundar roared for them to push back in turn. Jem did so, with all his might, and regained a couple of steps. Those in the rank before him furiously stabbed with their spears while those in the front rank held high their shields against the barrage. All at once, Jem found it the most terrifying yet exhilarating experience of his life. Here was the greatest battle of all, that between life or death, elation or... the end. Soon, the signal would come for him to move up and take his comrade's place.

Jem wasn't given a signal though. Instead, the blood of the man in front splattered across his face and into his mouth. Before he could spit it out, he was shoved forwards into the gap. A flurry of blows hammered his shield, and once they stopped, Jem hefted his own spear and thrust it over the shoulder of his comrade in the front rank.

All Jem could see was the narrow window his helmet allowed for. He could hear Gundar bellowing orders, people either side of him screaming in pain, in defiance. They spurred Jem on, and over and over he lunged with his spear, striking shields, armor, and once or twice, he was sure, flesh. But step by step, the Yurrish were being pushed back, and they were running out of room.

To Jem's right, the line faltered. Two Yurrishmen fell in quick succession, a gap opened up, and the Karrabans poured forth like a river burst free of its banks. In that moment, the fighting turned chaotic, dirks and swords slashing, fists and feet lashing out. Hands grabbed bodies and hauled them to the ground. Eyes were gouged, faces scratched, ears torn, noses bitten, heads beaten to pulps.

Over the clang of iron and steel, Jem heard Gundar's voice. "Fall back!"

Jem gave one last thrust of his spear and, along with a dozen of his comrades, turned and ran for the door.

The Karrabans chased them down.

Jem moved his legs as fast as he could, adrenaline his fuel. He reached the door and hurtled down a dark corridor, which opened up into a large rectangular chamber, lit by braziers. As soon as the last person crossed the threshold, the studded wooden doors were slammed and barred. Archers continued to shoot from inside the room, using loops and slits carved into the walls to pick off their targets out in the tunnel. Others thrust their spears through similar yet bigger holes and scores of helpless Karrabans fell, unable to see the dangers that awaited them.

Jem looked around the chamber. He couldn't see any doors or stairs to get out, only stacks of crates and barrels and a hundred or so bruised and bloody soldiers. This was it. Their last stand.

He looked at Gundar. The bear-like captain was bleeding from half a dozen wounds along his arms and legs, plus a couple to his face. His plumed helmet was lost. He was pale, hair thick with blood and sweat. He appeared a beaten man. Jem looked around the room and saw more of the same expressions. It seemed everyone already knew what Jem was only coming to understand. Never again would they see those they loved. Hug their family or friends. See their children grow old and happy. Hear the songs of bards and maidens, the jokes of jesters. It seemed so cruel, so dispassionate, so unnecessary. Why were the Karrabans attacking them? *Why?* What good would it do to lament now, though? The Karrabans were howling at the door, and soon they would blow it down.

Jem reached for the shark tooth around his neck and was relieved to find it still there, untouched by blood. He rubbed it, said a prayer to Eulé to keep safe his mother and friends when the Karrabans came for them. And he prayed for courage in facing his death, to die as his father and brother had done, defending those they loved. Thinking of them now imbued him with power, with the courage he yearned for. He rose to his feet, picked up his sword. They couldn't give up, not yet, not when they'd fought so hard and lost so much. Holding the shark tooth still, Jem said a prayer, one a fisherman recites before he faces a storm that blackens the sky and sends forth waves big enough to sink islands.

The Yurrish stood in the room, yet he felt alone. All of them looked ready to cede. All except Gundar, who, after drinking deep from his skin and pouring the rest over his face, looked to have regained his resolve. He hefted his blood-stained axe, walked toward the door separating the Yurrish from the marauding Karrabans, who pounded against the wood.

"It's times like these we learn what we truly love in our lives. Our mothers, fathers, children, husbands or wives. For some of you, that first flagon of ale." Despondent men and women looked up from the ground. "We all want to feel that love again, and that is why today is not our day. That is why you're better than these murdering Karraban bastards. They want to take and destroy everything we hold dear, everything we vowed to protect. I don't know about you, but I'm in no mood to hand it over. Let's stain these walls with the blood of these sons of harlots."

The hairs on the back of Jem's neck bristled. His body tingled. He began to pound the pommel of his sword against the wall, and soon, others joined in, banging spear butts against the floor, swords and axes against shields. "*Yurr, Yurr, Yurr,*" they began to shout, louder and louder until all were bellowing it from the top of their lungs. The beating against the door ceased, and in that moment Jem felt like he could bowl over the Karrabans with his voice alone.

Someone peered through a loophole.

"They're retreating!"

The Yurrish roar shook the walls, if not the whole cliff. Jem embraced those around him. Others dragged him into their grip. They jumped up and down with weapons aloft, a purge of stress, an embracing of relief and joy.

Amid the elation, Jem noticed the sudden change in expression on the face of the young soldier who'd announced the Karraban retreat. He began to wave and shout, but was drowned out and ignored. Jem hurried toward him, barging his way through bodies, and looked through the hole. All was black, until a Karraban brought up a torch. In its light, he saw a wooden cart upon which lay a long, black tube of what looked like iron. The Karraban looked directly at Jem, it seemed, then lowered the torch to the tube. Jem saw a spark. And then he realized.

Thunder.

Six

Tesh had grown used to the sights of a battle after it had ended. The trick, he had found, was to look only for results, to ignore the dead and snuff out the guilt. His Eastern slaves were busy carrying the Karraban dead from the corridors, recovering weapons and arrows. His men would have plundered everything of worth immediately afterwards, some even during, though Tesh made sure any who did never would again. Anyone not thinking of the whole was a threat to success. And what a success today had been.

The fort branded impenetrable by the ignorant fool Ashara and his pig-like mother, Alysa lay in ruins. The two great towers and adjoining battlements he had boasted of masterminding were now mere rubble. The trio of portcullis gates, which Ashara had branded, quite embarrassingly, 'Murder Alley', lay twisted and broken on the floor, the stonework around it crumbled and fallen. Body parts poked out from beneath the rubble, stained crimson. More Yurrish lay dead on the floor, blood sprinkled with pale dust.

Tesh stepped around the spiked roller. He found his gaze lingering over the morsels hanging from the spikes. A young Captain named Niemen approached them with a torch. He saluted Tesh and Iljasar, and spoke.

"Lord, I should warn you-"

"Don't worry, Captain," Tesh cut him off. He'd witnessed every horror imaginable on the battlefield. He'd learned how to switch off his emotions. The trouble, he found, was turning them back on. m

The sight further along the tunnel was indeed worthy of caution. Iljasar stopped and threw up. Tesh almost lost his footing on the slick floor, but Niemen offered a swift hand. The Karraban keeper gave a curt nod of thanks.

"They held us here before the gate gave way. The fire pots proved effective," Niemen said, his voice holding no emotion. The smell in here was the foulest yet. A blend of burnt hair and the latrine pit of a war camp. It was such an abasing act to empty one's bowls at the moment of death. Tesh would be sure to clench when his end came.

They didn't linger long in that chamber and Niemen led them up a winding staircase, the steps and walls stained red. At the top, they found the scene of another fierce battle. Karraban bodies were being removed, but even still there were at least twice as many of his own than Yurrish. They'd bled badly, yet they'd prevailed.

A Yurrish woman writhed beside the door, coughing feebly. Tesh looked down at her, watched as she clung to life. He'd always found it strange how some people hung on when death was so certain. Why didn't they just give up? He took out his dagger and pushed it through the woman's chin—the fastest and most merciful way. He cleaned it on the blue tabard of Yurr, staining its white lily red.

On they went through another door and along a corridor, again cluttered with dead Karrabans. The door at the end lay splintered and broken, the work of the brilliant rumblers. *What can they not destroy?*

"The Yurrish fought like animals here, Lord," Niemen said. "It was here we lost most of our men."

"A fox is fiercest when it's cornered. When it knows it has all to lose," Tesh said, taking in the dead around the room, slumped against walls, sprawled across the floor. He approached one big man in the center of the chamber. He'd died with his hands around the neck of a Karraban, a great battle-axe at his feet. Tesh could see more than a dozen wounds over his body and arms, and his face was a moist mask of red.

"Is that all of them?" he asked Niemen.

"Yes, Lord."

"No survivors at all?"

"No, Lord."

"Good. Burn everything. I want no hint this pathetic fort ever existed."

Niemen nodded and left. Tesh looked at Iljasar. The old warrior seemed fit to puke again. For a killer of men he had the weakest of stomachs. Life, Tesh found, had a knack of throwing up such contradictions. But indeed, what was man but a tangled mess of conflicting thoughts and feelings?

Tesh took a last look around the room. Something caught his eye beneath a beam of wood. He hefted the beam aside and found a young Yurrishman, face covered in blood from a wound to the side of his head. His body was stiff, skin pale and cold. Resting unblemished upon his chest, beside the white lily of Yurr, was a shark tooth.

Tesh yanked free the necklace and held up the tooth to the torchlight, feeling its serrations and the smoothness of its two sides. He found it a curious thing, and for some reason he felt compelled to keep it. He dropped it into his pocket and, without another glance, left, his mind already on matters further up the coast.

Episode Eight: The Gathering Storm

Men often speak of their fear of stepping into darkness. I have always embraced it. My lantern pierced the gloom, illuminating stalagmites and stalactites, lime-stained walls. A soft, sandy layer of salt and sediment covered the floor. The cave narrowed until I came to the unmistakable angles of a doorway. The rotten door lay slumped like a fallen guardian. I found it difficult to breathe along that confined passage, and the excited beat of my heart didn't help. I had almost given up. Now here I was, perhaps in the bowels of Uren's ancient city. The very thought left a smile fixed upon my face. When I stepped into a circular chamber, it broadened. The rotten husks of wooden crates and barrels lined the walls. And in the corner, a set of steps. I took them two at a time, smashing my shins more than once on their uneven heights. At the top, I arrived at a long and narrow chamber. Despite my urge to go on, I could not tear my eyes from what I saw upon the walls. Spanning the length of both sides was a mural. In part the paint had faded, yet the detail was vivid enough. It told a tale, and beside certain figures were names. Harada the Great. Ashara, Keeper of Yurr. I followed their journeys, tried to ascertain their triumphs, and at the end, reached a door, intact and firmly shut. I tried the handle. Locked. I'd come this far; a bar of iron wouldn't stop me. A firm boot did the job. I had no time to marvel in my manliness, for the sight before me dulled all thought.

From ***The Forgotten Daggers*** by S. T. Harris

One

ROBBINS AND FINCHES zipped amongst the bare branches
of the trees and bushes lining the road, singing and living in
peace without the worries of the world to trouble them.
Their uplifting tunes filled the cold morning air and created
an atmosphere more akin to spring, not late autumn. Edvar
watched with envy in his heart.

He looked over his shoulder along the line of cavalry.
With Baron Rijkard's men, the might of Ashara's army had
grown by eighteen hundred, though Rijkard himself was not
with them, nor two thirds of his promised soldiers. Rijkard's
barony was the largest and most sparsely populated; it took
days for the call to arms to spread. Then the warriors, many
of whom were farmers and shepherds, had to prepare, say
their farewells and march to Haberdam. Some wouldn't see
the rolling hills of home again.

Edvar had dropped back toward the rear of the column.
He'd grown weary of Ashara and Jarat's constant
speculations over people's loyalties and discussions over retaking the city. It all left Edvar with a knot of anxiety in his
stomach and the occasional feeling of needing to empty his
bowels. He couldn't ask them to stop; it was their way of
dealing with their own nerves. Similarly, he felt no comfort
riding with Isy, Vil and the Amast, who peppered him with
questions about plans and what was likely to happen at
Iscarta, none of which he knew the answer to. Again, he
could not ask them to stop. It was only natural to seek

reassurance when nervous or afraid. So instead, he retreated and sought comfort in solitude, though time alone allowed his worries to stew.

The riders sent to the other barons and baronesses of Yurr had yet to return. *Have the Council gotten to them?* Edvar could see the Grand Assembly at Iscarta going one of three ways. First, fearful of their own positions with Ashara ousted, the barons and baronesses would ignore the call. That would reduce Ashara's chances of retaking Yurrisa from slight to impossible. What then would they do? Give up? Find some quiet part of Soria to live out their days wondering what could have been? That is, if they weren't hunted down first. And Edvar would have to live in the knowledge that he'd failed his father, failed to preserve everything he had worked so hard to create. Destroyed by his incompetent son. And what of the Amast? They would surely be hunted down and killed. Isy and Vil too.

The second option: they all show up and pledge their loyalty to the Keeper and agree to march to Yurrisa—the most ideal solution by far.

Or third, in league with the traitorous Council, they show up and capture or kill Ashara and everybody else.

Each possibility felt just as likely to happen.

They arrived at a pebble-filled stream, and Edvar stopped and dismounted while the column rode on. He let his brown courser drink while absentmindedly he stroked her white-haired mane. He missed his time spent alone. Privacy, he had learned, was non-existent when marching with a group of over a thousand people. He splashed his face with the icy water, wet his fringe and pushed it back out of his face. The last hooves of the column clopped against the moss-covered bridge. Edvar looked up to find Camos upon the bank, a toothless grin upon his grey-bearded face. He dismounted and let his piebald rounsey join Edvar's horse at the water.

"What's funny?" Edvar asked.

"I feel like I've lived this moment before."

"I don't recall previously being in such an awful situation."

Camos laughed. "You're Harada's son alright. You look more like him every day. He was a man who spent much of his time in the realm of speculation. It's a place you can easily get lost in. Some people lose their minds altogether. Paranoid wrecks that lock themselves away in towers until their skin pales and withers, and their hair turns white and wispy."

"You're a bit of a poet when you're sober, Camos."

"Who says I'm sober? What I'm trying to tell you is to deal in the cold, hard facts instead. That's what a warrior does, and it was always my advice to your pa. Sometimes he listened, other times he told me to jog on."

"And what is it you believe I should do next?"

"Nothing. There's naught you can do. If them damn barons and baronesses don't show, we're screwed. If they do, we're saved. There's nothing more to speculate about. Worry when it matters. Now isn't that time."

"What of contingencies and a dozen more 'what ifs'? I respect a warrior's swiftness of thought, but it's foresight we need now."

"You aren't hearing me. It's all a waste of time. Unless you can see the future, you're pissing in the wind."

Edvar's sense of dissent evaporated. Camos was right. Their fates were in the hands of others. "What do you think will happen?"

Camos gazed at the swift moving water of the stream. "They'll show."

Edvar hoped the old warrior was right.

At a leisurely pace, they rode on and soon caught up to the train of supply carts and camp followers—smiths, carpenters, chirurgeons, and a few harlots. Camos filled the time with stories of battles of old in which Camos and Edvar's father had fought together. Some Edvar hadn't heard before. His father rarely spoke of his battles, even the most glorious ones. In times of peace, when the cries and horrors of the battlefield were years behind, he still avoided the topic. Camos, though, was much more open, and he seemed to enjoy Edvar's inquisitiveness. Indeed, Edvar had never seen the old soldier so talkative and animated, describing battle maneuvers and tactics, even dismounting to demonstrate heroic moments. Wine skins were passed back and forth—Camos seemed to possess an endless supply—and the conversation continued as they made camp that evening in the shadow of Iscarta. It was too dark to see the fabled knoll. Upon its peak stood the ancient stone henge known as the Circle of Iscarta. It was here, long before the War of the Damned, that the nation of Yurr was forged into being, when the kings and queens of the realm united under one banner. Yurr, it was said, meant 'union' in the tongue of the Ancients.

Edvar decided to share a fire with Camos. He needed a night away from Ashara and Jarat. The pair chatted more than bored fishwives. As Camos had pointed out, there was nothing to be done until tomorrow. Tonight, for a few hours at least, he could forget.

The painful need to piss awoke him sooner than he wished. As soon as Edvar sat up, pain and dizziness struck his head, forcing him back down. The biting chill dissuaded any more effort, so he tried to slip back off to sleep. His bladder didn't cooperate. In a daze, he clambered to his feet and staggered past Camos, who soundly snored.

Edvar made for the trees at the edge of camp. Dawn provided a weak grey light and a thin veil of fog that hung over the dew-tipped grass. Edvar fought to stop his teeth chattering. It seemed his piss would never end. As soon as he was done, he hurried back toward his tent, eager for water to wet his dry mouth. His grumblings were soon forgotten when he glimpsed the hill named Iscarta. Upon its flat peak loomed the great rectangular stones of the henge, each one glowing in the light of the dawn sun. At the base of the knoll were two almighty trees, their boughs leaning toward one another to form an arch over a path that wrapped itself around the hill and led to its peak. Edvar marveled at the structure, a place of such significance and still so influential, yet one so simple and, in terms of design, quite bizarre.

"Master Edvar," came a voice that cut through his thoughts. He turned to find one of Jarat's messengers hurrying toward him. Edvar sighed and nodded. No explanation was required. He returned to his camp, packed up his things, buckled on his sword belt, and left Camos snoring.

"What happened to you yesterday? I had a dozen messengers looking for you." Ashara asked as Edvar approached his tent. The deposed keeper was sitting before a growing fire, dressed in his leather armor, with a heavy cloak lined with furs draped over his shoulders. He looked as if he'd been awake for hours, if not the whole night.

"There was nothing more to be done that I could see, so I had some time off."

"Quite. I can smell the wine on you from here." Ashara smiled.

"You seem relaxed about things."

"I have made my peace with the situation. Like you say, what comes next is out of our hands. All we can do is hope they show. I have holidayed in their keeps, supped in their halls, hunted on their lands, stood beside them in battle. We are friends. Surely they will not betray me, too?"

"I'm finding it hard to trust anyone at the moment," Edvar said. "I fear that Rijkard will betray us. I fear the barons and baronesses will too. And even if they do pledge allegiance, I fear it's a ploy to lure us into a trap."

"You must silence that voice of paranoia, Ed. It will ruin you. It plagued me for a time too, and I lost myself. I succumbed to it. It is a voice of evil, but inside of you resides the power to banish it."

Edvar looked at the flames. Ashara's words, as they so often did, rang true. Edvar knew he was being foolish, but no matter what he told himself, no matter what he did to move on and heal, the wounds kept re-opening. To know Ashara had experienced the same and had overcome it, though, made it less daunting, and imbued him with a sense of hope. Edvar gave Ashara a grateful smile.

They broke their fast with bread and sausages—it wasn't a Yurrish breakfast without sausages—and watched the camp come to life. One by one, the orange glow of campfires lit up the misty haze of dawn and beat it away. Edvar spied a flurry of activity at the northern edge of the camp and saw a Yurrish flag raised. It fluttered in the breeze and attached to it was a smaller, white flag. The sign of a returning rider. Both Edvar and Ashara leapt to their feet and hurried to meet the scout.

Breathless, the rider dismounted and saluted.

"Sire, Baronesses Jalden and Ura are a short ride away. They expect to arrive by late morning."

Before the scout could finish the rest of his report, word came of Baron Agon's imminent arrival, and then of Baroness Ilda and Baron Reska's, whose baronies were furthest south of all. The latter pair would be with them by early afternoon, and were marching double time to arrive sooner. Edvar risked a smile. One of his fears was off the table—they had shown up. But there was still one missing. Rijkard.

Two

Midday came with no signs of the barons or baronesses. Edvar, Ashara, Jarat and their contingent of guards climbed Iscarta in silence as thick grey cloud moved in to smother the late autumn sun. Every few steps, Edvar's eyes turned to the horizon. The climb was short and by the time they'd reached the top, he felt ill.

At the peak they beheld the Circle of Iscarta. The great stones, discolored by time, dwarfed even the Amast. In the center of the circle they formed, was a smooth and tall stone. It served as the dais, upon which the Keeper stood.

A single blast of a horn interrupted the quiet. Heads snapped around to look in the direction from which it came. The first of the barons and baronesses had arrived.

Before long, they had each climbed the stone steps and entered the henge. First came Baroness Jalden, a stout woman with fair hair tied in a loose knot. The lines of age showed at the corner of her amber eyes, which glinted like the points of two blades. She clasped Ashara's hand and bowed.

Baroness Ura followed. Tall and straight-shouldered, she had a shock of curly grey hair and drooping cheeks that reminded Edvar of a hound. A cloak of wolf fur embraced her broad frame, and a sword hung at her hip. She bowed before accepting a gentle kiss on the forehead from Ashara.

Next, Baron Reska. He was a slender man of forty summers, with a pointed brown beard and bushy eyebrows to match. He shook Ashara's hand and nodded with an air of rigidity.

Baron Agon almost bowled Reska over in his haste to greet Ashara. The bear-like man had grown heftier around the waste since Edvar had last seen him, but looked strong as ever, despite his grey-shot hair and beard. A scar cut across his right eye, the eye itself permanently white. In his booming voice, he bellowed his hellos and hugged Ashara like a lost brother.

Last to arrive was Baroness Ilda. Edvar hadn't seen her in half a decade and back then her mother had ruled the barony. She'd since grown into a fair maiden, not to mention a fierce-looking warrior. Long-legged with a pale complexion, she had straight, flowing hair that matched her amber eyes. Like Ura, a sword hung at one of her hips, and on the other, a quiver stocked with arrows. She bowed deeply and kissed Ashara's hand.

Still no sign of Rijkard.

The barons and baronesses took their places in front of the pillar pointing in the direction of their own baronies. Ashara climbed the stone dais. And then another horn sounded. A short time after, a red-faced Rijkard huffed into view. He strode by Edvar, who was standing with Jarat and Camos outside the Circle, with the other advisors and guards of the barons and baronesses. Sweat lined Rijkard's forehead. His face was gaunt, eyes heavy. He looked as if he'd ridden from Haberdam without stopping. He straightened his jacket and fox fur-lined cloak, then stepped into the Circle, bowing in all directions and to Ashara most deeply of all.

"Please forgive my tardiness."

Ashara descended to shake his hand and slap his back. "Thank you for racing here, Rijkard. It's most appreciated." With Rijkard taking his place, Ashara began.

"Thank you for coming, and at such short notice, but as I'm sure you're aware, time is no longer a luxury we enjoy. You may already have received word from Yurrisa, but the account you would have received will differ from the truth, and that is what I wish to share with you today.

"I have been betrayed by my own Council. Rakar, Mara, Levanwe, and Malfan together have plotted to take control of the nation and of the Vault. I fear they seek to open it for themselves. Power has corrupted them. They have tried to kill me, manufactured a riot, killed a fellow Councilor, attempted to kill another, and ambushed me in my own throne room.

"Malfan is dead, Levanwe gravely wounded, and I still possess the Key of Ulara. The Vault will remain sealed, for now. Outnumbered, we had no choice but to flee the city with the aid of more victims of the Karraban madness, people who have remained hidden from us for centuries— the Amast, a noble people who have pledged to support our pursuit of justice.

"And it is justice I seek. The removal of these traitors, and an end to the danger they pose to all of our people and Yurr's future."

Edvar studied the faces around the Circle. Reska was frowning and seemed incensed by something. To Edvar's dismay, the feeling was mutual amongst all bar Rijkard, who looked anxiously at Ashara. Panic sprung to life in Edvar's chest. Did they resent Ashara for losing his seat of power and exposing everyone to such danger? Had they lost faith in him, just like the people of Yurrisa? But why then would they come? Unless...

Edvar looked at the chosen guards around him, seeking hands moving toward hilts, nods or eye signals, feet shuffling forward.

Baroness Ura cut the silence. "I'm sure I speak for everyone when I express my sympathy for your situation, sire, but this issue seems trivial compared to the news we bring, and news, I assume, you have not heard."

Edvar looked to Ashara, who glanced in his direction. A mix of worry and confusion filled his eyes. Ura went on.

"Sire, Novoro is destroyed, so too the defenses upon the Green Steps. A great Karraban fleet marauds the coast, laying waste to every town and village, pillaging, burning, raping and enslaving."

"Impossible!" Ashara said. "Novoro is built into the cliff. It is impregnable. I designed the defenses myself!"

Agon spoke up; Novoro lay in his barony, and the man no doubt would have felt the pain of every lost life. "It is true, sire. It's as if the whole cliff crumbled into the sea. A handful of survivors made it to Lera. They are mad, all of them. Their wits have abandoned them. They forever tremble, scream out in the night, breakdown into tears at the slightest knock or bang. They mutter about thunder and ships and flashes of fire."

"Reports of the same litter the coast," Reska said. "My towns and villages have been hit by Karraban raiders, and it's said they carry terrible weapons. Weapons, people say, must be creations of magic."

"It's true," Ilda said. "On our way here, we met a train of people heading inland from Dungarvia. They said the town's stone walls were reduced to rubble by great and terrible weapons that clapped and rumbled like thunder. They too said they were creations of magic, for they had heard nothing but the sky make such sounds before. They named them 'stormers'."

"Which means one thing," Ilda said. "Tesh has unlocked the Karraban Vault."

Silence descended. A breeze plucked at hair and cloaks. Ashara looked lost for words, gazing at the ground with a frown, shaking his head.

"I agree with Ilda. To craft such weapons must surely require magic," said Agon. "How else can the might of thunder be channeled into a weapon that can bring down a cliff? It reeks of the power of the Dagger of Silusa."

"We do not know enough of these weapons to call them creations of magic. Tesh is cunning and fierce, but he is no fool," Ashara said.

"He may be no fool, but he is merciless," Ura added. "I remember his visits to my keep as a child. He would beat other children with sticks until someone pulled him away, and all the while he laughed. There is a murderous streak in him. Something broken."

Reska spoke. "Could it be possible that your traitorous Councilors have allied with him, sire? The timing seems like more than mere coincidence."

"It seems more and more likely," Ashara murmured.

"We waste time trying to understand such a man," Jalden said. "He is capricious. Such thoughts that flow through his mind are beyond our comprehension. All we can do is stand up to him and send him back whence he came."

Nods and noises of agreement sounded from the barons and baronesses. The focus returned to Ashara. The Keeper offered no response. Each heartbeat felt like a turn of the moons. Ashara was seemingly stumped by what he had heard. And indeed the news was grave. Edvar didn't want to believe it either. It threw everything into the air. All the talk and planning was aflame. What in Soria were they to do now?

Ashara, at last, found his voice.

"If what you say is true, then I fear our options are few. If Tesh has unlocked the Karraban Vault, he sails to Yurrisa with the Dagger of Silusa, and there is nothing to stop him from trying to break open the Vault of Iron. With the might of two daggers, he would be unstoppable. Everything we know and love would be ended. And if he has carried out this madness, who is to say he will stop there. Will he march north? Will he cross the Green Deep and conquer the world? He must be stopped."

"If indeed Tesh has opened the Karraban Vault, should we not open ours too? How else could we match his power?" Reska said.

"My mother taught me that to open the Vault would unleash a terrible magic that would change everything it wrapped its tendrils around," Ashara said. "You no doubt have read the work of Layafwich. My mother believed his words to be true, that we Yurrish did not always look like this. Our frames were slighter, our eyes and ears smaller and narrower, and our skin naked of hair. It was during the War of the Damned that we began to change. The Karrabans experienced the same, and it served as one of the reasons the two nations came to a peace, and an agreement to lock away the Daggers, with the leaders of each nation to be the keepers of the keys of those vaults." Ashara took out the Key of Ulara from under his shirt. It hung upon a chain that glistened in the firelight.

"You do not know how many times I have been tempted to toss this into the Green Deep, to hurl it into a furnace, to leave the Vault forever sealed. The world would be better off without the threat of destruction hanging over it." Ashara sighed and tucked the key under his shirt. He went on.

"Tomorrow I will march to Yurrisa to re-take the city or die trying. We do not yet know if Tesh and the Council are in this together. We could watch and wait to see if they attack each other. Or if, as I fear, they are in league with one another, then the city's walls would be nigh impossible to take, with the Karraban forces defending them too. So I say we act fast and retake the city and hope that Tesh has not yet arrived. For all of Yurr, for everyone who has lived before us and all that hope to come after we are gone, will you stand beside me?"

The barons and baronesses looked to one another.

Agon spoke first. "All of us know our family's histories. We carry that familial vow to always uphold peace and to keep the Vault sealed. I will not be the one to break what tens of thousands died for." He fell to one knee and bowed his head to the ground. "My loyalty to you is unwavering. You are the true keeper."

Rijkard, who had yet to speak in the exchange, stepped up to Ashara. "Our great grandfathers stood side by side in the War of the Damned. We have stood shoulder to shoulder in the front rank, and I will do so again. He drew his sword and pointed it into the ground, kneeling down to rest his head on the pommel.

One by one, Reska and the baronesses stepped up and pledged their allegiance too, and by the end, Edvar felt a fool.

Tears welled in Ashara's eyes, and Edvar's filled a little too, though he was quick to wipe them away and cough to rid himself of the lump in his throat. Were they tears of relief or of fear? At that moment, it felt like both. They had allies, an army, but they had two armies to face, as well as weapons terrible and great, potentially forged by magic. There was a reason the Daggers had been locked away in the pits of the earth, and Edvar feared they would soon discover it.

Three

Waves crashed against the jutting rocks of the Yurrish coast. Salty sea water soared into the air, only to be scattered by gales and gusts that swept over the Green Deep. Gulls cawed above, determination to find a scrap of food overwhelming the need to seek shelter from the deteriorating weather. Their gazes were fixed on the thousands of men disembarking from the Karraban ships, on the pulleys and wooden cranes hauling from bilges great nets filled with trunks, barrels, crates and amphorae. And, of course, with the greatest care of all, the rumblers.

Tesh watched on from the hill overlooking the cove, playing with the shark tooth he had taken from the boy in Novoro. It was a fine landing point, wide enough for two dozen ships to beach at once, and sheltered from the worst of the waves. It was, however, thirty leagues from Yurrisa. The rest of the coast from here to the city was sheer rock face, with no way to disembark. *It will be worth it*, he told himself.

Tesh couldn't rely on Rakar to deliver on his promises. The deal was that Rakar would capture Ashara and give him up to Tesh, in exchange for Tesh's military support in taking over Yurr. Rakar would serve as leader of Yurr and vassal to Karrabar. Only, the man was as untrustworthy as they came. He'd betrayed his own keeper and intended to betray his co-conspirators too once this was over.

There was no way Tesh could rule out that Rakar had made plans for him upon his arrival. A typical Yurrishman. Rotten to the core. Instinctively dishonest. So Tesh had come up with his own act of betrayal. Once Rakar handed over Ashara, Tesh would take the city for himself and put somebody he could trust in charge. But it wouldn't be straightforward. Only a fool would admit a foreign army into their walls, and for all his flaws, Rakar was no fool. Instead, Tesh planned to surround the city by land and sea, and if and when the time came, he would reduce its walls to dust. Memories of walking through the gates of Yurrisa as a child were still vivid in his mind. How his father had marveled at the height of the sandstone walls, the looming towers and cunning defenses. Tesh had won the man wars and had received less acknowledgment for his efforts.

"We seem to be faring well," said a voice behind him.

Tesh turned to find Iljasar walking against the wind. His great battleaxe hung on his back, and he wore black leather armor with a mail shirt tight around his broad muscles. A greatcloak hung over his shoulders, the end snapping in the gust.

"Your organization never ceases to impress me, Iljasar.

"A life in the military, m'lord. Most of the men are up in the fields. The town just over the hill is called Dunmiska. Our scouts report no sign of resistance. Shall I send a raiding party?" Iljasar asked.

Tesh rubbed the shark tooth. "No. If we kill every Yurrish fool we see, we'll have no one left to rule. Ah, they're unloading the Hammer." Tesh's lips curled into a rare smile.

In the cove below, two wooden cranes with scores of ropes thick as a lazy soldier's waist raised the greatest weapon to have been built since the War of the Damned: a rumbler with a barrel wider than a round shield and longer than two men stretched from head to toe. The wrought iron creation was black, kept together with a series of metal bands painted Karraban yellow. The stone and iron balls it fired almost reached the knee in height and took a quad of men to lift. It had taken several years and twenty master smiths to get the design right, plus six months to build it, amounting to the cost of a thousand permanent soldiers. Tesh had seen the damage it could do, and longed to see it against the famed defenses of Yurrisa. He would shatter its walls as he intended to shatter Ashara.

As the beast of a rumbler was lowered, one of the ropes snapped, and the iron tube jolted forwards. Men shouted, and those below leapt out of the way. It didn't fall, though, and was carefully dropped upon a huge, eight-wheeled cart, pulled by a dozen field horses—big, muscular creatures with long fur that were bred in the Northern Hills of Karrabar. The whips cracked them into motion, and Tesh could hear the grunts and whinnies from upon the hill as they struggled to pull the wagon. The wet sand made it doubly difficult.

Upon the slope which led to the fields, men dug trenches and filled them with logs to provide some grip for the wagon's wheels. The horses gained momentum, but hitting the rising gradient, struggled to a halt. The whip cracked and cracked. One step, two steps. And then a piercing wail erupted from a horse. One of its legs had snapped, the strain too much. It tumbled backwards into the other horses and a writhing tangle of equine bodies rolled down the hill, hauled backwards by the weight of the Hammer.

Tesh laughed. Not at the pain-filled cries of the horses, nor the chaos that his men struggled to control, but at the fact this weapon had caused it all. So big it took more than twelve horses to pull. He turned to find Iljasar looking at him, wariness in his eyes.

"Relax, Iljasar. I am not yet mad. It is a laugh of excitement. Here we are, on the shores of Yurr, with a great army and weapons more powerful than anything since the War of the Damned. I have dreamt of this moment for three decades."

"A long time to wait, sire."

"Indeed. Time has not dulled my appetite for revenge as so often it does. I only wish Jessy was still alive. In one week, Iljasar, we will rule this nation, and revenge will be mine at last."

"I hate to say it, sire, but I cannot see us making it to Yurrisa in a week. It's taken the best part of a day to unload the ships. We're marching in late autumn, and it seems to rain here every damn day. The roads will be muddy and hauling all these supplies and rumblers will slow us down. There's a good chance we'll run into resistance too. They won't be a match for us, but if they fight it'll take us time to clear them out."

Tesh ground his teeth. It was everything he did not want to hear, but he knew it to be true. *Damn Iljasar and his pragmatism.* "No doubt you are right as always. I want us there as quickly as possible. See that it's done."

Iljasar bowed and took his leave. He always knew when he was done with. Tesh liked that about him. He hated lingerers. His gaze returned to the cove below. Those horses too injured to carry on had been killed and dragged into the surf where the water around them had turned red. Now, men had been drafted to help haul the wagon by rope, along with the horses that survived.

At last, the Hammer crested the rise. It was time to march.

Four

That night, the valley buzzed with apprehensive activity. Word had spread of the Karraban fleet sailing to Yurrisa and of the thunderous weapons they carried. Around camp fires, people debated whether the Karraban Vault had been opened, whether the Yurrish should unlock their own and harness the power of the Dagger of Ulara, and what that might mean for them all.

"The Karrabans have opened theirs and they're all fine."

"They're murdering innocents. What's fine about that?"

"But without the power of our own Dagger, how are we to stop them?"

Funnily enough, Edvar had heard few conversations about how they would actually retake Yurrisa, the immediate priority, and the one that plagued Edvar's current thoughts. To lose control of the Dagger would be an end to everything, and to stand a chance of stopping that outcome, they had to reclaim Yurrisa before the Karrabans arrived to bolster the defense.

Something else was giving Edvar a headache: why was Tesh doing this? Power, greed, control, revenge? An opportunity offered to him by Rakar? To answer the question, Edvar needed to know more. Ashara had revealed little about his history with Tesh, and Edvar sensed that there was something the Keeper wasn't telling him. He was sure the answer was there, locked away. He just needed to find the key.

As he had that morning, he found Ashara beside the fire before his tent. He was sitting forward, elbows on knees, gaze lost in the flames. When he heard Edvar approaching, he snapped out of it and looked up.

"Good to see you're keeping a clear head tonight," Ashara said.

"I can't hack two nights in a row."

"Your father was like that. He might have been able to fight a dozen warriors alone, but a night of drink knocked him out for the count."

"Another useless thing that we have in common."

Ashara looked at him. "You're more like him than you think, you know."

Edvar had no reply. He sat down on the stool facing Ashara, who handed him a skin.

"Yurrish Red. A gift from Baroness Ilda."

Edvar took it. "And you castigate me for indulging."

"In these stressful times, we all need a release, a way to forget for a few hours. Alcohol is a convenient means of doing that."

With brief reluctance, Edvar took a swig. The sweet, fruity liquid went down too easily. Edvar handed it back to Ashara. "A keeper must have his release too."

"I have enjoyed too much of it these past few years. No more. At least, not until this mess is sorted." Ashara waved it away.

"All they talk of in camp is Tesh and the Daggers. You said you knew him well. Do you think he'd open the Vault?"

"No." Ashara grimaced. "Or so I hope. The truth of it is, we spent much of our youth together—our widowed parents were fond of each other. We competed with one another, helped better each other. Yes, things became sour, particularly over Jessyia, but would that be enough to provoke him to unlock the Vault and sail an army here?" He turned to Edvar, a pleading look in his eyes. Love could give someone strength they never knew they had, help them achieve impossible things, and, Edvar knew, give them the conviction to march an army to war.

"Could it be the case that he's seen things differently to you all these years?"

Ashara gazed into the flames, considering Edvar's words, until his eyes closed. Slowly his head sunk into his hands, and for a while he remained silent, until, without looking up, he spoke.

"Tesh never wanted to 'compete' with me, did he? I will not deny that I enjoyed beating him. It lifted me up, and I never stopped to consider how it put him down. My mother and his father constantly showered praise on me, and now I come to think of it, I cannot recall them ever doing the same for him. His father used to scold and embarrass him in front of us and Tesh's cheeks would turn beetroot. He would glare at me with hateful eyes that twitched with anger. The same twitch I saw when we faced each other in that bout for Jessyia. And I saw it again when we met in Wender to sign so-called peace. It's a desire to inflict pain, to kill. A desire that has festered for years. He must hate me more than anything in the world. And how can I fault him? I no doubt wrecked his childhood and stole his love. In his eyes, I have taken everything from him, and now that he is Keeper of Karrabar, he wants to take it all back." Ashara looked up, tears in his eyes.

Edvar wasn't sure what to say. Ashara, if anything, was at fault. But things made more sense now, at least.

"If Tesh is using the power of the Dagger, would you open the Vault?" Edvar asked.

"If what they say is true, then I suppose I would have to. I can see no other way of matching that power. If I did not, all of Yurr might fall, the people I vowed to protect killed or enslaved."

"But one thing I've never quite understood is how it could be used. It's just a dagger. How can a dagger defeat an army?"

"Ulara is an old Yurrish word for 'souls'. The Daggers steal the souls of those they slay and that energy can be harnessed and channeled into weapons, such as these tubes of thunder the Karrabans have crafted."

"And do we know of any way of doing so ourselves? Even if we unlocked the Vault, how could we develop such weapons in the little time we have?"

"Different ways were developed during the War of the Damned. Each more terrible than the last." Ashara shook his head. "Weapons could be crafted, but I take your point. Time isn't on our side." Ashara took the wineskin from Edvar and drank deeply. "Not once did I ever think things would come to this, Ed." Helplessness and doubt raged in his black-ringed eyes.

Here and now, Edvar realized the terrible responsibility that weighed on the shoulders of the Keeper. Edvar had always seen keeping the Vault secure as a benign duty, and to unlock it as a power that would never be exercised. Yet it was a power that had the potential to murder thousands indiscriminately.

Five

Things made sense to Edvar now, but tomorrow they were still marching to war, and chances were, to his death. The wine had helped to numb that realization, and before he left Ashara, the Keeper had given him another skin. Now Edvar wandered through the camp, looking for Isy.

Darkness had settled, and so too a faint mist from the breaths of thousands of people and horses. The stars and moons pockmarked the raven-black sky above, the lack of cloud lowering the temperature further. The camp was the quietest it'd been since leaving Haberdam, but laughter rang out somewhere, songs too, and someone strumming a lute. Edvar headed toward it, and it transpired the merriment came from the Amast camp.

Around a large and roaring fire sat the Amast, Isy and Vil, and with them a score of Yurrish men and women. The conversation was in full flow, as was the laughter. The Yurrish shared their wine skins, and the usually rigid, stony faced Amast were like teenagers after their first ale—arms around each other's necks, singing, laughing, joking. It was like a carnival, a world away from the seriousness in Edvar's mind.

Isy spotted him and called his name. Others picked up the cry, and he was beckoned to the fire.

"He has wine!" Tulasc said, and everyone laughed and cheered. Edvar sat down beside Isy, who was clearly drunk from her loose movements and heavy eyes.

"Where have you been? I thought you'd gotten bored of me," she slurred.

Edvar smiled. "Well, I couldn't find any books about, so you'll have to do for entertainment."

She laughed, and Edvar found the sound brilliantly uplifting. They shared his wine skin, catching up on the past few days while Vil tried to show Tulasc a Yurrish dance called the Siege of Discura. The pair ended up in a heap. A Yurrishman bet another Yurrishman that Pekira couldn't lift him above her head. She did it with ease. The Yurrish sang songs, taught the words to the Amast, and likewise the Amast taught them some of their own. Together their voices joined in harmony, and the wine continued to flow as the moons inched across the sky.

"After seeing the riot in Yurrisa, it seems hard to believe that this is actually happening," Edvar said.

"I was thinking the same thing! My whole life people have mocked and abused me for looking different. The whole way to Yurrisa I was afraid the people would react to the Amast as they react to me. And it happened. It was like a nightmare come to life. I've never had much faith in people, and after Yurrisa it went altogether, but this is helping to change that."

Isy asked him about the meeting at the Circle—she hadn't been allowed up the hill, despite her best make-believe reasons. Tongue loosened by wine, Edvar told her about the Karraban fleet, of the tubes of thunder they carried, of their suspected use of magic, and his fears that they will seek to open the Yurrish Vault once they reach Yurrisa.

"But how would they get into the Vault if they don't have the key?"

"I'm guessing they'll force their way in. They've made great weapons which people say are powered by the magic of the Dagger of Silusa. It is hard to know for sure. The tales all vary."

"Would Ashara use the Yurrish Dagger?"

"I don't know. Maybe. If the circumstances justified it. Like if everyone was going to die."

By this point, the wine had gotten the better of most people. The Yurrish and Amast had either retired or passed out around the fire. Just a handful remained, talking quietly or enjoying the flickering flames.

"What is this dagger you speak of?" Kora asked, sitting down cross-legged beside them. Edvar had seen him drinking all night, but he did not appear in the slightest bit drunk. "I have heard talk of dagger all day. And of thunder."

Isy repeated what Edvar had told her, with Edvar adding details here and there. Kora listened without comment, and when they were finished, he sighed in his peculiar Amasti way.

"This is sad news. The Amast once had weapon of such power. It is a tale I have told Isy." With Kora's help here and there, Isy retold the story of the Amast to Edvar. Kora continued when she had finished.

"Its power corrupted us. It turned us against each other and then it began to change us physically too. Our bodies and features became what you see now. It is because of the Dagger that all this happened. You cannot use it."

"But what if the Karrabans are using theirs?" Edvar asked.

"We know of your Great War. We witnessed the terrible power wrought against one another. Everything was nearly lost. Do you want that again?" Kora went on. "I cannot tell you how to act. Only what I know. You have helped save my people and we will always stand by you for that, but please listen to these words. If there is another way, you must find it."

Edvar looked up into Kora's bulbous eyes. "I think you should speak to the Keeper."

Six

Isy thrust her spear, pulled it back and ducked her head below her shield. She stood, lunged again, ducked once more. Over and over, back and forth. Her spear arm grew weaker with each strike, and her shield felt heavy as a sack of stones. Camos called the drill to an end, and Isy almost sank to the floor. She fumbled with the straps of her shield. Edvar removed his own and helped with hers.

"I used to hate doing these drills," he said. "Still do. But it's good for strengthening the muscles and getting used to fighting in formation."

Isy drank deep from her water skin. The breeze on her sweat-lined face was cool and refreshing.

"You're making this gangly fool look like a puppy, Isy," said Camos, grinning at Edvar. "A few more sessions and you'll be fighting in the front rank."

Fighting in the shield wall was a prospect she did not relish. Trapped on all sides, slowly shuffling forward towards death or glory. *Just like life itself.*

Isy looked out across the meadow at the army's camp for the night. They'd left Iscara five days prior. The plan was to march west toward Yurrisa and meet the armies of the barons and baronesses at the Plains of Lital, a vast stretch of grassy land cut in two by the winding River Haber. During the winter, the river often burst its banks, and much of the Plains became a wetland, but it was the only place to muster such a large force so close to Yurrisa. It was a bad time of the year to wage war, Isy thought, but time wasn't anybody's willing companion.

Yurrisa was a two-day march from the Plains. Returning to the city still seemed a distant and surreal prospect. What they would find waiting for them they could only speculate on, and that allowed Isy's mind to wander to the worst-case scenario. It had dawned on her that she was marching to war without any real knowledge or experience of fighting or handling weapons, and that instilled in her a helplessness that kept her awake each night. It was why she had sought out the help of anyone willing to teach, and when she saw Camos and Edvar practicing, had approached them for guidance. Camos had taught her with patience, and Edvar, her sparring partner over the past few days, had given her confidence, encouraging her at every turn.

Edvar was wiping his face with a rag when a messenger appeared around the tents.

"Master Edvar, Keeper Ashara has requested your presence as a matter of urgency."

Isy bade him farewell and watched him go.

"What is this you teach Isy?" The accented voice belonged to Pekira. Isy turned to find her looming over Camos, resting on her spear. The veteran met her gaze.

"How to fight," he said.

Pekira looked at Isy. "Everything he shows you is wrong."

Isy spat water, stifling a laugh.

Camos shook his head. "I need a drink."

Isy smiled at him as he left, and Pekira approached her.

"I will show you how to fight, if you wish."

"Please do," Isy said, making sure Camos was out of earshot.

Pekira demonstrated to Isy what she described as a dance. She began by bending her knees and stepping forwards, backwards, left and right in different sequences, all in tune to a song she hummed. It was a means of teaching stances, methods of attack and defensive movements, she said. Basic, yet effective. Pekira bobbed and weaved and twisted her body like a writhing snake. Watching her was hypnotic. Isy copied her with the grace of a bull. Whenever she got it wrong, Pekira tutted and said something in Amasti that Isy didn't understand. A curse or insult, she suspected.

After half an hour, Isy found it easier, and Pekira began to smile. An hour later, Isy could do the dance without Pekira leading her. By then, Yera had joined in. Vil got involved too and made a decent attempt until he stumbled into a spectator and fell in a heap. Everyone stopped and laughed, but they were quick to help him up and pat him on the back. When Kora and Tulasc joined with their double-edged spears, the crowd of intrigued spectators swelled. Indeed, it was a sight to behold. Isy had never seen them properly fight. Their speed was blinking, spears blurred shapes that whooshed through the air, spinning, rotating in their palms and around their fingers. When they finished the sequence, the crowd burst into cheers and applause. It seemed to Isy that everybody felt as she did—awe-inspired. What Karraban could stand up to them? Could a dozen even take on one alone? Hope blossomed in her chest. They may have a chance after all.

Isy moved through the press, exchanging nods, smiles, pats on the back. Yurrish and Amasti laughed and joked. For those few moments, at least, everyone felt joy instead of worry and despair. A welcome thing in a military camp, she imagined, where it seemed that, at some point each day, the thought of whether tomorrow would be their last day entered everyone's minds. Isy looked around at the different smiling faces and felt nothing but warmth and love. She would die for these people, and she didn't doubt they would do the same for her.

A group headed to the river to wash, and Isy, Vil and the Amast went with them. The water was as fresh and clear as it was in Haberdam, and just as cold too. Isy stripped to her loose-fitting shirt, which fell below her waist, and took it off as she slipped into the water. The cold snatched her breath. The Amast disrobed naked without any qualms and dove off the bank. Nobody took a second look at their unusually hairy bodies and dark carapace back. Their good nature was infectious; more than a few Yurrish men and women jumped in after them. Something of a water fight broke out, though a sour-faced officer quickly shouted it to an end.

Isy dipped her head underwater, and after bringing it up again, set to scrubbing her body with her hands and nails. Content she no longer smelled of sweat, she clambered up the bank and wrapped herself in her fur cloak, hopping on the spot to dry and build some body heat. Vil, who had chosen not to get into the river, wrapped his own cloak around her. That eased her chattering teeth a little.

"Thanks, Vil," she said. Vil smiled.

Isy quickly dressed. She caught Vil looking away as she did. Other men and women didn't. She glanced at her friend again. He was unusually quiet.

"Everything okay?" she asked.

Vil opened his mouth, only to close it again.

"What is it?" Isy said.

"Have you thought anymore about going home?"

"No," she snapped, though she found herself frowning at her reaction. Vil's brows were furrowed too.

"Let's face it, Isy. We aren't fighters. Practicing with Edvar and that washed up soldier is one thing, standing before thousands of people determined to kill you is another. And what squad or company in this army will have us? We have no place here. I'm not afraid to admit that I'm terrified. We're marching to *war*."

"Well, I'm not afraid. If anything, I'm content. I'm surrounded by my friends. Helping them with a cause that truly matters. This time last year I was so miserable I felt like drowning myself in the Haber. Now my life feels like it matters. What me, you and everyone else is doing matters. I cannot walk away. I will not." And with that she spun on her heels and stormed back to the camp.

Anger rumbled in Isy's chest, though she wasn't quite sure why she had reacted as she had. Maybe Vil was right. Maybe she was ignoring the facts. Maybe she was afraid and refusing to acknowledge it.

She passed a group of archers, all women, loosing arrows at targets with tremendous accuracy. Isy slowed, taken by their camaraderie, their support for one another after each shot, clapping and encouraging and joking. One of them, a lean woman about Isy's own age, with raven black hair that contrasted boldly with her pale, delicate skin, spotted her looking. Her eyes were like plates, amber and black-ringed. There was a fierce beauty to her, but something else, something in the way she stared that grabbed Isy's attention and refused to let go.

The woman waved her over. Isy looked around, and realizing she stood alone, approached.

"You know how to shoot?" Her voice was deep, a little raspy.

"Sort of," Isy said, looking at the other women, all busy loosing arrows. "I've not tried in years."

"Here," she said.

Isy turned back to find a longbow shoved into her hands.

"You look like you want a go."

The yew longbow matched Isy's height. The copper-brown limbs were smooth and polished, the grip made of bone. It was the finest bow she'd ever seen. She gave the archer a hesitant look and received an expectant expression in return. Isy stepped up beside the other archers, picked an arrow from the closest basket, and nocked it. The fibrous bowstring dug into her first three fingers as she drew and aimed. She'd forgotten about the strain it placed on her back, and her bow arm trembled a little, already weak after the day's drills. Panicking at the embarrassment, Isy sent her arrow way over the target and into the thicket of trees beyond. The string snapped against her left forearm and she recoiled in pain. The beautiful bow dropped to the ground. Isy was afraid to turn back to the archer, and even considered running away.

"Try again," said the archer, picking up the bow. Isy nocked another arrow and this time the woman stepped up behind her, brushing up against her. She used her feet to alter Isy's stance so her hips were straight, adjusted the height of her elbow to level her aim, guided her as she drew back the string so the tip of her index finger touched the corner of her mouth.

"Breath in with the draw. Exhale when you loose," the archer said down her ear, almost in a whisper, and stepped away. Isy loosed her arrow and watched as it whistled into the heart of the target. She couldn't help but beam.

The archer slapped her shoulder. "What's your name?"

"Isy."

"I'm Ess. Who are you serving with?"

"Erm..."

"Where are you from?"

"Haberdam."

"So you're with that miserable prick Rijkard then?"

Isy shrugged. "I'm more with the Amast."

Ess laughed. "The giants? Have you seen them fight?" Curiosity filled her voice.

Isy nodded. "When we were attacked by a flock of blue ravens."

"A flock of what?" said one of the other archers. In fact, they'd all stopped to listen, and at that point, moved closer to circle Isy.

"Blue ravens. The Amast call them paska."

"I have. My grandma used to sing me a song about them. Never knew they were real," said another of the archers, a small woman with arms like a lumberjack's and short hair cropped over her ears.

Isy recounted the tale of the attack on the Amast camp and how they'd fought them off. They clung to her every word, something she was unaccustomed to.

"Glad they don't come down here. I'd be spending all my time shooting the bastards. I'm Flor, by the way," said the short woman, shaking Isy's hand with a crushing grip.

The others introduced themselves in turn: a tall hook-nosed woman named Glic; a woman with pockmarked skin named Bela; another young woman named Gummy, who didn't appear to have any teeth; and another woman named Dera, quieter than the rest, who had a horizontal scar across the center of her face, leaving her with a stub of a nose. They asked Isy some more about the Amast, passing around a skin of wine as they did, and Isy loved it. She felt like she was sat on the bench with the other girls in Haberdam, sharing the latest gossip.

"You should fight with us, Isy. Let the men do the dirty work with their cock-shaped sticks," Flor said.

"Aye. They don't call the Darts of Pleasure the best archers in Yurr for nothing," Bela said.

"What does that name mean?" Isy asked.

Flor piped up. "Basically, we all got fed up of men sticking us with their own 'darts of pleasure'", she signed with her fingers, "so now we devote our time to sticking them back with darts of our own."

"Only ours are more deadly than their small, shriveled pricks," Glic said.

They all laughed, Isy too.

"We know how to stay alive, that's the difference," Ess said. "And Dera's right. You should fight with us. We can never have enough arrows in the volley, and with a bit of work, I can see you hitting a few more targets."

Isy wasn't sure what to say.

"Think on it," Ess said. She gave Isy a lingering smile, then turned and headed toward their group of tents. The others shook her hand, slapped her back and bid her farewell till next they met—soon, they hoped.

Isy returned to her camp in a jubilant mood, until thoughts of her argument with Vil trickled into her mind. She had to apologize to him. He didn't deserve such a selfish reaction, one utterly devoid of empathy. It just frustrated her how he hadn't listened when first they discussed going back to Haberdam. Usually he never missed a beat, but he was afraid, and fear had the power to deafen ears and stifle rational thought. The sky darkened as she searched for him, though on the ground the light of thousands of fires beat away the gloom. It proved fruitless. Nobody had seen him either. *Has he left?*

Worry and regret grew within her heart and mind, though when she found Edvar sat by the fire before her tent, roasting sausages, she couldn't help but smile. He turned to her, smiling.

"Hungry?"

Isy nodded and slumped down on the blanket next to him.

"How was your afternoon?" he asked.

"Busy. But interesting. I can't find Vil. Have you seen him? I'm worried about him."

"I haven't, sorry. Did something happen?"

"We got into a bit of an argument at the river. Well, it was kind of my fault. And then I stormed off and got talking to these archers. They were all women, and they were amazing. The best I've ever seen."

"Ah, they must be Baroness Ilda's famed Darts of Pleasure. And I agree—the best in the realm. I've heard a story about their captain... Ess I think is her name. Shot the wings off a moving butterfly from a hundred paces."

"They asked me to join them."

Edvar turned to her, an impressed look upon his face. "Will you?"

"I want to fight with the Amast."

"I fear they will be close to the heart of the fighting."

"What makes you say that?"

"It's what I heard today, when we all met to discuss plans."

"You mean to say they're going to sacrifice the Amast before themselves?"

"That's not what they intend. You heard Camos talking this morning. The best fighters have to be on the frontline. I have not seen them fight, but from what I hear of their bouts in the camp, each one of them counts for ten warriors. Are you ready to fight in the frontline too?"

Isy fell quiet. Edvar turned the sausages.

"I have never fought in a battle either," Edvar said. "Heck, until a few weeks ago I hadn't even hit another person. My father told me what it's like when the shield walls clash, and the spears thrust and lunge and tear flesh and throats, when men get crushed beneath the feet of their comrades, when all you can see is what's in front of you, hear the sounds of death and fear all around you, and all you can smell is blood, piss and crap. I will happily admit it—I am terrified. Does it not scare you?"

Isy did not respond for several heartbeats. "Yes. It scares me so much that, if I allowed myself to think of it, I would never leave this fireside. All I've done since we left Haberdam is think of anything but. I have filled my life with distractions, but whenever there is a free moment, the fear returns. A sense of dread. That soon I will die."

Edvar nodded. "When I wake up in the mornings, I have to battle with myself to get up. Each day is as daunting as the last. But once you begin to face it, the problem is never so bad. Everything feels worse when you're comfy and warm in bed.

"There's still a mountain yet to climb, but I think we can do it. Well, I hope we can. I suppose that's all we have in all of this—hope. The fuel that's keeping everybody going in this camp. Hope that we can be victorious, despite the odds. Hope that we will not be the ones to catch a stray arrow or the tip of a blade, that we will ride through the gates of Yurrisa as heroes. Hope can lift a defeated army, can unleash the energy to force a person back to their feet after being knocked down. Anything is possible while hope is alive. Once it fades, we lose."

"Do you think we'll win?"

Edvar handed her a couple of sausages, their skins nicely browned. "I have a plan," he said, and his eyes glowed in the darkness.

Episode Nine: Besieged by Woe

It was an archive. A library. A gateway to the past. The history of a forgotten people. The stacks of books were countless, lost in the gloom. It was one of the most significant archaeological discoveries ever made. And I had found it. Then I realized the dagger must be real. It must exist. And somewhere in this cave it may reside. How had this happened? How had an entire culture fallen from the face of Soria?

I did not sleep. I did not eat, nor drink. I became lost in a fever of want. Every waking moment I searched, and when not looking, I read. The language of some tomes I could not decipher, yet others I knew enough to make sense of. They spoke of a great war, the deaths of tens of thousands, the burning of forests, the destruction of mountains. And it spoke of the Dagger of Ulara. A weapon that stole the souls of those it killed. I read those words several times and became suddenly aware of my tired, weary-eyed self, hunched like a gremlin around my campfire.

I began to wonder whether I'd lost my mind.

From ***The Forgotten Daggers*** by S. T. Harris

One

A CHILLING WIND tore and howled at the canvas of the tent, its cold touch finding its way through rips and holes to send shudders down the spines of those within. Small fires burned in iron braziers to warm Edvar, Ashara, Jarat and the barons and baronesses, who were sitting in a close circle around a parchment-covered table. Edvar had lost track of the time they'd spent discussing plans and speculating on outcomes and rumors. He needed air, but he couldn't leave. Not with battle looming over them. Besides, he didn't quite fancy the weather.

That morning, they'd crested the final rise and beheld the rest of the Keeper's army upon the Plains of Lital, below. Twenty thousand proud Yurrish men and women united as one, prepared to die for the cause. When they saw the Keeper's banner, their roar shook the ground.

But was it enough? They had to take Yurrisa and then defend it from Tesh. Unless Rakar had drafted mercenaries, he had no more than ten thousand soldiers to defend the city. As for Tesh, rumors were flying around camp of how many soldiers marched behind him. Some said sixty thousand, others as many as a hundred. From the estimations of idle soldiers and delirious survivors, Edvar reckoned the figure to be around thirty thousand. More than what they had.

If Tesh made it to Yurrisa before them, they'd have little hope of succeeding. If he didn't, they would have a chance, but their window of opportunity would not be wide. A drawn-out siege had to be avoided at all costs. Edvar believed, or rather hoped, that he had a way to do just that. It was by no means guaranteed, and they would get only one chance, which would come with great risk. But with risk came reward.

"Siege engines cause too much damage. How can we defend the walls from the Karrabans when they lie in heaps of rubble, the gates without doors?" Ashara said, his voice bringing Edvar's wandering mind back to the present.

"I see no swifter way to overcome the defenses," Baroness Jalden said—a rationalist, if ever there was one. "The last thing we want is to besiege the city only for the Karrabans to march up behind us. We quite literally would be stuck between a rock and a hard place. Speed is everything."

"I agree with Jalden," Agon said. "How else can we breach the gates and walls in our time frame without bringing them down? If we relied solely on ladders, we wouldn't have an army left to face Tesh. There would surely be enough time to plug a hole in the wall before the Karrabans arrived?"

The conversation lulled as everyone considered Agon and Jalden's words.

Baroness Ura broke the quiet. "What are we to do if they're already there? The last we heard was that Tesh and his army were attacking Jackson's Pond and the villages around it. That would leave them what, five or six days from Yurrisa?"

"We're two," said Rijkard.

"Not the most generous of windows," Ashara said.

"It is only an estimate. Like I said, they may already be there," Ura added.

"That'll become clear when we arrive at Yurrisa," Ashara said. "In the meantime, I want scouts sent out to try and find where exactly they are. Hopefully our riders can return to us in time."

"What if we met them in the field?" Reska said in his drawl voice. "Leave Yurrisa and take on Tesh. We may be outnumbered but we can decide the battlefield."

"And risk Rakar coming up behind us?" Jarat said.

"That worm won't leave his hole," Rijkard said.

"Rakar is an opportunist. We lack the numbers to fight on two fronts, and once he learns that, he will come and we will be slaughtered," Ashara said.

"So retaking the city it is?" Ilda said.

The creak of chairs filled the silence in between the gales that continued to shake the tent. Too many unknowns plagued their decision-making.

"Would we need to worry about the state of our walls if when we retook the city, we evened the odds?" Reska said.

"Are you suggesting we open the Vault?" Jalden, seated next to him, asked with a look of incredulity.

Reska nodded.

A wave of unease spread around the table.

"I understand the fear of facing a great enemy," Ashara said. "When I became keeper, I made a vow to keep the Vault secure. Our ancestors fought and died to lock away the Daggers for the good of everyone. The power of those weapons changed us, and if we grow reliant upon it again, it will consume us. I have learned as much from our new allies, the Amast. Once upon a time, they looked like us, and the Dagger their people possessed broke apart their civilization and transformed them into what we see now. Its power corrupted them, turned them upon themselves, and nearly drove them into extinction. I do not wish to be the one to set us on that course, and if that Vault is opened, that could be the outcome."

"But it could save us. Surely we could return it to the Vault once we're done?" Reska asked.

"If we were to somehow wield the Dagger and succeeded in defeating Tesh, I fear we would not relinquish the power that saved us. Some would no doubt argue that it would keep us safe from future threats. Threats that may never materialize. And what then? We slip into the days of old."

Ashara sat forwards. "I know how it feels to have only a stick in your hand while facing a foe with a loaded crossbow. Just because we despair at the odds it does not mean the outcome is certain."

Since the beginning of the exchange, Edvar had wanted to interject. He hadn't told Ashara of his plan for fear he'd reject it. To present it now, when other options were lacking, made it harder to dismiss outright. If his plan worked—and the 'if' was significant—it would be quick, effective and would save lives.

"Sire, my lords and ladies, if I may, I have an idea," Edvar said. Ashara nodded for him to go on.

"There is, I believe, a secret way into the city."

"The tunnels we escaped through? Surely we would be spotted moving through the outer city?" Ashara said.

"No. Rakar knows of them. They will be sealed. I always remember seeing a tunnel on one of my father's old maps which led in from the sea. It reveals itself during low tide and leads up to the sewers beneath Igbut. The northern gate is less than a mile from there. We could sneak in only a small force, but I hope enough to take the northern gate. The chances of success would be greater if we could draw some of the defenders away, say, by launching an attack on the southern gate. We could then admit a large portion of our army through the northern gate, take the eastern, neutralize the siege engines, and then take the southern."

"Have you been through this tunnel before, Edvar?" Agon asked.

"No."

"So how can you guarantee it exists?" Ura said.

"I can't."

"Do you have the map with you now?" Jarat asked.

Edvar shook his head.

It roused a rare laugh from Reska. "How can we take you seriously, lad?"

"From what I can see, you don't have a choice. If Tesh isn't already in Yurrisa, you've got mere days, if not hours, to take the city. There's no time to construct the number of siege weapons we'd need in order to breach one of the gates, and we all know about the wasteful slaughter of trying to take a wall with ladders.

"I may not have been through this particular tunnel, but I have traversed every single other one on that map. My father had it made and I trust him with all my heart. I do not deny that there is tremendous risk involved. If spotted, all involved would surely die. That's why I volunteer myself to lead." Edvar turned to Ashara. "You trusted me before, sire, and I let you down. Now let me make up for it."

Ashara looked around the circle. Edvar couldn't bring himself to do the same. Instead his gazed at the ground.

"It is a fine plan, Ed. Indeed, just like one of your father's," Ashara said.

"No," Ura said. "It is better. Harada was all thrust and pump. This is clever. I give you permission, Edvar, to take your choosing of my people. Whoever and whatever you need is yours."

"As goes for me," Agon said.

One by one, the others agreed. Until it fell to Jarat.

"If it pleases you sire, I would like to join Edvar."

"Jarat, with all due respect, we need you on the battlefield."

"If there's one thing you're not short of, sire, it's brilliant leaders. I was born in Yurrisa, grew up on its streets. I know every alleyway, every street, every junction. Edvar and I will make sure those gates get opened."

Hope fluttered in Edvar's chest. "It's true, sire. With Jarat, our chances of success would increase massively. We need all the help we can get."

"I too would volunteer myself to go, sire."

Edvar's head snapped around to look at Rijkard.

"I have experience in this kind of warfare, and I would be honored to stand beside Jarat and Edvar."

Ashara pondered in silence, thumb rubbing against the bristles of his grey-shot moustache. "Very well. With the three of you, I have no doubt you shall succeed. And it matters greatly that you do. For all our sakes."

Two

At the sound of a horn, the camp sprung to life. Men and women hurried into organized companies. Isy and the Amast stood still, bemused.

"Should we be going somewhere too?" Yera asked.

"I don't know," Isy muttered. "Let's see what's going on." She wandered toward the closest group of assembling warriors. The captain, a brown-haired woman with a strong, angled face, was standing upon a stool at the head of her company, addressing those under her charge.

"We march for Yurrisa in an hour. At the city, we will join Keeper Ashara's regiment in the attack of the southern gate. Once we're inside, we march for the keep. Your lieutenants will brief you further." She dismissed them and stepped down. Isy turned to the Amast. Nobody said a word.

Solemnly, Isy packed her things, her mood still miserable after her argument with Vil. She had yet to find him, and two days had passed since their argument. No one else had seen him either.

Worry plagued her thoughts, and it had begun to creep into her sleep. The night previous, she'd dreamt of chasing after Vil, only for him to be killed just as she caught up to him. *Where are you?* Vil hated the woods. Surely he would not have gone off alone. Or had her words been that painful for him?

Isy bit her lip. Guilt racked her chest. Vil hadn't deserved that reaction. Compassion and empathy had abandoned her and left selfishness in their stead. The reality was that Vil was scared, just as she was. She should have hugged him, told him everything was going to be fine, that soon they would be exploring the vaults of the Grand Library together, without a care in the world. What a truly awful friend she had been.

To further dampen her spirits, the realization was dawning that these next hours could be her last. That soon a great many people she cared about might die. Only her will and determination to defend those she loved kept fear from swallowing her.

One of Baron Agon's messengers appeared before them, a spotty youth with mousy brown hair and a noticeable underbite. He gazed up at the Amast, cap falling off his head, and stuttering, he asked them to follow him to Agon's regiment. Kora nodded his agreement and turned to Isy. He held a bunched fist over his chest, and the other Amast copied. And then they were gone, lumbering through the crowd, leaving Isy all alone. She slung her travel sack over her shoulder and headed toward the camp of the Darts of Pleasure.

Her pondering whether to accept Ess's offer had been short. Deep down, in spite of the risks, Isy wanted to fight with them. She wanted to share their togetherness, their bond. She had spent that morning shooting with them, and as the hours wore on the more certain she had become in her decision. They had made her feel like one of their own and kitted her out with a complete set of russet leather armor to match the other Darts. Their drilling had been arduous, and at times, tedious, but their patient guidance had been masterful. All of the training from her youth quickly returned, and she built upon it with the different things they each had to show her.

"Isy!"

She spun around to find Edvar weaving through the press of bodies.

"I'm guessing they went with your plan then?"

Edvar smiled, though it didn't linger.

"Myself, Jarat, Rijkard and Yurr's best will make the attempt."

"You're going? You never mentioned that!"

"I must. I know where the secret tunnel is, or so I hope. It is my plan; the responsibility is mine."

Isy bit her lip. Pain stabbed at her gut. She didn't want to lose him.

"I'm guessing you're shooting with the fabled Darts of Pleasure?" Edvar said. "The bards will sing of you yet. How do you feel?"

"Sick."

Edvar smiled. "I'm not feeling too sharp myself, but we can lament when we're in the grave," he said. His brows furrowed, and he looked to be searching for his words. Slowly, they came. "Before we march off, I just want to say that the happiest parts of my days these past weeks have been talking to you. I just hope, when all this is over, we can do the same again."

"Me too." Isy met his deep amber eyes. He met hers. Their gazes locked.

Edvar stumbled forwards, banging heads with Isy. Pain flared in Isy's forehead. No warm stickiness of blood, thankfully. A burly soldier carrying two stakes upon his shoulders had bumped into Edvar.

"I'm so sorry!" Edvar said.

Isy felt as if she'd just been slapped out of some intoxicating spell.

"It's fine," she said, rubbing her head. And then arms embraced her. Edvar hugged her tightly. Isy reciprocated. Tears came to the corners of her eyes.

Without another word, Edvar left.

Three

The wandering moon was near full, its icy rays a blessing and a curse. They lit up the cliff face and allowed Edvar to seek out the secret tunnel, but they also illuminated their rowboats for any watchful eyes. Edvar sat at the bow of the lead boat, clinging onto the edge. Nausea churned in his stomach and it wasn't to do with the constant rocking up and down.

Edvar glanced at the towers atop the cliff, punctuating the great sandstone walls that enveloped the city. Torches and braziers burned along them. He couldn't believe their half dozen rowboats had not been spotted. Despite the slow and steady rhythm of the rowers, Edvar was afraid they were making too much noise. Their numbers were mostly made up of Jarat's finest. Rijkard and his chosen few rowed at the back, lost in the murk.

Since the Amast camp, the old baron seemed a changed man. Certainly, he frowned less. Edvar knew he should have more faith, but no matter how much he told himself so, the thought remained lodged in his mind that the Council had gotten to Rijkard first, that they had offered him the independence he longed for, and that now he was guiding them into a trap.

"How much further, Edvar?" Jarat muttered, raspy voice like a growl. Edvar didn't reply. Heat began to rise to his cheeks. He strained his eyes, trying to penetrate the darkness, and through the gloom spotted a jagged piece of rock jutting out into the sea to create a sort of miniature bay. Edvar recognized the shape from the map and hope flourished in his chest. He directed the rowers closer, his heart beating faster. They crept along the cliff face, hope ebbing like the tide, until there, tucked into a corner out of sight, was a crack in the rock barely wide enough for a row boat to scrape through.

"Are you sure?" Jarat asked.

"Yes," Edvar lied.

Oars in, they pushed themselves through the gap, hands on rock, and soon the tunnel widened. The sound of the waves fell away, and a pungent smell of seaweed tickled Edvar's nose. He widened the shutter of his lantern, revealing a long and narrow tunnel which led off into darkness. The low ceiling was lined with stalactites of various sizes, and here and there, on rocks that rose above the water, stalagmites climbed to meet them.

"Remind me again what this was used for?" Jarat asked.

"It may never have been used. Or not by Keeper Bientas, who built it. He had a knack for rubbing people the wrong way. You know the kind: high taxes, brutal justice."

"Bastard."

"Indeed. So quite rightly he felt threatened and had this secret escape route built."

"Did he ever have to use it?"

"No. He drowned in the bath tub."

"Drowned?"

"If you believe the chroniclers."

"And you don't?"

"Whoever controls the flow of information can manipulate things however they please. They can re-write history, erase people and nations from time. How can we, hundreds of years on, verify that what they say is true? Do we just accept it?"

"What choice do we have?"

"That's the problem. Many lack the choice. But not us. We have the means to uncover the truth and disprove the lies. We have a duty to do so."

Jarat smiled.

"What?" Edvar said, a little offended. "Something my father used to say?"

"No. He was never that wise."

"Ahead, sirs," muttered one of Jarat's keener-eyed soldiers. She pointed to a small wooden jetty ahead, which led to a closed iron door.

They swiftly disembarked without a rattle or clink thanks to their padded armor and scabbards. Edvar gripped the iron ring of the door. It wouldn't twist. A nearby soldier loaned a hand, and with gritted teeth, they forced it to turn. The door creaked inwards, and a cool and bitter draft escaped from within.

Hope stirred in Edvar's chest. The fact that the Council hadn't barricaded or sealed the door surely meant they didn't know of it. Knowing Rakar and Mara, though, there could be something else. An ambush may be waiting for them further ahead. It made more sense, after all, to wait for them to move into a position of no escape.

They reached a fork in the dank passageway. If Edvar's recollection of the map was correct, left would take them to the keep and right to the old city walls in Igbut, which at the time of this tunnel's construction, was Yurrisa's perimeter.

Edvar ordered a halt. Silence fell around him. He walked on alone a few paces, shining his lantern down both passageways. Holding his breath, he half-expected his light to fall upon waiting warriors.

Nothing.

Edvar flashed his lantern—the signal to move—and led on down the right-hand tunnel. With each step, his confidence grew. The tunnel meandered left and right until at last they reached the end—a circular metal grate. Edvar peered though it to find a sewer tunnel. The stench of feces and piss confirmed it.

"Shine the light here," Jarat said, fumbling with the grate. "I think I see a latch." Edvar did as asked and soon heard a click as the grate swung open. One by one, they hopped down.

"How far? The sun will rise soon," Rijkard said.

"Once we're up this ladder, it's a short run to the warehouse. The gate's a few minutes from there."

The riskiest part came next—seventy-two soldiers navigating the streets of Yurrisa without being seen. Edvar could sense the tension amongst the group. He grabbed the first rung, swallowed hard, but a firm hand grabbed his shoulder.

"I'll go first," Rijkard whispered.

A sudden sense of fear gripped Edvar's chest. Rijkard was halfway up the ladder before Edvar could muster a protestation. Was he about to let off a signal to the defenders? Would they all be killed here, in this stinking pit, without a chance or hope?

Tense minutes passed. The smell of sweat and excrement was thick in the air of the confined sewer. Edvar decided to go after him, until Rijkard's head appeared.

"Hurry."

There was no hurrying a company of so many up an old and rusty ladder. At the top, Edvar found himself in a narrow alleyway cluttered with rotten refuse. Rats twitched and somewhere in the gloom, a cat hissed. His chosen warriors looked at him expectantly, and his heart thudded against his chest. This was the part he was least looking forward to. Losing in combat at the gate was one thing. Getting spotted before they even got there was another. With fear clawing at his resolve, Edvar took a deep breath and set off along the route he had meticulously planned, ducking down adjoining alleyways and avoiding streets at all cost. When they did have to cross a street, they moved in pairs, sprinting from shadow to shadow. They had timed it perfectly. It was the hour before dawn, the darkest of all, and the moons had fallen to cloud.

Soon the murky form of the abandoned warehouse came into view. They hurried inside, and stillness returned to Yurrisa. A peace that would end at dawn.

Four

No matter how much water Isy swilled around her mouth, the bitter taste of vomit lingered. Like that last bit of pottage that wouldn't budge from the base of the cauldron. She laughed to herself. How far she had come from scrubbing pots. She was glad that she was no longer in that miserable house in Haberdam, even if today she was to march to her death.

With the great sandstone walls of Yurrisa looming in the hazy dawn, fear found its voice. Retching and farting sounded throughout the loose press of waiting soldiers. Isy was glad she wasn't alone in feeling nerves. Around her, people comforted each other with smiles, jokes, pats on the back. Isy wished Vil was with her. There was still no sign of him. *He cannot make it back to Haberdam alone. What have I done?* To make matters worse, she couldn't leave and go after him. She would never abandon everyone in their time of greatest need. *But Vil needs me too... Or maybe he doesn't.*

"Isy," a deep Amast voice said, tearing her away from the torment in her mind. Tulasc, Kora and Pekira carried shields that looked able to withstand a battering ram, and their bodies were clad in a bizarre assemblement of armor. The smiths travelling with the army had broken apart greaves, cuirasses, pauldrons, and mail and refashioned them to the Amast's size. The jobs had been hastily done, and there were a great many leather straps flapping about them, but complete with their huge double-ended spears, looked like gods of war.

"Wow. If I saw you charging at my gate, I'd let you right in. What fool would stand in your way?" Isy said. Some of her fellow archers laughed.

They smiled in their strange, grimaced fashion.

"We have come to say goodbye," Kora said, kneeling before her. The others copied. "You helped us when we needed it most. You gave us an opportunity to save our people. That will never be forgotten in the hearts of any Amast. But I thank you for something else. You have shown me something, Isy. For too long the Amast have lived in ignorance of the world. Life is a struggle, is a fight in itself. And for some it is much greater than others. If you do not fight, you will succumb. We must do something we vowed never again to do—fight. Fight for our futures, for yours and everybody else's. If we do not, we all shall perish."

Isy hugged him. Tears fell from her eyes, and she buried her face into the nape of his neck. "This will all be over soon, and then we can help your people build their new home. Be careful."

She hugged the others in turn and watched as they fell in amongst the press of soldiers moving forwards into battle formation. Nothing would happen to them, she told herself, and she would make sure she would play her part in ensuring they stayed safe. At the end of the day, she would embrace them all again. *This is not goodbye.*

Isy felt strong in her leather armor, complete with vambraces and fingerless gloves. Her russet leather breeches were tucked into knee-high boots—by far the comfiest shoe she'd ever worn. Hanging from her hip was a quiver full of arrows, feathered ends pointing forwards—a tip offered by Ess. "Foolish men point them backwards, and when they come to shoot, realize their arrows have fallen out." Another canvas-covered quiver was fastened to her belt at the small of her back. Over her shoulders was a woolen seaweed-green cloak. Isy found it just as warm as her fur Amast cloak.

Every archer in the Darts of Pleasure wrapped their right arm in white material—the mark of the company, Ess said. "If ever you get separated on the battlefield, look for a white arm and head to it. Remember, we survive by sticking together. And if you get injured, it serves as a bandage to bind your wound. No man has ever come up with that idea."

The horn of the Keeper reverberated through the cold morning air. Everybody knew what it meant. The din of conversation died, and the soughing of the wind over the fields surrounding the city dominated the void it left. The horn rang out again, and the march forwards began.

Isy's knees trembled. She felt as if she would chew through her bottom lip. She looked at the women around her, their faces like stone. Isy could only imagine what her own must look like. A part of her wished she'd left with Vil. Who was she kidding? Over the mass of moving bodies before her, she saw the giant Amast and her fear fell away. *This is for them. This is for all of us.*

Five

The bells rang loud and panicked across Yurrisa. Hidden in the shadows of the abandoned warehouse, Edvar and the others lay in wait. He peered through a crack in a boarded window at the cobbled street. Echoing along it came a shout. Another. Steps rushed toward him, and into view burst a group of soldiers, breaths billowing mist in the cold morning air. They charged right by the warehouse, heading straight for the gate. Edvar looked at Jarat, Rijkard, and the others sitting and crouching in wait. It was nearly time.

The waiting was insufferable. The fate of thousands of men and women rested in his hands. If they did not open the gates—and in good time—they wouldn't overcome the defenders. At the hands of the storm brewed by catapults, trebuchets and archers, they'd suffer dreadful casualties. And any of those who did survive faced the potential prospect of meeting a fresh Karraban army marching up behind them. One bad decision, one hesitant moment, could see that outcome happen. Everything his father had taught him was beginning to make sense. He slowed his breathing and tried to quell his racing thoughts.

Beyond the window, Edvar heard more hurried feet. The late risers. Dawn was a good time to fight. Disturbed sleep made for groggy soldiers. Any advantage was vital, and often the mental ones played the most significant of roles.

Edvar looked at Rijkard and Jarat. Visions of calmness, both of them. A look of acceptance in their eyes said they were content with whatever came next. He saw it in the faces of some of the more experienced soldiers too. Now he understood why they mocked him for being 'green'—for his face turning green with stress and nausea.

The time to attack the gate was Edvar's to call. His plan was to wait until battle had been engaged at the southern gate. Edvar hoped some defenders from the northern gate would be diverted. It was a risk, and it meant delaying while their comrades potentially died. But they had to make sure they opened this gate, and with fewer defenders to overcome, they'd have a greater chance of doing so. And then a quarter of the force would then be inside Yurrisa. After that, the battle would soon be over, or so Edvar hoped.

All had fallen quiet outside. Edvar tried to imagine what was happening beyond the walls. Ashara had half of the army at the southern gate. The rest of the force was split in two and lay in wait out of sight, at the northern and eastern gates. The plan was simple: once the northern gate was taken, neutralize the siege engines, and open the eastern and southern gates. And then it was to the keep, to put an end to this madness. All before the Karraban army showed up. Then it would be back to the walls recently reclaimed. If it worked, Edvar couldn't begin to imagine what the chroniclers would write.

Edvar could sense the unease in the room, the desire to move, to act. He resisted it, waiting for the right moment. He heard horns in the distance, and what he thought was the snap and creak of trebuchets. He tried his best not to think about their great stones landing upon Ashara and the others. In the room, every eye, it seemed, was upon him.

Edvar peered outside once more. He could hear voices shouting to one another.

"They're hitting the south with everything! The Captain said to hotfoot it there now."

With anticipation bursting in his chest, Edvar looked at Jarat and nodded. The General signaled and by the time Edvar turned around, everyone was up, ready to move. Jarat took the lead, and Edvar joined Rijkard in the line of soldiers filing out of the warehouse, running at a crouch toward the opposite wall, where the street was still bathed in shadow. Over the roofs of houses and shops, Edvar could see the sandstone parapets and towers of the northern gate. Its wooden doors were no doubt closed and barred, drawbridge hoisted up over the dry moat, portcullis locked in place. He could see archers on the battlements, eyes to the south, and a steady stream of men and women running along the walls in the same direction.

Jarat led the force the opposite way to which the defenders looked. Silently, they made it to the wall and moved along it to an iron-studded door. Inside lay the gatehouse and mechanisms that raised the drawbridge and portcullis. It was unlocked.

They moved along candle-lit corridors and through empty chambers with fires burning in hearths. Edvar couldn't believe they hadn't been spotted, though as the thought processed, the inevitable yelp of a panicked defender rang out. A gurgled cry followed, then the clash of steel. It was the trigger for everyone else to fill the air with cries of battle.

The press around Edvar tightened. Armored shoulders barged by him, shields buffeted him forwards. But Edvar resisted. He couldn't bring himself to reach for his short sword. His shield arm sagged to his side. The clamor around him faded. All he could hear was the violent pulse of his heart. Heat radiated all over his body. Lights flashed in his dimming vision, and his strength drained away, his armor doubling in weight.

The two forces met with a clatter of shields, swords wildly thrust over the top, and idle he stood, battling with himself. He heard his name, voice familiar. A voice he had not heard in a very long time. *Father...*

"Edvarrr!" The shout slowly registered. He blinked and saw Rijkard. The old baron grabbed his shoulders.

"Fight it, Edvar. Fight it with your sword in your hand, as your father would have." Those simple words broke something in him, cut through his fear. Rijkard slapped him on the back, pushed him forwards, and next he was racing down the corridor after the old baron. Edvar drew his sword. The hilt felt good in his hand, light almost. His body pulsed with a sense of strength, with the power of his famed father. He was with him then and there. Edvar knew it.

Edvar and Rijkard caught up to the fighting. The defenders were circled around the great cogs and wheels that operated the bridge and portcullis. Some of Jarat's soldiers had already stormed the staircase in the corner and no doubt were clearing the walls. The defending Yurrish were fighting as all cornered soldiers did—like deranged dogs. Only months before, everyone in this room had been allies, would have died for one another, and now they were cutting each other down with hate-filled hearts. Edvar wanted to shout out above the clamor for them to lay down their arms and join them in ridding the city of the traitors, but they showed no signs of surrender, and if anything, were cutting down more of Edvar's comrades.

Edvar was pushed forward into the fray, joining the press of bodies encircling the remaining defenders. The shields of men and women behind him pushed hard against his back, and he pushed forward with his own, lifting his sword arm high so as not to nick any of his comrades. The shouting and screaming grew louder in his helmet, and somehow he found himself in the front rank, struggling to maintain his balance with bodies lifeless and writhing cluttering the floor, as well as the slickness of blood. Edvar kept his head down beneath his wooden shield and, with gritted teeth, swung his sword, aim indiscriminate. The first time he cut air, the second rebounded against a shield. The connection sent a shock up his arm, and as much as he wanted to strike again, he had to take a moment to recover.

Something broke. The resistance he felt suddenly gave away and he was surging forwards with the pressure at his back. The defenders had collapsed. The attackers rushed to the great winches to lower the bridge and raise the portcullis, and another group went outside and unbarred the gate. More men and women were returning from their venture upstairs, but the alarm had been raised.

Edvar ran outside, following Rijkard, and heard the roar of four thousand soldiers as they rushed toward the drawbridge and open gate. Leading them were Jalden and Reska.

"With me!" Edvar bellowed, sword aloft, and they followed. Racing through the streets with a small army at his back and a sword in his hand, Edvar felt god-like.

To the south, the slow, rotating rocks of the defender's trebuchets filled the grey morning air. Each one was potentially the death of more of Edvar's comrades, of his friends. He had to stop them.

He glanced over his shoulder, and dropped back to Jarat.

"We need to stop the trebuchets."

The General's grim expression told him he'd already thought of it.

"Take a few hundred warriors and see what you can do. Rijkard and I will see the gates open," Edvar said. Jarat didn't question him, nodding and beckoning to his warriors to form up and follow. They headed right, uphill toward the trebuchet stations, and Edvar went left, toward the eastern gate. Turning the bend, they screeched to a halt.

The street was blocked by a line of shields, the defenders six deep. Archers, positioned upon the roofs of the houses, wasted no time in loosing a volley in their direction. Edvar brought up his shield just as a brace of arrowheads punctured the wood. Screams rang out all around him.

"Shield wall!" he shouted, and everyone rushed to stand shoulder to shoulder, locking shields with the person beside them. The incessant thrum of arrows hitting wood, punctuated by the cries of the unlucky, was all he could hear. His breath grew short. *What do I do?* Edvar cursed himself for sending Jarat off. He peered through a gap in between shields. The defenders were happy to hold their ground, archers picking them off one by one.

They could not just stand here and take it. They had to retreat or charge.

Edvar looked over his shoulder and recognized a captain named Misa, a capable woman, taller than most men and serious as crucifixion. Dedicated and reliable, Edvar had faith she would carry out the plan forming in his mind.

"Captain, take a force and head down that alley we passed. You should find another joining it halfway down. It'll take you to a street running behind these bastards. You know the rest."

"Consider it done."

Misa shouted orders and the shell of shields rippled as she retreated to the alley. Edvar hoped the defenders hadn't thought of it already.

Arrows continued to hail down. It was now or never.

"Form up, ready to charge," he shouted at the top of his lungs. He fixed his gaze on the shield directly opposite him, took a deep breath.

"Charge!"

Edvar set off at a sprint. At first, he thought he was alone, but the roar at his heels told him otherwise. Arrows filled the air. He raised his shield. Ahead, he could see faces amid helmets, the whites of eyes. He lifted his sword and leapt the final few steps.

Six

In any other situation, the violence of the wails filling Isy's ears would have frozen her to the spot. Now was not a time to be idle. Great stones smashed into the earth as if hurled by the gods, crushing a dozen soldiers at a time. Arrows filled the air like an unending swarm of angered hornets. Clusters of stone balls the size of a man's head showered down indiscriminately. And yet Ashara and his warriors still charged. They were a hundred yards from the wall, voices breaking with their cries of battle.

At the head of the onrushing force were the Amast, under the cover of a giant cat — a wooden shed on wheels which housed a battering ram stouter than any Isy had ever seen. Covering the cat was a density of hides, well-soaked to protect from fire, hot pitch and oil. That cat was the beacon of hope in the minds of every charging fighter, and as long as it remained intact, neither their courage nor their belief would falter.

Close behind the Amast were scores of ladders, hauled upon shoulders. Isy didn't fancy climbing up one of them. The odds of that, she hoped, were slim. She was at the back of the charging force, along with a third of the army's archers. The rest had been split into small companies and placed amongst the advancing infantry, to cover the assault.

Men and women fell as if plucked by the cold hands of death, their roars ending in gurgles. The cat reached the gate, the least defensible of the three, lacking a dry moat and drawbridge like the others. The first beat of the ram sent the giant wooden doors shuddering. Ladders slammed against the walls, and a barrage of arrows rained down on those trying to get up the rungs. The attacking archers were in position now, setting up their shields and loosing arrows in response. A dozen defenders fell from the battlements, knocking off some of those scaling the ladders.

Isy and the Darts moved forward. Her heart was like thunder in her chest.

"We join the forward archers and cover the cat," Ess shouted. They would need to hurry. A shower of rocks and stone balls descended from the walls onto the cat's roof. Most rebounded, a few sat on top. One or two big stones smashed through. Isy gasped.

She could not bear to think of the damage it would do to the Amast. The thought put an extra stride in her step, dispelling her fear. She formed up with the other archers. Shield planted in the ground before her, she nocked her first arrow and drew her bowstring. Ess's commands were clear, precise. As one, they loosed upon her order, the volley raining down upon the battlements where a catapult was being reloaded. Isy lost sight of her own arrow, but bodies tumbled over the edge where she thought it had gone and the catapult did not spring its load.

Once more, Ess directed the volley. It struck with deadly accuracy, creating a kill zone upon the battlements above the gate. The pressure on the cat ebbed, and more ladders managed to grapple onto the walls. Attackers fearlessly shimmied up them.

Still the trebuchets and catapults flung their deadly loads. Too many died before they saw action. Isy wasn't lacking for it. The shooting was incessant, and only a few times did arrows come their way in return. The gate still stood.

The Amast were no doubt giving everything they had. And she knew from their stubbornness they would sooner die than give up. *That gate has to give. Please give.*

The defenders upon the gatehouse battlements had changed tact. They'd taken to dousing the cat with oil, pitch and fire. At first the wet hides resisted the flames, but with so much fuel, fires began to burn.

Seemingly from nowhere, a wave of defenders surged onto the walls and drove the attackers back. Ladders were poled off. Men and women fell to their deaths. Some on the ground were crushed by their bodies.

Ashara bellowed rallying calls, his voice carrying above the clamor. The tide was turning against them.

Where are you Edvar?

Seven

Blood filled Edvar's mouth. A firm blow from a shield had beaten back his heroic leap into the fray. His nose was broken yet again, but the fire within him still burned, and if anything, even hotter. He got behind his own shield and pushed back, thrusting low with his sword under his foe's shield. He felt a brief moment of resistance as it struck armor, before it slid forward through flesh. His enemy fell.

Edvar's comrades were at his side. The clap of shields sent his ears ringing. The defenders were forced back a few steps, and the fighting turned fierce. Hacks and chops and lunges. The combat was too close for spears, the streets too narrow. Shield, sword, axe and mace rained down, bludgeoning and dismembering, hammering against shields and armor without any grace.

Edvar couldn't catch his breath. He felt a tap on his shoulder and an iron-faced man offered to take his position. They exchanged places, and Edvar dropped back a few ranks to assess the situation, holding shield aloft from the arrows that steadily rained down. The archers were stood upon a flat-roofed apartment block. The next house along, closest to them, rose above it, not too high to jump from.

Further back through the ranks he dropped, ordering a half-dozen soldiers to follow him. Without a second thought, he burst through a door and landed in a heap on the floor. The next man behind him, a fair-skinned youth with an impressively-neat beard, helped him to his feet. They moved up the floors and climbed onto the roof, crouching as they approached the edge. The archers stood on the roof of the adjoining building, the drop about fifteen feet.

Edvar counted down with his fingers for the others to see, and then he jumped. He aimed his feet at the closest archer and landed upon him, arse awkwardly connecting with his neck to promptly snap it, as he struck the ground. Edvar's comrades dropped down too, and before he could get to his feet, the archers had been cut down.

Below, the fighting was fierce, but they were winning. The defender's line was thin and was close to breaking in the center. He saw Rijkard swinging his longsword, and his bear-like northerners hacking with their axes.

Behind the defenders, a group appeared from around a corner. Misa. The steel of her axe glinted in the morning sun as she hefted it in the air and brought it down into the neck of an unwitting defender, sending a streak of blood over his comrades. The butchery began, the skirmish won.

Edvar climbed down with the help of the others and met a blood-covered Rijkard. None of it appeared to be his own. They nodded and, without a word, headed for the eastern gatehouse.

A token force lay in wait in the cog room. It took no time at all for the portcullis to be raised and the gates opened. Attackers swarmed inside the city, the bear-like Camos in the front rank beside Ura. Edvar was pleased to see the old warrior.

On the south side, he had no clue what was happening. He staggered up the battlements, using his hands on the steps, his legs weak. At the top, the sight reduced him to his knees.

Black smoke plumed. Catapults hurled their loads from upon the walls, but the trebuchets had ceased. Jarat had succeeded, it seemed. But judging from the sounds drifting toward him, the fighting was still fierce at the gate. How was Ashara faring? Were Isy and the Amast okay? He had to find out, he had to help. Edvar pushed himself to his feet and began to run along the battlements.

Eight

Flames consumed the cat, but still the ram battered the gate. At the base of the wall, bodies had begun to pile up. Some attackers had used their dead weight to support the ladders. Crows and gulls circled above, and even with battle still raging, some had the courage to swoop upon the fallen.

Isy was running out of arrows. Her first quiver hadn't lasted long, and now she had just a dozen left in her backup. They continued to shoot at those upon the walls, each volley bringing death, though Isy hadn't seen a single arrow of hers land. She may well have killed someone. Maybe killed a bunch. She had no time to ponder the morality of it. Ess's orders flowed like a stream, clear and consistent. But as well as they were doing, the same could not be said for the rest of the army.

Ashara roared with a breaking voice, but he was too far back for the attackers to hear. Edvar had said they had to force the Keeper to agree to hold back, instead of leading the attack. For him to die would render everything pointless, all these deaths meaningless.

Still the Amast battered the gate, fire consuming the cat. Tears welled in Isy's eyes. Kora was in there. Her friends were in there.

"Look!" someone beside her shouted and pointed. There was fighting upon the battlements, defenders hurled over the parapets at the eastern side. The arrow storm from the defenders eased. And then she realized the trebuchets had stopped too. In a few heartbeats, the battle had turned. The gates swung open. The burning cat was hurled into the air, and from underneath the Amast emerged, coughing, falling to their knees. But alive.

Nine

Someone handed Edvar a waterskin. His arm trembled as he raised it. The cool water washed over his sweaty face. He slicked back his hair and looked down at thousands of his comrades streaming through the gate. Amongst them, upon his black mount, was Ashara.

"Welcome home," Edvar shouted down, a grin upon his face.

The beaming Keeper waved his sword and spurred his horse through the gate. Edvar picked up his sword and turned to the city, to the great keep upon the hill, shielded by its three walls. Any army would bleed out before taking it. Unless they knew of the ancient tunnels that led inside.

Ten

It took less time and effort to breach the keep than it did the city walls. It was clear Rakar and Mara hadn't thought they'd get this far. Either that or they'd committed too many to the defense of the walls and left none in reserve. Malfan was dead, and he was their military mind. Neither had commanded an army in battle, let alone defended a city from besiegement.

The underground passageways were unguarded, to Edvar's surprise. Rakar knew of them, he was sure. *Had he simply not thought of it?*

The attackers stormed through the tunnels and into the keep, fought off the few defenders that manned the gates and walls, and admitted the waiting army. Edvar met Ashara in the final bailey, not far from the entrance to the Iron Tower. They embraced.

"You were like the shade of Harada The Great upon that wall. It stirred my soul to see it. You have won us this battle, Ed. Now it is time to put it to an end. Where do you think they'll be? The Tower?"

"The Great Hall. Upon the thrones."

The door to the hall was closed and barred, but a group of warriors reduced it to splinters with battering rams and axes. They streamed inside. A small force of defenders put up a fight, but they were quickly overwhelmed. Soon it became apparent who it was they were defending.

Rakar sat upon Ashara's throne, crown upon his brow. His face was pale and gaunt and, as ever, he wore his plain black robe. Sitting to his right, in the throne once used by Ashara's wife, Jessyia, was Mara. Her pale, bony hands rested on the arms of the chair and her head was tilted down to sit on her chest. The front of her green dress was stained red with blood. Edvar had seen a lot of dead bodies today and she appeared to be another.

Sword in hand, Ashara walked toward the seemingly unarmed Rakar. Edvar tailed behind.

"I honestly never thought I'd see you in this throne room again, unless on your knees, in chains," Rakar murmured.

"It'll be the last time I ever see you in here," Ashara spat back, continuing his walk. He stopped at the bottom of the steps leading up to the thrones. Blood pooled at Mara's feet. "Are you satisfied with what you've done?" Ashara screamed, holding out his arms.

Rakar was silent a while. He looked up, past them. "I have failed. My only regret is that I should have planned it better."

"So this is your doing alone? You trying to kill me?"

"I had help, of course. But they were never part of *the* plan. They were tools. A means to an end."

"You really are a traitorous bastard."

"I knew you would come back with your army of ignorant loyalists to reclaim your seat. Do you think me that much of a fool?" He smiled, looking down at Ashara. "Why do you think Tesh is on his way here? To secure your demise, of course." He laughed, sat forward in his chair.

"Why, Rakar? Why betray your own and ally with the Karrabans? You had power, you had influence, you had wealth."

"But I was not the keeper. You think what I had was power. What is power without control over the Vault, over the Dagger? Just imagine what we could become if we used the Dagger properly. It is a gift. We are fools to ignore it. Your stupid mother should never have named you her successor. And all you have done is prove me right ever since. It is the Council that stopped you from foundering sooner. And all along you believed it was your divine self? The gloriously noble keeper. You are nothing but a fool."

"And there it is. I respected you, Rakar. I trusted you with all my heart, and for that *I am* the biggest fool in Soria."

"Tesh will show you no mercy. He hates no man more than you. Do you even know why, Ashara? Or has your naivety and ignorance blinded you to that too? You ruined his life. You and your wretched mother. He believes you turned his father against him and stole his one love. For years he has been sitting out in the cold, biding his time, plotting your end. This I knew and turned to my advantage. So please, I may have failed, but you will not succeed. Kill me now and be done with it, or let me live so I may see you die."

Ashara fell quiet, his shoulders slumped, breathing slow and heavy. Edvar could see him at any moment hefting his sword and loping off Rakar's head.

He didn't get an opportunity to do anything.

Into the Great Hall poured the reverberant clangs of the city bells. The same bells that had rang out that morning as they marched to battle. It meant only one thing.

The Karrabans had arrived.

Episode Ten: When All is Lost

As I padded about that lightless ancient library in search of this soul-stealing dagger, haunting the aisles like the ghosts of its creators, my desire began to wane. I wondered about the people who had once lived here. About the great city that had stood upon the cliff above my head. What had happened? Was the Dagger of Ulara responsible for their end? What were the bounds of this weapon, if it could wipe a civilization from the annals of time? Should its power once again be unleashed upon the world? Or should it remain forgotten, beyond the fingers of the corrupt?

But it would mean so much to our understanding of life. Imagine the secrets it could reveal. Are we now better able to handle its power than those that once lived? Or is that the question of an ignorant fool? Humanity has not changed in thousands of years. The lure of power over others is greater today than no doubt it was then. And if history has taught me anything, it's that those people who seek power rarely embrace the responsibilities that come with it. It is power alone they want, power to do whatever they want. Would this dagger be a curse to us all? Would it doom humanity to its end?

I came to a stop. A want to find the dagger and a sense of foreboding clashed within me like warring armies. I needed to make a decision.

I headed back to my camp, but faltered, turned back round, back again. My mind was afire. I could only imagine what Uren would do if I told him of this place. He would raze it to the ground, hunting for the dagger. And what then if it was found? In hundreds of years, could someone like me be walking through the vaults of our own past? The blame for it all would be mine. That final thought sobered me, and conviction emerged.

I packed up my things, and from my travel sack pulled out my last stick of dynamite. Before I lit the fuse, I looked once more at this ancient archive, the history of a forgotten people. With a sigh, I lodged the explosive into the wall and fled its sizzling. When at last the explosion came and the ceiling behind me collapsed, a pang of sadness struck my heart, yet I knew that I'd done the right thing.

From **The Forgotten Daggers** by S. T. Harris

One

EDVAR AND ASHARA hurried to the battlements, where already scores of people had gathered. Eyes looked to the coast. A fleet of ships filled the horizon, the yellow sails of Karrabar unmistakable. To the east, smoke plumed in the direction of the Yurrish military camp, empty save for a few chirurgeons, craftsmen, and followers who had stayed behind. The Karrabans must have found and torched it. And now, marching through the fields where a few hours before Ashara had led the charge, was an army to dwarf their own. Thirty thousand at least. Bannerman and standard bearers stood at the head of each Karraban unit, yellow flags snapping in the breeze as they marched in time with the beat of thousands of drums.

Edvar's elation at retaking the city disappeared into an abyss of dread and despair. His fatigue came to the fore, bruises throbbing, joints and muscles aching, cuts stinging. They needed more time to prepare. Defensive plans hadn't even been agreed. The focus had all been on retaking the city. Panic grew in Edvar's chest, but he breathed deep. Fear was speaking from the podium, and he had to silence it. *Of course we can defeat them. We must. Otherwise, all the deaths, all the pain, the torment, everything father and Ashara had worked hard to build, would be for naught.*

Ashara had already won his own internal battle. He growled like a bear robbed of its salmon and began to bark orders. "Put that swine Rakar in chains and lock him in the prison tower. You, get that southern gate reinforced. Jarat, where's Jarat? Find him and tell him to divide every able-bodied fighter amongst the three gates and docks. You, get those trebuchets manned. Where's Bertan? Bertan, see to it that the tunnels are collapsed."

"But sire, how else are we to flee if we need to?" Edvar said.

"I have no intention of going anywhere, Ed."

In moments, the bailey cleared as officers gave instructions to their underlings and preparations for the defense began. Their biggest problem was obvious: a lack of bodies. Taking back the city had bled them, and although for many the fighting hadn't been the fiercest, the battle had been taxing, physically and mentally. No doubt everybody—Edvar included—dreamed of ripping off their armor and soaking for hours in a hot bath, free of blood, sweat, and grime. *Will I ever get to do that again?*

Ashara set off through the gate, down toward the city. Edvar caught up to him.

"Are we going to the walls?" he asked.

"Not yet, Ed. Something must first be done. The people have lost faith in me, and no doubt they'll now see me as a tyrannous bastard come to reclaim my throne. If they do not trust me, they will not stand by us, and if that happens, we lose. Besides, we need their help. I am no fool, Ed. I have seen how many of us have fallen. Thousands lie dead outside the walls and in the streets. We are outnumbered, and we have too much wall to defend."

"What will you say to them?" Edvar asked as Ashara lengthened his stride. A squad of riders had tacked their horses outside the final gate. Ashara picked a chestnut mare and hopped upon her back like a man twenty summers old.

"The truth." He kicked his horse into a canter and disappeared along the cobbled street. Fighting with the foot holds and reins, Edvar mounted another chestnut horse and followed.

Two

"People of Yurrisa!" Ashara bellowed over and over again, standing in the saddle as he travelled along the streets. The windows of the houses and apartments were closed and shuttered, some boarded up, doors firmly secured. "This is your keeper speaking," he roared, his deep, booming voice echoing off the buildings. He darted along different streets and through squares, repeating his cry. Edvar tailed behind, and as he went, began to see doors and windows creak open.

"Come to the Keeper's Square!" Ashara called.

Edvar picked it up. "To Keeper's Square," he shouted as he sped along. He looked over his shoulder and saw heads appearing in doorways, bodies stepping out into the street, pointing after him. Edvar beckoned them to follow. One by one, riddled with fear and hesitancy, they did. At seeing people leave their homes, more emerged. Windows opened wide and heads thrust out in curiosity. Tens became hundreds.

Edvar joined up with Ashara at the heart of the square. The place where it had all fallen apart. A growing din of voices filled the air, and in the distance, the Karraban drums rumbled. It didn't take long for the square to fill.

"People of Yurrisa. I am sorry," Ashara began, standing in his stirrups, commanding voice carrying across the square in a manner that Edvar could only dream of. "War has come to these walls. Our Treasurer Rakar has plotted with Keeper Tesh of Karrabar to remove me and take my place. Now Tesh has brought a great army to our gates and a fleet to our shore, and he carries with him weapons we fear are powered by the magic of the Dagger of Silusa."

Gasps and exclamations rippled throughout the crowd. Ashara raised his hands to quell them. He had to shout to regain silence. "But they can be defeated, and the only way to do so is if we're united.

"It was Tesh who divided us. Had I known what I know now, I would not have treated for peace. It is clear he wishes to bring back the days of the Damned. All of our ancestors died and struggled for an end to those days. It'll be over my dead body to let Tesh bring them back. I will not let him raid and burn our homes, destroy and deflower what we love and hold dear, and above all, he must not be allowed to unlock our Vault and have the unchecked power of two Daggers."

Voices turned hoarse with their roars of agreement. Fists punched the air. The people, it seemed, were with Ashara, yet Edvar found himself frowning. Ashara wasn't telling them the truth, that what he had done to Tesh in years past had caused this now. Instead, he was blaming him, painting him as an embittered monster.

"Outside our walls is an army to dwarf our own," Ashara went on. "In our harbor lies the greatest fleet you will ever see. They can be stopped, but it is not possible without your help.

"We lack the numbers to man our walls. We need people to help bring arrows to archers, reload the catapults and trebuchets, carry the wounded to the chirurgeons, bring water and food to our weary warriors. If we stand together, we win. Can you help us defeat these Karraban bastards?"

They cheered. A resounding yes.

"Go out and spread the word across the city. Head to the barracks closest to your home or to the walls and help defend our home!"

Ashara reared up on his horse and rode through the roaring crowd back up the hill toward the keep. Edvar rode alongside him.

"What was that?" Edvar asked

"What do you mean?"

"That wasn't the truth."

"Do you think they would have reacted as they did if they heard that I am to blame? If we survive this, they will come to learn the reality, but right now I need to inspire hope and confidence, and if they knew the truth, that wouldn't be possible. What's done is done, Ed. Now come on, we have too much to do."

Three

At the top of the Iron Tower, the true scale of the threat dawned on them. The Karraban infantry surrounded the city, a great mass of bodies slowly dividing into rectangular units, in preparation for the attack. Behind the marching soldiers were horses lugging heavy carts, some of which were much larger than others. Edvar, to his great frustration, could not make out what they were, but he guessed they were the thunderous weapons they'd heard about. Upon the waves, the Bay of Yurrisa was sealed by a line of Karraban ships. More lingered beyond, in case some lucky bastard somehow got through. The Yurrish ships—not that Yurr boasted much of a navy—had sailed out to meet them before the harbor gate. Forty-four ships in all. The Karrabans had three times that, at least. *This is madness.*

The door to the chamber opened, and the barons and baronesses walked in, Jarat too. The war council had come for its final meeting. Edvar left the window and took his seat.

Ashara acknowledged them all, and with one swipe of his arm, cleared the desk. Cups clanged against the floor. He went to a cupboard and picked out a large sheet of parchment, which he unfurled to reveal a map of the city. Without saying a word, Ashara began to place objects upon it. He used coins for the locations of the trebuchets and smaller coins for the catapults upon the walls.

"We have twelve trebuchets, two dozen catapults, forty-four ships and thirteen thousand able fighters. Against a hundred and fifty ships, thirty thousand men and whatever else the Karrabans have."

"It looks like they're going to attack on all fronts," Agon said.

"I agree," Ashara said. "We need to divide ourselves up. Rijkard and Ura, can you take the eastern gate? Jalden and Reska, can you take the northern? Agon and Ilda, the docks? Jarat, Edvar and I can take the southern gate. That's the weakest point of defense after our assault." Ayes and nods rippled around the table. Ashara went on. "Should any of us fall, we retreat to the keep, slowing them down any way we can. Should they breach the gates, it's to the Vault."

A suffocating silence flooded the room. Ashara didn't need to say what came after that; everyone already knew.

There was an expectant look in the eyes of Reska and Ura. Edvar knew what thoughts ran through their minds. *What about our own dagger? When will the Vault be unlocked and the dagger wielded?* For all his flaws, Ashara wasn't an oath breaker. But Edvar wondered whether temptation would get the better of the Keeper if it came to that final stand before the Vault? *Will I survive long enough to see what happens?*

"Do we have an update on the number of volunteers?" Ashara asked to dispel the silence and change the subject. Reska and Ura, it seemed, lacked the courage to voice their thoughts.

A messenger, young, fair-haired and slender for a Yurrishman, stepped forward. "Sire, they have counted nearly eight thousand and the queues are still growing."

Edvar smiled. That was more than he thought. A lot more. Not all of them would be fighters, but still, it evened the odds a little. The talking raged on, hurried and panicked, as the details of the plan were thrashed out. Edvar contributed in parts, but for all his studying, Jarat and the barons and baronesses possessed far superior experience of warfare.

Bits and pieces of information about the volunteers kept coming in. Twelve thousand now, seven thousand of which could fight. They were quickly divided amongst the group, treated like pieces in a game of Warlords. Indeed, the men and women around the table were warlords, only they played no game. There would be no starting over if things went wrong.

The beat of the Karraban drums grew louder in the room and then fell silent. Eyes met, glanced at the windows.

Ashara stood. "This is our home. These are our people. Our ancestors vowed to protect the Vault, even if it cost their lives. We've inherited that burden, and just like they did in the time of the Damned, we must face our own test now.

"Together, I do not doubt that we can repel whatever Tesh throws at us, magical thunder or not. The Yurrish spirit cannot be broken." He raised his wine cup. The others stood and copied.

"For Yurr," he said, and together they echoed it, voices filled with fire, some breaking with passion—Edvar's one of them. A tingling sensation spread out from his chest, up and down his spine, to his fingertips and toes. It dispelled his hesitancy, his fear, and imbued him with power.

Four

With numbers stretched, the Darts of Pleasure had been
assigned to the southern gate. As Ess had promised before
the assault on the city, everyone in the squad lived, and
everyone seemed fresh enough to defend the walls, except
for Isy. Her legs cried out for rest. Nerves churned in her
stomach. She did her best to hide it. The growing tide of
adrenaline helped, too. Her quiver was stocked, and in
between herself and Flor, who was to her right, stood a
barrel packed with more arrows. A young lad named Igar, no
more than sixteen, tufts of a new beard covering his cheeks,
had the responsibility of keeping them supplied. The
knowledge that she wasn't going to run out relaxed her. She
could take more chances with her shots, put aside her
hesitancy to loose. Ess said they needed to shoot as fast as
they could, if they were to win the day.

Isy found some comfort in the knowledge that the
Amast were also stationed at the southern gate. Indeed, they
were serving under the Keeper himself and stood at his
flanks upon the battlements, gazing down at the Karrabans
who had halted on the fields before them. They formed a
dense line of pikes, billhooks and spearmen, with archers at
the rear, and ladder bearers in between. Thirty thousand
strong, at least. Behind them were what looked like giant
mole hills. Objects sat upon them, slender and dark; too far
for Isy to see what exactly. The scores of yellow swallowtail
flags didn't help her view either.

A bright sun hung in the pale sky. Dusk was still a few hours away. On the eastern horizon, grey clouds gathered, threatening rain. The breeze stiffened; the flags of both nations snapped violently, the only source of noise. Everybody on the battlefield was still and silent as the next, waiting. Isy felt a peculiar sense of togetherness. Even the Karrabans would be experiencing what the Yurrish were— thinking of home, of those they loved, of getting through this alive. Isy thought of Vil, of all the time they had whiled away wishing for adventure, for excitement and for a life beyond the miseries of Haberdam. Not once did she ever believe they would get it. And here she was, upon the walls of Yurrisa, about to fight in the greatest battle since the War of the Damned. Seeing the world, meeting people, facing fears and overcoming them. Now she understood. She had *lived*, and that made the prospect of death a little less scary. Still, she wished Vil was here beside her.

To her left, Flor nocked an arrow, and beside her, Ess looked on unfazed. The gate itself was about a hundred feet to her right. An archer was positioned in every narrow window of its two towers, with a catapult at the top of each. Isy could see Edvar standing atop the gate. He wore black leather armor underneath a coat of scaled plates. A conical helm with a nose guard sat upon his head. He had a roundshield on his left arm, the white lily of Yurr emblazoned upon it, and in the other hand, a spear. He stood beside Keeper Ashara, who was dressed in gleaming plated armor with a lightning blue trim. He held a visored helm underneath his arm, blue horsehair plume hanging from its peak, and he walked along the line of defenders, slapping shoulders, shaking hands, embracing, giving words of encouragement. He looked resplendent, a true leader.

Once the attack began, Isy and the others were expected to climb the parapets and onto the wooden hoardings that projected out over the wall, to give a greater shooting angle. Further along the line, on the stretch of wall above the gate, a conveyor of men and women lugged wooden barrels up the stairs and stacked them beside the murder holes. Within them, pitch, oil, rocks. Igar and the other runners hurried along the wall with wicker baskets of arrows upon their backs, topping up and handing out spares. Some handed out waterskins. At the foot of the wall, city side, Isy could see a group of people making stretchers out of wooden poles and canvas. A nauseating heat struck her, and she took a swig from the waterskin set down before her. That flash of vulnerability permitted fear to speak, to remind her that these could be her final moments. No matter how much she struggled to overcome it, to silence the nagging voice in her head, it was always there, opportunistically waiting.

Isy wished once more that Vil was beside her. She'd squeeze him tight, tell him how much he meant to her. How truly grateful she was for him being her friend, for coming after her, sticking by her side and helping the Amast. Instead, all she could do was hope that she lived to tell him.

With a long blast of a horn, the Karraban lines began to advance, and once more the beat of the drums sounded.

Dum, dum-dum; dum, dum-dum.

"This is it," Isy muttered to herself. With a trembling hand, she nocked an arrow to her string.

Five

Tesh's body tingled. The beat of the drums flowed through him, each thud bringing a wave of strength and determination that for days he had found waning. Setback after setback had taken its toll. First, the incessant rains, and then the gods-awful roads. Thousands of men, horses, and wagons had churned them into a quagmire. Digging wagons laden with rumblers, iron balls and barreled supplies added days to their journey, and the unruly Yurrish hadn't helped matters. Tesh had decided before this began that he would not punish the Yurrish people for their cretinous leader. Some rulers would eliminate the dissidents, rule with fear. He wanted to show these people he was worthy, as he had done with his own. He'd ordered his men to avoid harming them, but when they were ambushing and killing his own, he had no choice. Tesh would have a tough time getting them in line.

Rakar had promised that Yurrisa would open its gates to Tesh, and they'd agreed on a signal to confirm it—the removal of every Yurrish flag from the towers and walls, and the hoisting of the Karraban one over the southern gate. All Tesh could see were the blue flags of Yurr, with their damned white lilies, rippling in the breeze. The gates were firmly shut and an army lined the walls. At the base of those walls lay hundreds of dead bodies, feasted upon by crows and gulls. Between there and the Karraban front ranks, great stones of trebuchets lay sunken in the earth.

Tesh had discovered what had happened earlier. Off to the north, they'd found a military camp of significant size. Enough for twenty thousand, at least. From the captives of the camp, Tesh had learned that Ashara had escaped from Yurrisa, returned with a great army, and only that morning had retaken the city. The leather of Tesh's gloves creaked as he clenched his fists. Had they not taken so long to get here, he would have faced Ashara in open battle. Just what he had always dreamed of. Still, a siege wasn't a challenge. Not with the rumblers. And he couldn't say he was all too disappointed. Ashara and his mother never ceased to boast about how great Yurrisa's defenses were. How Tesh had longed to reduce them to rubble, to step into the city with a sword in his hand and an army at his back. The prospect roused a smile from the blackness of his mood. He would show Ashara who was the better man once and for all. How wrong his father had been to shower that pompous Yurrishman with love and praise. He would shatter Yurrisa's walls as he intended to shatter Ashara's soul, and he would grind down what remained with the heel of his boot.

The drums continued to beat, louder and louder as his army neared. He had divided his force into three, eighteen thousand in all, with another eight thousand in reserve. Iljasar's doing. If Tesh had his way, he'd have thrown everyone at the Yurrish. When the footmen reached three hundred or so feet from the walls, a horn sounded, and the drums ceased. In perfect synchronization—the result of constant drilling—shields were locked together to form a sturdy wall, with others locking theirs in place above, to create a single great shell. Captain Piskin, a dark-haired man with more courage than sense—an ideal candidate to look after the rumblers—looked to Tesh for the order.

Tesh nodded.

Piskin gave a long, deep blast of his oxen horn, and the air began to sizzle.

Six

Isy squinted at the objects lying upon the mounds of dirt behind the Karraban lines. They looked like tubes of some kind. Karrabans fussed about them, some jabbing at one end with a pole twice their height, and then, as those carrying torches stepped toward them, everyone fled. The flames were lowered. Sparks flared.

The air clapped with a thunder so loud her helmet rattled. The stone beneath her feet shook. Scores of small objects flew toward the wall, and before Isy could think of anything else, she was thrown to the ground. Dust plumed into her eyes and mouth, gritty in her teeth, scratching her throat. Her ears rang like a thousand bells, and over it came deep, resounding thuds. On and on until, at last, they ceased.

Curled in a ball, Isy refused to move. A hand grabbed her arm, urging her to stand. Water splashed her face, and she wiped her dust-filled eyes clear. She discovered carnage. To the right of where she had been standing, the parapets had been destroyed, a semi-circular hole in their stead. There was no sign of Dera or a handful of the other Darts. More parapets and crenellations had been shattered. Holes gaped in the towers either side of the gate. Catapults had been reduced to splinters. Motionless bodies lay beneath chunks of stone. Some survivors crawled across the floor, desperate to be off the wall, blood trailing behind them. Nearly all the wooden hoardings were broken, gone or unstable. A thick smog of white smoke, carrying with it a sickly smell of burning coal, swirled around the parapets and obscured the Karrabans beyond.

With the ringing in Isy's ears subsiding, she could make out other sounds, like that of thousands of running feet and the rattle of weapons and armor. Ess heard it too.

"They're advancing," she shouted at the top of her lungs. "On your feet! Arrows ready." Her courage dispelled the fear in the others. Everyone stood, had an arrow on their string and was seeking targets. But the smoke remained, shifting, twisting, playing tricks with the eye. The sounds of the Karraban charge ceased. Silence fell again. Tension constricted Isy's chest. In her armor she felt stifled, underclothes glued to her body with sweat.

A hiss filled the air.

"Down!" Ess shouted.

Before she could finish, the barrage resumed. Twice as loud, even more destructive. Isy fell to her knees, bundled her head into her body and covered it with her hands. Thunderclap after thunderclap ruined her hearing, each one followed by the smashing of stone, brick, mortar and bone.

"Archers, ready," Ess bellowed and one by one, the Darts mustered the courage to stand. Isy's knees and arms trembled. She couldn't nock her arrow.

"Loose!"

Isy aimed high into the smoke like the others, their volley of darts lost.

"Again," Ess shouted. They nocked and loosed while the Karraban barrage continued. More archers upon the wall found courage and composure, and, together, the defenders sent forth a thick swarm of darts. Over their heads, the great rocks of the trebuchets rotated in the air and plummeted down into the smoke. Whether they hit anything was anyone's guess, but the Karraban thunder subsided.

"Hold!" came the order, and the stream of arrows ceased. Silence once more fell, or as close to silence as Isy's ringing ears would allow. She scanned the shifting clouds of smoke, seeking anything. There, a flash. A spark of blue and orange.

Isy dropped to the ground as the bangs erupted, and heartbeats later, dust, rocks and mortar struck her prone form. The Karraban thunder obliterated more crenels and hoardings. Great chunks of stone fell from one of the towers, crushing a dozen or so people standing on the wall below. Her ears rung more than ever. And then, as it had before, the thunder ceased. The dust around her settled. The parapet to her left was gone, so too half the wall.

A deep, ominous blast of a horn rang out beyond the wall. It was met by the roar of thousands of Karrabans.

Isy scrambled to her feet. She found her bow covered in dust on the floor by the crenel and snatched an arrow from her quiver. Armored bodies appeared through the smoke, running like madmen toward the wall, shields and billhooks in their hands. Behind them, others carried great wooden ladders, their ends tipped with sharp metal hooks.

Isy drew, aimed and loosed. Her arrow punctured a man's chest; he fell away and was trampled by those flushing forward. She gasped. *I've just killed someone.* She had no more time to consider it. An arrow zipped by her head. She ducked, nocked another. The surviving Darts were all on their feet. Ess, Glic, Bela, Flor, and the rest, shooting like goddesses. Isy took courage from them all.

Before she could draw another arrow, the top of a ladder thudded against the wall before her.

Seven

Ashara bellowed words of encouragement, doing his utmost to quell the fear in his warriors. Edvar's senses still reeled from what he had just experienced. Power beyond anything he could have imagined. *The Dagger. It has to be.* How else could Tesh have created weapons of such destructive might? The gate beneath his feet, three feet thick and studded with iron bolts, was punctured with scores of wide holes, but still standing. The portcullis had suffered a similar fate, its iron bars twisted and bent.

Upon the battlements, archers furiously loosed. Citizen volunteers carried the wounded away on stretchers—men and women with limbs missing, broken or crushed, bleeding from cuts or punctured by arrows. Edvar looked to his right and saw Isy with her bow in hand, loosing as fast as she could. And then he realized who she was shooting at. Resting against the broken section of wall to her left was the top end of a ladder.

Edvar spotted Camos, a cut to the side of his head. Edvar shouted him. The old man looked and Edvar waved him over. Camos grabbed a couple of spearmen and hurried. Ducking below the parapets, Edvar held up his shield as he ran. An arrowhead pierced through the wood a few inches above his arm. The force nearly knocked him off balance. It did not deter his charge, though. He could imagine any moment a Karraban leaping over the top of the wall and slashing at Isy.

His fear came to pass.

The top of a Karraban helmet sheened in the afternoon sun. Edvar strained every sinew to lengthen his stride. The Karraban hurried up the last few rungs and leapt onto the wall, thrusting with the long, dirk-like point of his billhook, and with the sickle-like hook projecting from the side, he swiped and slashed. Isy hopped back and knocked into another archer, who sent an arrow wayward—with so many attackers below, it probably still landed.

Two more paces and Edvar was there. He lunged with his spear at the Karraban's chest. His foe leapt to the right and swung his billhook, head height. Edvar brought up his shield just in time. The horizontal spike lodged in the wood. No matter how much the Karraban yanked and pulled, it would not loosen. Out of the corner of his eye, Edvar saw another Karraban reaching the top of the ladder. He had no more time to ponder his next action. He brought up his spear and thrust it into the Karraban's gut. The point glanced off his scaled armor but at last found a gap and sunk into his flesh. The Karraban gasped and fell to his knees. The second Karraban stood upon the edge of the wall. Edvar readied for a charge, only to be overtaken by Camos and his warriors. With their spears and shields, they forced the Karraban over the side, and with a desperate scream, he fell away. Together, straining, they tried to heft the ladder off the wall. The weight of the Karrabans climbing up kept it down. Edvar joined in the push, Isy too. They tipped the balance and slowly the ladder descended into the white smoke of the battlefield below.

Isy, bow back in her hand, hair unkempt and covered with dust, smiled at Edvar, and he at her. For that brief moment, at least, he was ignorant to the chaos around him. Until another thunderous bang rocked the wall. Edvar and Isy ducked behind a parapet.

"We need to stop those weapons," Isy said to him.

Edvar peered around the stone. "Any ideas?"

Isy looked too. The smoke had shifted, and Edvar could see a wagon with an iron tube resting upon it. Beside it was a man, a torch in his hand. Isy stood, arrow nocked, and loosed. Her shot flew straight and true and struck the Karraban in the chest. He fell backwards and dropped his torch on top of a barrel.

A heartbeat later, a tremendous explosion sent Edvar ducking down again. The sound dwarfed any other that day. Flames rushed and roared, and when he stole a glance, saw a tower of fire rising high into the sky. Black smoke swept over the killing fields below, choking and stinging eyes. The Karrabans, those not caught up in the blast, were stunned and rattled. But further along the wall, the fighting remained fierce. Another squadron was struggling to fend off Karrabans streaming up a ladder. Edvar ordered his group to follow. He looked again at Isy. "Keep shooting, and use fire if you can. Aim for those wagons! If we lose the wall, make sure you get to the keep." And then he was off after his warriors who already were engaging with the Karrabans.

Over the clash of steel, the screams, grunts and shouts of men and women, Edvar could hear Ashara.

"*Fight. Fight with everything you have. Fight till your last breath! Fight for your homes. Fight for those you love.*"

And they did. The Yurrish met the marauding attackers with cold iron. Edvar didn't get a chance to bloody his spear again. The Karrabans were cut down and the ladder sent whence it came.

Everyone upon the wall ducked at the next great explosion. On the battlefield before them, not far from the gate, flames roared into the sky like the blast of an angry dragon. Dark smoke plumed, sending even those upon the walls coughing. When it shifted, Edvar saw a deep crater in the ground. Around it, charred and burning bodies. Isy and the Darts must have dealt a telling blow.

The two explosions halted the flow of the attack—many of the Karrabans at this stretch of wall at least, had been killed or wounded by it. And then Edvar heard the horns. The Karrabans began to pull back.

The Yurrish had won the day.

Eight

"What in Soria happened?" Tesh raged at Iljasar.

Grim faced, his second-in-command kept his eyes to the ground. He'd had a lifetime of admonishment; he knew how to get through them. "The barrels of powder caught fire, m'lord."

Tesh shook his head, anger pulsing through his body. "If they could explode, what fool thought it sensible to place them beside the rumblers?"

Iljasar gave no reply. He knew it was a question he could not successfully answer.

"Get me Piskin. I want answers and assurances that this will not happen again. We could have taken those walls if not for stupidity killing our own men!" Tesh slapped a tankard off the small table in his tent. A few drops stained Iljasar's yellow tabard.

"Aye, m'lord."

"And where are my siege towers?"

"They're almost ready. Tomorrow they should be finished."

"*Should*?!"

"I'll see what I can do."

"You best see to it, Iljasar, because at dawn we attack again, and if those towers aren't ready, I'll be firing those carpenters from the barrel of the Hammer! People are not doing their jobs, at a time when they need to more than ever. Will the Hammer be fixed for tomorrow?"

"I have been assured it will. But, sire, if I may say, there is no rush to take the walls. We have them surrounded. Word from the docks is that nothing remains of their pitiful fleet and their harbor gate is ruined. They are on their knees and have nowhere to go. We can do this on our own terms. In a few days, they may even surrender."

Tesh listened to the veteran. Often the man's words swayed him, but not this time, for Tesh was of another mind. He agreed that the Yurrish were on their knees, but when an enemy was down, he wasn't one for giving them a chance to get back to their feet. Especially if that enemy was Ashara. "I appreciate your counsel, Iljasar. As ever."

Iljasar knew when he was dismissed. He bowed and took his leave, gaze lingering over his keeper as he went.

Today was, perhaps, Tesh's worst day on the battlefield. Yes, damage had been inflicted on the Yurrish, but the cost was great. Nearly four thousand men lost. He hated losing anyone, let alone *thousands*. For the first time since this campaign began, doubt entered in his mind. A sense of uncertainty that bored into his thoughts and feelings. It constricted his chest, sapped his focus and resolve. A question kept on circling his mind: *is it worth it?*

Of course it is. Had those fools not placed flammable powder beside the rumblers they would have taken the city, of that he was sure. Tomorrow, the siege towers would be ready, the Hammer working. It would all be different, and it would end with Ashara pleading with him for mercy.

Nine

A solemn atmosphere hung over the city. Edvar was weary to his soul. Now he understood his father when he used to say that nothing was more exhausting than battle. And tomorrow he would have to get up and do it again.

Not long after the battle had ended, the war council convened and determined that the walls could withstand the thunderous weapons another day. The greatest vulnerability was the dock. The Yurrish fleet had been destroyed, and so too both of the outer towers and gate. It would have been worse if not for some of the Karraban ships bursting into flames after being struck by the great stones of the trebuchets. Edvar suspected the projectiles had triggered a similar reaction to what had happened on the battlefield. Fires had spread to neighboring ships and put the attack in disarray. Tomorrow, though, the Karrabans could sail right into the harbor and gain a foothold with all but three inner towers and another gate to keep them at bay. The biggest problem for the Yurrish was they had too few warriors to cover all fronts, and the more stretched they became, the greater the chance of a breach. They had to repel Tesh, or that was it. There was no help coming. They were on their own. The walls had to hold. It wasn't a matter of how long.

Adrenaline waning, Edvar realized he hadn't eaten since dawn; even that had been just a few anxious nibbles. He headed for the Great Hall. Night had long since fallen, and through a veil of cloud, he saw the glow of the wandering moon. The smell of fire still hung heavy in the air.

A handful of officers were sitting upon the long benches in the Hall, sipping from tankards, their conversation muted. A gruff man, hair braided with beads, had a bandage around his head. The slender man opposite him had a bound thigh. No doubt they were trying to enjoy what could be their last night alive. No amount of ale could change the reality, though. Edvar spotted Isy close to the hearth. She was staring idly at the food in the bowl before her. Edvar helped himself to a bowl of the stew that was simmering in a cauldron over the fire and approached.

"Everything alright?" he asked.

She jumped, straightened, but gave him no smile. Only a nod. Edvar sat down opposite her. Her face was pale, eyes red with tiredness, or from tears. Both, perhaps.

"It's been one bastard of a day," Edvar said, with a sigh. Again, Isy did not respond. It was as if she'd locked herself away inside her mind and was peering through the windows that were her eyes. "Did you lose anyone?"

"A few of the Darts," she said.

"I'm sorry."

"Thanks... Eat, if you want." And she gave a flicker of a smile.

Edvar took measured bites instead of the guzzling chomps his stomach urged him to take.

"Thank you for helping me today. When I saw that man at the top of the ladder, I thought I was done for."

"You don't have to thank me."

"You were the bravest person on that wall today," she said.

Edvar shook his head in disagreement, but his cheeks burned all the same.

Isy fell quiet as Edvar ate. And then she went on. "I killed someone. I can still see my arrow sinking into him, and him falling down. When I close my eyes it's all I see."

"I still get nightmares about the first time I killed someone," Edvar said. He paused, gazed into the fire. "I can still see him falling, hitting the ground. The blood. I feel guilty, even though he was trying to kill me. I don't think it's something I could ever get used to, killing. The idea of playing creator sickens me."

"How do you deal with it?"

"Try not to think about it. When I do, remind myself that it was me or them. What choice did I have?"

"I'll remember that when I'm on the wall tomorrow." Isy poked at her stew, breaking up the film of grease that had settled on the surface. "Do you think we'll make it through tomorrow?"

Edvar swallowed a mouthful of stew and looked into her bright amber eyes. "Yes."

"Edvar." They turned, and at realizing who it was, stood and bowed.

"Do you have a moment?"

"Of course, sire."

Ashara nodded to Isy, Edvar likewise, and then he followed his keeper out of the hall, to his private reception chamber. Ashara fixed them some wine, then led Edvar to the fire burning in the hearth, the room's only source of light.

"Those... weapons today," Ashara began. "Their might was beyond bounds. Never have I seen such dread in the eyes of so many Yurrish. It must be as they say—they're powered by the magic of the Dagger of Silusa. That Tesh has violated the most sacred of oaths to wreak his revenge upon me. Upon us all.

"I have driven this man to madness. How do we stop him, Ed? If he is using the Dagger, how do we stop him? Do we refuse to wield that which could save us?"

Doubt consumed Ashara. Edvar could see its corruption in his eyes. "To unlock the Vault of Iron would make you just like Tesh, if indeed he has unlocked the Karraban Vault. From what I saw today, their weapons killed hundreds of their own. What good are magical weapons if they do that? And if they do so again, will Tesh's men continue to support him? Plus, what I saw suggests that these weapons may have a weakness we may be able to take advantage of—fire.

"We took a beating today, but we are far from defeated. We are Yurrish, sire. Fearless and brave and we do not give up, no matter the odds. Tomorrow we must remind the Karrabans of that."

Ten

The jangling of the city bells broke Isy's fitful sleep. She sprang upright in her bunk. An officer shouted into her room. Others were already out of their beds and dressed, throwing coats of mail over heads, strapping on armor and hurriedly fastening weapon belts and baldrics. Bow in hand, Isy joined the stream of bodies heading for the bailey. She stepped out into the racket of the bells, and immediately the chill morning air stung her cheeks. Dawn was yet to come, though a faint grey light to the east suggested it wasn't far off. When the bells at last ceased, the void they left was filled by the distant rumble of the Karraban drums.

The Darts of Pleasure formed up before Ess. Her right leg was heavily bandaged. Isy had heard she'd broken it, but Ess had refused to stand down. Isy looked around and saw fear and weariness in the eyes of many, yet backs remained straight, shoulders broad. Limping, yet without complaint, Ess led them through deserted streets to their post of the day before, at the southern gate. With every step, the Karraban drums grew louder. By the time they'd reached the battered walls, the day was brighter, and once at the top, they beheld the enemy. Isy gasped.

The Karraban lines were twice as deep and wide as the previous day. Looming behind them like giants, pulled by horse and ox, were square wooden siege towers, taller, it seemed, than Yurrisa's walls. Between the towers, horses lugged wagons upon which sat the thunderous Karraban weapons. Isy couldn't see any of the barrels that had caught fire and triggered the explosion. The Karrabans had learned their lesson, it seemed. Isy's heart sunk. That was a weakness they had hoped to exploit.

Isy couldn't see anybody around the mounds upon which the Karrabans had placed their terrifying weapons yesterday. There was, however, a crowd gathered around one great mound—indeed, it was more of a knoll— directly facing the gate. Upon it was a monstrous weapon, dwarfing the Karrabans around it. Eyes wide with fear, Isy looked to Flor and Bela beside her. Their eyes were fixed on the enemy, expressions unreadable.

"Men and women of Yurr," a voice cut through the tense quiet. The Keeper. He was standing upon a parapet, glimmering longsword Runas in hand, clad in his polished armor. The blue plume of his helm almost glowed in the weak morning light. Despite the Karraban drums, his voice carried loud and clear along the battlements.

"This will be the most testing day in all of our lives. A day we look fear in the eye. When pain will seek to break us. But we shall not be broken. This is our *home*. The people within these walls are *our* people. Our families, our friends. Those we love more than anything in the world. We are all Yurrish. And now our very existence has been pushed to the edge of the cliff. Do we fall, or do we fight?"

A few soldiers close to Ashara muttered, "Fight."

"Answer me!" he roared.

"Fight!" came the cry.

"What?!"

"Fight!" Even louder this time.

"What do we do?" Ashara roared at the top of his voice into the sky, sword aloft.

"We fight!" Isy bellowed, voice joining a deafening cacophony, made even louder by the Amast who unleashed the full force of their great lungs. Hilts were bashed against shields; spear butts hammered the ground. It expelled their fear and replaced it with courage and defiance.

Isy's body tingled. She felt invincible.

Eleven

Over the beat of the drums, Tesh could hear the roars of the Yurrish upon the walls, could see arms and weapons punching the air. And standing tall above them all was Ashara, looking like a rooster with his blue-plumed helmet. Tesh's lips curled into a smile. Their cheers would soon fall quiet.

"Prepare to fire."

The first horn rang out, and the advanced infantry, positioned much further away from the rumblers than the day before as a precaution, took a knee and awaited the wave of devastating projectiles.

Tesh's gaze turned to the Hammer, awaiting the signal that they were ready. Captain Piskin raised his hand.

"Fire!" Tesh roared.

The drums ceased. An ear-piercing hiss sounded first, and then an explosion that stunned the senses, a flash so bright Tesh had to cover his eyes. White smoke billowed forth from the Hammer's muzzle. Fractions of a heartbeat later, a giant iron ball shot forth to smash into the tower to the right of the gate. The stone walls imploded. The tower crumbled. Great chunks of rock hailed down upon those on the wall below. The weight of the falling stone destabilized the wall. The parapets began to topple. The Yurrish cheers had turned to screams, ringing out from the debris-filled smog the collapse had stirred. When at last the dust settled, Tesh found the whole left-side of the gate ruined.

The barrage from the smaller rumblers came next, positioned closer to the wall upon wagons. Dozens of explosions and bangs sent Tesh's ears ringing even further. He had never known such noisy warfare, though he couldn't care less. He watched with a satisfied smile as the weapons of his own making brought down the walls of Ashara's city. And then it was the turn of the Hammer again.

Tesh didn't hesitate to give the order. The ground beneath his feet shook, and a moment later, the great wooden gate was ripped from its hinges. Tesh grabbed the horn from Iljasar's hands and blew with all the air in his lungs. The roar of thousands of his men answered it. Tesh shoved the horn back into Iljasar's grasp and mounted his horse.

"Come, Iljasar. We have a city to take," Tesh said, with a grin that had become fixed on his face. He paid no mind to the unease upon his old friend's face. Instead, he donned his helm, kicked his horse into a canter, and rode into battle.

Twelve

A hand grabbed Edvar's arm. The metallic taste of blood filled his mouth. His ears rang like the warning bells, and with consciousness returning, he realized the warning bells were indeed ringing.

Edvar opened his eyes. He was on the floor, like scores of others. He could see lifeless bodies and shields, spears, bows and arrows, scattered, broken, without wielders. Rocks and stones were everywhere, some covered in blood. And around them swirled clouds of dust and smoke.

"Master Edvar!" said a voice that cut through the ringing. Gingerly, Edvar looked about and found Nikson, one of Jarat's men. Blood seeped from a cut to his eyebrow. With his aid, Edvar regained his feet. Somehow, he didn't seem to be injured.

"The gate is breached, sir! We must hold them off or retreat to the keep."

Retreat, the voice in Edvar's head said.

"Where is the Keeper?" *And Isy, where is Isy?* He looked along the ruined, rock-strewn wall, scanning the bodies upon the floor, and the faces of those courageous enough to still be shooting. He couldn't see her.

"In the street below, awaiting the Karrabans."

Another wave of thunder struck the walls. Edvar and Nickson ducked. Luckily, their aim was further along the wall. Edvar glanced beyond the parapets. He could make out dark shapes rushing toward him through the smog. And beyond them, he could see something else, looming tall and moving at a slow, foreboding pace.

Siege towers.

They needed the trebuchets. With nearly all the catapults destroyed, they had no other means of taking them down. He looked back toward the city and saw the great wooden arms hurling their stones toward the docks, the most vulnerable point. He dreaded to think how the battle fared there. *It cannot be much worse than here.*

Edvar looked down toward the gate, city-side, and saw Ashara plugging the breach with a dense shield wall. Camos was there too, making sure spears and shields were raised and ready. Standing tall amongst the press were the Amast with their huge spears, shields and makeshift iron armor, ready for the charge. The Karrabans would not get through easily. The bigger threat was upon the walls, and the siege towers were closing, now clear of the smoke. Hope flickered in Edvar's chest. They weren't covered in wet hides. They could be torched!

Edvar raced along the wall to the nearest and still functioning catapult, and ordered the operators to hurl barrels of oil at the approaching tower. Then he ran back, ordering archers to douse and light their arrowheads and aim for the towers.

The catapult released with a snap. A trio of barrels rotated in the air and shattered against the side of the tower, drenching it in oil. Archers loosed their flame-tipped darts and fire engulfed the wooden frame.

The tower continued on toward them. At its top, a half-dozen archers appeared behind a wooden wall and loosed a volley through a haze of rising black smoke. People around Edvar fell. He hefted his shield and moved to the cover of the wall. A furious exchange of arrows unfolded as the burning tower rolled close enough to drop its drawbridge. "Shield wall!" Edvar shouted, and in a few heartbeats the rim of his shield was locked with others. Edvar braced himself, held tight his spear. He was in the front rank, the line six abreast.

Another barrel of oil struck the tower, close to the top. The drawbridge fell. Karrabans poured forth, roaring and howling, filled with a lust for blood. The Yurrish unleashed a torrent of fire arrows, and the top of the tower burst into flames, washing over the charging Karrabans and turning their roars to wails. Some jumped from the drawbridge to their deaths. Others continued their charge and hurled themselves onto the ends of Yurrish spears. The flames grew and grew, wood snapped, the fire spat, and the tower collapsed.

Shouts and screams rang out from the base of the wall. A furious battle had unfolded in the short tunnel of the gate, enemy shields locked against one another, shoving and pushing, with spears and billhooks thrusting and stabbing over the top and underneath. The wall above had been wrecked, but it still stood, and the murder holes were unblocked. With Nikson and a few others, Edvar rolled a barrel of oil to the edge of the hole and poured it down, drenching the press of Karrabans below. Someone else dropped a torch and fire erupted. Edvar could feel the heat on his cheeks. The most horrific wails he had ever heard drowned out his tinnitus. The fetid scent of burning hair and flesh stung his nostrils and made him gag. Edvar had no choice but to push it aside and helped the others roll another barrel of oil to the edge of the murder hole.

Fire had won the battle for the gate, but it would only rage for so long. And did their victory even matter? Edvar looked along the wall. Siege towers were docked, Karrabans disembarking, overwhelming the Yurrish. The walls were lost.

The realization sickened Edvar. They *had* to hold these walls, and they hadn't lasted more than a day. After all his efforts, none of it had been enough—like trying to hold back the tide with his arms alone.

Edvar stood at the edge of the wall and shouted down to Ashara.

"The walls are lost. We must fall back to the keep!"

PARIAH'S LAMENT | 379

Ashara looked at him with grim realization. He nodded and gave three blasts of his horn. "To the keep!" he bellowed.

Thirteen

Tesh rode through the ruined southern gate. The walls of the tunnel were black with soot, the charred remains of gate and warriors swept to the side. It was midday by the time the walls had been cleared and the gates opened. The fighting went on in pockets along the streets, but the bulk of the Yurrish force had retreated to the keep. Holed up with nowhere to go. Just as Tesh wanted.

The keep had three gates and three large baileys. His army could bleed taking it, but he had no doubt they would succeed.

Tesh dismounted in the square just inside of the southern gate. He looked at the looming walls, at the stone houses and buildings, and lastly, at the keep, rising high above all else. How he had dreaded coming to this place as a child, of walking through this very gate. And how he had dreamed of doing so again, just like this. A wave of euphoria filled his chest. He let out a roar of victory, of strength and power. He was close. So very close. And neither man, woman nor wall would stand in his way.

The strategy to take the city had long been planned. Those who had attacked by land joined those who came via the docks. Tesh's army swarmed through the streets, ignorant to the houses and buildings with their boarded windows and barred doors. Their orders had been clear— fight only those who were armed. No pillaging. No raping. Everyone knew the punishment that would befall them if they disobeyed. As Tesh rode up the hill toward the keep, he spotted eyes looking out at him through cracks and crevices. They were not his people, though soon they would be. Would they accept him? *They will have no choice.*

The outer wall of the keep loomed before Tesh. Arrows rained down on his men, who were standing with shields locked tight, resisting the barrage, waiting for the rumblers. Too many were falling, though, and of the rumblers there was no sign.

"Archers," Tesh bellowed. "Onto those roofs!" He pointed to a cluster of buildings not much smaller than the keep's walls. He grabbed the nearest soldier and ordered him to find out where the rumblers were. No sooner had he shoved him on his way did they arrive, mist billowing from the foam-lined mouths of the horses. With well-practiced efficiency, the mounts were unhitched from wagons, rumblers prepped and loaded.

"Fire!" Tesh roared, bringing down his sword, and the air hissed and clapped. The metal portcullis bent and broke. The wooden gate behind splintered, but held. On and on the rumblers battered the gate, all the while the Yurrish lobbed arrows in their direction. It seemed such a feeble response compared to the might Tesh wielded.

His smile widened when the bent and broken portcullis fell with a clang. The gate burst inwards, and the inner portcullis went with it. The awaiting Karrabans poured into the breach like ants over a dropped sweet.

The Yurrish met them with shields and spears. Arrows rained down from the walls, his men picked off in swathes. Then came the oil, the boiling pitch. Pockets of fire erupted, bodies consumed by flames. Pain stabbed at his chest at seeing each one of his men fall, scores dropping with each heartbeat.

"Prep the rumblers," Tesh shouted. The go-ahead came, and Tesh bellowed "fall back." His officers echoed the order, and those clogging up the tunnel slowly retreated. "Now."

In the confines of the streets, the combined noise of half a dozen rumblers almost burst Tesh's ear drums. The impact was devastating. The Yurrish line was fractured, holes gaping.

"Charge!" Tesh roared, and the Karrabans poured through the breach like water down a clear drain.

Tesh knew of the keep's three baileys. And this first, the biggest, was designed to be the main killing field. His men knew that too, and as soon as they left the cover of the gate, they moved into hedgehog formations, inching forwards with shields aloft, never stopping. Despite the projectiles from catapults and, closer to the wall, arrows, they made it to the next gate with few casualties. With the attention of the defenders consumed, the rumblers rolled up behind, and once again they employed the same tactics.

It took even less time to breach the second gate and, as Tesh stepped through it, he looked up the hill to the looming towers and marble buildings and saw Ashara upon the battlements.

Fourteen

Every part of Isy's body ached. She'd done something to her left knee, and whenever she bent it, pain erupted. Upon the wall, the collapsing tower had knocked her off her feet, and she'd struck her head on the edge of an arrow basket on her way down. She was afraid to touch her blood-matted hair.

Ess had ordered them off the wall soon after that, yet Ess herself hadn't made it. She had refused to leave her post, saying her broken leg would only slow their retreat. Glic and Flor had tried to carry her and Glic had received a hard shove in response. Instead, Ess remained, loosing shaft after shaft with grace and fluidity. Another thunderous wave had struck the wall as Isy reached the street below. When she glanced back, she could see no sign of Ess.

Isy and her fellow archers had been among the first back to the keep, and now they sat in the innermost bailey, listening to chaos unfolding, to death creeping toward them. As she sat there, taking in what could be her final moments, she realized something else. There wasn't a single one of the Amast in the bailey.

"How did I end up here? How did it come to this?" she muttered to herself, tears filling her eyes. A part of her wished it was all a dream, that any moment she would wake up in her favorite place in Haberdam, with her copy of *Myra the Maid*. But in these past few months, she had lived and experienced more than she had in her entire life. She had confronted her demons, conquered fear, had made a difference to the lives of others. Now, she had a choice. To finish her life as she'd spent much of it, or as the person she was now.

A group of Yurrish fighters charged through the gate, and then it was closed and barred, the portcullises dropped. Amongst them were Ashara, Jarat, Rijkard, Ilda, Ura, Camos and Edvar. Edvar's face was smeared with soot and blood, fringe glued to his forehead with sweat. His armor was missing scales, and his leather was torn at the shoulder where he'd taken a blow. He looked ready to drop, but he was alive, and the tension in Isy's chest eased a little. But of the Amast there was no sign. Her heart told her they were alive somewhere in the city. Or was that just a folly of hope?

Edvar slumped down against a wall. Isy brought him a waterskin and held it to his lips. He looked up at her, tired eyes slowly registering her face. She knelt beside him.

"We cannot hold them," he muttered. "There are too many. The thunder... How can we stop it?"

"We must, Ed," said a voice behind her. The Keeper. "When I felt as lost as you, it was your father who helped me find my way back. 'Do not despair for the end,' he said. 'Think only of the present, of those you love, those you wish to see again, and of the past, of times of peace and happiness, and fill your heart with hope that you will one day see them again, that beyond the struggle with darkness, there is light. Fight for it. With everything you have, fight.'" Others had stopped to listen.

"Our light has not yet faded. We are broken but we are not beaten." Ashara extended his hand, and Edvar took it.

Ashara's words stirred Isy's heart. Indeed, they stirred everyone who heard them. The pain in her body fell away, and instead, her aching muscles filled with vigor.

A wave of thunder hammered the gate. Iron groaned, wood splintered and snapped.

"Form up!" Ashara roared over the bombardment. "If we retreat, our last stand is the Vault. But it will not come to that, for we are warriors of Yurr, and this is our home!"

The Yurrish cheered.

"When they breach, we charge!" Ashara said.

Isy joined the other archers on the battlements, who were furiously loosing arrows at the Karrabans. Edvar, she could see, was standing beside Ashara and Jarat in the front rank. He'd been given a new shield, a spear and a helmet.

After another devastating barrage, the gate gave way. Limbs appeared through the splintered gaps, and moments later the beam snapped in two, the doors surging inwards.

"Charge!" Ashara roared.

The clash of wood was so loud Isy was sure everyone in the front ranks had broken their arms. The force of the Yurrish sent the Karraban line reeling a dozen paces, but bodies filled the space behind and pushed back. Isy and the other archers lobbed arrows into the press of Karrabans, picking off dozens at a time. The Karrabans fell further back, pushed whence they came by the last-remaining Yurrish.

"Fight! Fight for your lives!" Ashara roared, and they answered with renewed effort. The Keeper himself was like a force of nature, beating back the Karrabans with his giant roundshield, and pummeling and hacking with his blood-stained sword, Runas. By his side was Jarat, the fearless General displaying how he'd earned his title. Rijkard, Ilda and Ura were there too, axes flashing and spurring on those around them. Isy couldn't see Edvar.

Another voice cut through the clamor, deep and accented. A Karraban voice. Moving forward through the Karraban force was a man with a black helmet. The rest of his plated armor was black too, trim golden. He bellowed orders and encouragement, and he was inspiring belief. The Karrabans pushed forwards, one pace at a time. Wielding shield and sword, the black knight made it to the front ranks and, fighting furiously, began to drive a wedge in the Yurrish line. The Karrabans surged forward into it. The Yurrish resisted with everything they had, but the force became too much, and the line collapsed. Order was lost. In a heartbeat, the fighting turned frantic, desperate, gruesome, yellow and blue tabards battling with shields and blades, fists and feet, fingers and teeth. A struggle for survival. Humanity reduced to the basest of instincts.

Isy felt helpless. She could not shoot for fear of hitting one of her own. Some of the other archers upon the wall dropped their bows and drew shortswords, dirks, even knives. They hurried down the steps.

"We don't need archers no more," one woman said as she passed Isy, a curved dirk in her hand.

Isy drew her dirk, swallowed hard, and followed.

Fifteen

Edvar didn't know which way to turn, who to fight. He wanted to take off his helmet to see what was going on around him, but more than once it had stopped a few glancing blows. The yellow tabards of Karrabar were everywhere, but the Yurrish fought like gods and goddesses. Men and women roaring defiance, battling for their homes, for their lives, their futures.

He spun and by chance caught a blow on his shield. And then he was engaged. Spear long since dropped, Edvar swung his sword. Parried. The counter came swiftly, and Edvar brought up his shield, lunged beneath it, the tip of his blade sinking into the Karraban's gut.

Before his foe had fallen, the next was upon him, thrusting with the wicked point of a billhook. Edvar ducked behind his shield. His enemy hooked onto the rim and yanked him forward. Edvar fell off balance, but managed to duck, and over his head he felt the shaft of the billhook swing, and then a scream. The Karraban had struck one of his comrades in the face with his spike. Edvar seized his chance and plunged his sword through his enemy's unprotected groin.

Edvar turned, anticipating another foe, but there was space around him, and he used the opportunity to look for Ashara. Through a horde of dueling warriors, he spotted the blue plume, battling furiously with Tesh. Edvar was fifty paces away. His path was blocked by scores of dueling bodies, but that didn't deter him.

Shield up, Edvar weaved his way through furious battles. He hamstrung a Karraban poised to kill a Yurrish woman on the ground, and when he fell to his knees, she leapt upon him and plunged her dagger through his eye. A Yurrishman succumbed to a Karraban axe, and the subsequent blow was aimed at Edvar, who caught it on his shield and managed to slice his foe down his side, in response.

Edvar was no more than twenty paces away now. If he could get to Ashara and Tesh, he could stop the Karraban Keeper, and then all this would end. Edvar ducked by another dueling pair. As he rose, something hard struck his head. He staggered, hit the ground, but quickly regained his feet. Before him stood a short man, clad in plated armor. He held a battle axe that almost matched his height, the twin blades sharp as guillotines. His eyes held an ominous look beneath the rim of his open-faced helm. He was much older than Edvar, a veteran of war. A professional killer. He hefted his axe and swung for Edvar's neck.

Sixteen

The pace was furious, just as it had been all those years ago in the tourney. Each clang sent a shockwave down Tesh's arm. Ashara pushed, Tesh riposted then launched an attack of his own. Ashara parried and stepped away.

"Age has not robbed us of skill, if not our stamina," said Tesh, following it up with a slash to Ashara's neck. The Yurrishman hopped aside.

"It has robbed you of your sanity, though. How could you, Tesh?"

Tesh's eyes narrowed. "You cannot see how deserving you are of all this?"

"It matters not how I behaved, how we behaved. We were kids! Opening the Vault over such trivialities is unconscionable!"

Tesh laughed. He hacked and slashed with his blade and Ashara parried and moved. "What do you speak of, you damn fool? You think I unlocked the Vault of Bronze? All to get my revenge on you?" Tesh spat at Ashara. Anger raged in his chest. "Damn you to hell, Ashara. How arrogant are you? You think me some mad man drunk on power? I am a man of honor, Ashara. You should know that better than anyone. I would never betray the sacrifices my ancestors made."

"Then how else have you manufactured such monstrous weapons?"

"Is it so hard to believe that others can better you? That all the nonsense you spoke of impregnable defenses would not inspire in others a desire to break them? To prove that you're the idiot you truly are? They are weapons of my creation, forged of iron, as magical as the catapult that hurls a stone. They have nothing to do with the Dagger of Silusa. They are the result of years of laboring over ways to ruin your life, as you have ruined mine."

"Things were never easy between us, Tesh, and I regret my part in that, but I never intended to bring ruin upon you."

"You are blinder than I ever thought." Tesh's anger erupted. It came forth in a roar, and he swung his sword with all his strength. Ashara met it, and his next blow, and his next. Not once did he counter. Tesh's anger roiled, self-control lost. "You turned my father against me. You stole the only woman I've ever loved. We had planned our future, and you pissed all over it. And then you let her die. You took her, and you killed her."

Tesh marauded forwards once more, bashing with his shield, hacking with his sword. He pushed Ashara further and further back.

"For too long you have tortured my heart and soul, tainted my life, and now it will end." Tesh arced a blow from left to right. Ashara's sword only glanced the strike, and the tip of Tesh's blade bit into Ashara's shoulder. He dropped his sword, staggered to the ground.

At last, Tesh had him.

Seventeen

Edvar was camped behind his shield, praying the planks of wood held. The Karraban veteran's battle axe cut through the air once more. This time, Edvar parried it with his sword. The force almost numbed his arm. He hopped away, keeping his shield high as Camos had taught him.

His foe had no shield, and Edvar thought that would give him a chance, but he hadn't been gifted any opportunity to attack, and the constant defense was draining him. His foe was tiring too, though, and for a few moments, they both circled, catching their breath. Edvar stole a glance around him. The hulking form of Camos stood out from the crowd. A trio of Karrabans surrounded him, thrusting and hacking. Camos kept them at bay, until a crossbow bolt struck his leg. Camos sank to one knee. The Karrabans seized their chance. Camos gutted the first that came into range, parried the blow of the second, and the third ran his sword through Camos's throat. Even still, the bear of a man grabbed the neck of the closest Karraban, until he slumped to the ground to join the friends he had loved and lost. Edvar gasped, and his opponent preyed on his distraction.

Edvar ducked and rolled from the slash aimed at his neck. Fueled by the rage of seeing Camos killed, Edvar launched an attack—one of Camos's favorite combinations. He pushed back the Karraban veteran, and with his final blow, flicked the wrist of his sword arm and slashed his foe's leg, deep.

The Karraban fell, and with him out of the way, Edvar could see the blue plume of Ashara's helm. On the ground. With Tesh standing over him.

Urgency flooded him. He had to get to Ashara. But the Karraban regained his feet and once more stood in Edvar's way, albeit a little more unsteadily.

Edvar swung his sword, right down to left. His foe deflected. With his backstroke, Edvar aimed for the neck, and when that was blocked, he spun, fell to a crouch and slashed at his legs. His enemy tried to jump back, but the tip of Edvar's blade nicked him. He grunted but kept his feet and swung his axe as Edvar moved to stand up. The flat of the axe struck the side of Edvar's helm, sending him flying off his feet. He landed upon his shield.

Edvar looked up, only able to see through one eye—the blow had spun his helmet to cover half his face. The slender point of the axe rose up above him. It didn't fall. Edvar yanked off his helmet. The cries and clangs of battle rushed into his ringing ears. A stunned expression masked the Karraban's face. Slowly, he lowered his axe and staggered forwards. Behind him stood Isy. In her hand, a dirk, the blade painted red. Her eyes were on Edvar, not on the Karraban, who, with a demented look of rage, lifted his axe.

"Isy!" Edvar shouted.

Isy shot forward, pushed by a force that Edvar could not see. He caught her as he got to his feet and turned to see her savior.

Vil.

The Karraban had tried to cleave Isy in two. Instead, his blade struck stone. Now his focus was on Vil. Boldly, Vil swiped and hacked with his sword, pressing all the time, but his lack of skill was evident, and the Karraban, although wounded, dealt with his attacks easily.

Edvar retrieved his sword, and as he came to stand, Vil parried a heavy blow. He staggered backwards, balanced himself, and with a roar of defiance, charged at the

Karraban. The veteran stepped forward to meet the charge and thrust the spike atop the shaft of his axe through Vil's stomach. With horror, Edvar watched the Karraban lift Vil off the ground, the point protruding from his back. Vil hung there, before he fell like a rag doll.

Edvar charged, and in his ear he heard the cry of Isy as she followed. He unleashed a furious combination, moving with a speed he didn't know he possessed, twisting, slashing, up, down, right, left, and with each strike he pushed the Karraban back, into the backs of battling pairs, staggering over the fallen. Edvar's attacks consumed the Karraban's focus and Isy seized her chance. She waited for their blades to clash, ducked low and plunged her blade into his groin. The Karraban fell forwards, axe dropped. Edvar looked at her, too short of breath to say thank you. And then he remembered.

Ashara.

Eighteen

Ashara's sword lay beyond his grasp. So too his shield. On his back, breathing heavily, he clasped his bleeding shoulder, trying in vain to stop the flow. Tesh couldn't help but smile. The Karraban Keeper looked around at his conquering army, battling still but crushing the Yurrish. He turned back to his old enemy.

Tesh had at last bested the perfect Ashara. Had made a sham of all his boasts. Tesh would never bring Jessyia back, would never get to return her safe to Karrabar, to hear her laugh, to see her smile, to lose himself in those grey eyes he found so deep and sad—a sadness caused by Ashara and her bastard father, who'd forced her down a path she had not wanted to take. Ashara had ruined their future, and now Tesh would end his, and in doing so, end the pitiful line prolonged so feebly by Ashara's idiotic mother, Alysa.

"It does not need to be like this, Tesh," Ashara said.

"This is the only way that delivers justice. You are a curse on my soul, Ashara, since the day you entered my life."

Karraban horns rang out behind the wall, their blasts frantic, short, urgent. Something wasn't right. Tesh couldn't help glancing across the bailey. He sought Iljasar. Pain jabbed at his chest. His oldest friend was lying face down in a pool of blood, axe at his side.

Terrible wails echoed over the walls, drawing Tesh's attention to the broken gate. His men surged through it, running in fear. And then fighting erupted. Giant bodies, two hundred or more, raced across the threshold of the gate. They dwarfed his men, twice their height at least, wielding spears big as young trees. Dark hair covered most of their slate grey bodies and they wore furs, leathers, and homespun clothes. They cleaved through the shield wall, men unable to resist their might.

The fighting turned frantic. Tesh's men hit the ground quicker than they could swing their weapons, and even when they did land a blow, they seemingly did no harm. The giants moved with unbelievable swiftness, each stroke taking out two, three, four at once, stabbing, slashing, bludgeoning. Nobody could get near them. With defiant roars, the small group of Yurrish attacked as well.

Tears welled in Tesh's eyes. Tears of anger, of frustration. He roared his laments. But he would still have his revenge...

He turned to Ashara and felt a cold sting in his gut. He looked down to find the tip of Ashara's sword embedded in his stomach. Warm blood flowed into his breeches, down his legs. Sudden weakness struck him, and with it, a chill that cut to his bones.

"I loved Jessyia too," Ashara said. "She meant everything to me. If I were in your position, I probably would have marched an army into Karrabar to save her. But she would never have wanted that. I am sorry, Tesh. From the deepest reaches of my heart, I am. I will carry the burden of what I have done for the rest of my days, which may not be much longer."

Tears obscured Tesh's vision, but not enough to see his men dying. He had won. Surely, he had won?

Ashara slid free his blade, and Tesh sank to the ground beside his eternal foe. His eyes grew heavy, and when he closed them, he saw Jessyia.

Nineteen

Half a dozen Amast, including Pekira, who was looking beaten up with a bandage wrapped around her head, and Kora, whose right leg was bound too, volunteered to carry Vil to the pyre. Resting upon a wooden platform, his body was draped in a blue flag emblazoned with the white lily of Yurr. Upon the shoulders of the Amast, he rose higher than anyone else. Befitting of the man who had helped save them all.

Lying beside Vil were the bodies of Agon, Reska, Jalden and Camos. It had taken ten Karrabans to bring down Agon, Isy had heard, and Reska had held a staircase at the eastern gate alone until finally his wounds overcame him. Jalden had been found with an axe still in her hand, defiant even in death. Every one of them had died so that others might live. Isy would never forget them all.

Isy had learned after the battle that, on his journey back to Haberdam, Vil had encountered a group of over four hundred Amast. They were survivors of the Karraban attack who had fled in a different direction to Kora and the others. They had fared better than their kin, and after establishing themselves a new home in the north-western forests, had set out to look for fellow survivors. It was then that they ran into those from the camp who were on their way to Haberdam with the Yurrish. When they learned of Kora's plight, those willing and able to fight headed for Yurrisa. And that's when they ran into Vil on his way back home. The chronicler's assistant hadn't wanted to fight, and yet he came back. It cost him his life. But he made the difference. Had he not guided the Amast to Yurrisa, they would have arrived too late, and the outcome would have been very different. She and Edvar would probably be dead. She would make sure the chroniclers recorded Vil's bravery. Although he had left in cowardice, he overcame his fears and fought like a hero from the stories he had loved so much. *You have earned your place amongst them, Vil the Vanquisher.*

Isy had wept for her friend for the past two days. But it wasn't just for Vil she shed tears. Tulasc and Yera had fallen too. The pair had held the Karrabans back while the Yurrish retreated to the keep. In the end, they had given themselves up defending those who rejected them, who revolted at their very sight. It was just so moving to see how many people appreciated their sacrifices. Isy swore that they would never be forgotten in the minds of any Yurrishman.

Her eyes had remained dry until this moment. A gentle hand touched her back and gave it a reassuring rub. Edvar. He smiled at her, black and blue rings around his eyes, arm in a sling. She smiled back, though it lasted fleetingly on her lips.

A bandaged Jarat, along with a dozen of his finest soldiers, had given Vil a guard of honor. Hundreds had gathered around the pyre. Edvar had sent word around the city for any family of Vil's, but nobody had come forward, save a solemn contingent of chroniclers that had schooled him in his youth. They stood to the left of the pyre, in the shadow of hundreds of Amast. Kora's brother Gyapa, who had led the force that broke the Karraban siege, stood beside his sibling.

Standing at the head of the pyre was Keeper Ashara. His resplendent armor seemed a world away. Now he wore a muted black robe, his bandaged arm hidden beneath a russet cloak.

The Amast set Vil down and took a step away. Ashara spoke.

"Young Vil was not what you'd imagine a warrior to be. He succumbed to fear before the battle of Yurrisa. It's a struggle we all face. An eternal duel within ourselves. Some of us never succeed. Others overcome it with ease. Some need to build or find the strength. Vil was one of those people. In the time I knew him, I watched him struggle with crippling fear, watched him resist and fight back. When he found Gyapa and the Amast, he found something else too— the strength we all need to fight against fear and defeat it once and for all. Unshackled by its restraints, Vil became the hero he always dreamed of being. Never will his sacrifice be forgotten in the annals of Yurrish history."

Ashara bowed and took a step back. It was the cue for the Amast to begin their song. The same one Isy had heard them sing on the night of Japha's cremation, the night that Vil had entered the lives of the Amast, and had cemented himself in Isy's. The soft, harmonious tone quickly set her weeping, and when the flames washed over the blue linen, her sobs became unchecked.

Isy could stand neither sight nor smell and pushed her way through the press of people. She heard her name called, footsteps on the cobbles, and found Edvar hobbling after her. He said nothing to her, just wrapped his arms around her and held her close. It was everything she needed.

When her tears had eased, they walked, his arm around her.

"Every time I think of him and how he died, a knife of grief pierces my heart. All the pain he must have felt..."

"He died a hero, a man without fear. If there is any way to die, it is like that. People will sing of the little chronicler's assistant who saved Yurr. How he protected his friends when they needed it most. He is a true example of how we all should be."

They paused by a fountain, sitting on a stone bench. The square was quiet. Many people were at the city walls or down at the docks, picking through the ruins, searching for survivors. Early estimates were that a fifth of the buildings in the city had been damaged. The defensive fortifications were altogether wrecked.

"Would you stay here, Isy?" Edvar said. She lifted her head from his shoulder and looked at him.

"I... don't know. I haven't thought about it." She genuinely hadn't. Her entire focus had been on surviving the battle, and in the days after she had been consumed by grief. The idea was new in her mind, and it scared her. Could she seriously move to a place with over ten times the population of Haberdam? It would be a different beast altogether, and she had experienced how the people had reacted to her and the Amast already. She didn't want to endure that again.

Isy knew in her heart that she would never go back home, so where else? With the Amast, wherever they relocated to? Stay with the Darts? She bit her lip.

Twenty

He heard a sound, gentle and soft. A bird, chirping to itself. A delicate breeze touched his cheeks. He opened his eyes and found himself in a bright room, the windows tall, curtains open. A silhouetted figure stood in the light at the end of his bed. Tesh's eyes adjusted.

"Have I not climbed the Spire high enough?" Tesh asked, realizing how dry his throat was. "I thought myself dead."

"The wound was shallow."

Ashara walked around the bed, filled a bronze cup with water, and handed it to him. Tesh hesitated for a moment before accepting it. Ashara sat in a chair at his bedside, facing him.

"Why have you done this?" Tesh asked, waving his hand over the room.

"I feel no ill will toward you, Tesh. Only regret. Regret that goes back to the day we first met. Indeed, I do not blame you for any of this, though it saddens me deeply that so many had to die for what happened between us.

"My father died when I was nine years old, and from that day forth, my mother said to me, over and over, that the future of the kingdom was in my hands. The security of the Vault was my responsibility alone. The lives of those in Yurr depended on me and my decisions. Pressure suffocated me.

"My father had been a great man, how could I begin to emulate him? And then you and I met, and our parents pitted us against one another, innocently, I do not doubt, but I regret that, for me, it was a means of proving myself capable, of proving to my mother and to the world that I was befitting of the role of keeper.

"You were better in every way, Tesh. You could do things that I had spent years trying to achieve, and it had taken you half the time and effort to do them. I knew I had to improve to best you, so I worked and worked until we were equals, and that charged our rivalry. I should have been your friend. We had both lost a parent after all.

"What happened with Jessyia... I loved her too. I knew it from the moment I first saw her. I could not take my eyes from her. And she had such a profound effect on me. She calmed me. Improved me. There was no one better to play the role of devil's advocate. She saw much more than I. Indeed, she was twice the leader I ever was."

"And me too," Tesh said.

Ashara smiled. "We are old men now, with the grace of hindsight. We both loved her, for she was indeed the finest woman in Kohrem. But know that there was nothing I could have done to save her. She died giving birth to our son. He too died." Ashara's voice cracked. "I thought my world had ended that day."

Tesh felt a stab of grief in his chest, as he had when he saw Iljasar... and then he remembered it all. His greatest friend dead on the floor. What had happened to his body? How many of his own had he led to their deaths? All because of his blind rage, his bitter memories gnawing away at his resolve, his sanity. Tears trod a path long barren and reached the corner of his eyes. He blinked them away.

"What was your son's name?" Tesh asked.

"Edvar." Ashara sighed.

"I'm sorry," Tesh said. The words did not pain him as much as he thought they would. "Jessyia and I had grown up with each other. Our families had been close. I never knew my mother, and my father never showed me affection or love. The only person who ever did was Jessyia. I never doubted that we would marry and spend our lives together. I had never known another woman like her. She gave me a feeling of joy in my chest that I have never been able to rekindle.

"I still remember the day you arrived in Karrabar, when she looked at you for the first time. I saw something in her eyes that I had never seen before. A longing that she had never looked at me with. That look struck a blow greater than any battleaxe. She loved you more than she loved me."

Uttering the words shattered his emotional dam. Tesh did something he hadn't done since the duel with Ashara all those years ago. He sobbed. And he could not stop. He buried his face into the pillow and wailed. All before his truest enemy.

When at last his tears eased, he felt different, lighter, free of thoughts and feelings that for too long had weighed him down.

"I was a fool to allow myself to be sucked in by Rakar," Tesh said, steadying himself. "He knew I longed for revenge. I was weak to listen to his words. Bitter. Depressed. Lonely. And for the first time in my life, I had the power to act." Tesh sighed. It was as if his mind had sobered after a long state of drunkenness. "What will you do with Rakar?" he asked.

"I am not yet sure."

"It was always his intention to overthrow you, he simply lacked the means. He believes you unfit for the role of keeper. He believes that your mother never should have named you and should have named him instead. When I became Keeper of Karrabar, he came to me with his scheme. The skirmishes in the Borderlands, the assassination attempt... all his idea. He intended to overthrow you with the aid of his fellow councilors and grant Yurr to me in exchange for military support—he feared the barons would rise up against him. It was his intention to kill the other councilors and rule for himself. He is a snake in the garden. Do not let the flowers around him deceive you."

"I appreciate you telling me this."

"We must learn to cooperate."

"Can we agree on an end to this madness then?"

Tesh looked hard at Ashara's amber eyes. The hate he had always felt at the sight of the man was no longer there. He offered a weak, pallid hand to Ashara, who stood and shook it in the warrior's grip.

"Now rest and recover," Ashara said. "And enjoy peace, at last."

Twenty-One

By the Keeper's orders, the Amast had been given free accommodation at all of the inns in the Square of Ilanda. As hard as the innkeepers tried, they could find no beds or rooms big enough. It hadn't taken long for canvasses to be erected in the square itself, and many of the Amast spent their time outside, warmed by braziers supplied by the innkeepers, and waited on hand and foot by serving girls and boys. The people of Yurrisa had embraced those they had once rejected. They were, after all, the saviors of Yurr.

The atmosphere in the square was quite the opposite to how Isy felt. Songs sounded in one corner, lutes, flutes and drums too. The air was thick with the smell of roasting and frying meat, as well as the pungent scent of nuts that seemed to follow the Amast around everywhere. She caught sight of Pekira standing before a shelter.

Pekira saw her coming, and the once cold, unloving Amast woman grinned and embraced her.

"It is so good to see you, Isy. We have looked forward to your visit."

"I am sorry it's taken so long."

"Never apologize. You have done too much for us ever to be angry with you."

Isy smiled and her cheeks flushed. "Where is everyone?"

"I will take you to Kora."

They made their way through the carnival-like atmosphere, the Amast singing songs in their own language. "They sing of our fallen," Pekira said. "Tulasc and Yera included. They all died true heroes, defending our kin and the people of Yurr. We will sing of them forever."

Some of the Amast recognized Isy and shouted her name. Others joined, and soon two dozen of them were chanting her name, banging their giant hands on tables and stomping their feet. One woman gave her a string bracelet with a beautifully carved token.

"You have helped secure our future, Isy, and for that every Amast loves you," Pekira said.

Isy spotted Kora sitting at the edge of the group, a tankard of mead in his hand. He smiled and stood as she neared and they embraced. Pekira went to fetch her and Isy a drink.

"I'm so sorry to hear about Tulasc and Yera," Isy said as they sat, wiping tears from her eyes.

"They will always be missed. Many of my kin fell in this city. Two hundred in all. Their bodies will be taken to our new home. We will celebrate their lives and their sacrifices for eternity."

Pekira returned and handed Isy a frothy tankard. She sipped and was surprised by how much she liked it. Kora went on. "We became separated retreating from the walls and got trapped battling in the streets. That's when Tulasc and Yera fell. They gave their lives so that we could live. We thought all was lost until we heard the horns of our kin. They are made from the horn of tura, the goat that lives high in the mountains, and they make a sound known only to us. I've never been happier to see my brother's ugly face."

Isy laughed. One of the Amast had made a joke—the time of strife really was over. A group of Amast were listening in and cheered at the climax of the tale. Isy still couldn't believe how things had turned out. In the moments before the Amast arrived, Isy had known what true helplessness and despair was, hunched in a tight knot of a few hundred fighters, many wounded and struggling to stand. She had thought her life over.

"And we have more good news," Kora said. "I have met with Keeper Ashara and Baron Rijkard, and they have gifted us lands in the north for us to start again. We want to know if you will come with us, to help us build our new home, and a home of your own, filled with the love and happiness you deserve."

Isy opened her mouth but found no words. Kora had been the first person to make her feel alive, feel that she mattered. He appreciated her and what she did, and so did the other Amast. Every one of them was a kind and gentle soul, selfless beyond measure. If she went with them, she could have everything she had always wanted—a loving home and family.

But she felt hesitant. And she didn't know why. Did she really want that? Perhaps it was what she *had* wanted, when she lived in misery in Haberdam. But that felt like an age ago now, a different time. She had experienced the world; lived an adventure only the bards sang about, or that she'd read about in books. She wasn't sure if she wanted to give all that up, and settling down with the Amast felt like it would be doing just that.

And then there was Edvar. Isy sighed.

"I understand your hesitancy, Isy," Kora said, smiling. "We will not be offended if you do not come. Know that always there will be a home for you amongst the Amast."

"When do you go?" Isy asked.

"Tomorrow morning. We have much to do, and our people still need help."

Isy looked down at her ale and bit her lip.

Twenty-Two

Edvar had never seen the pair together other than at that tense peace meeting in Wender, which seemed so long ago. After everything that had happened, it didn't seem right that Ashara and Tesh were standing side by side, looking content and at ease, smiling, whispering jokes and comments in each other's ears. Edvar couldn't ignore the anger it triggered. The whims of these men had caused all this death, destruction and strife, and now they stood here as if none of it had happened. Why did any of it have to happen at all?

Edvar wondered whether he would ever truly understand it. He still hadn't spoken at length with Ashara. But whatever had occurred behind closed doors between the keepers, they had come out with peace renewed, a treaty signed and thousands of copies made and distributed around Yurrisa. At its heart, was a solemn promise that Yurr and Karrabar would never again war; that the rights and sovereignty of the Amast would forever be upheld, and; that the Vaults of Iron and Bronze would remain forever sealed. There was even rumors of the two keepers destroying their keys, though that was the talk of the people, not the keepers themselves. But it signified the atmosphere of hope that was spreading through the streets. War was, at last, over.

Ashara and Tesh shook hands and patted shoulders as they parted. With the docks ruined by the Karrabans, Tesh was due to sail from the town of Dunmiska further down the coast. The thought had occurred to Edvar that Tesh was play-acting. Feigning repentance and contrition, doing all he could to haul himself out of the snake pit, only to get back home to Karrabar and begin rebuilding and plotting. Only time would tell.

Also gathered in the bailey were the Amast. A long line of horses and wagons packed with barrels, food, tools and supplies awaited them. Hundreds of Yurrish craftsmen had volunteered to go with them to help build their new home. And as part of the peace treaty, the Karrabans would send further supplies and aid. Whether the Amast would accept them was another matter. Edvar wouldn't be surprised if they didn't, but knowing what he knew of the Amast, they would find forgiveness somewhere.

Standing with Kora and Pekira was Isy, cloak over her shoulders, travel bag in her hands. Edvar's heart sighed. He could not blame her for going with them. They revered her, and she had a deep connection with them, a familial love. But he wanted her to stay. She had gotten him through these terrible months. All the time they'd spent together didn't feel like enough. He wanted to hear her laugh, see her face light up in delight, to help her with her worries and concerns and share his own. *Why didn't I tell her any of this? Why didn't I just be honest with her?*

She saw him and waved, and headed toward him. Edvar choked.

Isy unshouldered her bag and stood beside him.

"What's up with you?" she asked. "Sad to see them go?"

"What? Er... yeah," he said, blinking furiously to hide his tears.

Isy eyed him. She fell quiet and watched as the train of wagons and wains set off. The people of Yurr had come out in force to see off the Amast, and as they wound their way through the city, they cheered and clapped and showered them with flowers. The sight filled Edvar with pride, pride that his people had seen the error of their ways. Things were now how they should be.

He looked at Isy and saw tears rolling down her cheeks. "Are you not going with them?" he asked reluctantly.

She wiped her cheeks and smiled at him. "You thought I was going?"

"Well, you're dressed for a journey."

"They turfed everyone out of the barracks, so technically, I'm homeless. I think after saving your life and helping save the kingdom, you can sort me out with my own tower."

Edvar laughed. "I don't even have a tower."

"But you don't deserve a tower, Edvar. Look at the mess you created. It's me who got you out of it. So a tower it is. Non-negotiable."

"I'll see what I can do." A grin had locked itself in place upon his face.

The last of the carts trailed out of gate. "Shall we watch from the battlements?" he asked.

"I'd rather not. I've had quite enough of walls. Let's go to the library. There's a book I've been wanting to read."

Discover more epic fantasy at:

http://ofmetalandmagicpublishing.wordpress.com

Greetings from Of Metal and Magic

If you've come this far, you must have enjoyed what you read! At OMAM, we strive to publish the most thrilling, adventurous, and exciting stories. If you liked this book, you can do us a big favor by leaving a review on your preferred platform, such as Amazon or Goodreads.

Of Metal and Magic Publishing was founded in 2020 by veteran authors Richie Billing and JM Williams, with a focus on quality epic and high fantasy fiction.

The collaboration began many years prior when Richie, JM, and a handful of other authors came together to create a new fantasy world. Our international menagerie crafted stories which all took place in the same epic fantasy setting. We developed a unique method of storytelling that involves writing in the same shared fantasy universe, which we each populate with our characters, cultures and stories. Through hard work and heated debates, we developed a unified canon and history for our world, SORIA.

Though they are designed as stand-alone works, our stories all influence the greater narrative of our shared world, even directly referencing or overlapping with each other. We refer to these Soria stories, relating to our original fantasy world, as *Of Metal and Magic* CORE stories.

But we do much more than our CORE series. It is this innovative and unique format of shared worlds that *Of Metal and Magic Publishing* wishes to build on. In addition to seeking out new voices and the best talent in the traditional fantasy genre, we also seek to craft new worlds for our authors and contributors to relish and share. Every single story published by OMAM has the potential to grow into something greater, a new epic world of shared narratives.

The OMAM team has been writing and publishing for years and felt that, with all of our combined experiences, we could create a publisher which could give opportunities to new and exciting voices in the world of fantasy, help and support writers with their careers, and above all, contribute to the world of writing in new and exciting ways. To that end, you can check out our sponsored podcast, *The Fantasy Writers' Toolshed*—available on Spotify, Google Play, YouTube, and other major podcast hosts.

As a publisher, we are always looking for submissions from new authors. In addition to publishing novels in our signature flavor, we also publish short fiction on our website and in occasional anthologies. We are also not averse to fantasy verse. If you're a fantasy author, whatever your chosen format, send us your work.

To find out more about who we are and what we do, or to submit your work for potential publication, look us up at http://ofmetalandmagicpublishing.wordpress.com, or on Facebook at: https://www.facebook.com/ofmetalandmagic.

ABOUT THE AUTHOR

Richie Billing is from a city called Liverpool, a place known mostly for The Beatles and football, yet it's one with a rich history, some of it good, some of it bad, and as a result, it's a gold mine of inspiration. He got into writing fiction in about 2015 and fell completely in love. Now it's a part of his daily routine. He gets grumpy when he doesn't get time to write.

Fantasy has been the genre that has captured Richie's attention most. The book he has the fondest memories of reading as a youngster was *The Hobbit*, and he grew up in the *Harry Potter* and *Lord of the Rings* age, so imaginative stories were what he knew and loved. As you've seen in this book, Richie doesn't just write fantasy. If he gets an idea and thinks it would make for a good story, he'll write it, regardless of genre, though often he finds himself yearning for the fantastical and the endless possibilities it brings.

Richie studies the craft of writing as much as time allows, and over the years he has read book after book, stacks of articles, attended lectures, seminars, workshops, courses and more. Much of what he's learned has been shared on his blog, *The Writer's Toolshed*, and writing manual, *A Fantasy Writers' Handbook*, a detailed guide to writing fiction, the fantasy genre, and the things a writer can do to build their platform, market their scribblings, and get their stories published. Some people say it's good, but you can see for yourself.

His debut novel, *Pariah's Lament* will be published by *Of Metal and Magic Publishing* in early 2021. If you like an underdog's tale filled with intrigue, conflict, and a hearty dose of action, I think you'll like this. You can find out more on his website, https://richiebilling.com.

Drop by the site if you'd like to keep in touch or want to send Richie a question or comment. He's got lots of helpful things on there, including a free ebook on the craft of writing and lists of publishers and book reviewers. You can also joing his mailing list to be the first to learn about updates and additions to those resources, new blog posts, news on nifty writing tools, and special offers and opportunities.

PRAISE FOR RICHIE BILLING

For *THOUGHTS ON WRITING*

"This is a really inspiring book."

For *FLYING ON THE GROUND*

"Billing knows human nature, he understands our light and dark sides, relationships, love, loss, hatred and jealousy, comradeship, living in the moment, and when we reach for the stars or hide in the shadows."

"His stories make me feel so light like I'm walking on air at times, then the darkness settles and really gets your adrenaline rushing. I love his writing style."

For *THE FANTASY WRITER'S HANDBOOK*

"Written in a friendly, uncluttered style, Billing has managed to accumulate and present a huge amount of useful information in a way that perhaps a favorite lecturer might do."

"This is an ideal, accessible source for tips and advice and practical resources for the aspiring fantasy author."

MORE BY RICHIE BILLING

APPENDICIES

Soria Background

All *Of Metal and Magic* CORE series and stories are told from the perspective of the Sorian "modern" period, a Victorian-like era of industry and imperialism. The year is 2336. Telsemar University, one of the oldest and most prestigious institutions in the world, is celebrating 500 years since its founding. The city-state of Drumnaught controls the world's most powerful navy.

The Zanbaq Empire is long passed, but its effect is still felt in the daily life of all Sorians. For example, the common words for the days and months are derived from Old Zanbaqi.

DAYS
Ahyd-ya (day one)
Tahan-ya (day two)
T'lath-ya (day three)
Arbe-ya (day four)
K'ham-ya (day five)
Ste-ya (day six, the day of rest)

MONTHS
01 Zara-shar (flower month)
02 Haya-shar (animal month)

03 Ma'an-shar (water month)
04 Yufa-shar (wind month)
05 Alhara-shar (heat month)
06 Esifa-shar (storm month)
07 Alawn-shar (color month)
08 Jali-shar (ice month)
09 Fariga-Shar (empty month)
10 Qi'ama-Shar (resurrection month)

The date system of Soria is based on a significant event in the world's history referred to as *The Exodus*. This was the year when thirteen tribes were forced to flee the early Zanbaq Empire and the continent of Elitor altogether. Twelve of these tribes arrived on the continent Kohrem, seeding new societies and setting the stage for a dramatic, and magical, evolution.

But to learn more about this and Soria's other mysteries, you'll have to read our stories.

OMAM Pronunciation Guide

This guide lays out the rules for all non-standard names and words used in any OF METAL AND MAGIC series or story. If you have any questions on how to pronounce a non-English word, or non-standard name, look here.

VOWELS

Vowel phonetics are based on languages with less complexity than English, such as romance and East Asian languages. As a rule, each vowel group is a single sound, either a single vowel or diphthong. An apostrophe between vowels annotates two separate and distinct vowel sounds occurring one after the other.

For example, "chaos" in an American accent would be *kei'as*, "triage" would be *tri'aj*, "buoy" would be *bu'i*.

VOWELS		
Letter	Sound (IPA)	Example
a	ah (ɑ:)	car, hard
e	eh (e)	bet, send
i	ih (ɪ)	hit, sitting

y	ee (i:)	need, team
o	oh (əʊ)	go, boat
u	uu (u:)	doom, fruit
uh	uh (ʌ)	gun, Monday
ei/ay	ay (eɪ)	face, rain
ai	ai (aɪ)	sight, kind
ae	ae (eə)	hair, stare
au	au (aʊ)	house, cow
eu	eu (ɜ:)	hurt, third
oi	oi (ɔɪ)	joy, employ

CONSONANTS

Consonants are less complex, but still each letter only corresponds to a single sound. As such, some unconventional spelling is required for names and exotic words.

For example, "c" always has only a hard sound, and only "s" can be used for the corresponding soft sound in words such as "center" or "sh" for words like "conscious". Likewise, the letter "g" only makes a hard sound, the corresponding soft is written "j", so the word "gauge" would be written *geij*.

If a word has two separate consonant sounds appearing side by side, or a glottal stop in between the sound, it is spelled with an apostrophe.

COMMON CONSONANTS

Letter	Sound (IPA)	Example
k / c	k (k)	car, kill
g	g (g)	girl, green
j	j/g(dʒ)	juice, stage
z/initial x	z/s (z)	zoo, nose
sh	sh (ʃ)	shoe, fish

Soria Timeline

Dawn of Creation

First Age of Light

First Age of Darkness

The Medallion War

Second Age of Light

Establishment of Zanbaq Empire

Jaysem's Discovery

The Exodus

Flourishing of the races

Founding of Telsemar University

MODERN ERA

~6000 BE

~4500 BE

1213 BE

1200 AE

2336 AE

AE=After Exodus
BE=Before Exodus

This is the calendar used on Kohrem by the twelve tribes since the Exodus, which has been exported to the rest of the world.

Lightning Source UK Ltd.
Milton Keynes UK
UKHW011837010921
389863UK00003B/73